I0687870

A PLACE of SAFETY
(Volume One)
Derry

Kyle Michel Sullivan

KMSCB
Buffalo, NY

Disclaimer

This book is a work of fiction. Though it is written as if an autobiography and is set during a difficult period of history in Londonderry, Northern Ireland, the main characters and their names, places, incidents, and situations are products of the author's imagination. References to actual historical events, real people, and real places are used only in a way to illuminate or further the story. Any resemblance by the fictional characters to actual events or places or persons, living or dead, is entirely coincidental. All rights are reserved to the author, including the right to reproduction in whole or part in any form, manner, or concept.

Cover design by JamTheCat
ISBN: 979-8-9923177-0-1

LIBRARY OF CONGRESS CATALOGUING IN PUBLICATION DATA
Sullivan, Kyle Michel (1952-   )
A Place of Safety - Derry / by Kyle Michel Sullivan
Buffalo, NY : KMSCB, 2024 | Summary: Set between 1966 and 1981, Brendan Kinsella just wants to live his life, but he was born and raised in Londonderry, Northern Ireland, and history keeps intruding.
Library of Congress Control Number: 2023922596
(print) ISBN: 979-8-9887577-1-9 (Hardcover; alk. paper)
Historical-Fiction | Narrative Fiction

Acknowledgements

Thanks to Dawn Greenfield Ireland, and Carrie Armstrong for assisting in the editing and proofing of this book.

Thanks to Eamon and Martin Melaugh for allowing me to pick their brains and use their knowledge of the times to keep it as true as possible.

Thanks to CAIN, PRONI and *Derry of the Past* on Facebook for their excellent attention to the period and collection of images and information.

A Place of Safety
(Volume One)
Derry

Table of Contents

About the Author

Other Books by This Author

In the Beginning

Those who knew Eamonn Kinsella—and were truly being honest with themselves—had to admit that were he born but ten miles to the west or north his murder would have been seen as the fitting end to a hard and brutal man. As his son, I do not make this claim lightly. Nor is it merely from spite. While it's true he near twisted my arm off when forcing me to turn over a pound note I'd just received for my tenth birthday—his need to drink himself into another stupor far more important than my pain—that does not factor into my opinion. All it does is prove that my father was very difficult, in many ways and with everyone.

The fact is, as had long been known, it could take little more than a wrong word, here; a wrong look, there; or even a wrong touch on his shoulder to call forth some beast within. Then suddenly you'd find yourself on the floor with a split lip or blackened eye, and it would be your own fault for his reaction, no matter how improbable the cause. So expect no apology. With his height at well above six feet, weight of more than fifteen stone, and back still carrying the strength gained from a long-past position as a navvy, few were they who would take the dispute further. That was why as word of his death spread, the first thought on many-a-mind was he had finally focused his anger on the one absolute truth of existence—that there was always somebody bigger, stronger, meaner, and better with his fists than yourself, and that one day you were sure to meet.

His body was found off the Limavady Road, down a farm trail that would have offered a pleasant view of the River Foyle had it not decided to turn so sharply to the east. The morning air was cold and blustery, and the fields around him bleak and gray despite recent whispers of snow and the brightness of the sky. He had been dumped in a ditch, his coat pulled down his arms and his hands bound tight behind him. Rumors flew that he had been emasculated, never to be confirmed one way or the other. It *was* verified that every bone in every finger was broken, several ribs were shattered, an elbow had been dislocated and his face pummeled into the merest hint of a human visage. Blood soaked his shirt to his trousers, the knees of which were torn and scraped as if he'd been forced to crawl on them. Or been dragged. And it was said not one tooth was left in his mouth.

As for the Coroner's release on the manner of his death? It was the purest embodiment of callous simplicity. "Mr. Kinsella perished from the result of a bullet being fired into the crown of his head."

Mr. Kinsella *perished*.

He was not *murdered*.

Nor was he *killed*.

Or even *slaughtered* like a cow in the abattoir.

He merely *perished*.

A charming word you'd hear more often on the lips of someone claiming they're *perished from the hunger*. Or thirst. Or cold. Or the mere seeking of a job. Not once until that Coroner's comment had I ever connected the damned word with death. Which sent me to the library to dig into their dictionary and discover it actually *was* defined as such, with synonyms being *expire, wither, shrivel, vanish, molder* and *rot*, any of which might have been just as inappropriate.

He had lain on his back in a slight trail of dirty water until his clothing was soaked through and solid with ice. One unseeing eye open and tinted by blood, the other swollen shut. Well-preserved, he was. Refrigerated, even. Therefore, time of death was difficult to establish. That somewhere between midnight and four of that morning was decided upon brought forth a great explosion of anger, seeing as how it had been two nights since he was jostled out of McCleary's in his far-too-usual condition, just after last orders. And it was known that he had not returned to his hovel, nor had he been seen anywhere else, since. So to one and all it became a truth carved in stone that his torturers had enjoyed their game with him for two bloody days.

Adding to the horror of his lengthy demise was how the somewhat reticent undertaker handling the funeral arrangements had gently but firmly insisted on a closed casket.

"Considering the overall devastation visited upon him," he'd said to the widow, his voice soft and mewling, "well, there's only so much one can do, you know. And really, Mrs. Kinsella, it would be best to remember him as he was."

To which my mother began to wail, "My poor Eamonn." As was expected of her. Mrs. Haggerty, our immediate neighbor, was at her side. Which was how word of this travesty leapt from house to home with the speed of telepathy; that woman never knew a secret she couldn't spread faster than the BBC.

My elder brother, Eamonn, the younger was standing in the room, his fists clenched and his body tight. In a corner, my elder sister, Mairead, sat on a stool and wept. They both knew what he meant. I was also there, quietly leaning back against a wall, being quite the stoic lad, I'm told. But in truth I could make no sense from the quiet manner in which his death was being depicted by any and all concerned so had no idea how to act.

Oh, but did this news increase the dead man's stature. He turned from being a drunken bully to the truest of Irishmen, who did not release his hold on life as easily as others would have. Who fought to the end in order to return home to his kith and kin. Why, he even spat blood in the faces of his killers, that much was a certainty. Before the day was gone, he'd been elevated to the likes of Cu Chulain and Michael Collins and every other hero of Ireland's past, with any and all recent grievances forgotten.

Throughout the afternoon and evening, many a pub mate dropped by to offer kind remembrances of my Da's bleak eyes and long face, a visage that brought to mind tortured poets and sad balladeers. They wistfully spoke of how he could sing so well as to make the angels weep. Elegant tunes of Ireland's ruined past and her dead future. Others provided gentle smiles as they told stories about the stories he could weave. Melodious tales of fairies living in oak glens that once spread forever across the land. And of gods who roamed her once glorious green fields and forests. And exciting events wrapped around Grianán Aileach, the ancient ring fort but six miles and a hundred worlds away from town.

Oh, he had a true Irish heart in his use of words, was the general sentiment. And to a man they swore that in another time and under better circumstances, he'd have given the likes of James Joyce and Sean O'Casey a challenge as the nation's bard, for each tale had been brought to life with such beauty and perfection you'd have thought he lived through each and every one.

Which put me off. I'd heard Da's stories and singing voice, and not been much impressed. But when I said so, the usual response was, *Oh, you poor wee lad, how could you know?* Or, *What a thing to say about your poor dead Da.* Or, *This is what happens when you're simple.* The last one usually followed by a wink and nod to whomever was seated next to them.

Simple! I was labeled that thanks to my mother, and once you have the reputation you cannot remove it. But would a *simple lad* be smart enough to know now was not the time to remind the bloody hypocrites of the money borrowed but never repaid? Or drunken rants along the road, or the beatings and the bursts of howling fury and the theft of any money we'd managed to pull together, all in the service of drink? Would a simple lad wonder at how much viciousness and cruelty could have been poured into one man in fewer than thirty-six years, while others just accepted it as part of him?

I grant you, he was hardly the only Irishman filled with anger. It was the one honest emotion those like him were allowed to hold. And if my mother was seen at market with fresh bruises, or was out in the cold night air walking us around till our lord and master had sworn himself into weary, drunken sleep? Well, her nails had left scratches deep on more than just his back, and her quick use of an iron skillet to the head had not gone unnoticed.

But still it hit me wrong. It wasn't till years later that I truly understood how hypocrisy is just good manners, at a wake. So the bad of my father was made quiet and the best cried aloud.

His funeral was well-attended and partially paid for through the intersession of our priest, Father Demian, who'd so often visited our home in times of distress. The rest was provided by the widow's one sister, Maria Nolan, who had rushed over from Houston.

Texas.

It was she who'd sent me that pound note.

She saw that everything was arranged as well as possible in our sad little hovel, and kept my younger brother and sister at her hotel room to give them peace from the nonstop clamor of adults in the house.

She was also shocked at the condition of our two-up-two-down wreck of a home. So when she spoke to the press, she emphasized that the new widow had five children, with another soon due, yet was living in a structure that was all but condemned and had no prospects for better. She was vocal enough that she actually shamed the bastards who ran the town like their bloody fiefdom into at least promising new lodgings once the last tower of the Rossville Flats was completed.

If there were room still available on the queue, of course. *Can't make promises one might have to keep.*

I think they expected that, as with most catastrophic events, soon all would be over and done with and life would return to normal once the confusion surrounding us had drifted away. Then they could continue ignoring our plight. And would have but for one small and final detail that proved more than important.

Eamonn Kinsella lived and died in Derry, in the North of Ireland. *Londonderry* for those who cannot be bothered to learn the city's true name. A Catholic town taken hold of by Protestants in the way an abusive man might take hold of a woman he fancied, refusing to let her go even if it meant her destruction. So when it was learned that my Da had been killed by two drunk Protestants, that well-mannered hypocrisy and general anger turned to fury.

It didn't help that the bastards swore to heaven and earth they'd only meant to have some fun with the *Taig* and it was his own fault things got out of hand to the point he had to be shot. Like a mad dog. Which was accepted as *the most reasonable explanation* by the powers that be, despite his vicious and extremely well-known injuries. So thus was the martyrdom of Eamonn Kinsella to Mother Ireland manifested as the truth of his former existence vanished like a ghost.

The year was 1966, when several other Catholics were killed for being Catholic and Catholic schools were attacked by Protestant fools, all because the Catholic minority in the state had the nerve to want the same rights as any Protestant. It was as if the latter thought continuing to hit the former, who are only asking you to stop hitting them, would make them shut up and let you continue the beating. To add to this insult, Protestant leaders insisted the Catholic population was, itself, responsible for the discrimination against it so no quarter would be given to make amends for the past transgressions they, themselves, had caused.

It never ceases to amaze me how easy it is for too many people to refuse to see the reality of what is happening around them. That trying to keep their world as it had long been was no longer an option. That if they would only compromise a little, nothing more would be needed and everyone's life would be so much better. But to follow that course would have taken intelligence in a land where arrogance and stupidity held sway. So what followed was all but pre-ordained.

Already being one to keep to himself, I was unaware that my world was building to an explosion of the most vicious death and cruelty, ever. An explosion made only the worse by it happening in a supposedly civilized part of the fast-dwindling British Empire.

But what child of ten can see the growth of history around him when few adults can? Things happen, and you either rejoice when it ends well or weep when it doesn't. Thus, my father's death held resonance for me in only the most selfish, limited, and inconsiderate of ways—that a man I feared was gone, and I could now live my life in the manner I chose, that of a lad filled with hopes and dreams and prayers and promises, thinking himself to be in a place of safety.

1966-68

Child of the Groundhog

I've heard it said many a time that in order to truly know Derry, with her meandering streets of deteriorating terrace homes and ramshackle shops laid about the north and west areas of town, you had to have been born there. To which I give no argument. Within the great, thick, near four-hundred-year-old city walls was a town center like any other in the UK—brisk, neat, and functional. As were the shops lining Abercorn, Foyle and Strand Roads. It was the crooked little streets in The Bogside and Brandywell that were built like some drunk had wandered about to designate *this* alley as a Walk, *that* enclave as a Way, and *those* steps as a Terrace which made it preposterous. One might claim that since many such streets were now vanishing into redevelopment it would help simplify everything, but that only expanded the confusion.

The city was nestled along both banks of a bend in the River Foyle and once did some fair commerce in shipping from her port. That is, until the British decided Belfast was more suited to their control. The river provided a natural barrier between the Catholic Bogside and Protestant Waterside, with only the Craigavon Bridge allowing access from one to the other. Further along, the Foyle became a lake and then opened into the North Atlantic.

There was a joke, that if you stood on the south shore of the lake and looked to the north, you'd see the South. Of Ireland. Since the border separating the North from the South ended at Muff, just as the river flowed into the lake's expanse.

I was born Brendan Kinsella in the Bogside on the 2nd of February, 1956, a date which brought my Aunt Mari no end of merriment when she heard. She'd been four years in Houston, at the time, four-thousand miles and five worlds away. She and my Uncle Sean met when he was at the American Naval Station in Clooney and got themselves wed, then he took her home with him.

Ma had not been pleased.

"Sold herself to an American," I once heard her say to Mrs. Haggerty, when they were discussing a third child my aunt had borne. "She should have stayed here to help me. Married a good Irishman, not run off across the water."

"I thought her husband was Irish," Mrs. Haggerty had responded.

"He says, but looks Swedish, to me."

"Still, couldn't she bring you all over? It's far better opportunities in America than here."

Ma had pointed to her cheek and said, "This come from me suggesting as much to the mister. Says Ireland is his home and he'll not be run off, like so many others."

"What nonsense. More shame's in *not* going where there's work."

"I know that. You know that. But himself? Even Belfast is too far a jaunt for him, now. The sooner he's gone from us, the better for us all."

"Bernadette, don't even think such things! Say a quick prayer."

"I have, more than once, this day."

Oh, and that is how I learned my mother's Christian name wasn't Ma. And to be clear, I was but seven and seated on the stairs repairing a watch, with a step up as my worktable, while they were on the divan. So I could hear every word they said.

Each had a mug of tea refreshed from a kettle hanging in the hearth. At the time, Ma had just started with my younger sister, soon to be Maeve, and Mrs. Haggerty had put something in her cup to help with the morning sickness, even as Ma had let her know how much less of a burden this new pregnancy was.

"I've not been near so tired," she'd said, "or ill, in the mornings. Far better than with that one." And from the side of my eye I'd noticed her nod to me, but as was my habit I paid little attention. I was having a devil of a time getting the watch's back off.

"Well, the more you have," Mrs. Haggerty had said, "the easier it becomes."

"No, with my two eldest it was nearly nothing, and his little brother was the same. But then, after *that* one I could have passed an elephant with less trouble."

"And with your Brendan such a wee lad." She'd said with a

smile in her voice.

"I feared his brother was going to be like him, he was so quiet," Ma continued. "But he's become quite the reader. *That* one, it's only tearing things apart he cares for."

"But look how he puts them back together."

Ma had snorted. "He pays no mind to anything else. I can talk at him an hour and he won't hear a word till I flick his ear. Then he looks at me, huffy. Like, *How dare I interrupt him?*"

I'd finally got the back off that watch and seen how dirty the inside of it was, from sweat and muck, so my full attention had shifted to that as they'd kept up their chattering. It's so much easier to just ignore the voices than to try and make sense of what they're saying.

I had just finished and was screwing the back onto the watch when Ma flicked my ear.

"I said, it's time for supper," she snapped. "Clean up, or do you care not to join us?"

It was only then I'd realized Mrs. Haggerty had gone, my brothers and sister were at the table, and Ma had probably been talking at me for half-an-hour without a response.

Another reason they thought me *simple*.

Anyway, the cause of Aunt Mari's merriment was, by all accounts, I become intent on being born a week late. She had been notified Ma was finally into labor, so had called Mrs. Rafferty to see how the birth was going. That was on the 31st of January. She had to call twice more before the midwife could tell everyone I was finally of this world.

Seems I'd started to come out that morning, taken a glimpse of what was awaiting me, and slipped right back into my mother's womb till it was half seven and what little light there was had stopped drifting in through the window. That's when she'd laughed and told them of this odd American custom where if a groundhog pops up from his burrow and sees his shadow, it's six weeks more of winter.

As if I'd planned it all.

Had I really been able to do so, I would not have kept my mother in labor for near fifty hours. It gave her something hard to remind me of any time I did something she disliked. Usually followed by the thump of her middle finger to my temple.

She was born a Farrell, my mother, off Clarendon Street, near

Queen, next to the last child of a woman whose health forbade future pregnancies. But the church being the Church and men being men, their priest brushed aside the warnings and my one grandmother died bringing Aunt Mari into the world. And never was it spoken of without also saying it was God's will.

Funny how that translates into what men prefer and not women.

Da was born in Belfast and hated to return there. I found this out when Mrs. McCory was sniping at him for coming home paralytic in the middle of the day and his response had been, "Feck off, ye ol' cow. I'm off t' bloody Belfast, t'morrow's bus, an' won't have the chance to partake. The bloody nuns'll see to that. Nosin' about. Makin' sure I work to the bone. All women do. To the feckin' bone, an' fer nothin'."

I was five, at the time.

We knew nothing of his family, which was very unusual. In Derry everyone knows your family back fourteen generations and are happy to tell you about it with even so much of a hint as to being interested. So I had sought Mrs. McCory out and asked her if they'd been told of his death.

She had patted my head and said, "That's not for you to worry about, lad."

Then I'd asked, "Are they not coming to Da's wake?" I very much wanted to meet them.

Her only response had been to take me to a wreath that wore a banner saying *In Sympathy* across it, and said, "They're here in thoughts and prayers."

Which told me nothing. It was from St. Ambrose, not people. Which I had pointed out. She'd grown stiff and told me to be still. I'd huffed, in irritation, but asked no more.

I was later to learn St. Ambrose was an orphanage near the Belfast harbor. It was there Da would room because he could stay without cost, having once been a tenant. By some agreement, the nuns would take his day's wages and hold it till he was due to leave, then swear him to take every farthing home with him.

Which sometimes worked.

He had been left at their door when he was but five, with a note pinned to his ragged shirt—*Eamonn Alwyn Kinsella, borne 9 September 1930.* An older couple had brought him, rung the bell and hurried off. No one knew who they were, and young Eamonn was of no assistance, for he wouldn't speak. But there he stayed for eleven years.

Nothing more was known. Some even questioned if his name was truly Kinsella, for they could find no link with him to any they knew of that name. Him being from Belfast, there came rumors he'd been born a bastard and been given *Kinsella* as a way to cover for the family's honor. Whatever the truth, Kinsella is how he remained, and how each member of the family was listed, in the register.

I was fifteen before I thought again about what Mrs. McCory had said, so went looking to ask her, but by then she'd been moved up to Portalow and it was a devil of a time to find her. There was more trouble to get her to answer my knocking. I only kept at it because I heard a woman calling, inside, "Ma, the door. Get the door! Answer the door!"

When she finally did, she had dropped to half her size and twice her age, and had no idea who I was or what I was asking her. A moment later, her daughter by marriage came up, wiping her hands on her filthy apron, and took her by the shoulders, gently telling me, "She's had a stroke, lad. Her memory's gone, and if you press her too hard she may grow upset. Who did you say you were?"

"Brendan Kinsella. We-we lived near her, off Nailors."

The daughter nodded and said, "If she comes back, and she does on occasion, I'll let her know you called. So head along."

I did, kicking myself for not seeking her out, sooner.

Ma's first born was Eamonn the younger. Da's namesake, as noted. By his sixteenth year he was showing a solid feel of Da, in looks but had an easier temperament and searching eyes laid upon him by his mother's mother. One could see it from a photo Ma had of her parents, framed and hanging next to the prayer corner. Large and brown, they held a careful vision of the world that could bring all but the hardest heart to want to comfort him, and by passing his Eleven Plus had shown himself to be set for primary education, making him far more intelligent than Da, to my mind.

He also showed a willingness to work. On many a morning, he'd be off early to lie about his age, so as to shift coal at the docks, before classes. I think the local masters liked how he was there but a few hours and was quick with his hands. How he cleaned himself, after, was a secret he kept from us all, but once home only the darkness around his nails would reveal he'd been working, that day.

Which Ma would notice, demand he hand over his wages, then use her scrub brush to finish cleaning his hands before Da could see them, all the while snarling, "You're not to say a word to your father."

"But can't I keep a couple sixpence for a run with the lads, ma?" he'd all but beg, his voice tight from the pain of her vicious scrubbing.

Ma would just jab him with a finger and snap, "Be still. We need this money to live on, not go galavantin'."

He'd hush. Soon he'd stopped bothering to ask.

While I could see Ma's point, it still felt unfair. Da's work was occasional, and him keeping his wages and taking from the dole was made worse by Ma's willingness to let him. So on a couple of occasions when I'd had the scratch from one of my repair jobs, I'd pass some along to my brother.

It was a joyous little secret between us, and he'd tell Ma nothing more than, "One of me mates bought the tickets and drink." Not really a lie, since that mate was me. Then at night, as we lay in bed, he'd tell me what film he'd seen and describe it as if I was seeing it, myself. I especially liked his joy over *Thunderball, What's new Pussycat?* and so many others.

"There's this girl in *Swingin' Summer*," he'd said one night, "she's got to be the hottest bird ever. Raquel Wells, or somethin'. We're thinkin' of seein' it again, just for her, 'cause she wears this bright miniskirt cut up to-to-" He'd groaned to complete his thought.

"Can I go see it?" I'd asked.

"Dunno. You're but nine. Still, it had songs and silly stuff in it. I'll check the rating."

It was gone from the cinema before he got around to it.

Ma wanted Eamonn to quit school when he made fifteen and a half and get a steady job with John Allen on the quay, but wanted to try for Queens, in Belfast. She raised a fuss about the cost and waste and on and on, but in one of the few times I ever saw Da take Eamonn's side on anything, he'd said he should. Of course, that led into one of their worst rows, which both my brother and I stupidly intervened in. I suffered a bloody nose from it, though to this day I don't know which of my parents gave it to me.

My brother's lip was cut, as well, but he'd mastered the art of removing his shirt before it was stained and could put a plaster over the damage quick enough the stop the bleeding.

On that occasion, however, it was my older sister, Mairead, who calmly stepped between our parents and silenced them both with a simple, "Stop it." Done in a way I'd not seen before.

"Now, Ma," she'd continued, "you know Eamonn is old enough to make his own decision about Queens. Which means you'll have to give him your agreement, anyway. So why argue about it? And Da, if you truly wish to support him, take on shifting coal so he can focus on his studies. If he graduates University, his earning potential is much greater. Don't you both think that would be best?"

They had been so shocked at her controlled manner, they had dropped onto the divan and just looked at each other for five minutes before each giving a shrug of consent. I was too set on pinching my nose to even think of saying a thing.

For the next two weeks, Da had actually gone down to the docks and done what was needed. Ma never saw a farthing of his wages, but when the dole came she was able to use most of it to pay debts and put aside for other expenses.

When later I'd asked Mairead where she'd learned how to silence our parents like that, she had said, "You know Sister Joseph?"

Know her? She was half my size and I wasn't large, and she'd scared the life out of me just by looking at me, more than once in primary school. I'd been so very pleased when she moved to a college that I would not be attending. So I'd nodded.

"Well," Mai had continued, "she once told me that you should know what you're saying and mean what you say. And even if you don't, you should act like you do."

"I don't get the sense in it," I'd responded.

She'd patted my cheek and said, "Nor did I, till now."

Which was all I could get from her in explanation.

But that was Mairead. Second born and referred to as *a handsome lass*, since she also had our father's look about her. Straight brown hair down the length of her back, practical in all matters from clothing to housework to our supper, and no time for foolishness. By the age of fourteen she was already blessed (or cursed, if you prefer) with a figure well-noticed by boys half again her age. She knew it and laughed at them, but unlike our father, her eyes never held anything but hope and love for any and all.

She had no interest in finishing her studies, our Mai, and often said so. "I could go to secretarial college, but it seems a waste of time. I think I'll get a job at Cooley's Shirts. Or Tilley's. Should happen before Eamonn enters Queens, so I can fill in for him when it comes to money."

Which is what she did, but with Hogg and Mitchell's.

Now comes myself—born after two miscarriages, and named after the saint rumored to have landed on Greenland, for some reason. My looks I seemed to take more from my mother, being small, darkly-fair and wiry even for a lad of ten years. My face was broader than my brother's, my eyes as wide, and my thick black hair so massed with curls it was always a struggle to keep from being tangled, unlike the rest of my siblings. Many a neighbor woman told Ma it was more a certainty that I took after her older brothers, though none had been around for decades and the few snaps of them were of poor of quality.

Her response had always been, "Not one of them had hair such as his. And all had their wits about them. And many a friend. He has none. Ignores the neighbors' lads. Prefers breakin' his toys and puttin' them back together."

"But the ones he has are such poor things," said one lady. Mrs. Cahan? "I'm sure he's just trying to make them better."

"No, he's just *simple*," Ma'd replied, with a sigh.

Ma was right about me not being much for playing with other boys. They liked to march and race about in games I could not make sense of. Like they're on parade. Or fight with sticks and dust bin lids as if they're Medieval Knights. Or fool with marlies—marbles. Crouched around a circle in the center of the earth rolling bits of colored glass at other bits of colored glass and it-it-it just struck me as a waste of time.

Nor did they want me about, as well. The names they used on me as much as said so, their favorite being *Looner*. I think that's a play on loonie and loner, but I never actually cared to know. I had far more fun in my world by reworking the spring on an old wind-up Castoy and having it go toddling off. It gave me a true sense of accomplishment.

And don't you think those lads didn't notice that I could fix theirs, as well, when needed.

I think Ma really preferred that I not muck around with them, so much; they were not kept as clean as she kept us.

"They can only come over after bath night and been done for nits," was her usual comment, which put her on the wrong side of more than one neighbor lady.

Thinks she's on the Queen's register.

Expecting a visit, is she?

There's such a thing as too clean.

And the like, though not to her face.

I was told by Mrs. Haggerty that she wasn't like this till after I came into the world. Said almost like an accusation. And with it was the hint that because she thought me simple, she'd been trying to wash the oddness out of me. Didn't work, of course, but she still got caught in the habit.

Mrs. Cahan responded that I was just a rare duck, for she noticed that by the age of six I could repair just about anything from clock to transistor radio to the ancient wiring for the electric light in the parlor.

Which we were not supposed to have.

We *officially lived* with Mrs. Haggerty, in one of her bedrooms. That was for the purposes of the dole and to keep our cost of rent low. But in reality, my parents had taken over an abandoned maisonette next door, not long before my birth. Then Da had run an extender from Mrs. Haggerty's so we could have electricity without officially paying for it. Which was really dangerous, so the moment I understood what had been done I replaced it with real wiring. All before I was ten.

Thus did word spread of my ability. And my low fees, of course, to the point where I began to feel quite the career man.

Of course, all that mattered to Ma was the bit of money I'd make, and she was adamant I give it over. However, I'd worked out on my own it's best to hold back at least half and hide it in little spots I'd fix up around the house when she was asleep or out. Then when we were down to farthings, I could slip some to Mai and tell her I found it, and she'd tell Ma it was her found it when she bought some eggs or spuds. I was quite the sneak in doing so, and fully enjoyed it.

Rhuari followed me by almost two years, being a near-Christmas baby. Ma grumped while he was building within her, but he came out in less than two hours so she felt blessed. His face and feel were plain and direct, with big eyes flanking a short nose. The reason Ma worried he might also be *simple* was how he could spend hours watching me work my magic on a broken wind-up toy. But then Eamonn and Mairead helped him learn how to read, and he found books to be far more interesting than myself, to Ma's relief. He was able to read quite well, long before entering school. What made him seem even smarter was how, if Ma asked him what the book was about, he could tell her. In great detail.

"Tells stories like his father, he does," she'd said to Mrs. Quincanon, once. Another neighbor lady. "Just easier to follow."

"And him but a child."

"It's natural with him. Clear and straight in his words. I can tell. Unlike *that* one." Said with a nod in my direction.

Which was a silly thing to say, since I never told stories. Mainly because when Da would tell them to us, he was usually lost in drink so jumped around and forgot parts of it. Like this one tale about how harpies came to live in the Cliffs of Moher. It was because the Dagda, the father of the ancient Celtic gods, had washed them away in the waters at the base of the Cliffs. His sins, he'd washed away, because he had been a sinful man and felt the need, but his wife, Morriggan, who was queen of the demons was angry used her magic powers—for she was also a witch—to make them into harpies. And now they come out during storms to feed on fish in the sea. Except there's also human sacrifice in it, thanks to Morriggan's three daughters, but they only did this to young male children. Because the Dagda had cheated on them all. Morriggan, not his daughters, for he wasn't the sort to do *that* sort of thing. And around and around until you had no idea of what the story was about.

Once done, I'd asked Rhuari what Da was saying and he'd just rolled his eyes and said, "Nothing. There are no harpies living in the Cliffs of Moher. They don't exist." And left it at that.

As did I. If that was story-telling, I wanted no part of it.

By the time of Da's death, Rhuari had proven himself to be the master of few words and simple gazes that all but cried *I know more than you think I do*. At first, I was cautious around him...until I heard Ma ask him a question about me and a clock I'd been repairing, and he'd simply said, "Ask Brendan," as he'd put a spoonful of porridge in his mouth.

"I'm askin' you," she'd snapped.

He'd finished chewing and swallowed his mouthful and then calmly said, "But how should I know about the clock? He's the one working on it."

From that point I knew he'd never be a tout.

He had yet to take the form or look of either parent, which led Mrs. Keogh, of Doolin Street by Fanin Court, to be certain he was from what she sweetly called *rumors of a friendship* between Ma and a *certain butcher*. I only knew she thought this because I came up with a lamp I'd fixed for Mrs. Cormac, her neighbor, who was nodding with pursed lips as they swept their stoops. Neither noticed me, at first, and when they did they laughed off any idea that I might have known what it was they were discussing.

I said nothing. It's best to let adults think what they want.

After Rhuari came Maeve, and so obvious the sister to him Mrs. Keogh's gossip extended to her. But by the time Maeve was set into motion, the gentleman in question had long encamped for Australia and the prospect of a better life. And the truth was, both she and Rhuari had gained the look of Aunt Mari, though my little sister was not the least bit calm and gentle like her. While she had Mairead's way of setting her mind in a certain direction and not wavering a bit, she was also confrontational, especially if she had some reason not to like you.

Fortunately, I was acceptable so she was never cross with me. When she was but five, I'd asked her why and she'd said, "You're Brendan. You fix my dolls."

Which I did. Like one that was missing both legs. I worked up new ones from some rusty springs that I cleaned and oiled, wrapped in wax and white cloth, and added pieces of sticks for the feet. I also rebuilt the arm and reconnected the cords, and she was happier than I'd yet seen her.

After four more miscarriages, the midwife had severely cautioned Ma against having another. But the church was still the church—where science and sense had no place in man's day-to-day life and *a woman is there for her husband and God will decide who lives and who dies, and to interfere with that in any way was hubris of the most blasphemous sort*—last came Kieran. Born not four months past the death of our father and growing up never to know the burning anger in the man's voice or the question of whether he'd meet the end of Da's fist or the back of Ma's hand, if either was in the mood. He arrived early, as if impatient to get started, and his looks were tainted by Ma with none of Da noticeable about him. Considering how long it took Ma to recover from his birth, leaving Mairead to care for us with Mrs. Haggerty's help, that was one more good reason Da was gone.

Ma's obsession with us being clean was close to a mania by this point. We bathed every other day then nits were removed from our heads, using a fine-tooth comb she would soak in alcohol. Then our hair was washed with a vinegar concoction none of us liked. Eamonn grew to hate even the smell of vinegar while Rhuari just let it all go and I didn't care one way or the other. The girls covered it with a hint of whatever flower was available. Clothes were washed hot and neat. The ragged floor scrubbed and sheets fresh on the bed.

"I can't believe the filth I've lived in," was her usual comment while at it.

To try and minimize Ma's fussing, Eamonn fixed the hovel up so as not to be too much of a danger to us, and I backed him. We knew Da had shored up the stairs and bedroom floors, and he'd slapped paper on the poor walls, early on. That had made it livable, but only just. For the last five years of his life, he'd done nothing more that I know of. It was Eamonn and myself who made it a fine enough shape, using materials *found* at the refuse sites. That is to say, my brother was happy with it; I felt it barely acceptable. Ma just huffed at our work, but that was the best compliment you could get from her. At least the upstairs floor creaked a bit less and the doors remained shut against the wind and rain.

You might think to have so many crammed into a maisonette only half-wired for electric and a toilet outside was horribly cramped, but it was a rather spacious situation for the Bogside. One family per room and sharing the kitchen and hearth and toilet and pump, and raising quite a hideous stench was not unusual.

Of course, my siblings and I were not in born in hospital or the infirmary. When it was my time, Eamonn and Mairead were sent to stay with Mrs. O'Canainn while Da was off using *the miracle of my birth* to cadge a few drinks at McReady's. Which extended into more than one day since my birth did, as well. And when he finally did come home, lost in his spirits, he and Ma had a great set-to despite her post-birth condition because nothing was left of the dole and there was no food in the pantry. Through which

I slept. I learned this some years later from a letter Ma wrote to Aunt Mari, complaining about my not listening to her.

Which had brought Aunt Mari's reminder of how I'd been as a wain, followed by, *What did you expect? He was born when the two of you were hard at each other, so from his first day knew the best way to deal with your fighting is to ignore it. Small wonder it extends to even now.*

To which, Ma had written back in her less than precise hand, *"You give a wain like him too much credit. I think I'll have him tested for deafness."*

Which she never needed to, and knew it.

Ma and Aunt Mari were the only girls amongst nine children of what was once a fairly well-done family, her father having owned a boot repair shop, up the Strand Road. That is, until his wife passed and he took to drink, and was dead before Ma reached the age of majority. Not a one of her brothers was living in Derry by that time, nor could they be easily located, so the two girls wound up under the care of the nuns. That branded Ma with a hatred of all her brothers, which we knew about but never truly understood.

I did catch hint of a reason thanks to Mairead...oh, *happening to get* one of Aunt Mari's letters while Ma was off on some errand or other. She was using the kettle over the hearth to steam it open and didn't know I was in the back, behind the toilet, making a new hideaway to stash my earnings.

When I'd come inside, I'd seen her and asked, "What you doing there, Mai?"

She'd jumped and cried, "Brendan! You gave me such a fright."

Then I'd seen the envelope and asked, "Is it another letter from Aunt Mari?"

She'd caught her breath and nodded.

"Did Ma say for you to open it?"

"I-I just want to see what's in it," she'd sighed back at me. "I-I noticed Ma never reads them to us, in full."

She had started to reseal the part that had come undone but I'd shrugged and said, "So let's see."

She'd hesitated then nodded. "Keep an eye out," she'd said as she returned to the kettle and finished the job.

I'd stood by the door, pretending to toy with the lock. Only to find it truly did need some oil, for it was beginning to stick. Not that we locked our doors, then. We were a community that looked out for each other and, honestly, had nothing worth stealing. But why live with something broken?

I'd been about to ask Mai if we had a paper left from last night's chippy, for the fish was usually slathered in grease, when I'd seen she was carefully opening the envelope to pull out Aunt Mari's handwritten pages. I'd snuck over to see them, and our aunt's way of writing was less precise than Ma's. Which made it hard to read. What had startled us both? With the letter had been a pair of ten-pound notes and a photo of a man in Brisbane.

"That's Australia," I'd said, having just learned about the place at the Brothers' school.

"He's one of our uncles," said Mairead, quickly reading the letter, in wonder. "There's seven of them but only the one, there, and Aunt Mari's saying, *I thought you'd like to know, anyway.* Anyway?"

Suddenly, she'd grown nervous and slipped the money, photo and letter back into the envelope and resealed it, saying, "You're not to tell Ma I did this. Promise me?"

"When have I ever touted anyone?"

She'd cast me smile that said *Sorry*, then written Aunt Mari's address on a scrap of paper from the chippy and set the envelope atop the divan before starting that night's supper.

She'd stayed lost in thought throughout the evening, our Mairead. So as I'd helped her wash dishes and Ma settled the wains to bed, I'd whispered, "Mai, whatever you learn, will you be telling all of us?"

She'd cast a wary look at me then softened. "You, I will. But I don't want Ma to know I'm doin' it, yet, and Eamonn. Well, he couldn't keep a secret if his life depended on it. The others are too young to know, yet."

I'd chuckled, feeling very adult at being in on this with her. "What's his name, then? The one in the snap?"

"Claren."

"What kind of name's that?"

"First of my questions to Aunt Mari, if I can work the price of a stamp from Ma."

"Should've kept the money."

"Oh, I couldn't. It'd be stealin'."

"But it's for us all, isn't it?"

"For Ma to use as she sees fit."

That had made me scowl, truly angry. "No wonder Da was always in drink."

"Bren, I don't think he knew."

"But twenty pound, and for how long? Once a month, maybe? Since Da died? Before?"

"I don't know. I doubt she sent that much, each time. But I'll see if I can find out."

"What'd Ma do with it? She could've bought new uniforms for all of us instead of scrounging through the church cast-offs. Real shoes instead of sandals."

"I don't know. She gives Father Demian an envelope, at mass."

"Good luck asking him—wait, is Ma passing all of it on?"

"Oh, no, Bren, don't let your imagination run wild. I'll ask Aunt Mari about it. In a quiet way."

"How much is the post to America?"

"I'll have to find out. Why?"

I'd slipped back behind the toilet to pull a shilling from my hiding place and handed it to her. "You think it's more than that?"

She'd cast a surprised look at me. "...Brendan...?"

I'd just looked back, plain. And *simple*.

"I-I'll let you know," she'd finally whispered.

Which she had the next day, and given me the change.

I don't know when Aunt Mari's reply came, but it turned out our seven uncles truly were spread around the world. She was in contact with four of them and hoping to hear from the other three, soon. Their names?

Claren, in Brisbane, who managed an international freight company.

Tomas, in Cape Town, who worked in an office for the same company, there.

Shamus, in Toronto, who was a cabinet maker for a furniture company.

Michael, in Sheffield, who worked in the iron smelters as a master welder.

James, in London, who was well-up in a bank.

Robert, in New York, who was a police captain.

Joseph, in New York, who was a police sergeant.

Uncle Claren was the youngest, and Aunt Mari had just heard from him for the first time, hence the photo. The last three were the oldest, and the ones she'd not yet heard from. And Aunt Mari also confirmed Ma had not cared to know anything about them.

She feels they abandoned her and myself, she wrote, *and wants nothing to do with a one of them. But they are happy I've made contact, again. They had no idea where Bernadette and I had gotten to. I want my brothers to know of my three, and I'm sure my sister will come around some day. That you know is a good sign.*

No need to mention how we'd found out.

But then in Aunt Mari's next letter, she'd asked Ma to tell Mai she'd finally heard from James. No photo.

Guess who else couldn't keep a secret?

Of course, that set Ma on a tear when Mai came home from school. Ranting and raving, she was, her nails digging into Mai's arm. But my sister, despite not yet fifteen, calmly and quietly said, "Ma, we should talk in lower voices so the whole street doesn't hear, and do so in private."

Her manner was so absolute and certain, Ma stepped back and looked straight at me. "Go down McCleary's and get a haddock for supper. Take Rhuari and Maeve with you."

When Ma's voice was that tight and controlled, I knew better than to say a word. So I pushed my brother and sister out the door then motioned for them to wait, whispering, "Be quiet. Say nothing to Ma and I'll get you a sweetie."

Big eyes and quick nods from both let me stay by the window and try to listen in as Ma and Mai spoke, *woman to woman.* But their voices were too soft.

Until I heard Ma growl, "You can't let the Corporation know about this!"

"It's twenty pound a month, Ma," Mai shot back. "How do you account for the extra funds?"

"I don't. Those bastards think we cover the rent and eat on the pittance we get on the dole!"

"Don't they check on it?"

"Mrs. Haggerty knows a worker at the Bru and lets us know when they're coming by, so I'm in a bedroom with Kieran, Maeve and Rhuari while you lot are off with friends. They accept it."

"How much do you give to Father Demian?"

"That is none of your business."

"How much, Ma?"

Ma huffed and rumbled but finally said, "Ten pound, and my sister knows about it."

I would swear I heard Mai growl as she said, "He'll take two from now on, and not a farthing more."

"It is not your money!"

"It's the family's. We can use it to feed ourselves, well. To make this place even better. Get decent clothes for the wains from Armours instead of scrounging."

"I'll not spend a farthing on this place! They'll be tearing it down, soon, probably with us inside. Look at what they've done to Ann Street and—"

"Your own should come first, Ma."

"There's naught wrong with giving to the Church. Father Demian, he-he's done far more for us than anyone."

"And knowin' how hard off we are, he still wouldn't turn down a penny."

I think I heard Ma slap her, which angered me and I was about to go inside when Mairead's cool, calm voice took over. "I will speak with Brendan about some more repairs."

"You'll do nothing of the kind!"

"And I'll take the wains to get new winter coats. I'm sure Father Demian will appreciate you giving him two pounds a month. Of course, I could speak with him, if you prefer."

"Are you dictating to me how I spend my own money?"

"Family money. I'll write Aunt Mari and thank her for what she's sent us. Let her know what we plan to do with it, from now on. I'm sure she'll be pleased. So when Brendan returns..."

"You put too much store in him, being simple."

"He is not. So I will ask him what he can do and to look into the costs. With him and Eamonn doing the labor, it shouldn't be much."

I could tell from Ma's voice she was angry and this might grow violent. But Mai wasn't giving an inch. I'd seen her handle Ma into silence many times before, so now I could herd Rhuari and Maeve down to Carlito's Sweets. Then I left them outside McCleary's as I picked out their best haddock and a tin of peas. We already had potatoes cooking in the hearth, and that night we feasted well.

Now that I knew how much Ma had given the church, I was even more determined to keep part of what I'd make on whatever short repairs were sent my way. I just told Ma it was a third of what I actually charged, and I let the clients know I was doing it cheap, so they shouldn't tell my mother for fear she'd demand I charge more. It worked out well.

As for the house, we did nothing major. Fresh paper on the walls. Paint as needed that was...well, *found sitting around* in some of the construction sites. During a midnight ramble. With materials from the waste areas to...to *supplement*.

Mai managed to get a decent woven rug to cover the broken tiles in the parlor. From Devlin's. Eamonn and I even put a shelf up over the hearth to hold a vase of flowers. To my surprise, suddenly there was a little Dresden figurine of a lady dancing under a tree in the middle of it. And over the next year, our now neatly papered and painted wall along the stairwell became dotted with more framed photos of the family. Included was one of us all, taken just after Maeve's birth, with Da standing behind me and Eamonn, his hands on my shoulders as I looked at a Corgi car that I'd begun to take apart. It had what looked like a new frame instead of one bought second or third hand, and was next to the one of her parents. To my mind, it appeared Ma was glad Mai had given her the excuse to provide less to the church.

Oh, she still helped keep St. Agnes clean, and when it was polling time she still dragged Eamonn down with her to help. Though never me.

Unless something needed fixing. I wasn't too simple for that.

So within a year of Da's passing, our hovel was almost livable. And to be honest, on more than one occasion I was sorry that he hadn't left us much earlier.

Which is something no child should ever think about his father.

Expansion Demanded

As mentioned, never was I the sort of lad who sought friendships. I had more important things that needed my attention and would have been happy to pass through life on nothing but a name basis with those around me. But Eamonn decided he fancied a girl he'd met at The Embassy, while dancing one night, and found he knew her uncle, Mr. O'Faelan, who drove an old black cab. He also learned she lived in a house that overlooked the pitch where Derry City played their home games.

So one day, when I was but eight, Eamonn stormed into the parlor, freshly washed, and said, "Come along, Bren! Derry City's playin' and I know a place we can watch."

I waved him off and kept my focus on unwinding the spring to Mrs. Campbell's alarm clock. She'd wound it so tight it was frozen and might even have been bent so may need a new spring, if I could get the old one out and-and-and never mind; that's not important. It's the sixpence she'd promised that was.

But he simply picked me up, slung me over his shoulder and swatted me arse, saying, "We're off to watch the match, Ma!"

"Leave off me!" was all I got out before Ma headed up the stairs, also freshly washed. When had the two of them done that? I wondered, for I'd been working not so very far from the basin.

She was smiling as she said, "Good. Get him out for a bit. All he does is sit there and tinker with things. Drives me mad. Be sure to keep him there till it's done."

Then I heard, "Bernadette, I'm callin' yous," in Da's voice, from upstairs! Eamonn carried me outside just as I saw him look over the railing at her. When had he returned from Belfast? Then I realized the house was quiet. Where were Mairead, Rhuari and Maeve?

Eamonn waved to Da then out we went and I wound up seated on his shoulders, ferried like an invalid child all the way to

Brandywell. Enroute, he told me, "I just want to spend some time with a lass named Ailene, Bren. Slip away and talk. Will you help me, here?"

"Why can't you talk to her without me?" I snarled.

"It's complicated."

"What's that mean?"

"Don't the Brothers teach you English?"

"I do well enough."

"All right, all right. It's just, I want to talk with her without her parents breathin' down my neck or her friends all about is all."

"And you need me for that? I was trying to—"

He yanked at my legs to shut me up. "I told Mr. O'Faelan I'd bring you. He's heard how you like to fix things and he'll probably ask you somethin' about his cab."

"I don't fix cars."

"He may still ask."

"He can ask what he wants; I don't fix cars."

We were at the front door to a nice terrace house before he let me down. An older lady answered Eamonn's knock and he said, "Good afternoon, Mrs. Mooney. I'm Eamonn Kinsella and this is my brother, Brendan. Did Mr. O'Faelan tell you we might be droppin' by to watch Derry City, with him?"

She just huffed and said, "He's upstairs, front bedroom. I'll bring you all some tea." Then she headed back to what looked like a real kitchen, from what I could see. Very posh.

So up the stairs he dragged me. Hesitated at an open door, to the back bedroom, and smiled at a pretty girl with red hair, inside. Then led me to the front.

It was nice and comfortable, with two windows and lace curtains pulled aside. Two boys huddled around one and a boy and man were at the other, chattering some nonsense about how the match was going. The man was Mr. O'Faelan, who was tall, ruddy, neatly dressed and smoking a cigarette. The boy with him was Colm, a lad my age who was also ruddy and block-solid. I'd seen him about school with a pack of mates. He was one of those cool lads whom no one would test or question.

At the other window were Danny Gallagher and Paidrig Hurley, both my age. While Danny was trim and fair, Paidrig was more fat than not and darker. Neither was at my school, but I'd seen Danny at my parish, and they were having full fun rooting our team on.

Eamonn introduced me to Mr. O'Faelan, who shook my hand and said, "I hear you're something of a fix-it lad."

I just shrugged.

"My *For Hire* flag won't stay up. I have to bind it then unbind. But if I take it in for repair, it's going to cost me a new one. Maybe even put in an electronic."

"Don't you know someone who can take it apart and see what's the problem?"

He smiled. "They all tell me to get a new one."

"Well, I won't know what I can do till I see it."

He smiled and nodded. "I'll show you after the match."

"You'll have to take us home. I don't have my grip or turnscrew with me." And I shot an angry glare at Eamonn, who smirked and ducked out of the room.

The man just nodded and pulled up a chair to sit and watch what he could of the match.

I didn't really understand the rules of football, for sports had never much interested me, so Mr. O'Faelan explained it as the first half continued. Colm cast me a few wary glances then joined Danny and Paidrig, seeming to be irritated.

At the mid-point, score was 0-1 and not looking good. Mr. O'Faelan was smoking hard and fast and growling in very angry tones. Not even Mrs. Mooney's tea and cake settled him. Not until I noticed some mistakes made by the opposing team's fresh goalie, in the second half. I had no idea what to call them but I'd say things like, "He's at the wrong side of the net," and "Looks like he's aimed for the middle of the pitch." Nine times out of ten, watching the players do their back and forth runs and kicks and bumps, I could say where a goal would be attempted.

Mr. O'Faelan, noticed and asked me to pay special attention to our goalie. I had to stand on the chair to get a better view of him, and I found he was more aware of the other team's strategy, and was trying to get his lads to pay better attention.

Colm and Danny came over to flank me at that window, fascinated, as Mr. O'Faelan stood behind me. Eamonn was, as I suspected he would be, still gone.

"D'you play?" Colm asked me.

"Never have," was my response.

"Then how can you tell what they're up to?" Danny asked.

"How they move on the pitch. Looks they cast each other."

Colm frowned, his eyes sharp on the players. "We have a strategy that's tight."

"Not like theirs."

"Will we be winning this match?" Mr. O'Faelan asked.

I nodded. "Probably. Derry City's not on top of it, but the other goalie's shite."

He chuckled, said he had to make a phone call and hurried downstairs.

Colm smirked after him. Eight years old and he knows all his Da's betting quirks. Then he turned back to me. "I've seen you at school."

I shrugged in answer.

Danny added, "And at mass. Off to yourself, you and your family. Always quiet. Except around the grown ups."

"Ma don't like noise in church," I said.

"He's the looner, hi," said Paidrig, whom I'd forgot was there.

Colm frowned at him. "What d'you mean?"

"That's what the lads call him. I know the White brothers and they pick on everybody but him, hi. Scared he might hex 'em or somethin'."

"I don't know them," I said, even though I did and they had tried to pick at me, a few times, but had backed away when all I'd do is just glare at them like they were insects.

"You want to play some footy?" Colm asked. "I'm with a team at Doire Youth Club. Play at Long Tower and we could use another."

"See how you do as real goalie," said Danny.

"I'm usually it, but I'm not good with strategy."

"Or quick," Danny laughed, and got a shove in response.

"Never played before," I said.

"It's easy," Colm laughed. "Keep the ball out."

I huffed. "Like what I've been telling you he was doing or not, the whole match?"

Colm and Danny both laughed.

Paidrig helped himself to a last slice of the cake.

I actually smiled but still said, "I don't know."

That is when Eamonn was shoved into the room by Mrs. Mooney, as she snarled, "You'll stay here or be out on your arse."

Mr. O'Faelan was right behind him, shaking his head and fighting a smile as he murmured, "Oh, Eamonn. Eamonn."

By this point, the match was near finished and we were up by one. Try as they might, the visitors could not land a ball in the net, thanks to the only real defense coming from the goalie. When it was done, Mr. O'Faelan was grinning ear to ear.

"Get done with your tea, lads," he said, "and we're off to home." Then he looked at me to add, "You're by Nailors, right?"

I downed the last of my cup, nodding. I also noticed Paidrig's pockets seemed to bulge a bit and there were cake crumbs laced on them. He'd helped himself to more than just two slices.

"Come along, Bren," Danny said as we headed from the room. "Won't know if you like being goalie till you try it."

I huffed. "Who told you that?"

"Father Demian."

"But he's right, you know," said Colm. "He's one of the coaches and does well."

"It's funny, hi," said Paidrig, "watchin' him run up and down the pitch in his cassock."

Eamonn overheard and asked, "What's this about?"

"We want your Bren to join our team," said Danny.

"He's great with strategy," Colm added.

"You *should* take him with you, lads," Eamonn said, smirking at me. "Get him away from his tools for a minute or two. Be normal."

"I am normal," I snapped.

"To yourself," he said, with a chuckle.

I shrugged and huffed some more. I didn't like people talking about me.

Mr. O'Faelan took us home. I did an examination of the *For Hire* flag and saw that I could not take it off without breaking the government's seal, which would invalidate it. No wonder no one wanted to touch it. But it was easily worked around by securing a hook to the box's body and around the flag's arm, to hold it. He knew a man at Nixon's who could do a good solder on the catch, so I showed him how to wrap a wire clipped from a clothes hanger around to hook onto the catch and hold it in place. No charge, since we'd got a ride and I really didn't do any work on it. He still gave me sixpence, which Ma promptly took.

A few days later, Colm and Danny appeared at my door, to

go with them for a practice at Long Tower. I was in the middle of rewiring a transistor radio so didn't really pay attention to Ma telling me this until she grabbed me by my ear and dragged me outside.

Da was seated on the divan, combing his hair, so just looked at me as Ma snarled, "Do you better than being inside, all day." Then she'd slammed the door shut.

Colm put an am over my shoulder and pulled me along, saying, "Come along, Bren. It's best to make your mother happy."

"You don't have to play," said Danny.

"Just watch and tell us what we're doin' wrong."

"We've yet to win a match. Maybe you got ideas."

"All Father Demian has us do is run around after the ball."

"I don't know the rules," I grumped, as we went.

"Me Da told ya," Colm said.

"They the same for your club?"

"Almost," Danny said, then he filled me in as Colm let me know rules were for breaking, whenever possible. If that was the case, why have them?

But they gave me a fair idea, and after ten minutes watching their plays, with the adults having no answer when I ask why the center was in striker position while the strikers were doing nothing at all, I took over as goalie and kept the ball out every time with little effort. Father Demian saw it all and agreed to have me join the team, with the church paying my few expenses.

"Boys should be outside playing with friends," he'd said with a pat on the head. "The healthier you are, the better."

Ma seemed to like me being part of Doire, and never once complained when I came home filthy from grass and mud. Danny was usually with me as he lived up the hill from us, so he would recap what happened in our match, with Colm's comments, whenever he was with us. Me? All I'd ever say was, "It was fine."

But she would be in a fine humor, especially if Da was off working. I'd still get a scrub, head checked and combed despite my curls, and given my supper, after they were gone. Then I'd up to my room and return to whatever I'd been fixing.

Another mate of theirs—wee Eammon, who was smaller than me with red curls and freckles—cheered us on. He couldn't play much for the asthma, and even just yelling had him make use of an inhaler two or three times. Paidrig would hold the towels and water for us all.

We wound up with another pair of mates, Gerry and Billy, who lived in The Fountain just around the Walls from us. They stumbled into our group while we were having an after-school match at Long Tower. Both were on a bus to a Protestant School in the Waterside and they got let off closer to Gerry's than Billy's, but being Proddys didn't keep them from joining in on a match, once Doire was done. After that, it was usually a gather in front of Colm's house on Dreaden Alley (nice and flat with few cars passing) or down the Brandywell.

On bright spring days, sometimes I'd join them just running up and down the hill by our hovel, for no reason. Then in winter, we'd use sleds made of scrap tin to slide in the mud or snow. All of it was mindless to me, but I soon found that if I had a repair problem to work out, every time I'd find the solution by joining with my mates and not thinking on it. I even got to where I enjoyed just running about as much as them.

For the most part.

There were some occasions they'd make terror up Butcher Street and down Shipquay, laughing and shoving each other and acting the maggot while I wandered along behind. I was always confused at why they would think that was fun, which added greatly to my reputation as an odd one. But I was never harassed over it; I was always just Bren, who could fix whatever they broke and make it better than before.

They introduced me to wee Johnny's to see comics. We'd pool our coin to buy a lemon drink or two as Danny or Colm read a new DC to us, and when we did buy one Colm would keep it at his place. *For safety*, as he put it. Which actually was a good idea. Ma had no time for such nonsense and would have thrown them out.

I got comfortable with these lads. They let me be who I was, as if they understood my need at times to just be quiet. I found this out during Da's wake. They all came over, said the nice things that are expected to Ma, took some of the food people had brought, then dragged me up to one of the bastions to smoke fags Colm had snuck away from his Da. Well, wee Eammon couldn't smoke, thanks to the asthma. And his mother was a trial—the only one I'd seen who was cleaner than Ma—but he liked to be part of the group, and we liked having him for he was always well-mannered.

Anyway, we'd just sat there, looking out over the Bogside, nibbling at sandwiches and cakes and biscuits, sharing a couple bottles of Orange Crush, saying nothing until darkness was falling and I could face Ma's weeping and wailing, again. Then wee Eammon had started coughing and shivering, so we'd walked him down to his home, still in silence. That was the day before Da was put in the ground, and it was exactly what I'd needed.

Colm's family seemed the most bent on abandoning Derry, like Ma's brothers had. He often talked of joining his oldest brother in South Africa when he was of age, but only in a vague manner that meant nothing. He didn't even know which town he lived in.

"Pretoria, I think," he once said, "though I'd swear me Ma said it was Durban. She says I'm imagining things."

"Can't you ask her?" asked wee Eammon.

"She thinks South Africa's a city and these are parts of it."

"That's daft," I said.

"Bren," he snarled, half-joking, "don't say that about me Ma."

"But I saw them on the globe at school, and South Africa's ten times larger than the whole of Ireland."

"Don't be daft, yourself. Makes it bigger than England, that does."

But the next day I'd shown him on the globe in Brother Thomas' office, and he'd huffed and puffed but had to agree.

The good point of his family was, his brothers would send money home to supplement his father's work driving a cab, so Colm and I were usually the only two with more than a thruppence on us.

Danny's mother was sickly and a bit too precise in her ways, so she had but one daughter and two sons, with Danny the youngest and purest of them all. I only say this because I once overheard Father Demian tell his Da he had the look of Caravaggio's *Cupid*. Which I'd thought odd. Sister Margaret had shown us paintings of Love's Messenger, and he was usually a fat baby, not trim and neat like my mate.

His Da worked for the Diocese, who paid him little enough to live on, though better than the dole. He was an altar boy for Father Demian, our Danny, and even began thinking about taking the mantle. More-so once his Da got a better position in the office.

"Would you be Father Daniel, then?" wee Eammon had asked.

"No, we take new names," Danny'd replied. "I like the sound of Father James."

It was a cold day and we were up by Roaring Meg, in the bastion, filling the chill air with smoke from Blues, all so very world-weary in thought and attitude. I was actually in mind to be finishing up the cleaning of a clock for Mrs. Dean, but at the same time I liked the simpleness of the moment and the peace of the chill air, with just my mates and me.

"We could call you Da Jim," Colm laughed, his breath dancing away on a soft breeze to join the smoke trailing from chimneys not so very far below us.

"Catch yourself on," said Danny, soft and suddenly shy. "It's just a thought."

"I wonder what I should call myself," Wee Eammon murmured, "were I to take the mantle?"

"Father Tim," I'd said. I had just finished Dickens' *A Christmas Carol* and it just popped out. Then I blew smoke straight into the air, like a train engine.

Danny had read the book as well and shot back, "Then you'd be Father Scrooge, the way you are with money." He was smiling when he said it, so I just laughed.

Colm had leaned back against the damp cannon and sighed, "Naw, he'd be Father Tommy. Always with the doubts."

At that, I huffed. "Why? Because I don't let people tell me just anything they want and think I'm fine with it?"

Paidrig popped in with, "You never say anything, hi. Just look at 'em like they're fools."

Colm took another drag then said, "Which fits what I said." Then he winked at me.

I grinned and nudged him. "Then you'd be Father Bugger It, not caring a damn."

Colm busted out laughing as Danny cast me an exaggerated look of horror. Paidrig said nothing more, just nodded, and Wee Eammon took a shot from his inhaler.

Wee Eammon was an only child of an *abandoned woman*, about whom the less said the better, as everyone loved to say. He was the only one smaller than me, with eyes like emeralds, and an open grin of crooked teeth. I never once saw scowl on him.

"Has the look of a leprechaun, that one," I once heard Mrs. Keogh say to Mrs. Cahan as we passed, aimed for the Long Tower.

"No pot of gold for his kind," was the reply.

"I dunno. Could be it was one of the little people sired him."

"Oh, you are awful!" Spoken with a laugh, the old cows.

Fortunately, wee Eammon had been at the front of our pack so I don't think he heard them, and I said nothing to him about it. I liked how he was always the happiest among us and felt no need to hurt that.

His mother worked out having a proper flat in the second tower of the Rossville Flats, with two bedrooms, sitting room, kitchen and indoor plumbing. Probably because she was master at playing the sad thing in need of protection and comfort. On more than one occasion she had used it to get me to fix something of hers at no charge, despite me swearing, each time, I never would, again. Ma could have taken pointers from her on how to deal with the Mayor's residential allocations.

I think the Mayor's office was suspicious of Ma's claims and supposed residence being a single room in Mrs. Haggerty's. Especially after Da's death and Aunt Mari's comments to the press. But rather than do anything about it, they simply put our name to the bottom of the list, even though we were almost as bad off as Paidrig's family.

Paidrig's attitude of avoiding anything that would take effort could be extended to his full family. Granted, jobs were hard to find, with the shirt factories preferring to hire women and only the most menial of labor set aside for Catholic men, but his Da was not the sort to seek work with much effort. Like my own Da. So they lived in one room of a three-level building on Fahan, next to another room holding his older brother, sister-in-law and kids, with no prospects of that changing till the last tower of the Flats was completed. If then.

They would always be on the dole, that family, begging or borrowing what they could and blaming their lot on those who hated the Pope while moaning about how meager their pantry was. But all of them were fat and strong despite swearing they never had enough to eat. In fact, Paidrig wound up rounder and heavier than wee Eammon and myself, put together, which is a mystery for the ages.

He was the least clean of my mates, so there were times Ma

wouldn't let him in the house before she'd sponge-washed and combed him, herself. He never fought her. He never fought anyone. But soon, on the rare times he did come to my home, he preferred to wait outside.

Billy's Da kept bar in a pub on Spencer so was bringing home a steady wage. Billy took after him, in his long, fair, narrow looks. Of course, the best benefit of his Da's occupation was how the man was loath to touch any alcohol, since he always saw how it affected others. They were saving up to move into a new home on the Waterside, soon as one was available. Which he never tired of pointing out.

"Mates for years and can't wait to be quit of us, eh, Billy?" Colm often shot at him.

"Don't be daft," was always Billy's response. "We're mates, forever, hi. And there's busses 'round the Guildhall."

Sounded like he'd worked it out, well-enough. But none of us really believed him.

Gerry's Da drove a lorry for Arann Express, making trips to Belfast and back three times a week. They were all fair complexioned and sturdy builds, with round faces, quick smiles and calm tempers. They were in line to move to a new estate being built on the Waterside; with Gerry having but one younger brother, we knew they'd soon be there.

But the only time any of us paid mind to the other's religion was when Danny would cross himself each time we passed a church, be it Catholic or Protestant. Then Paidrig would laugh and say, "It's Father Danny with us, again, back from drinkin' his holy blood."

Danny would just sneer him away and Colm would jostle him for it and we'd keep on. We were our own little pack. all of us poor and living in tight quarters, so were equals in each other's eyes. When I was out with them, I was happy and at ease, so wasn't worried about completing whatever project I was repairing.

Well...not much worried.

The Chinas

Things were going well, overall, until this one day after school. I was heading for home to complete the rewire of an old lamp for Mrs. Carnahan and felt there'd be no footy, today, for I smelled rain coming. But my mates all caught up to me and wanted me to join them for a match at Long Tower. I was thinking *yes*, only Ma had just come out the door and seen me, and called down I was to watch Rhuari. Then off she went with Maeve and Kieran to plague the mayor for housing, again (as she'd told Mrs. Haggerty, Mrs. Cahan, Mrs. Keogh, the Raffertys, and every other person she'd seen as she left, sure to make a ten-minute walk to the Guildhall take near an hour). Rhuari came over to join us, a book in hand.

"Is it just you here?" I asked him.

He nodded. "Eamonn's out with his mates for a gander while Mairead's off to Devlin's. Looking for a small bed for me and Kieran."

That surprised me. "We got room for another bed?"

"Mai thinks so."

"But won't it be a price?"

He just shrugged, then stopped, frowning. "It's gonna rain..."

"Aw, not so much," Colm laughed.

"Come play with us," Danny added. "Be a sweeper."

"No, I think I'll just sit," Rhuari said. "Read my book."

"What is it?" wee Eammon asked.

"*Irish Folk Tales.*"

"Are you testing for it?" asked Billy.

Rhuari shook his head. "I just like it."

He showed it to Billy, and *that* is when it came a sheeting rain. We ran back down Nailors around to my home since it was closest, slipping, sliding and laughing in the muck and mud. By the time we piled inside, we were soaked and filthy, and Rhuari was upset because his book was wet, and it was the library's. He sat as close as he could to the hearth and held it flapping open, shivering and saying nothing. His glasses were wet and splattered till I cleaned them.

Then I added turf to the hearth, to build up the heat, and we stripped to our shorts. I made tea. Soon the room was warm, and we could lounge comfortable on the woven rug. Then I rushed up to my room to bring down a wee tin of biscuits I'd bought. I liked to have something to nibble at as I worked on a radio or Hoover, and kept it hidden behind a loose board in the wall.

As we'd arranged our clothes around the fire, I'd noticed Colm also had a paper book stuffed in his jacket pocket.

"You carry books to read, now?" I asked him as he took a biscuit.

He laughed and said, "Me brother sent it from South Africa. He's in Port Elizabeth. Said Ma shouldn't see it."

"Why not?"

"Dunno. Just kept it in me jacket, like he said."

Danny frowned, saying, "I thought your Ma said he's in Durban."

"Aw, she thinks they're next to each other and ain't even close."

"I think she just likes the sound of it, hi," said Paidrig. "It's almost like turban."

"What's a turban?" wee Eammon asked.

"It's like the hats his mother wears," Danny sighed, a fag smoking in his lips and combing his wet hair in a very Steve McQueen kind of way.

"Yeah, all round and wound up on top, hi," Paidrig added, "like she's a Paki."

I don't think wee Eammon understood him; still he smiled and shrugged an okay.

But Colm frowned, saying, "Don't you be callin' me Ma a Paki!"

Paidrig blinked and said, "I wasn't..."

"Men with turbans are Sikhs," Danny huffed, "From India, not Pakistan."

"What're they seekin', hi?" Billy asked, laughing.

"It's a religion," Danny snapped. He'd been fair moody, of late.

"And who told you that?" asked Gerry.

"Father D, hi?" asked Billy. He would never say Father Demian's full name.

"No, I-I just learned it, is all."

Colm snorted a chuckle. "Probably *was* Father *Demian*." He shot the name at Billy. "He knows all and is all, and don't ya forget it."

I was taken aback at Colm's smirk. And how Danny was glaring at him in a nervy way, so I popped in with, "What d'you mean?"

Colm cast me a side glance and said, "You're just now eleven, right Bren?"

"Next month."

"But *you're* not an altar boy, like our Danny, are ya?" Colm asked.

"What if I'm not?"

"It's just that near every lad in Derry is and..."

Danny cut him off with, "What're you saying?"

"Well, you are, ain't ya?"

"What if I am?"

But he was getting truly angry, so I grabbed Colm's coat and pulled the book from its pocket. The title was *Borstal Boy*.

"What's this about?" I asked, far more chipper than I felt. I did not want a fight in Ma's home, not with her Dresden over the hearth.

Colm took the book from me. It was wet and a bit torn but not too badly so.

"An IRA lad's time in a British jail," he said. "I've poked through it, here and there, but a lot don't make sense. Guess you have to read it from the start. You want to, Bren? The writer's got your name." Then he added with a wicked grin, "But he says he pronounces it Br-br-br-brendan when he's scairt."

"I don't do that," I snapped back at him.

"No, you just do this—Bren-cough-dan-cough."

I smacked at his shoulder, even though it's true. When I was four, I developed this light noise that whispered up from within me, like I'm trying to clear my throat without anyone noticing. It only happened when I was nervous or scared, and it made Da laugh but drove Ma to distraction since it was she who usually brought it on.

"Leave him be," Gerry said. "You're in his home!"

"You do make a nice cuppa, Bren," said wee Eammon, cutting in. "Thanks."

I just nodded to him.

"So it's an IRA tale, hi," said Paidrig.

"Any bombs?" Danny asked, still not fully happy.

"Just the one he's smugglin' in, at the start, I think," said Colm. "I read part where he's in borstal and gets to be friends with this Brit named Charlie and they call each other China. You know why, Bren?"

"No," I said. "Why?"

"No, I'm askin'," Colm said.

"Askin' what?"

"Why they call each other China?"

"I haven't read it. How would I know?"

Which got Billy in on the confusion. "Why would they call each other that, hi? Ain't they all English?"

"How's it written?" asked Danny. "Is he angry when he says it?"

"Fine, here," Colm said, flipping through the pages. "He says—uh, here ya are—*stickin' up for your China.*"

"Away on, Colm," I said. "Sounds like another word for mate."

Which got Paidrig even more confused. "But they're English, right? They ain't from China, hi. Are they?"

"Like from Hong Kong?" Gerry asked.

Colm rolled his eyes and said, "That's why I'm askin' Bren. Maybe he can figure it."

"Why me?"

"You read."

"Not so very much."

"More'n me or any here."

"Oi, you don't know that," Gerry snapped.

"Ya read this?" Colm held up the book.

"Never even heard of it," Gerry huffed.

"I read," Rhuari finally said.

"Here, then, you read it for us." And he tossed the book to him, and my little brother caught it like it'd been tied to his hand.

"Colm!" I howled. "He's just gone nine. Rhuari, give it here."

I tried to take it from him but he bolted away, holding the book as if it were treasure as he said, "I read at an advanced level!

Better than any of you!"

"But there's jail, in it, and bombs and IRA. Ma won't like this."

"Yeah, Rhuari, give it over," said Colm. "Ask Eamonn if he'll tell us if Charlie's Chinese."

"Eamonn?" Which surprised me. "What's he to do with reading?"

"He's aiming for university, inn't he?"

"Not if Ma has a say in it. She's digging at him to work."

"But you said your Da wanted him off to Queens."

"Da's dead. Ma ain't."

"She been at him much, lately?"

Now that he mentioned it, I had to admit she hadn't, and it surprised me more to realize it. But it seemed since Mai had taken over the finances and worked in Aunt Mari's contribution, money was not so tight as it was and Ma's complaints had lessened. Some. She could still get in a lather, if she was up to it, but being on a political committee seemed to give her another outlet for her anger: berating the Unionists.

"Maybe you *should* ask Eamonn," Danny said to me. "My mother keeps telling me, if he's going he'll have no problem."

"How would she know?"

"She's working with some thinking of helping him with it."

I huffed and wondered why Eamonn hadn't said word one. And Mairead thought he couldn't keep a secret.

"Whole thing about *Chinas* sounds bloody stupid to me, hi," said Paidrig.

"*Peter Rabbit* more your speed?" Colm laughed.

I left the book with Rhuari, who sat next to the hearth to begin reading it, right there, and made myself a second cuppa, smiling. I felt very grand, at the moment. I'd found I liked my tea on the weak side with a sugar and splash of real milk. Ma had worked a small second-hand cooler out of Father Demian, for to keep some things fresh. Or maybe it was third hand, since it barely worked. I was still trying to understand its mechanics so I could fix it.

Paidrig helped himself to another biscuit, asking, "Does anybody else call anybody that, hi?"

"Dunno," said Colm.

"I like the idea of it," said wee Eammon. "Nobody here does that. It's all *mate* and *lad* and *son*. Normal things. This sounds special. Sets you apart."

Danny finally grinned and motioned to me, "Oi, me China, the biscuits—give us share!"

I laughed and shied one to him and he caught it—

Just as Ma came in the door, with Kieran.

Before we had a chance to even think of moving, she snapped, "What're you boys doin'? Why is it so hot in here?"

"Nothing, Ma," I said, scampering to put myself between her and the rest of us. "Just come in from the rain to dry off and get warm. Have some tea."

"Leaving mud all over my clean rug!?" And I must admit, it was kind of claggy with it. She also saw the mess of tea, milk, sugar, and biscuit tin on the table by the hearth, and her eyes cut into me.

Bloody hell, I was for it.

She quietly said, "Get yourselves dressed, boys, and away home; the rain's let up, and Brendan has much to do before supper."

All of them yanked their things on and snuck away, though wee Eammon did stop by the door to say, "Yours was the closest home, Mrs. Kinsella. That's why we come here."

Ma just nodded and said, "Off! Your mother was askin' after you."

That's when Colm popped his head back around the door, winked and smiled at me. "See you, tomorrow. Me *China*."

"Me what?" Ma snapped at him.

"Nothin', Mrs. Kinsella. Thanks for your home." He left.

Ma glared after him then turned to Rhuari. "Go upstairs. Put on fresh clothes."

"I'm fine here, Ma," he said. She cast him a look and off he went. I took vague notice of how he'd kept the book out of her sight.

I pushed the lid back on the biscuit tin as Ma lay Kieran in his bassinette and I wondered why Mai was off looking for another bed when he was still proper size for that, and damn if I wasn't giving off that cough. Then Ma sat on a chair by the hearth and motioned me over. I slowly went, her eyes locked on me. "We can barely feed ourselves, but you give those boys half of what we have?"

"Just tea, Ma (cough). The biscuits I bought on me own."

"With what?"

Oh, shite. "A-(cough)-a shilling I got for fixing Mrs. Hill's old telly. It needed a tube."

She shook me, angry. "You wasted good money on such an extravagance?"

"At least I earned it (cough), not like Da ever really did—"

She slapped me, twice. Sharp and stunning. My ears rang so, I could barely make out she was saying, "You do not talk to me like that! And never will you speak ill of your father! A poor man murdered by Protestant bastards merely because he wanted to care for his family, and they wouldn't even allow him that much dignity. So you will never spit on his name, again, master Kinsella. Do you understand me?!"

I made myself nod.

"Now, did you use the full shilling for that tin of biscuits?"

I was still shaken by the slaps so shook my head before I could think not to.

"How much?"

"Sixpence."

"That tin of biscuits only cost sixpence?"

"It was open and two taken. Mr. Owen offered it, for that."

"I'll ask him." That made me jolt into glaring at her. She noticed and grew stiff. Somehow I knew that had I said a word, she'd have whaled on me. "Now hand the rest of that shilling over to me, to make up for the milk and sugar you gave those boys. You'll also give me every farthing you've made fixing other people's things. And don't you think for one second I won't know the full of it. I had a nice bit of craic with Mrs. Rafferty and she tells me there's a number of people paid you twice what you told me. Now clean the mud off everything in this room, including yourself, or there's no supper for you."

So I did. As good as a lad of near eleven can be expected off a woven rug, which was still wet. Of course, it warranted me nothing but a cut of bread, lump of cheese and mug of water in my room as the others ate. And peace and quiet to finish Mrs. Carnahan's lamp. And for a week Ma told the neighbors how much trouble it had been for her to clean the floor and walls and cabinets and windows of mud after *me and my mates had destroyed her home, all without a thought for anyone but ourselves.* The sympathies she got were enormous.

To her face.

But a few days later, I was in the toilet and heard Mrs. Haggerty and Mrs. Connolly having a craic in her pantry. Oh, but was there some laughter at Ma's mantle of martyrdom.

"As if much really needed doin'," said one, "the way she is with soap and water."

"Aye," said the other, "there's such a thing as too clean."

"There's a wee want in her, on that."

After some laughter came, "She thinks no one knows about her making sport of the Bru."

"Fools will be fools, no matter how smart they think themselves."

"Speaking of Brendan..."

"Oh, what a horrible thing to say," mingled with laughter. Then came, "But he is odd. So few friends. Always in his room tinkering with this or that."

"My transistor's not picking up as well as it should. Has he done somethin' for you, of late?"

"Not a radio, but I bought a toaster from them thieving tinkers and it was burning bread, of course. He got it to stop."

"What was his charge for that?"

"Sixpence, so don't you let him charge you a bit more. I'd go for thruppence, were I you."

"You'd think he's a Jew, the way he is with money."

"Somebody has to be. Their father—oh, enough said about him."

"God rest him."

Then they moved into the parlor and I could hear nothing more.

So their true feelings were saved for laughing at Ma, when she wasn't about. And they shared her belief I was of limited mind and could easily be manipulated. *Only go for thruppence* to repair a transistor? I'd ask for a half-crown then let myself get worked down to a shilling. Let her think me simple, after that.

Another time without meaning to, I was trailing behind the family, enroute to Mass, when I heard Mrs. Murphy and Mrs. Rafferty speaking about us done up in our *Sunday-best*. True, our clothes were much worn but they were repaired as best can be.

By Ma, of course, as she often said.

"So you could see she's really tryin' so hard," said one in a tone that was not kind.

"Oh, but isn't she the one out to prove herself a holy mother?" In the same tone.

"It's Mairead made those rags acceptable, I'd say."

"No, Bernadette does have a good hand with a needle."

"She also loves a good craic."

"Even when there's work in need of doin'."

"Her Eamonn is growing up well, hi."

"He's after Queens College, I hear."

"He didn't get his smarts from her, did he?"

"Nor his craftiness."

"That's from his Da, God rest him."

"And enough about him, hi."

"Aye. But the lad does cut a fine figure, don't he?" And I would swear to it I heard a light sigh, after saying that, but I didn't know which of them did it.

"I wouldn't mind me a little of that."

"Oh, you're awful."

And that's when the laughter and giggles and whispering started, and they finally noticed me and shooed me off. Of course, this was before Mai had learned of Aunt Mari's contribution. After that, our Sunday best became much nicer.

As for Mass—well, I sang and knelt and prayed, like the others, but was more fascinated by Danny trying to keep the order of the ceremony in mind as he worked with Father Demian. Was it incense here? Holding the cross there? Lighting the candles from the left or right? Dousing them from the right or left? Not that it mattered. While Danny would wince when he did it wrong, Father Demian would always pat him on the back of the head and make the little corrections needed in as quiet a way as possible. Kinder than with the other boys. Other than that, it mattered not, to me, for Paidrig was now with Colm's parish and I don't think wee Eammon's Ma attended any service.

To be honest, the main reason I continued with it was how I would often get business. Like Mrs. Casey slipping up to me after the service to say, "Brendan, my clock's been runnin' slow; give you thruppence to look at it." Or Mrs. O'Connor saying, "Brendan, my lamp is shorting out and you did such a good job with Mrs. Cahan's, do you think you could fix it for less than sixpence?" And I'd never turn them down—albeit with the caveat,

"Won't know till I see it."

A few shopkeepers were the same way, if I was by their door. "Brendan, the missus tells me you're good at reworking lights and I've one that won't come on, even with a fresh bulb. There's a shilling in it, if you can fix it right." And I'd do it then and there, since I now made sure to always have a turnscrew and grips in a pocket. Made me feel the proper man.

And if Ma was told different on what I said I was paid, I'd just say they weren't being honest with her. Besides, it truly irritated me that Ma still gave any of our pitiful funds to Father Demian, for *the poor children in Africa and Asia and South America and godless Russia* and on down the endless list of poor children who were anywhere but Derry and her own home. But the one time I was fool enough to ask Ma why she did it when her own needed the money more, I got a sharp smack to the back of my head.

"They're doing God's work," she'd snapped, "and you're not starvin', are ya?"

Not anymore. No, I never truly was. Somehow, we'd always had enough to eat, it's just—it was always the least amount needed to live on, and even at that age I was weary of it.

On top of this, Ma was spending more and more time working to help civil rights groups and in elections, like for Eddie McAteer, and dragging Eamonn in to help with polls. Which might be part of the reason he was being considered for assistance at Queens. But this also led her deeper into the church's Nationalist, anti-communist attitudes, and built up a stronger disdain for Protestants than she'd ever shown before. And Father Demian was in lock step with her.

Of course, the Protestant crowd was growing more and more difficult with us, in the Bogside. As if that would stop the marches and demonstrations and actions being taken throughout the year. It's like their side believed that to give us the same as everyone meant there would be less for them. There were also many on our side who said we should just keep ourselves apart from the Unionists, completely, with the comment usually followed by something like, *They cannot be trusted.* So I made sure to tell all my mates—no, my *Chinas* that religion and politics were to be kept from my house.

"If you don't," I said, "you're in for an hour's lecture about the history of Ireland in full detail, from my mother, and you do not want that. Believe me."

"Yeah," said Paidrig, "get enough from the brothers, hi."

"And priests," said Danny.

"Father Demian treats you to history lessons, does he?" asked Colm, jostling Danny.

Who just shrugged and said no more.

Fortunately, Ma never saw Billy with me, again. Which was good, because the gossip was growing about us being seen with him.

That one lives in The Fountain, don't he?

It's not good for him to be mingling in with our lads.

What d'ya think he's after, hi?

Somethin' sneaky, that's for sure.

That's a low thing to say about a child.

You sure he's Protestant? I seen him hittin' Proddies with stones.

He's the one with the catapult, hi?

Brand new, and a good eye with it.

Well, if he fires stones at them, he can't be a bad 'un, can he?

If he's a Protestant, he can.

It was funny, because I knew a lot of that gargle had come from this one Monday afternoon, in the summer, when Billy and I were alone on William Street and got caught in the middle of two gangs chucking stones at each other, one Catholic and one Protestant. I'd been near hit by a fair-size piece of pavement that came from my side, so howled at the stupid buggers and shied it back at them, without a thought. Then I'd followed it with more.

Billy had laughed and begun grabbing pebbles to fire at the Proddies, using that catapult. We were howling like loonies in the bin.

Till both sides forgot about each other and came after us.

Fortunately, we're also good runners.

I'd known Mrs. Bannon was home so I'd dragged Billy around a corner and up to her door and scurried inside, crying, "Mrs. Bannon, we've come for tea!"

She'd come tottering down the hall, an older lady in just her shift and apron, eyes wide and wary. "Tea?" she'd asked. "What do you mean?"

"Don't you remember, Mrs. Bannon?" I'd said, full innocent.

"You invited me after Mass, yesterday, for-for today at-at—" I looked up at this old grandfather clock of hers; it showed 1:49, so I continued with, "two o'clock, but I'm a bit early. Sorry if that's a trouble."

"I did?" She'd begun to frown at herself.

"Surely you've not forgotten?" I'd asked. "You wanted me to take a look at your radio?" She had an old one that still used tubes and was about to die. I'd fixed it but a few months ago.

"Did I?"

Billy had been about to fall into laughing so I'd jostled him and added, "I brought a friend, Billy, with me. I hope it's all right. If it needs a new tube, then he can run off to get it."

She'd huffed then smiled and shrugged and said, "Come along. Have a look. I was about to have my luncheon. Would you care to join me?"

That had made me hesitate, but Billy'd said, "That'd be smashin'!" He was always hungry, like Paidrig.

So I'd made a big show of looking in the back of the radio and noticed one of the tubes had come loose. Didn't mean anything, but it gave me the excuse to say that was the only problem so all was well.

But then she'd fed us part of her roasted chicken, warmed from yesterday, with mushy peas and carrots, and a fine Ceylon Black and I started to feel bad because now I was sure she'd intended this to be part of her meals the full week, and there I was lying to take from her.

Only my mind was taken by how she'd used a knife and fork to cut the meat off a leg, to eat. It so fascinated me, I'd tried to emulate her. It seemed much nicer than tearing at the meat with your teeth and fingers, like Billy was doing with a wing. She was kind enough to give me direction on how best to use the cutlery. Not to grab it but to hold it like you were going to poke a lad's arse with it.

Which had made Billy and myself laugh, to hear it come from her.

"It's so much nicer this way," she'd said. "Isn't it?"

Well, it certainly had been, and the mechanics of it were simple. Dig the fork deep into the meat and slice between it and the bone. Carefully. Like working with a transistor, to make sure you didn't cross any wires. I'd felt very grown up, doing it.

Billy had grown silent and watched me and her work our finest manners. We had a lovely chat about how glad she was we'd stopped by, despite all the noise and carry-on. She also had four cats that came strolling out, one after the other. All orange tabbies, of course, and only one willing to be touched. None tried to get on the table but instead placed themselves around her, standing at attention, almost like they were guarding her. Then each had been given a bite of chicken, which they would only accept from her. When we'd finally left, she'd made us swear to come, again, and next time she'd be sure to remember inviting us.

I'd determined I would, and I'd bring something from the chippy.

Billy had laughed at me the whole way home, saying over and over, "I can't believe you did that, hi!"

"Got us away, didn't it?" I'd said, proudly. "And well-fed."

"Me mother's gonna wonder why I'm not hungry, now. And where I was."

"Tell her we had tea and cakes at the Diplomat."

"Yeah, she'll believe that. You're loop-de-loop, me China."

"Maybe next time I'll let you get pummeled."

"I'm faster than you in a run."

I'd only laughed at him, because he was right.

We'd crowed about our battle to Colm and Danny, the next day, and they'd told me I was mad. To which I answered, "I was. The bloody stone missed me by an inch. Whoever threw it should get glasses or training."

Then since I had no jobs lined up, we'd hit up to Long Tower and had a fine game of footy.

I began to work on my jobs for Protestant clients late in the night, to keep Ma from knowing of them. I actually preferred to work at night, in the dark, with only a torch on my project and the stars in a clear sky to accompany me. I found I liked having my world carefully divided up in this orderly way—work, me Chinas, school and dealing with Ma, and all was well and good. Kept it like that for months, till one day Ma learned I'd repaired another old radio with tubes in it, for Mr. Willis. He'd paid me half a crown without comment, and I'd said nothing to Ma, but his wife was not happy and, probably in her most condescending manner, let her know I'd overcharged them. Which was nonsense.

Ma had grabbed me the moment I got home and demanded I

explain why I hadn't told her anything about it, like she'd ordered me to do. She was not fond of the Willis family being Protestant, but I didn't care about that so long as I was paid.

Fortunately, she'd learned of this two days after I'd done the work and the half-crown was well-hidden, so I'd told her, "I don't know what you mean. I was paid a shilling and did the work at their home. They bought the tubes it needed and sat me there ten minutes as it warmed up so they could check it."

"You're lyin'," Ma snapped, shaking me.

"You believe Protestants over your own son!?"

That caught her up. "And just where is this shilling?"

"I give it to Mairead, for the household." This had actually turned out to be a good way to sidestep her.

She'd given me another shake, but for once there were no slaps. "You will tell me of every job you do, for this day forward. Do you understand me? Even those not handled here."

I'd nodded, but inside I knew there was no way I would. What cemented my decision was she'd asked Mairead when she came in if I'd given her the money. Mai had merely said, "It's in the jar, Ma, for tomorrow's shopping."

She had checked and seen a few coins in it so accepted the story.

For now.

I know this reveals me as anything but a perfect angel. Or child. What money Eamonn made, running errands for shopkeepers or neighbors and the like, or Mairead made for watching the wains of others, went straight into the jar for the household. I don't think they held anything back, so I'm sure I should have done the same. But with Ma allowing us to be deprived for so long, not only by Da but also the church, I had settled into this belief that if I gave all of it over, it would not be well-used. And even with Mairead now running our expenses, I could not shake that idea. So kept half to myself, and to this day I am not sorry I did so.

✳✳✳✳✳

Things began to change between us all on a day in mid-spring. Me, Colm, Paidrig, Billy and Gerry were headed for the bridge to cross and watch the train arrive. Danny had been called into another meeting with Father Demian, for some reason or other, and wee Eammon was kept home by his Ma, who was keeping him away, more and more.

As we passed Tillie's, at the head of the Craigavon Bridge, four older, strapping lads were coming up the other side of the fountain, aiming for town. Probably to walk the Walls and toss pennies on Walkers Terrance or Nailors Row, just for the hell of it. We ignored them till one was fool enough to yell, "Bloody Taigs," at us. So Colm shied a stone at him. Clipped him in the shoulder.

I knew he could throw well, but this made me jump with joy. "Jesus, Colm, you should be a hurler!"

He laughed and went looking for another stone, but Paidrig cried, "They're comin' over, hi!"

We looked about to find all four lads rounding the fountain, aiming straight for us. With five of us and four of them, we were ready for some fun. Even me, for a change, since it was helping my Chinas.

But then Billy yanked Gerry back and yelled, "What're yous doing? We're not Taigs," then off they ran, leaving us three to face down four.

Which we didn't.

We ran the circle, leading them along and laughing and splashing water and cursing as cars whisked past, honking, madly. It was great fun—until a lad got struck by one and slung to the ground, screaming in pain. That is when we ran off, fearful the RUC would blame us for it.

Which they did.

They came for Colm and myself at school and pulled us down to Strand Road, snarling threats the whole way; Paidrig wasn't in class that day, nor at home, so it was just us two. And they made it sound like we'd killed the lad.

In the back of the car heading to jail, the two of us sat still and unbending. Then Colm whispered, just loud enough for me to hear, "They chased us is all."

One of the peelers looked back at us, snarling, "What was that? What'd you say?"

"Just tellin' me mate you're a right bastard," Colm smiled.

The *right bastard* cuffed him by the ear then glared at me. "Got anything to add?"

I said nothing, just looked at him, making myself smile with all innocence.

In the station as they told us of all we'd done and how we'd go to borstal for it till we were too old to walk. I couldn't understand how they knew it was us involved while Colm was keeping his cool attitude on, for they had accidentally let slip the hurt lad didn't even have to go to hospital.

Finally, I popped off with, "Why're we to blame? We're heading for the Waterside and they shie stones at us and call us Taigs, then start chasing us? Were we supposed to stand still for a lashing? It's only peelers like you get to do that, isn't it?"

That got me a smack to the head, but also a chuckle from more than one of the constables, and a look of awe from Colm.

Fortunate for us, his sister was seeing a lad whose uncle was a barrister in Liverpool, and he called over and got us released with naught but a warning.

As we left to walk home, the city windy and damp, Colm shook his head at me, smiling. "Jesus, Bren, barkin' like that at those bastards?"

"I tried to make it funny," I said. "No sense of humor, them."

He laughed. "You are mad. I never know what's up in that head of yours."

I shrugged, said, "Neither do I, half the time," but inside felt very proud.

The next day, we caught up with Billy and Gerry by Long Tower, and Colm calmly took Billy by his jumper to ask, "What the devil was that, yesterday? You don't stick up for your Chinas?"

"What'd ya have to shie stones at 'em for, hi?" Billy snapped back at him. "They was just yappin' at yous."

"Was it you told the peelers that?"

"No! Colm, I'm no tout. I only told me Ma."

"It's the same thing, me China," I sighed, as world-weary as I could be.

"No! She'd never turn me out!"

"Toss us, again, you'll get a wild kickin'," Colm sneered.

Then Billy all but pleaded with, "Gerry!"

"I-I'm sorry I run," said Gerry, "but I know the brother of one of them lads, and he recognized me."

We all shifted focus to him, shocked. I felt as if I'd been

punched in the chest.

He continued with, "It must've been him let the peelers know so they went to me Da, for information. Me Da's got worries enough at his job without being asked why I'm runnin' with a couple of-of…"

That set *me* to glaring at him, daring him to say it. Colm was also worked up in a quiet, scary fashion, so Gerry backed away.

"Lads, c'mon," Danny said, pulling Colm back. Paidrig helped, but also shot dirty looks at Billy and Gerry, both. "We're mates, here," he continued. "All Chinas. No need to go raging anymore."

That settled everyone, but not by much.

Until it got back to Ma that the reason I was hauled down to Strand Road was due to a Protestant lad I was running with. No need to repeat her howls and curses and furies and slaps at me having dared bring two Protestants into her house. After she was done with me, she spent three days cleaning everything in the foyer, including her Dresden figurine. I was tasked with clearing out the hearth and starting a new fire, and I was kept from school for a week thanks to my bruises, which would have been worse had Eamonn not come home and stopped her physical punishment of me. While he wasn't as perturbed as she when he found out about Billy and Gerry, I could see he was not happy, either.

I was warned never to go near them, again. But I still considered them me Chinas. Two of my few real friends. Which now looks to be very childish of me. For I knew things were growing worse between the two sides. And I had little problem with them wanting to play it safe. Besides, after that Gerry was never around for a game of footy, and a few months later he was moved to the Waterside.

As for Billy, since his Da was working so steady, now, he spent most of his time with his uncle, one of those fat fellows who's never held a tool for work in his life but was happy enough to call Catholics lazy, and who was mad for this Belfast minister named Paisley.

I was at Billy's house, not long after, and we were going to go for a wander soon as Mrs. Corrie tested a lamp I'd rewired. They had a smaller place that backed up to the Walls, as if trying to hold them up or hold the march of time back. Furnished well-enough and neat, with an actual kitchen, but on the shabby side.

I noticed this newspaper I'd heard of, *The Protestant Telegraph*, lying on a table and read some of it, and grew ill. Paisley hated O'Neill as much as we did, but only because he didn't deal *hard enough* with the *papist scum*, and a lot more like that.

When Billy hopped down, pulling on his coat, I showed him the paper and asked, "You read this?"

He brushed it off, saying, "Bren, you know I don't read, hi."

Mrs. Corrie came in, saw me with the paper and snatched it away, her voice cold and hard as she said, "You shouldn't handle other people's things!" Then she shoved two sixpence in my hand and rushed us out the door.

Outside, Billy gave me a backhanded swat on the shoulder. "What'd you do, Bren, get me mother thinkin' we're snoopin' and—?"

"It was there," I snapped as we headed around to Bishop's. "I just read it for something to do. That paper's got some harsh words in it."

Billy shrugged. "My uncle says sometimes exaggeration's the best way to make your point, hi."

"How does that work?"

"I dunno. I guess it means making things up to make it easy for people to understand."

"Sounds like lying, to me."

"Ian Paisley's a man of God, Bren. Would you like me to call your Father Demian a liar, as well?"

"Call him what you like," I said. "My father's dead."

Then someone ran up to tell us about a massive demonstration of unemployed men happening in the city center and we rushed off to see what that was for and how the RUC would handle it. Not that we were hoping for violence, just some excitement, for there was little enough to do in Derry when you're a lad.

It wasn't till the following year I really understood who Ian Paisley was, and see the fullness of his evil.

Life Sideways

I'd just gained my twelfth birthday and my present was Ma finding all my hiding spots for my scratch and taking it. Then she gave me a hiding for not handing it over, as she'd demanded. I think she also kept the card Aunt Mari usually sent me, with a pound note in it. So I was bruised, limping and bust, with nothing lined up to fix, and not in the best mind. The day was cold, gray and bitter, so Colm took pity on me and thought he could beg a couple shillings off his Da so we could pop over to Woolies for hot cocoa.

Only we found he was in a foul temper, cursing and slamming his fist against the front wings—uh, fenders of his cab. He was parked near the bus depot and having trouble with the heater, so was jumping back and forth from under the bonnet to beneath the fascia to see why it wasn't warming the ten-year-old piece of junk. Colm was of a mind to just let him be, but I got a curiosity up and peeked under the bonnet to see what he's doing.

"Don't touch a thing, Brendan," he snarled at me. "This bloody beast's already jabbed me twice with shocks."

"Isn't it grounded?" I asked.

"Somewhere a wire's touching metal, now and again. I think it's shorted out the heater's motor."

That made no sense to me. In a lamp or radio, it's easy to find a shorted wire. Why not in a car? Being small, I dropped to my back, despite my aches, and was able to slip under it to get a look.

Colm jumped into a rage. "Bloody hell, Bren. We're not here for this!"

"Sure, Colm," was all I said, not really listening.

"You'll dirty yourself, and your Ma's already in a state."

I only nodded, as if he could see me.

He kicked my foot, for that. He had become neater than I and was well on to being adult in body if not in brain. Me, I thought it odd him talking about having to shave when I had little more than soft down about my chin, yet, and us near the same age.

Anyway, I got a look at what I later learned was the back of the core, and it was one holy mess of trash, with half the floor of it rusted away. I cleared it to get a better view and found a wire hanging there. I noticed a similar wire on the other side attached to a spot and had a cover over it, so using the edge of my turnscrew, I put it back where I thought it went and said, "Mr. O'Faelan, have you something to put over this wire down here? It's missing a cover."

He crouched low to look under the car at me. "Brendan, if you've made a muck of anything, I'll box your fuckin' ears."

"Right here, see? This wire was loose and caught in some twigs and leaves. It's missing the cover."

He looked hard and could just see what I was pointing to. "It's a glove, the cover's called," he said. "Get out from under."

I did and he started the car up and turned on the heater as I tried to brush off the mud and dirt and oil that'd caught my coat. Colm gave me a look-over, rolled his eyes and stormed off without a word. He wanted to be nowhere near me when Ma saw it.

In truth, now my brain was caught up with my body, I didn't want to be near me, either. I took off my coat and laid it over one of the fenders then grabbed some snow from nearby to wash at it.

That's when an estate car parked behind us, in the area meant only for cabs. Mr. O'Faelan cast it a quick glare but said nothing, just focused on the heater—and in a moment, he almost smiled.

"It's working, so far," he said.

"I'd not run it till you put a glove on that," I answered, half-paying attention. The coat only looked dirtier. "Not if the other wire has one."

"Right you are." And he turned off the heater and the motor, then he got a look at me. "Aw, Brendan, your Ma's about to be right sore with you."

I saw the grease on my hands had streaked my shirt, as well. Nothing massive, but what could I do now except to laugh and shrug? "It'll wash." Not really thinking about the coat being wool.

Then I crouched down to grab a bit of clean snow from the gutter to scrub my hands, and looked up to see an older lad lifting some bags into the estate car as a woman of maybe Ma's age trudged up to the passenger side. Both were big and looked very much like mother and son.

But caught between them was this girl. Silky golden hair drifting down her back caught in the chilly breeze. A deep red beret atop her head. Form enough to her body to make even the simple coat and bell-bottom trousers seem perfectly female. She handed a last parcel to the older lad, and then turned to reveal a face of clean skin, rose-hued cheeks, and eyes bright enough to fill a room with sunshine.

Then she saw me.

Washing my hands in the gutter.

Her eyes grew wide and surprised.

I jolted to my feet at realizing the sight I was making.

She almost laughed, her full expression dancing with humor and no judgment. Lips red as cherries without a touch of rouge, without the hint of anything on her face that might hide her elegant complexion. What could I do but laugh back, spread my arms and shrug as if to say, *I'm a slob*?

"Joanna!" The bark came from her mother, whose hard cold blue eyes glared at me. "In the back!"

She whispered into the estate car and her brother hopped behind the wheel, casting me a frown that seemed to mix both wariness and condescension. As they drove off, I heard her mother say, "It's not right to make fun of little street urchins, like that."

"I wasn't," was all I heard her say back.

And my heart went with her.

That is when Mr. O'Faelan gently popped the back of my head, a half-smile on his face. "You'd be aimin' high with that one. She's Waterside, and well-off."

I looked at him, confused, and said, "I-I dunno what you mean."

He just shook his head, still smiling, and tossed me half a crown. "I mean learn to keep yourself clean and smellin' good."

"I smell?"

"No. But a touch of Old Spice, makes the girls think twice."

"Birds really go for that?" I asked, feeling quite cool as saying it.

"Woolworth's'll have somethin'. Or Wellie's. I'll drop you."

I noticed my trousers were also wet, and for the first time caught the idea that maybe Colm had the right idea in keeping himself extra tidy. You never know who you'll run into in Derry. If I did chance to see her, again, it probably would be better if I was presentable.

"I'd best walk. Don't want to dirty your seats."

"Not a worry. They're Naugahyde, from America. Easy to clean."

"What kind of animal is that?"

He burst into a laugh. "You're a daft one, Kinsella."

I chuckled, still not sure what he was talking about, and pulled on my coat as I backed away. "Well, next time you need something fixed on your car, Mr. O'Faelan, this daftie'll handle it well enough."

"No doubt. But it is somethin' you might consider. You have the touch for motors."

I stopped. "You think so?"

He nodded. "Good future in it. They'll always need fixin'."

"What won't? Thanks." And I flipped the coin then headed up to the Diamond, my limp almost gone.

I stopped in the Woolworth's and found some strong soap for my hands and a small bottle of oil that smelled of spices. It used most of that half-crown, but after I washed myself, that night, I just knew Prince Charles couldn't feel any better or cleaner or more pleased with himself than I, and Ma's anger over my coat drifted into the shadows.

I snuck into the bed beside Eamonn. He was dead asleep atop one of his course books. He'd been pushing the studies a lot, as of late, and Ma was more than a little irritated at him for it, since it also meant he was spending less time at the committee.

This one time I heard her going at him for it, he'd responded, "What am I doin' there? Makin' sure that people who already have their mind made up about somethin' keep it made up, when they'll always have it made up. McAteer's sure to be re-elected because the church is tellin' people if they don't vote for him, they're goin' to hell. It's too bad it's him in their pocket; he couldn't even get the university extension set here instead of Coleraine! Bloody accountant."

"Watch what you say about him and the church," she'd snapped. "They've done well by us."

"As little as they could, and nothin' to help me at Queens. Father Demian as much as said so. I'm glad he's leavin'. And the poor help I'm gettin' from the committee is—well, what good are any of them?"

It was at this point I'd expected to hear Ma slap Eamonn, but instead her voice had grown cold. "This is what I raised? Naught but sons of selfishness, you and Brendan. When De Valera came to Derry, I held you aloft to show him his namesake, and he smiled at you and I thought that a blessin'. But now? Now I see it was a curse. He knew, even then, you would never hold Ireland as dear as he. Shameful. The both of you."

Eamonn had said nothing, just gone up to his room and not even come down for supper. Mai took it up to him. What they spoke of, I don't know; I'd had a clock to work on and was doing it in full view of Ma, so she could see what effort there was to it. Mrs. Bannon had given it to her to bring to me, so she'd accepting whatever they were willing to pay for its fixing. But when Mai had come down, Eamonn was with her and his face was easy.

"I'm not abandoning Ireland, Ma," he'd said, his voice easy. "I'm out to make her even more proud. Isn't that all right?"

Ma had just finished washing up and was drying her hands on a fresh towel. "In what way?" she'd asked, wary but not sharp.

"I thought I might learn business and help John Hume with the credit union. But after speakin' with Mai, I'm after tryin' for law."

That...had cut through Ma's reserve. "Solicitor or barrister?"

"I'm thinkin' the latter, maybe. It'd be years of work, but—"

"A barrister." Ma's voice had taken on a near reverential tone and her eyes focused on something a hundred yards away as a smile touched her lips. "Wouldn't that be a blessin'?"

"So should I continue on?"

She'd looked at him, fighting that smile, and said, "You won't find me stoppin' you."

And there had been peace, again.

It didn't hurt that Mai was now on at Hogg and Mitchell's, and she used a friend's address on Fahan as her official residence. This kept the welfare from cutting back on Ma's dole, since they didn't know any better. She also said naught about the money sent by Aunt Mari. So we were doing better, despite Ma's nattering on, and I could see no reason for him not to continue on with his studies.

"Are you really trying for law?" I'd asked him on Boxing Day, last. He'd just sent off his application, and we were having tea by the hearth, where it was warm and comfortable.

"Dunno yet," he'd said.

"Are there Catholic barristers?"

"Of course there are. Still, never hurts to have more on our side. Are you thinkin' of University?"

"No, not me. I fix things, is what I'm good for."

"You're smarter than what you think, son."

I'd smiled and settled into the divan "I just want a happy life. Anything more is-is hard to figure."

He'd ruffled my hair and dipped in close to whisper, "So what's these little secrets goin' on between you and Mai?"

"What d'you mean?" I'd asked, knowing full well what he was hinting at.

"I've seen you two sharin' a bit of craic, and I know you also give her money you won't give Ma."

I'd just shrugged. "If Mai has something to tell you, it's up to her."

He'd grinned and looked hard at me, saying, "One of these days you'll let me know what's goin' on in that quiet little brain of yours."

I'd snorted. "Well, when you find out, will you share it with me, then?"

He'd laughed and hugged me close and I'd never felt so happy and grown up.

So that night, I watched Eamonn breathe in deep and softly let out. His hair had grown long and it suited him. I still kept mine short because the curls drove me mad, getting in my face. Now I wondered if there might be something at Woollie's to better control it. Or maybe the chemist's, close by. They might even have a suggestion on how to smooth it out, let it be like Colm's and Danny's and Paidrig's. Even wee Eammon's was longer and finer than mine. I was beginning to feel last year around them, now.

I looked out the window over the Bogside. It had grown a clear sky, with touches of clouds just visible, and colder. Under moonlight, the rows of houses took on an aura of gentleness and mystery, streaks of snow breaking up the nonstop lines of the roofs and quiet empty streets. Even the waste lots had the right look to them, bright and open. With the stars shining down, a form of tenderness came over me. But the night always did that, for there was less clutter to see and have to deal with.

I still ached from Ma's slaps and couldn't get comfortable enough to sleep, so I carefully slipped the book from under my brother, thinking I'd read it for a bit. The title was *A History of Ireland*. It started thousands of years ago and carried up to modern day, if the table of contents was to be believed. Maybe he'd let me read it once he was done.

He had read *Borstal Boy* and said I should, as well. But Rhuari had already given me a detailed synopsis of it, despite there being parts he didn't understand—like when it sounded as if Charlie was calling for Brendan to help him and Brendan did but it turned out to be a mistake of some kind.

"Why would Brendan apologize to Charlie for trying to protect him?" he'd asked.

I'd asked Eamonn about it and he'd only said it was just a misunderstanding, but in a tone of voice that told me it was something he did not want to discuss. So I'd had Rhuari show that part to me. And I'd understood. And I'd told him, "He was dreaming and Paddy woke him."

Rhuari'd given an *I don't believe you look* but said nothing more.

I flipped through a little of Eamonn's book and it seemed good enough, but I couldn't really concentrate, and it wasn't from Ma's beating. My mind kept drifting back to that girl.

Joanna.

I knew girls around my area who were just as pretty and wore clothes just as nice, at times. Moira down the way was already looking like Mai in figure, and her being my age. Colm certainly noticed her. And sometimes I'd catch him chatting her up in a way that seemed very adult, a fag tucked in his ear and her acting like a simpering thing. I mean, I liked the image of her but this girl.

Joanna.

Christ, she was more than lovely, and the longer she was in my mind, the more perfect she became. And the more my heart grew close to bursting with the idea of her. I could still see the way she tossed her head, making the spun silk of her hair whisper about like something ghostly. The flow of her under her coat made the more wonderful by its being atop bellbottoms that emphasized the line of her legs from her elegant hips. I could picture us, lip-to-lip, gentle and loving. I ached to hold her.

That was a first, for me, wanting to hold a girl close. I'd

always had a tight focus on my work, and my Chinas took time enough away from that. But now? Wanting to just rest my head in the crook of that girl's neck? To breathe in her perfume? It brought a stirring that began behind my heart, moved through my chest and down my belly to tingle across the insides of my thighs. Without thinking, I crushed my legs together and felt lightning jolt into my crotch then ricochet up to my own chest. I almost laughed at the glorious sensation of it all. I felt my tadger grow, which made me a bit nervous so parted my legs. I thought I'd cut off the blood to it and it was swelling from that, for it was also beginning to ache.

I lay still. Focused on the book since I was nowhere near sleep. Tried to force the sight of Joanna from my brain. But that only made things worse. I kept imagining her looking at me. Smiling at me. Then crossing to me to slip her hand around the back of my head and pull me into a kiss that held a promise of heaven and the lightning exploded through me, again—

And daggers of pain ripped into my tadger.

I grunted, trying to keep quiet and still. Any thoughts of Joanna vanished from my mind thanks to the sudden stabbing hurt. I felt like I was being cut to bits, down there, and it was getting worse. I rolled onto my back and began to moan, not knowing what to do. Rhuari and Kieran would have slept through an atomic bomb, but it woke Eamonn and he turned to me.

"You all right, son?" he murmured.

I managed to gasp out, "Eamonn, I-I think I-I think Ma did me a real damage."

He sat up a bit. "What d'ya mean?"

"My-my tadger..." And I grunted from the pain.

He looked at the covers and saw the lump, and laughed. "It's all right, son. Happens to all us lads."

"Is it supposed to hurt so?" Then I cried out as more daggers shot into me.

He looked closer at me. "You're sweatin'."

"I-I think it's comin' off."

He felt my head and frowned and said, "Hang on," then slipped away. I heard him knock on Ma's door and finally her sleepy voice snarling what the fuck he wanted. A moment later she came in and dragged me from the bed. I screamed from the pain, and that woke the others. She yanked down my pajamas, looked at my—at me and snarled, "Have you been abusin' yourself?"

"What?" I had no idea what she meant.

Eamonn piped in, "Ma, that's not what happens."

"And you know, do ya?" she shot at him.

He smirked and said back at her, "I'm healthy enough to."

She flicked him with her finger, snapping, "Don't be vulgar." Then she looked hard at me then nodded. "The Raffertys have a phone. Go call casualty and have an ambulance sent."

Eamonn nodded and left, then Ma turned to me. "You have trouble passin' water, do you understand me? Do not tell them you were abusin' yourself and bring shame to us. You're havin' trouble passin' water." I nodded and carefully pulled up my bottoms. "Now put on your robe and slippers, nothin' else."

Twenty years later, though I'm sure it was but half an hour, an ambulance came. Ma was dressed and I was lying on the divan, shivering from the pain. The attendant checked me over, saw my bruises and cast a hard look at Ma. "Have you somethin' cold?"

"What?"

"Have you or no?"

Mairead was up and said, "We only have a cooler."

He sighed. "Bring me a wet cloth, then. Straight off the tap. It'll make the ride easier for the lad."

She grabbed a wash cloth and went out the back as a constable appeared at the door, glared at me and asked, "So what happened?" His voice sounded like Belfast.

I gasped out, "I-I'm having trouble passing water."

Ma added, "He's always had weak kidneys."

"Look like he's been in a fight," the constable said.

"Have ya, lad?" the attendant asked.

"I-I-I fell down the stairs." Cough.

The attendant barely kept a scowl to himself. "That must've hurt."

I nodded.

"He's young for stones, inn't he?" the bloody peeler asked. I could tell he was thinking something else had happened, something criminal he could blame on me, but the attendant shrugged him off.

"Could be any number of things," he continued, his eyes now kind. "So we'll be taking you to casualty and they'll check you out, and I'd say in a few days you'll be right as new."

Then Mairead returned with a wet, icy towel. He guided me to a stretcher and gently lay me down then set the towel on my crotch, which bloody hurt and made me scream, again. Bloody hell, was he trying to kill me? I was close to hitting him. Finally, he called, "Hey, Murray, we're ready."

A second attendant popped in, smelling of cigarette smoke, and took the other end of the stretcher, and Christ, I would have killed for a fag, right then. Something to take my mind off this pain.

Ma said, "I'm ridin' with yous."

The first attendant looked at me. "How old are you, Brendan?"

I managed to say, "Twelve."

"You want your mum along" And I knew he'd have let me say no.

But I looked at Ma, and her expression would have killed him on the spot if he'd seen it, so I said, "She-she's no other way. To get there."

He nodded and said to her, "Then you can join us, missus."

"And why could I not, me bein' his mother?" Ma shot back at him before she turned to Mairead and said, "Leave Kieran with Mrs. Haggerty on your way to work. I'll fetch him soon as I'm done with himself."

"Aye, Ma," she said

Then as they carried me out, I glanced up the stairs to see Eamonn standing at the top landing, smiling and moving his right hand in the signal for wanking. Jesus God, I would've killed him if I'd been able to get past the pain.

I barely even noticed the crowd gathering outside to watch me being carted away. Oh, there would be some good craic, tomorrow, with me at its center. What a joy that would be.

And for once I was sorry I'd miss it.

The ride to Altnagelvin was fast and the care I got was quick, with them even giving me a pill to ease the hurt. Then a doctor examined me. He seemed nice enough, but the way he kept feeling up my tadger made me highly uncomfortable.

"Well, the problem's obvious," he told me, his voice carrying a curious accent I later realized was Scottish, and derided myself for not knowing it, at once. "But I've questions for ye, first. When ye bathe, do ye clean inside yer foreskin?"

"I bathed, tonight," I said, wondering what he meant.

He nodded. "Have you no' had an erection before?" I still wasn't sure what he was talking about, but this time I told him so. "Your penis, Brendan. Has it become hard or felt strange prior to tonight?"

"Never," which wasn't the exact truth. I'd woken a few times recently with something odd going on down there, and it not being comfortable, but nothing more'd happened. I'd been meaning to ask Eamonn if he knew what it was but he'd been so lost in his A-levels, I hadn't found a chance.

He nodded and stepped out to talk with Ma. They spoke softly, but I heard every word.

"Brendan's problem is Phimosis, Mrs. Kinsella. That means his foreskin is very tight, much too tight for a lad his age."

"What if it is? What's that mean?"

"Well, when he has an erection his foreskin can't expand correctly, meaning the head of his penis can't push through, or if it does, it breaks the skin, causing bleeding and infection. With Brendan, it's a case of his head not being able to make it past the foreskin. The best way to handle this is to remove it, and as quick as possible. That'll eliminate the problem. Have ye other sons?"

"Three."

"I suggest ye have them examined."

"What? Is this catching in boys?"

"Oh, no. No, it's something he was born with."

"Oh. Of course." And her voice was all but derisive.

"I seriously doubt any yer other sons will have the same trouble, but better safe than sorry. Since Brendan's here, now, I'd like to go ahead and schedule it."

Ma agreed. And neither of them said a thing more to me, so that morning, I was circumcised. They kept me a week, to be sure there was no infection or any other trouble. And I slept very well, thank you, having the whole of the bed to myself. True there was nothing but curtains separating me from the next patients, but it all felt so luxurious, I had to fight myself to keep from sighing over the pleasure of it.

However, everything else was fucking torture. I had shots in my arse, every day, and pain pills to keep the daggers from coming back, and meals worse than even Ma could make, with nothing to do except coursework dropped off by Father Jack, this younger, fitter, happier priest who was taking over from Father Demian, after Holy Week. No visits till I was sent home, and once there it was up to me to keep myself clean with a medicated soap and taped with gauze, changed twice daily. Which I did, at first, but each time I removed the gauze it was like pulling my flesh away, again, so the third day I just lay the gauze around me. I still bled but it wasn't as hideous to work with.

Ma had to get me y-fronts to keep everything in place, and she was not happy at the expense. I managed not to smile about it, for they cost near all that she'd taken from my hiding places.

It was another week before I could return to my classes and another fortnight before I could walk without thinking of the surgery I'd had. Naturally, I fell behind in my coursework and the brothers allowed no excuse for it. Which made for many a walloping on my hands.

But the week I was home, Colm, Danny, Paidrig and wee Eammon would drop by after school to talk and play *Monopoly*; Danny's Ma had bought it for him at Woolworth's and it was wicked fun. We'd sit around the hearth and chew gum and smoke French fags that Colm provided. I asked him, once, where he got the ciggies and he just said he'd show me when I was *old enough*, like it was some massive secret. Then he and I would usually bankrupt the others and face off to the death—which I won as often as not.

For some reason, Ma didn't mind any of this. In fact, I once caught her watching us as she came down the stairs. Colm was seated on the divan, facing the hearth, and the others had moved another chair around for me before sitting themselves on the floor. He had a ciggie in his mouth, our Colm, and the room had grown thick with smoke. Like it would from Da thanks to his Gallaher Blues. Also seated on the divan before the fire, for hours, as Ma brought him tea and sandwiches.

Colm was growing much faster than I, already strong, dark Irish, and her expression on him was almost tender. Which for some reason made me wonder if he reminded her of Da. Even though he was nothing like the man. I determined to ask Eamonn what he thought about it, sometime, but never did.

Of course, the neighbor ladies also heard I was at home and available, so began dropping by with odds and ends that just *happened to need fixing*—radios and clocks and the like. I focused on those and made near three pounds the first week, none of which I could keep, for Ma knew of every farthing.

"Pays for those ridiculous underdrawers you just had to have," she had snapped.

I didn't understand her problem with them. I actually liked the feel and decided I would wear these, from then on.

And after my two-week examination, when the doctor removed the sutures and said I could return to school, I asked him, "What for, when I'm making a fine livin' now?"

Ma had flicked me in the back of my head and snapped, "You'll do as you're told, and that is that."

And so it was.

As usual.

Still, from that point on I did only the minimum course work necessary to get by till I was fifteen and six and could decide for myself. I thought it'd lead me to be assigned to the Brow, since that was where those with no hope of learning were sent. However, despite my lack of interest I managed to do well enough to stick with the smarter lads.

One teacher chuckled at me after a test and said, "It's good you like to read." Which was true, I suppose. I still couldn't play footy and there were stretches of time where I had nothing else to do, so I'd begun reading everything I could, like Eamonn and Rhuari were doing. I'd drift away in the worlds they would build, and I guess I gained knowledge enough to get by on my courses.

Still, this caused Father Jack no end of irritation, for he told me over and over, in the kindliest of fashions, that I was *not living up to my potential*. But as I'd told Eamonn, I'd seen the course of my future, and it wasn't following him to Queens. That was a certainty. Especially as word got around at how a transistor radio sounded better after I'd worked on it than it did when it was new, and that when I replaced the tubes in a television set, they stayed replaced. It made me feel good to know people were happy with what I could do.

An added feature? While working on a radio, I had to test it so would use the BBC's News, which let me know what was happening around Northern Ireland and the world. Riots and demonstrations in America. War in Vietnam. Bombs testing by Russia and the US. It made you dizzy trying to keep up with it all.

I was foolish enough to ask Eamonn for more information concerning the May riots in France, which I'd caught a little about on the BBC. Father Jack overheard me, and that is when he became set on managing my life for me.

"It's good to learn all you can about the world, Brendan," he'd said as he lent me books on St. Thomas Aquinas and Thomas More. Which were more religion-set than I liked...but I read them.

When Colm saw me with one, he'd snicker, "Told you you'd be Father Tom."

"I'm never changing my name," I'd shot back. "I was born Brendan and will be till I die."

He'd just laughed and jostled me, and we'd run off to meet Danny at another demonstration by the Guildhall.

But that did get me to thinking and I finally caught on that Father Jack only saw me as a smaller version of Eamonn, to be molded and formed and polished. Silly of him, for I was doing it more from boredom while my brother was a sponge when it came to history and sociology and politics and things such as those. His choice of books showed that. I had the feeling he was building his own thoughts about the future of Derry, possibly to join more with John Hume and Hugh Logue.

Sometimes it was a joy just to sit next to him and watch him think as he explained himself. Explained civil rights and the goings on around the world as equality was being pushed for all. I caught myself smiling many a time, and being able to refer to things I'd heard on the radio made me feel a greater part of our conversation.

Anyway, having Father Jack insert himself into this melee was confusing, to say the least. I liked him, well enough, for Father Demian was a man I'd never felt comfortable around. His hands had been a bit too free and easy, at times, which is half the reason I never joined Danny as an altar boy. He also smelled of whiskey more than once when around me, and his eyes were as cold as unburned coal.

Ma had finally decided my reluctance about him was further proof I was simple. But Eamonn had nudged me and whispered, once, "He's a bit of a mad dog. Best to avoid so you don't get hydrophobia."

"Mad dog?" I'd asked, not sure what he meant. "I've not seen him much in a temper."

"He's not one for that. He just like bein'—oh, let's say he's a bit too friendly."

"In what way?"

"Don't be dense, son. Hands on knees. Pattin' your arse."

"Was he so friendly with yourself then?"

Eamonn had shaken his head. "But there's stories I've heard, so caution is a virtue."

I'd huffed. "How can you be cautious if you don't know what you're being cautious about?"

"You'll know."

And we'd left it at that.

But it had reminded me of what'd happened early last year, just after my eleventh birthday.

Ma had opened the card Aunt Mari sent me, and if there'd been money in it she'd kept it. From her attitude she was all but daring me to say a word about it. Well, two could play at that. I'd found a radio *discarded* in the muck from redevelopment, so I'd repaired it after Ma was to bed, and made a quid off selling it. I hadn't wanted to be around her, just yet, so I'd jaunted over to Danny's to see if he'd join me in a wander. His Ma'd said he was at St. Agnes and there I'd gone—and caught a glimpse of him and his Da by the hutch behind the church. Their voices growling and low as Danny'd been trying to pull away while his Da gripped him hard by the left arm, snarling.

I'd kept behind the stone wall, for he'd not want anyone to witness that. I know I wouldn't have, were my Da still alive and roughing me up.

Then I'd heard Danny cry, "You don't care; I'm nothin' to you!" followed by a number of slaps. Which had startled me. I hadn't figured his Da was like mine. A moment later, Danny'd busted onto the street and raced up the hill.

I'd started to follow him then stopped. I'd had no idea what to do or say and had no idea what was going on.

Until I'd noticed fresh spots of blood on the pavement.

Danny was bleeding? I'd known what that meant and how that felt and it was settled. I'd run after him, calling, "Danny, hey, me China!"

He'd made me run the length of that bloody street before he slowed and finally leaned against a high wall. When I'd caught up to him, I was full winded but he was barely breathing hard.

"Jesus, Danny, didn't you hear me calling? I saw you down the street and-and was thinking I'd like to-to..."

That's when I'd noticed his lower lip was split open and blood covered his front. He'd never had a mark on him before, not like me and Ma and Eamonn. It had shaken me.

He'd turned away to wipe at it, as if ashamed, then for some stupid reason I'd popped out with my old excuse of, "Did you-did you not watch where you were going and run into a post, again?" The best cover's always to make it seem like something stupid happened.

He'd cast me half a glance, hesitated then nodded, sharp and hurt.

"Well it don't look good," I'd said. "You want to go in the clinic?"

He'd shaken his head. I'd nodded and looked around. Four houses up lived a friend of Ma's, so I'd taken a gentle hold of his jumper.

"Then let's clean you up."

He'd let me guide him up to the door, where I'd knocked. A round woman Ma's age but with tender eyes had opened it and gasped.

"Don't worry, Mrs. Kieffer," I'd said, "Danny was-he was just playing the cod, and it looks worse than it is. Can we come in to wash him off?"

"Of course, son, Lord preserve you," she'd said, all but dragging us back to the kitchen, rattling on about God, the saints and the belovéd mother of Christ. At the time, it had seemed she had gone on forever, but in truth it had taken but a few minutes to wipe off his face. Did it as tender as he were her own child. Then off had come his jumper and shirt, to soak, swearing she'd take them down to his mother's soon as she had a moment. Then she'd gently put a strip of plaster on his cut lip.

She was one of the unlucky women who could start a child but never keep them till birth, for she'd have made a fine mother. Even at that age I'd felt a bit sorry for her.

Finally, he was clean and almost back to smiling, and she'd been trying to figure out if he'd fit one of her husband's jumpers. I'd had to choke back the laughter at that, for the man was larger than she. So I'd taken off my coat and offered it up.

"No, Bren..." Danny'd said, and those were the first words

he'd spoken since I arrived.

"It's just to Woollies," I'd said. "And-and I've a jumper on and it's just past me birthday and I want a bit of fun so you can help me with some grab and mix. I've a pound on me. Come on."

"I'm not after a sweet, right now," he'd muttered.

To which Mrs. Kieffer had laughed. "By all the saints, a lad not wanting a sweetie? Is it the end of creation?"

"Well I want some," I'd shot back at him. "So come along. I'll buy you an orange crush at the counter."

"Jesus, Mary and holy St. Joseph, Daniel," Mrs. Kieffer had spit out between gales of laughter, "you'd best take him up on it. The local Jew boy's partin' with some of his scratch, and without you havin' to beg!"

Well, that had set me wrong, her making sport of me like that. I guess Ma had been complaining to her about me, like she did to everyone. So I liked to put money aside, so what? Was that cause to call me a Jew? Or a bloody Scot, since they were known to be as tight with a farthing as any. All the things I'd fixed for her at half the price of the tinkers? Some gratitude showed, here. We'd just see if next time she burnt her toast I fixed her toaster for less than double what I'd charged the last time.

But the stupid joke had brought a crooked smile to Danny's lips, and he'd nodded. He'd slipped on my coat and we'd wandered down the lane, Mrs. Kieffer's laughter ringing after us, mixed with, "I'll get your shirt and jumper to your mother, Danny. I'm sure the blood'll come out."

The air had taken on more of a chill as night approached, but Danny's humor had grown better, and we'd jumped and run about like pups at play, dancing through Butcher's and crossing the Diamond down to Woollie's. Then we'd slammed straight at the grab and mix of candies and began filling a bag. Soon it was packed and paid for, using half the pound I'd made.

"You'll have to help me eat this," I'd said as we headed out.

"No, Bren, it's all yours."

"It's too much for me, alone. Come on. It's a sin to waste it."

He'd smirked at that and picked out a nougat wrapped in clear, asking, "Venal or mortal?" as he'd bit into it.

"You tell me; you're the one gonna be a priest."

His face had frozen. The look he'd shot me was cold and hard. He'd spat the nougat out, grabbed the bag and slung it to the pavement, then crushed it with his shoe.

"Bloody hell!" was all I got out before he'd bolted back up to the Diamond.

Others passing by were eyeing me. I'd been embarrassed by the sudden trouble so let him go. I was sorry I'd wasted the half-pound on him.

The next day, he'd given me my coat at school and started off, but I'd stopped him and asked why he'd done it. To my shock he'd frozen and started to breathe ragged. His hands shook as he whispered, "I don't wanna talk about it."

"But why was your Da rough with you?" I'd asked, being stupid.

Danny had glared at me and yanked away, snarling, "I don't wanna talk about it!"

So I'd let it be, complete, but it hadn't take much to work out that Father Demian was involved in some way. For Danny had soon quit as altar boy and even stopped attending Mass. Now Father Jack was our priest, and while his hands weren't free with you and his words were always kind and caring and suggestive of the greatness within you, his nosiness put me in a place where I felt the need for even greater caution than with Father Demian.

And I also grew more certain that I'd go my own way, despite them all, so I borrowed no more books from Father Jack.

Mr. Motor-boy

I started working on cars more when Willie Pringle's handbrake assembly broke on his A35 van and he gave me a go. I had to borrow a few tools from a lad I knew at Nixon's, but I took it apart, saw how it fit together, and was able to rebuild it with the assembly from a crashed one. Willie got a mate to bring me the parts so it only took me one evening, and I tossed off studying for a maths exam to do it. Still got a decent grade 'cause it's just the way numbers work and—well, had I studied I'd have done better.

Which Father Jack let me know, for days.

Didn't matter. The first time Willie set the handbrake, he busted a smile and kept resetting it and releasing it, over and over till I said to him, "Have a care, Willie; you'll need the whole of it adjusted, again."

"No, Bren," he said. "It feels solid and strong, better'n when I bought this pile shite ten year ago, and new at the time."

I patted the bonnet and said, "Now you see, there's your problem. You treat the van like she's worthless. Speak kindly to her and you'll have no more troubles."

He gave me a wary look and said, "That spell in hospital— are ya sure it wasn't for the loonies?"

"What d'you mean?"

"Well, that's what you're called, inn't it? And you don't exactly think the same as the rest of us, do ya?"

I laughed. "You should hear what I say to the radio as I'm about to make a soldering. *This'll only hurt a moment, and then you'll be all better.*"

Willie hesitated then saw I was making sport of him and joined my laughter. "You are daft."

He paid me two pounds and drove off. I hid one in my y-fronts because, sure as shakes, when I went inside, Ma asked, "How much did you charge him?"

"Just a pound, Ma."

"If I learn you're lyin'—"

"He's Paidrig's uncle, and he bought the—"

"Arra, you know nothing about money. Hand it over." Instead, I dropped the one in my hand in the household jar. Her glare would've cut steel. "Now wash up and set the table for supper." Then she looked out the kitchen window into our tiny square garden; Mairead had been toiling it as best she could, still it was a stretch to call it that.

"Mairead!" she called out. "Get the wains and come on in, now!"

"Eamonn's not home, yet, Ma!" she called back. Through the window I saw her rise, and her hands and shift were black with mud, but she looked pleased. Maeve was almost as dirty.

"Where's Rhuari?" Ma asked.

"Here, Ma," came as a whisper.

I looked back to the parlor and saw him seated on the divan, using the fading light to read by. "Eamonn's not yet home."

"Nor will he be, until late, so he'll make do with it kept warm on the hearth."

He'd been out much, lately, running with a pack of lads from Creggan and Brandywell, who were as clean and neat in their latest fashions as any and not silly about it, like the London crowd. They'd all been accepted to Queen's, in Belfast, and I was now ashamed I'd once thought him as big a slug as Da.

So we had our supper and set for bed, then I began tinkering with Mrs. Smith's alarm clock; she'd wound it too tight, again, which was easy to repair. I'd snuck it into the house because I didn't want Ma to know about it so I could keep the florin I'd been promised.

It was past midnight when he came creeping into the room. He saw me at the window and froze. I showed him my turnscrew so he relaxed and pulled off his boots. His voice was soft, so as not to wake the others. "Ma know you're up?"

I snorted at him and turned back to the clock. "Your supper's on the hearth, probably dry."

"I put it away. We got carryout. Chinese."

"Which one?"

"Base of the Flats."

"Any good?"

"Oh, yes..."

"How'd you pay for it?"

"John did. Well, his wife."

"Who's that?"

"Hume."

"Oh, yeah. Yeah."

"You should come to a meeting, sometime."

"Ma won't let me. *Too young.*"

"There's other lads around, your age and younger."

"The ones she thinks're hooligans?"

He chuckled as he said, "No doubt. Tell her it's for to learn more Irish history. That might bring her to your side."

"She won't believe that, from me. Rhuari, maybe."

He pulled off his trousers, watching as I screwed in the last tiny bit. Then I checked the winder; it was just right. He shook his head, doffed his shirt and pulled an apple and his knife from his coat and cut off chunks to eat. "You're good at that."

"Dunno why people make such a fuss," I said as I put its back plate on, actually feeling very proud. "It's like a, b, c."

"Not for everyone." He offered me a slice of the apple.

I bit it from his hand. It was bright, sweet, and juice ran down my chin. Near perfect.

"Who's teachin' you all this?" he asked.

"I just see how it comes apart, figure it goes back together the same way, and then it works."

"You'd be happy doin' that, wouldn't ya?"

"It's a future to it."

"What about when computers take over? What then?"

"Things'll always need fixing."

He wrapped an arm around my head and hugged me close, chuckling, then popped another bite of apple into my mouth. "C'mon, let's to bed." Then as we were climbing in he asked, "How you feelin' down there?" He nodded to my crotch.

I shrugged. "Hasn't hurt for some time."

"Is it back to workin'?" He had a smirk on his face that told me exactly what he meant.

I blushed. "I'll wager mine works better than yours."

He laughed, silently, and kept cutting the apple. "You haven't had the right use of it, yet."

"I've had use of it."

He leaned over to murmur, "With a girl?"

I'd have to say *no* to that, so instead I asked, "Have you?"

He sighed and leaned back, playing up the man of the world aspect of it. "Not a girl. A lady."

I felt my heart quicken and something stir down below, so I lay face down on the bed and half-buried my head in the covers to whisper, "Eamonn..."

"Near twice my age, she is. And well-versed in the art of love." Then he leaned close to whisper, "And married."

"Eamonn!" It came out almost like a hiss.

"Her husband's in Hong Kong, has two mistresses and sends her barely enough to live on, the right bastard, and—" He looked at me, sharp. "You're not to say a word of this to anyone, you understand?"

Oh, I could just hear Ma's neighbors having a good craic over this.

Well, he's a wild one, ain't he?

Cattin' 'round with a married woman.

Some lad she's raised.

First time he pulled this with me, he'd of seen the back of my hand.

Which would set Ma off to the moon, and not at those old cows.

So I just sneered, "Yeah, I'm the neighborhood tout, sure." He ruffled my hair, his hands sticky from the apple's juice, and I couldn't help but ask, "What's it like?"

He took a moment to answer, cut two final slices off the apple and gave me one then whispered, "It's the same as a drug. It pulls you in and builds you to a joy that's double the pleasure from when you take care of yourself."

"You mean?" And I did the wanking move with my right hand.

He nodded. "Have you really experienced that, yet?"

I huffed and lay my chin on my arms. "The one time I even come close to it, the bugger nearly come off. I don't think I'm meant to do that sort of thing."

He jostled me, smiling, again. "All lads're meant to do that sort of thing. But I'd not go braggin' about it to Father Jack, at confession."

I snorted. "That, I already know. He's not pleased with me."

"*Not fulfilling your potential?*" He chuckled as he said it.

"Said it to you, has he?"

Eamonn cast me a grin nodded. "He thinks I should try for Trinity. *Queens is too easy a way, for me. I've more smarts than I let on.* He likes the idea of me being a barrister."

"He likes the idea of ordering about the lives of others."

He eyed me, wary. "Do you not like him?"

"He's all right. And a much better deal than Father Demian."

"Him, you kept your distance from. Right?"

I shrugged. "Ma drags us to Mass and that's enough."

"Your Danny's not at the altar, anymore. Give up on the church, has he?"

I just shrugged. No surprise he hadn't noticed till now.

"So no communion for you? No confession?" His voice was distant, soft and thick.

"You think I got something to confess?" In truth, the answer would be *Yes*, but no need to go into that. Is there?

He took in a deep breath and cast a side glance at me. "No idea. I never know what's goin' on in that quiet little head of yours."

I just smiled. I had to admit, Danny had been more pleasant since Father Demian was gone. And Ma was taking Father Jack sweets she made. None for us, but for him? The start of the week brought the aroma of another cake. Or scones. It was like she'd become a girl, again.

Of course, Mairead, being our Mai, she asked Ma if she could help her make some, to which Ma agreed because a time or two her work got a bit charred. What's nice is, by this point Mai's cooking had grown fine. Because she had so much practice with it, I'm sure. Soon she was making all the sweets and putting some aside for us, not bothering to let Ma know till after she'd made her pilgrimage to the rectory.

Of course, the first couple times Ma made a fuss, but Mai had only smiled and told her, "I make food for us all, Ma, not just a few. It's how I've always done it. But if you'd prefer to make the next batch for Father Jack on your own, that will be fine, with me."

Which shut Ma up, nicely. I could take lessons from our Mai on handling our mother.

I finished the apple and turned to watch my brother dance with slumber, and I couldn't help but ask, "Eammon, this lady of yours. Is she at your meetings?"

He sighed and nodded.

Then it struck me—he hadn't kept his lover secret; he'd told me. And yeah, I'm not one to spread gossip, but it was suggestive of his true nature. Always had to share and be part, in something.

But I still had to ask, "Do the others know?"

"And add to the gossip? Naw, we just keep it quiet."

"Not even Ma knows?"

"You'd be hearin' of it, if she did. Helps they're all too busy yammerin'."

"What about?"

"Aw, goings-on in America. With civil rights. Martin Luther King. Bobby Kennedy. Killed. Settin' up marches. Organizations here to help us all get equal treatment. Ways to make Stormmount pay mind. Like we've been doin', of late." He cast me a half-asleep look. "Don't you pay attention to. To what's happenin'?"

"Yeah. Been to some of the demonstrations. And the protests at Guildhall. The one last week, I heard Mrs. Keogh talking about it with Ma."

"You weren't there?"

I shrugged. "Mrs. O'Malley's toaster wasn't popping up, like she'd been promised by Mr. Teenan, so..."

"You had other—what's the word? *Priorities*. Don't matter, anyway. Mayor's payin' no attention."

"So where's these marches gonna be?"

"Nothing's settled. People still talkin'. Maybe in a few months."

"I could come on one, couldn't I?"

"Yeah. Like I said. There's always lads. Like you. Dancin' 'round on the sides." And he drifted off to sleep.

I'd been one of those lads, a time or two, and frowned at how he described us. Like we were hangers-on who scattered when things went rough. Which, in truth, was how I'd been. No backing up of the marchers. It wouldn't do for it to continue.

I rolled over and looked at the ceiling. The paper covering it was stained and wrinkled, some of it torn and drooping down. I thought it was time to do something about that, so it doesn't fall on us in our sleep and we think it's a rat come calling. That may cost nothing more than some paste. Use some old newspapers and whitewash over them. I could ask around, in the morning. See if

Mairead would put up some scratch for it, from the jar. I only had a couple pounds hidden away. Which I could use. Except then Ma would wonder where I got it since I'm supposed to be skint. Better to do it the official route.

Or just not bother. Maybe cello-tape would be all it needs. Be cheaper and probably look as good. Certainly would cost less.

I smiled at the thought of it, and watched the midnight shadows fill its creases. Not with sadness and neglect, but with spaces for new ideas to come. Making room enough for a new world to begin. Where all could fit. One where if a Catholic boy saw a Protestant girl, he wouldn't have to give a second thought to going up and asking her for some time together, and vise-versa.

The moon whispered behind a cloud and the shadows in the ceiling shifted into Joanna's face for the first time since that night. Green eyes that shone like emeralds. Lips bright and red as cherries. Cheeks as round and soft as peaches. A nose pert and outlined with freckles. She could be a poster girl for Lady Bell Ice Cream, with her smile. A smile she was sending me. Seeming to agree with my hopes and dreams. I wondered if I could tape the paper into her form or visage? It might be worth a try.

I felt the same sensations as before, but this time without pain or discomfort. In fact, touching myself made everything so much finer as I lay there. Seeing her. Thinking of her kissing me. Thinking of her hands caressing my face. I could picture myself tracing my lips down her neck, like in the cinema, as we held each other in the ways only the gods understand. As my hand traced up and down myself, almost without thought, drawing me deeper and deeper into happiness and beauty.

What I was thinking, I don't remember. What I was seeing drifted away from my sight. Shadows increased and became more real than anything else in the room. Silence surrounded me. Beauty and grace of a kind greater than any church could provide built within me. Every part of my being tingled as I did all I could not to move too much. To hold my sudden grunts and groans and gasps and huffs as quiet as humanly possible until...

Until...

Until...

A feeling exploded through me unlike anything I'd ever known and I gulped and coughed and gasped without thinking and shivered and drifted along, the bed like a gentle sea and—

I froze.

Dared not move.

Something liquid had shot from within me and I'm thinking, *Oh, Jesus, I've probably gone and undone everything the doctors fixed, and now I'm bleeding.*

But when I finally found the courage to look at my hand, the wetness on it was clear and sticky and smelled odd. Like day old meat.

I glanced at Eamonn. His breath was deep and steady. No answers coming from him, not just now. So I wiped it off with my sheet and lay back. An odd sense of peace surrounded me as I softly drifted into the best sleep I'd had since coming home from hospital.

Marching Season

It seemed from that night protests were happening all about the city. The Action Committee held one at Guildhall, after which an MP named Austin Currie staged a sit-in at Caledon, not far from Derry, because some Protestant girl was offered an entire house for herself when whole Catholic families were still confined to one room. He was dragged out by the peelers.

Then there was a comical one over a weekend, where a caravan being lived in by the Wilson family was drawn onto the Lecky Road by lads who were part of the Housing Action Committee, blocking it. There were four in that tiny thing, with one of the wains sick. It stayed in place, till Sunday. Guarded by the lads. Daring the constables to do same as in Caledon.

They didn't.

Which was disappointing, so it was repeated the next weekend, by which time the press had learned of it and the publicity was building. I only got to see it after the caravan was in place, since I was rewiring a lamp on Abercorn.

This time the Wilsons got their house.

The next big one was some days later, on the Craigavon Bridge. A new lower level was being dedicated and Councilor William Beattie was set to cross it, but some lads blocked the path, holding up placards comparing the man to Hitler. One fellow who was smaller than me, Finbar something, got himself arrested, but that was the extent of the RUC's pushback. If the HAC was expecting violence from them, it wasn't coming.

There were others, and I was there, usually with Eamonn and my Chinas at my side. As were Ma and a number of the neighbor ladies, who'd show up to support some family threatened with eviction for not being able to pay their rent or gas. It was turning into quite a movement.

Most of the time, once things began to wind down, Colm

would wander off to talk and smoke with Eamonn and lads he knew, few of whom I did. I felt deep within that I ought to also be doing that, but Eamonn never asked me if I wanted to and Colm's not the sort to need an invitation to do anything, so I just stayed back. It didn't feel as if I was needed, really. Colm also milled about with the leaders of the movements, asking them questions about logistics and numbers and intentions, Paidrig always hanging at his side. It struck me he was laying a path into politics, himself, and him but the same age as myself.

At some of these gatherings, the crowds could be overwhelming and the anger in them strong enough to feel in your skin. That's when Danny and I would stick by wee Eammon, as a quiet protection. Other lads we knew were about, as well, but these two were me Chinas and I'm not ashamed to say that at times the murmuring and calling of the people surrounding us could make me cough and want a way out of it. What tempered my nervousness was the understanding that all of this was in hope that our peaceful actions would lead the way a solution for the—how did John Hume put it? "The inequities of the current situation in our fair town."

Of course, these were on weekends, when factories were closed and people had leave. School was also shut, guaranteeing a fine turnout.

So long as Derry City didn't have a home game. One had to have priorities.

Then an organization called the Civil Rights Association, in Belfast, set up a march that August, to Dungannon. Everyone was so caught up in the excitement of it all, we paid scant attention to the Apprentice Boys' March, that month. Oh, the pennies still flew off the walls and stones were slung back and forth and the press called some of it rioting when it was really little more than skirmishes where the RUC chased us and not them, but we had other things to dream about than whether or not a rock hit a rotten Proddy.

Eamonn was to join that march, starting in Coalisland, and insisted I not come. "Paisley and his bastards're gonna make trouble," he'd said, "so it's best you not be in harm's way."

I argued with him but to no avail, especially since Ma took his side. So off he went. What was funny is, it turned out there was no trouble to be had because the RUC wouldn't allow the marchers anywhere near the loyalists.

The next day there was already talk of yet another march in Derry, and no one could keep me from that. If it happened. There was much argument about whether or not it should.

By this point, Eamonn had settled on a degree in law, leading to the level of a barrister. He and his new mates had been in long talks about it with Father Jack, who had also joined forces with the HAC and CRA, *though not in an official sense*, as he put it.

"There are those in the church who consider your actions communistic, so I cannot be seen taking your side," he said, "but that does not prevent me from observing what may prove to be a momentous advancement in the lot of Derry's people."

Which to me sounded the opposite of what he was actually doing, being part of the marches and sit-ins and arguments and so forth. But he was the priest and I was only a boy who refused to go along with what he wanted for me, so my opinion was of no importance.

Then I overheard him talking to Mrs. Quincannon, who sorely disapproved of the DHAC's actions and was upbraiding him for letting them use the church for meetings.

"No fear of God, in those commie scum," she said. "Nor simple human decency or respect. It's one thing to help people get housing; it's another to want to run the government and kick out the church."

Mrs. McKinley was next to her and said, "You're a fool for not seein' they're only doin' what's needed. Waitin' for them Loyalist bastards to keep the promises they keep breakin' is gettin' us nowhere but to the grave."

"And spittin' in their faces is a better way to go about it?"

"If it's manners they want, they should talk to the Marquis of Queensbury, shouldn't they? Might remind them of what happens to those who help themselves, too much."

Father Jack calmed them both by saying in his smoothest voice, "Ladies, sometimes words *are* insufficient and must be followed by actions. Never forget, our Savior not only sat with his flock to reveal his teachings, he went into the crowds and into the wilderness and into foreign lands to perform his miracles, and in doing so, showed the world what the one true faith is. Should we do any less?"

And yes, he was just that poetic and overdone. You'd think

he was writing a book.

But I also noticed that while such talk managed to hush the old cows when he was around, it also helped build a wall against those who disparaged the protesters or feared their rash actions would cause grief for one and all. Almost as if he were giving the protesters a sort of protection.

Ma took the side of action, railing on about England's persecution of the church from the times of Cromwell and the settlers who stole Irish lands to enrich themselves and the Great Famine that was really nothing more than genocide and the lies about Parnell being an adulterer. Of course, mingled in was a fear and hatred of communism, even as those pushing for action were considered exactly that. It was almost comical how she could talk well of both sides at the same time.

As for Eamonn, now that his path was settled he went from being foolish to becoming the next de Valera. "But much better lookin'," she added. "I remember thinking, when he came up to visit, that time, that he looked more of an accountant and not leader of Free Ireland."

"Your Eamonn has grown up fine, Mrs. Kinsella," said Mrs. Haggerty. She and Ma were each on their stoops, wrapped in aprons and shawls, slippers on their feet, scrubbing them. "And imagine havin' a solicitor in the family."

"Barrister," Ma huffed, more than a little pride and condescension in her tone, sitting back on her knees and gazing into the distance in a manner I'm sure was meant to seem romantic. "I'll put him to work on the Mayor with his snail's pace of gettin' us a decent place to live, no thanks to that one." At which point she nodded to me. "The way he'll happily work with Protestants is an embarrassment."

I was fair certain she held me up as the reason we lived in such a shambles, and never mind I was the one who kept it from collapsing around us. Thank you so very much, Ma.

Mrs. Rafferty had joined them, laughing, and said, "But by the time your Eamonn has his certificate and can face them down, even your Kieran'll off to Queen's."

"No, I think he's best suited for Trinity, myself," Ma said, with an even greater touch of self-importance. "He wasn't born simple."

I rolled my eyes and wondered if I should up my scores in

school and plan for my A-levels just to prove to her I wasn't a complete fool.

Nothing I could do about it, right then. I was outside at the window waiting for Danny and wee Eammon to come, so was using the sill to hold some of my tools and an old clock I'd found in a dustbin behind a shop. The levers were rusted near solid but I had finally worked them apart. Its wooden body was split but could be filled in and painted over. And since the face was in such perfect condition, being this painted porcelain with old-fashioned brass numbers, my plan was to clean it up, make it work right, and sell it to Mrs. Donaldson's shop down by Waterloo. She had second-hand goods in the back area that only looked half ready for use. I thought doing this might also show her I could fix those things up, as well, to bring her a better price, and maybe a steadier line of work. So I was only half listening to their craic.

I had my little work box at my feet to set everything into at a moment's notice and an eye up the road towards Danny's home. But then Ma just had to say, "It's a pity not all my sons're like Eamonn, strong, smart and sure of themselves. Livin' their lives to make the lives of others better. When he shifted coal, every shilling he made was handed over without a word of complaint or me havin' to fight for it, not like with that one."

I looked around to find her glaring straight at me as she offered up that lie. And Mrs. Rafferty appeared to be in what appeared to be complete agreement. Both got a glance of disbelief from me, for I remembered full well how many times Eamonn had asked Ma to let him keep a little of his wages, and her reply had been that he was a selfish child who thought of no one but himself when she had to scratch the earth to keep kith and kin from having to eat grass like they did in the famine, and on and on and on. Oh, she could lay on eloquence as well as Father Jack, when she had a mind to.

So without a thought, I popped out with, "Oh, aye, Ma, between you and Da's drink, there was no one could keep his own wages."

She hissed, bolted up and yanked me by my hair then struck me hard in the face, snapping, "You dare talk of your own father like that? A murdered saint of a man?"

I tore away from her, wiping blood from a cut on my lip. Saw Mrs. Rafferty shake her head in horrified agreement, saying, "The mouth that one has, Bernadette. You've a trial with him, there's no question."

Mrs. Haggerty rose to her feet, wiping her hands on her apron, wary but silent.

Rhuari appeared at the door, looking at me as if I were mad. He must have been in his usual corner, reading. He didn't yet have the ability to block out Ma's words when he was lost in a book, not like I did. A couple of neighbors also popped their heads out to see what fun there was to be seen.

I'd have left it there but Ma was not yet content in my punishment. She grabbed up the clock's face from the sill and smashed it against the wall, shattering it, causing Rhuari to race inside. Then she glared around at me, a vicious grin on her face, and snarled, "Now you'll come back here and clean this filth up!"

That look—that crooked, snarling smile—it tore something apart, inside me. I'd seen it when she was fighting her worst with Da, a couple of times, almost like it was a pleasure to her.

Again, without a thought I snarled. "I could have made two crowns off that clock, Ma! For one so concerned about money, you seem not to give a tinker's damn about that!"

Jesus, God, did her face grow red and twist with anger. Which I expected—but not the true joy dancing in her eyes, as well. Cold and vicious. Anticipation of the damage she now felt license to do to me.

It kicked my mind with a memory from when I was but nine years old. The night of September Equinox. Da'd been gone much of the summer, and it was not long after the Belfast bus had arrived that I'd heard him coming up the hill, singing a fight song. I'd warned my older brother, who'd picked up Rhuari and headed for our room, saying it was time for his bed. Mairead and Maeve were already in theirs, reading, so for them we had little worry; Da rarely aimed his fists at them, and then only when he was in the worst of ways and seemed not to know any of us. As for Ma in the back? I'd shot a quick, "Da's coming," to her then scurried up to our room, hoping to have covers enough to cushion against his blows.

Only he hadn't burst through the door, raging. Instead, I'd heard him clomp inside, drop his sack, exchange soft words with Ma, all of which was followed by a confusing silence. Then he'd jumped upstairs to crash into their room. Moments later, my sisters were screaming. My brother and I had burst to the door to see what was wrong only to find a shaken Mairead carrying a weeping Maeve downstairs. Then my brother had jolted and tried to cover my eyes, but not before I'd seen Da come out and stand at the railing to bellow, "Bernadette! I'm callin' to yous!"

As already noted, this was not the first time I'd heard him say it and have my sisters banished from their room, but this *was* the first occasion where I'd seen him full naked. With his tadger pointed straight from between his legs.

To say it had jolted me would not be a lie.

I'd just moved away from young Eamonn's hands when Ma had come all but leaping up the stairs, in her shift, her hair wet and streaming down her back. She'd called over her shoulder, "Mairead, wrap yourselves in the shawl on the divan. I'll let you know when to come up."

We'd kept the door closed tight enough that she hadn't noticed us watching as she'd danced past and thrown herself into Da's arms. He'd grabbed her rear in a way most vulgar and they had kissed and she had smiled at him and then they'd stumbled back into the room and their door slammed closed, and for half an hour the creaking of their bed could have been heard clear to Armagh. And Holy Mary, Mother of God, she had borne the same bloody smile as she had on her face, now.

Young Eamonn had sighed, shut the door and turned back to our bed, where Rhuari was already asleep. I hadn't moved. Moments later, I'd heard he was also away from this world. Obviously, he had not been surprised by the actions of our parents.

At the time, it had made no sense to me, and yet within the same thought, it had. All of the times I'd been caught in the middle of their battles and hurt, thinking they'd hated each other and it was only the church refusing divorce that kept them as man and wife, to have witnessed the joy in their faces as they embraced was confusing, at best.

Then Kieran on his way and Da was dead. And I'd had no need to think about it, anymore.

Until now.

The smile on Ma's face after breaking that clock held the same joy as that night, when she'd flung herself against a man who'd brutalized her time and again. It was the same vicious grin. I now finally understood.

She had *loved* his abuse.

Loved abusing him.

They had hurt each other because they wanted to. They had hurt me and Eamonn the younger because we tried to keep them from doing it. They had gotten some bizarre form of pleasure from it all. A pleasure denied her since his death.

Was this why she was always at me? Was it not the long hours in labor and my quiet way of doing as I wanted, but that she needed someone to use for her abuse? She no longer had my Da, Eamonn had already become too much his own man, and Mairead was too calm in the face of her spits and snarls, so had that made her choice? Because I would simply take it yet still go my own way? Giving her even more excuse to vent her love of punishment on me.

Like I deserved it for staying to myself.

Well, we'd see about this. Let her come at me, now. I wouldn't flinch or cry. Let her cover my face with blood. Watch her tear me to bits, you fucking cows. Let's see how long you let her go before you call Father Jack to hurry and calm her anger, as Father Demian had done so many times. Let's have *him* see what was done to me. I would make bloody goddamned sure the whole world knew of it.

I think I began to smile at the joy of having Mrs. Rafferty and Mrs. Haggerty there to see it all. Da's attacks on myself and Eamonn were still fresh in my mind, and I would feel no shame in them witnessing my destruction, for it had finally become clear to me—they were aiding in it by refusing to end it. So here we would go, again, like the repeat of an old program on the telly.

Only Mairead appeared at the door, saying, "Ma, come inside for a sup of tea. I've some fresh made. And yourselves, ladies. You seem you could use one."

And my grandiose thoughts vanished as Mairead's strong, simple voice cut into Ma's anger. That smile vanished and she did nothing more than shake her finger at me as she went into our home. "I'll deal with you, mister. I'll deal with you."

"With a strap to his behind, I'd say," said Mrs. Rafferty as she followed Ma inside.

And the next time you need a repair, you old cow, you'll pay three times what I last charged, or off to the tinkers and see what good they do.

Then everyone slipped back to their business. No fun to be seen, here. I almost felt a disappointment, myself.

Danny and wee Eammon showed up, shortly after, to find me standing alone on the lane, still facing my door. Doing nothing. By this point, my lip was no longer bleeding. I'd wiped my face with my sleeve. My shirt was black so blood didn't show on it. I looked as if I'd just grown lost in one of my thoughts.

Which was somewhat the truth. Thoughts were still ricocheting through my head, but—

"Ready for us, me China?" Danny asked, his voice wary.

I returned to the moment, nodded and turned, and we walked down through the waste land to Fahan and Waterloo to find what sport we could in Guildhall Square. There wasn't much, with this demonstration. Just more loud voices and demands made. They had begun to seem all the same and a bit tedious. We stayed for a long enough while, paying little attention to the crowd or speakers, just smoking and saying naught.

Then we had a bite at a chippy. Danny and I let wee Eammon share in ours. More mine, really, for I wasn't so very hungry, and eating hurt my lip. After, we wandered along the Strand and the docks till half eight. That's when we returned to the Flats to drop wee Eammon off.

His mother was not happy he'd been out so long, and never mind he'd been with us. She smelled the fags on us was sure we were trying to kill him, if not from the asthma then letting him starve to death, and she would not hear of him actually having eaten. He just cast us a look of thanks before we were escorted out and the door slammed behind us.

We heard her saying, "I don't want you around those two, anymore!"

"Ma, they're me friends, and Brendan—"

"Enough! The trial that Brendan is to his mother is bad enough, and he's happy to make you one for me!"

Their voices grew too muffled to hear more.

Danny sighed. "I'm glad my Ma's not like that." Then he cast me a wink. "She's on tranqs. Maybe we should ask NHS to give some to wee Eammon's."

I just nodded and turned, not even trying to smile. I was numb. Just leaned against the railing and pulled out my last Blue. As I lit it, I heard barking, from below. In the twilight, I saw a pack of dogs chase a yellow tom cat across the courtyard. It tried to escape them, but they managed to surround it in a corner and were howling and snarling and lunging as the cat hissed and spit and clawed at them.

I held my breath. Five—no, six against one. I figured the cat was dead. I wanted something to throw down to stop them but had nothing and the elevator was slow.

Danny noticed the beasts and sighed. "I've seen that one chased a few times," he said. "Not a pleasant creature. Looks like he's finally been caught."

"It's not fair, is it?" I murmured. "A pack like that against one."

"It's nature's way."

"Yeah. I guess. Would that it were not so."

I watched the mongrels grow closer and closer to the tom, having their fun. Lunging. Snapping. Near grabbing his tail, once. He still spat and hissed and scratched, giving no hint of surrender. I wanted to turn away, but I couldn't. It would be dishonorable.

Closer they grew.

Louder.

Angrier.

People walked wide to avoid it, doing nothing to help or hinder. Like with me.

I felt a despair grow within. And anger. At everything. At nothing. I truly hated nature's way. It wasn't right or fair, just brutal and cruel. I hurt from the understanding, and my anger grew deep. I flicked the last of my Blue down at the howling beasts. To my shock, it twisted and spun and landed on one dog's arse. The mongrel yelped and turned and the others hesitated and—

The tom spun into a howling mass of fur and claws, startling the dogs. Howls and whines and cries of pain and soft whimpers then poof—the cat was gone.

"Jesus, Bren, did you see that?" Danny whispered.

I nodded, grinning, really fucking proud of myself, though it was pure luck the Blue had traveled as it did. "Never count yourself down, eh?"

"I guess not," he said, then fired up his own fag.

I didn't want to move. I wanted to stand there, in homage. Watch the dogs wander around, hurt and confused. How could it have gotten away? They had beaten the little beast, they knew it, but it had outdone them. They'd get no more go at it, and nothing could have pleased me more than to have witnessed it. I actually started to laugh, even though it hurt my lip.

I looked up and across at the Guildhall, sitting solid and uncaring. A symbol of all that was wrong in Derry. A Catholic town controlled by Protestants without a care for those who'd been here a thousand years before them. Beyond it, the Foyle whispered past, giving no thought to our pettiness and obscene behaviors. Nature's way was to let the strong destroy the weak? That tom had proven it a lie. No matter how badly you seem to have lost, you might still beat your tormentors.

Then wee Eammon's Ma burst out the door, howling, "Why are you standing there, smoking? He's got asthma, you know? Are you trying to kill him?"

"Ma, I'm fine," came from within.

I sighed and saluted her, then Danny and I headed for the elevator. At least my mood was lighter.

We were climbing back up the hillside to my house when Danny said, "You're in a better temper, now."

I shrugged. "Wasn't I, before?"

"Naw. Quiet. Even for you. Like you're a hundred miles off."

I stopped halfway up the hill and looked at my house. No light was on. I turned around. "I want another smoke, but I haven't any. Let's go to—"

"Here."

He let me have one of his Marlboros! I hadn't noticed that he'd been smoking Marlboros! Those were not inexpensive. I felt honored. I fired it up and stood there, looking out over the Bogside. Over the fading light. Finally, the darkness. The lovely darkness. With nightfall, I knew I'd be fine, again. Happy, again. Something icy was caught in my chest. Something empty. I needed space and silence and nothingness to let it drift away, and the shadows would fill that. So I said nothing.

Danny kept quiet. For a moment I got the feeling he was going through something similar. Maybe as bad as myself, maybe worse, but him not saying a word was the best thing he could have done for me. By the end of the smoke, the light was far enough gone to let me be completely at ease.

Then Danny whispered, "It's nice, here. The city's quiet and you can tuck your thoughts away to worry over, later." I nodded.

I could hear a smile in his voice. "You understand what I mean. I don't think Colm could. He's too caught in his—what'd he call it? *Forward movement?*"

I chuckled. "Sounds American."

He smiled. "That's our Colm, always with the latest."

I asked, "Have you seen him, today?"

"Naw, he's off with those new lads. Him and Paidrig. No idea who they are. Where they are. Why?"

I shrugged. Smiled. "You'll always be me China, won't ya?"

His smile joined mine, but with a bit of wariness. "'Course, Bren. And you, mine." He looked back over the Bogside, swaying a little. "When's Eamonn back?"

I had no idea so just shrugged, then asked, "You thirsty?" He shrugged a sort of *yes*. I grinned. "Y'know, I got a pound on me, still. What you say we find out if some old sport'll pop in the off-license and get us a little something? To drink."

"I don't think a pound's enough for the both of us," said Danny. Then he cast me a wicked side glance. "Let's to my house."

I shrugged and we went.

His was a decent maisonette. Mold on the whitewashed walls and chipped sills and stoops, without, but in through the green door you'd find a well-kept parlor with a small prayer corner next to the hearth, cushioned chairs and two lamps around a low table. Pictures adorned the walls and throw carpets covered the floor. A telly was in the corner nearest the window, its rabbit ears extended with tinfoil.

We said *hello* to his mother, who was focused on some cooking show on the telly so barely noticed us.

"Valium," said Danny.

"Wow," I said. "Y'know, I can copy me Ma's signature. You think we could get some for wee Eammon's? Like you said?"

"I think ya gotta see the doctor first."

Then we were up to his small room, where he had a plush bed to himself, table and lamp beside it, a wardrobe and a narrow desk with a wooden chair. His brother and sister were off to jobs in London. Posters of *The Rolling Stones* and *Lulu* and the like were pinned to his walls, and atop the wardrobe was a row of books...that hid three *Tennant Nips* bottles. He handed me one.

"How'd you get these?" I asked.

"Da's. Didn't notice I lifted them. He forgets how much he's had to drink, at times."

So we sat down and started up the radio and finished off his Marlboros and each had a bottle as we just listened to song after song after song. Not saying a word. I didn't get home till well after everyone was to bed.

The next morning, I slept on and missed Mass. Then Mai worked a full fry-up, the smells of which brought me bolting downstairs fast, I was so perished from the hunger. But the moment Ma saw me, she tossed what was to be my plate on the floor, breaking it. That it was one that was already chipped and cracked, I noticed. Of course, that set Kieran to wailing.

Mai's sigh of, "Ma, it's a sin to waste food," didn't begin to make her sorry for it, while Rhuari just looked at her as Maeve asked, "But how's he to eat it, Ma?"

"Hush and finish your breakfast," she snapped. Then she shook Kieran and said, "Be still or I'll give you cause to cry." Of course, he couldn't be, so she pulled him up from the chair and swatted his rear. He shut up, startled.

Silence smothered the room. It was the first time she'd struck him in any way. She almost looked flustered.

That's when I glared at her and muttered, "Beating a baby."

Now they all looked at me, in shock. Which made me grin. Then just to be a maggot, I sat cross-leg on the floor and ate every bit of that fry-up I could manage with my fingers. Like a dog eating its vomit, but with care so as to avoid the broken plate.

There was not a word from any of them, though a wary glint came Ma's eyes. I had to fight a laugh. If she thought me simple, before, now she was sure to think me mad. A true looner. And I loved it. Might give her pause, next time she thinks to lay hands on me.

After, I found my box was still by the stoop, as were the remains of that clock. I cleaned everything up, kept the brass numbers off the porcelain, and took it all up to my room. I had already determined to add a new face to the clock. It wouldn't be as pretty but would function well enough and show my capabilities to Mrs. Donaldson. And Ma would have to send me to my grave to get anything more than thruppence from me, again, no matter how much she knew of my jobs.

I made a pound, it turned out so well. Called it an antique, did Mrs. Donaldson. I had dug up a couple of stones in the yard as a new hiding place for my stash, and they covered my total of seven pounds six neatly.

The strong beat the weak? Like bloody hell.

Standoff

After that, days would pass with not a word between me and Ma, except for a direct order to clean this or fetch that. Mairead took up the washing of my clothes and fixing my meals, and I gave her more than half my earnings because I knew she'd use it right, for Ma was still set in giving part of our little bit to the church instead of use it all for us. She'd be content with burned toast and tea from twice-used leaves for breakfast if she had her way, as if it were a penance she had to endure and would see to it we endured with her.

But Mairead made certain we had eggs and jam and fish fingers and carry-out from the Chinese or chippy, on occasion. While Ma'd rather dig through the church's offerings of donated shoes and clothing for us to wear, our Mai saw to it Eamonn didn't have to rely on Da's old Mac, when he was off to Queen's. That thing was long and had been hand-cleaned a few too many times after catching dirt and filth when working the docks.

This is when my seven-and-six was useful; we'd found him a fine sports coat at Woolies that would go well with any and all occasions. Mai and I gave it to him on the day he left for his orientation, as his first classes were not till October. Oh, did he smile with joy. And Ma gushed at how smart he looked, never once asking how we paid for it.

While he was off, Mai worked her magic on cleaning the Mac and Ma used her skills to effect some repairs. For a short while they were like two ladies having a fine craic by the hearth. It would have looked like new, once they were done, had the material not been so worn.

He wore the sports coat home on his return, and did he look bright and happy. Mai had wrangled a table from Devlin's that had a slot where you could expand it along with six chairs. I've no idea how she paid for it because it looked almost new; she had to know someone there who would work with her, for her wages were not that good. So we sat around it, feasting on haddock, chips and peas as we listened to his tales of his future university life.

Two friends from Creggan were there, with him—Jackie Brennan and Aidan Dunn, all going for law, and they stuck together as much as they could in their course schedule. I knew Jackie by sight—tall, thin, ruddy and long straight black hair around a short face. He had an air about him that said, *Don't bother me.* So I never did. In fact, I was amazed he and Eamonn took on with each other. As for Aidan, it wasn't till he and Jackie swung by to join Eamonn on the trek back to Queens, that Sunday, that I put a face to the name—a lad not much taller than me, but stockier and plain in looks and temperament. His smile was not one I'd have trusted, but he and Eamonn got well enough along so I accepted them, for his sake.

They had already made some friends with both lads and girls from around the six counties, not all of them Catholic.

"They want the same things as us," he said, talking about this one fellow from Armagh. "Peace. Love. A chance at prosperity. And they understand it's the landed gentry usin' our distrust to keep us down in the muck while they live the high life. It's opened my eyes to the potential for goodness in people."

"Just you be careful of them Loyalist bastards," Ma shot back. "They smile to your face and nod to your words, but stab you in the back, first chance they get."

"Which is why Jackie and Aidan stick with me," he grinned. "We keep watch on each other."

"Good for you. Keep your head about ya." And for the first time in months I actually saw a smile on Ma's face. Not only that, she didn't cast a damning eye at me. I didn't know what to make of it.

After he finished telling us of this bright new world, one that sounded like he'd jetted off to a whole new planet, he slipped his fine jacket on and said he was off for a meeting.

"With Jackie and this Aidan?" I asked.

He gave me a sly grin and said, "We'll see who's there."

I wanted to join him, to hear what they were talking about, but Ma finally turned her cold eyes on me and said, "You'll help Mairead clean up and put the table back. It's too large to leave as it is."

I decided not to argue, but shifted the dishes to the pail, for washing, and brought in water to heat, and had the table contracted to near half its size and the chairs stacked in a corner, in two snaps. Then, while Ma was upstairs with Kieran, I had my parka on and was out the door to catch up to Eamonn. In the back of my mind, I knew I'd get some stick but I didn't care; I just wanted to sit close by and listen in as they talked so I'd be better able to discuss things with my brother on his own level.

They normally met at St. Agnes so I ran down the path to St. Columb's and across to Fahan. It was a brisk night with one of those vague, inconsistent fogs that carried fingers of thickness and then nothing and then thickness, again, lending an air of mystery to the never-ending rows of houses. There was even a cool feel to the refuse lots that were once homes and shops, now gone thanks to the slow spread of redevelopment. Work the Mayor's office was pushing to *upgrade the living quarters.* All they'd managed to do was make the houses still occupied seem darker and more alone, despite lights burning inside.

Few people were about, with the pubs being full and the fun crowd being at The Embassy, dancing to the latest music. I liked the solitude; it added to my sense of happiness and peace, and made everything almost magical.

I finally saw Eamonn striding down the dark street, ahead of me. Hands in his trouser pockets. Caught up in a band of the mist then appearing on the other side, like he was going through some sort of cleansing process. Smoke from a fag trailed behind him.

I slowed down so as not to catch up to him. The feeling around him was so pure and easy. So big and well-grown to me. So smart and filled with promise. For the first time I began to think maybe I would like to emulate him. It wasn't too late for me to do well on the Eleven Plus. I was unsure what future I might want for myself, aside from fixing things and building a family of my own, but Eamonn's new existence looked to be so full of promise and possibilities, I knew if I went to Queen's I could take the time needed to find any direction in life I wanted.

He continued up Fahan, pulling his coat's collar up. I smiled. The chill was finally getting to him. It didn't, me; I had to leg it just to keep him in sight, so I worked up a bit of a sweat. But we passed the turn to Father Jack's church and headed up Creggan. Then he made a jig to his left and a jag to his right, pulled his collar up around his ears, and shortly after, stopped at a house that had an old, pink and white Vauxhall Cresta parked in front. It had ridiculous sidewalls on the tires and lips above the headlamps so everyone on the Bogside knew whose it was. Then he knocked on the door and a woman answered and let him in.

He was visiting Mrs. McKittrick.

That confused me. Was the meeting in her home? I saw no one else around so-so-oh...oh, surely *she* wasn't Eamonn's lady. I'd only just fixed her portable radio, and while I grant she was a fine-looking woman, she was past Ma's age!

No, this couldn't be right, Eamonn and her. True, her husband had emigrated to find work, but I would never have connected her with Eamonn's description. She worked in a dress shop. Or owned it. I wasn't sure which. But that silly Cresta showed she was doing well enough. So I crept closer to the house and peeked through a window. There must be other people inside, and once I'd seen, I could put this nagging worry to rest.

The curtains were closed but I could see through a small space at the center and—

Oh, my God, was all doubt erased from my mind. She and Eamonn were on the settee, kissing and pulling at each other's clothing and-and-and then I saw what Eamonn was talking about when he wondered if I'd made use of my own tadger.

I jolted back and ran down the street, feeling as if I'd done something wrong. Like I had seen something I never should have. I was also feeling more than a little let down by my brother. The manner in which they'd grabbed at each other was just—it was ugly. Joanna would never pull at my trousers like that. Nor put her hands on my buttocks. And I'd never grab at her breasts like Eamonn had Mrs. McKittrick's. They looked more like dogs rutting in the street. Was that how men and women were when they made love? Grasping beasts lost in some mindless actions?

Really?

I had a shilling on me so I stopped at Geary's for some hot cocoa and hoped the crowd of dating couples would help put what I'd seen out of my head. But something about it also made my heart race even as my brain kept spinning. I'd look at lads with long hair and tight bell-bottoms trying to kiss girls in primped hair and patent-leather boots and-and then I'd see Eamonn and Mrs. McKittrick falling onto the settee, again, and had to shake the thoughts away.

I was still trying to make sense of how awful it was when Mr. Geary came over and said, "You sittin' there your whole life, Brendan?"

I shook my head. What was left of my cocoa was cold, so I got up, then stopped and just had to ask, "Mr. Geary, when men and women are together, are they always like animals?"

"What a question," he shot back. "What makes you ask?"

"Nothing. Just-just something I-I wondered."

He leaned in close and whispered, "Look around you, lad, and take note. Between you and me, men are dogs, and women are cats, and never the twain shall meet, except in the art of love." Then he winked.

It was all I could do to keep from saying, *That wasn't art I saw*.

So I just smiled and headed on, for this I knew to be nonsense. I'd seen how those dogs were with that tom. And yet—well, in truth, their snapping and snarling and hissing could be considered close to what I'd just seen, if the tom had been a female and the dogs all male. It finally made me laugh.

At least now I knew how she'd heard of my repair abilities.

I wasn't ready to return home. I knew Ma would not be easy about me sneaking off, so I wandered over to Colm's, but he was out. From there I went to Paidrig's and climbed all three flights to their rooms to find he was watching his baby sister and nephews. His brother and sister-in-law were at the Avco to watch a film so he was stuck. I had no interest in helping him; he lived in a place that wasn't good enough for rats and I feared some day we'd be pulling him and his family from its rubble, once it collapsed. I thought about wee Eammon's flat, up in the tower, but his mother had yet to forgive me for being his friend, and Danny had begun running with a new crowd, of late, so I just slowly wandered about in the growing ruins of Bogside.

We'd been learning about the Blitz and how even Belfast and Derry were hit by the Nazi bombers, so I wondered if this is how the city looked after such a catastrophe. Da was from Belfast. He might have drifted through ruins like these, though they'd have still been smoking from the fires and death within them. Perhaps that was why he wound up at the orphanage.

No. No, the war started years after that. I think. I only had rumors and gossip that he'd even been in an orphanage. He might have been taken there after his parents died in the bombings and...

Oh, it struck me hard how little I knew of his childhood. Little of his life except comments made while he was in drink. Nor had his stories or songs stayed with me. I'd once asked Ma after him, but all she'd snarled is, "There's nothing you need to know, and leave it at that."

Considering how angry she was when I did ask others, it was better I left it silent.

I did recall one moment that could be related to his early years. It was after one of their nastier rows, when he'd wound up seated on the divan, too drunk to rise. Father Demian had come to calm him while Ma was next door, being tended to by Mrs. Haggerty. Mairead had been focused on cleaning young Eamonn's face and I'd been seated on the top step, my shoulder handing me plenty of pain and my arm almost useless. When I'd finally seen a doctor, it turned out he'd broken my clavicle when he'd slammed me against the banister. But at that moment, I'd been listening as Father Demian said all the usual things about forgiveness and control and understanding, to which Da had only grunted. When the priest finally left, I'd watched Da stare at the door with absolute hatred as it closed, and heard him mutter, "Bloody bastards come at ya from nowheres. Call ya and come at ya. And naught ya can do to stop it. No place to go. Bastards. Bloody fuckin' bastards. Devils." Then he'd drifted into a stupor that wound up with him sleeping on the divan.

When Ma had finally come back in, she'd stood in the doorway and gazed upon him for a long time, then covered him with a blanket, her cheeks still red from his fists. Her face had been kind, in its expression, until she'd seen me still sitting there and snapped, "You should be in bed."

I'd been angry at him for what he'd done to us, again. And confused at the tenderness Ma had shown as she covered him. And there was how Da had never looked at Father Demian as he was being lectured. And now, mingled into my memory was how he and Ma had flown into each other's arms, that night.

Rather like Eamonn and Mrs. McKittrick.

Dear God, if they stayed together, would they wind up like our parents? Would he have some secret needing to be kept from one and all and her the only one knowing so willing to forgive him anything? Would Joanna and I become the same, were we to get together? Was that how life worked? Love worked?

I wanted answers, but who could I ask? Not Eamonn, that was certain. And Ma would fly into a rage. I didn't think Father Jack would be the right person, either. What does a priest know of real life? Mr. O'Faelan, maybe? No, Colm's knowledge of such things was obviously no better than mine. Nor would any of them know about me Da, except maybe for his pub mates who brung him home when he was paralytic. Like that one who told me about him being smart—what was his name? Perhaps he knew something about Da that could help me understand him, and if I did understood more about him, all of this might make sense.

The mystery of his early years began to pick at me, magnified by the blank walls rising above rough mounds of dirt and stone. History vanishing around us all. Our overlords insisting this was about nothing but redevelopment. Widen Fahan for better traffic flow. New lodgings for old, with indoor plumbing and windows tight against winter's chill and good wiring that could accept electric appliances for those who could afford them. So now half a block that once was a community of people living next to each other their whole lives, if not generations, had been made vacant and meaningless, their windows bricked or boarded up. The destruction was working its way closer and closer to my home, so it was only a matter of time before we were located into a soulless flat and ordered to feel grateful because it offered an inside toilet and hot water.

The fog grew deeper and more consistent, so that looking at some of these buildings made me feel more like I was staring at ghosts rather than dwellings where couples had been married and borne children and lived their lives in silence, always hoping tomorrow would be better. Or tomorrow. Or even the tomorrow after that.

Over centuries.

Was it like this in Dublin? Through all the Republic? I was fair certain it wasn't on the other side of the Foyle. Joanna's family was obviously doing quite well, for that estate car was almost new, and their clothes were up to date, obviously not from a second-hand shop. Were all Catholics so poor in wealth? Were Protestants really so much richer than us? The stories and gossip I heard were so filled with contradictions, I honestly couldn't say. It seemed to me I should travel down to Dublin some time just to see for myself what a nation of papists was like.

I was almost to Howard when I heard an RUC whistle blare up the hill, mingled with the sound of running feet. By instinct I stepped into a vacant doorway and glanced about just in time to see a couple of bikes appear from the mist. An old Schwinn and a banana bike. They whisked past followed by two odd-sized lads on foot, laughing, and all vanished into the darkness.

More footsteps came at a run.

It was Danny.

"Oi, me China!" I whisper-called out.

He skidded to a halt, a wild look on his face, saw me and hopped into the doorway moments before two peelers ran past.

He chuckled, out of breath, and punched me soft in the shoulder, saying, "You saved me, Bren." His face was bright with excitement, happier than I'd seen him in months. I noticed the collar on his jacket was torn, fresh. He pulled at it to look, saying, "Yeah, they almost caught me. Me Ma'll toss a fit."

"What was all that?" I asked.

"We took a wander through the old jail. They saw us and thought to snatch us. Bloody peelers. Weren't doing anything; just looking."

"Still after your mates."

"Won't catch 'em. By now they'd hit out to four directions."

"Where they from?"

"Shantalow." He grinned wider and said, "But I know where they'll wind up." Then he glanced after the peelers. They were long gone into the fog. "Come with me; I'll introduce you."

"Where?"

"Up Groarty across to the Republic. The circle fort. Haven't ya been there?"

Grianán Aileach. Once the grandest place in Ireland. Rivaling Tara, and centuries older. The seat of kings. The fort my father used in his stories. I knew other lads had gone climbing all over it, but I'd never been, though our class was supposed to make a trip there, later in the year.

So I shook my head and asked, "Isn't it far?"

"Not so very. So you comin'?"

I gave a shrug and nodded, and off we went.

Grianán Aileach

Danny kept a pace that was neither fast nor slow, but steady. His focus locked onto the road, ahead, looking neither to the left nor right. I almost asked him where he'd been these last few weeks, but the lovely silence of us just being together and the good clean air crashing into my lungs kept me from saying a word. I often preferred quiet, even when with my Chinas. Just liked to know they were there, and they seemed to respect that, in me.

A lot of the walk was up a hill, with grottos along the way. As we left the city's edge, the fog all but vanished. There was no moon out but the stars shone light enough to see across the parcels of cultivated land and beyond the dark clumps of trees. And because the air was cut only by the sound of our shoes on the road, it seemed as if we'd been taken to a new and amazing world of peace and tolerance. I slowed our walking to just enjoy every part of it. Let the beauty of it wander through me.

Thick hedgerows. Water trickling through ditches to each side. Slow hills and few trees. Pastures that were obviously green, even in the darkness, empty of anything that resembled life. Danny and I could have been the only lads left in the world, just then, and I'd have been fine with it.

We finally cut down this road just past the border that curled around and up a hill, and I could just make out a round shape bulging at the top, to our right. There wasn't a tree near it and the wind was brisk and bit at my cheeks. I had my parka on while Danny was in just a jacket, but he seemed untouched by the chill.

"Is that it?" I asked, my voice sudden and sharp against the quiet.

"Yeah," said Danny. "It's got walkways going up, inside."

"Me Da used to weave stories about it, in the pubs."

"Tell us one."

"It's been years, Danny. I don't remember much. How long

you been comin' here?"

"Some time. Night's best. Too many lads, in the day."

"Bloody hell, you do keep your own counsel, don't you?"

"I like bein' alone." He was smiling, but I felt it was soft and sad. "Don't you?"

I nodded. "So why bring your mates?"

"I didn't," he said with a sigh. "They just showed up when I was there. We hit it off."

I heard a swishing sound and turned just as that Schwinn raced up the gravel road and whipped past us, its pilot laughing. Another boy was on the handlebars. A moment behind them was the banana bike, a Huffy Penguin. A second lad sat on the rear of its seat. They stopped a bit ahead of us and jumped off, waving at Danny.

"Hey, Dan-O, who's the lad!" shouted the one who'd piloted the Penguin.

"It's Brendan," he called back. "I told you of him!"

They came back down the hill, to meet us, one tall, two my height, one smaller than Maeve, all dark and slim and looking a lot like brothers. It was the same group who'd been chased by the peelers. Their clothes were flashy and neat, something I hadn't noticed before, and their faces were all grins. The tall one grabbed my hand, saying, "So you're the famous fix-it lad."

"Can you work the gears on me bike? They rattle something awful," said one my size, who was the darkest. The other one my size was fairer and freckled.

I shrugged and said, "Won't know till I see it."

"I'm Tommy," said the tall one, "and this is Connor." He pointed to the one with the Schwinn then to his mate in size, who'd piloted the Huffy. "That's Shane. And last is Brian."

"Boru-to-yous," said the smallest lad, whose pants were actually a few inches too short for him and whose boots made his feet look comical in size.

"And Saint Brendan to you," said I, in return.

"He's not joking," chuckled Danny. He'd come quite alive.

They laughed and we cut through low growth that was thick and grabbed at my trousers, going up the last of the hill to the fort.

"I think I know your brother, Eamonn," said Tommy. "He's at university, now, inn't he?"

I just nodded, suddenly remembering what I'd seen in the

window. "I-I don't recall you being around."

"I met him on the march at Dungannon. Bunch of us Derry lads there. He's a passionate one. When things threatened to get hard between us and the Proddies, this one point, he helped convince us to back down and keep walkin'."

"We should've torn those bloody bastards apart," snapped Brian Boru-to-yous.

"Plenty of time for that."

We reached the base of the fort and circled around to a tiny opening covered with a grate. Tommy undid a couple of bolts and pulled it partway off, then we scampered through this cave-like passageway to the middle of the circle. It had stone steps leading up to three levels of walkways, the uppermost one only a few feet under the top. I climbed around and up to look out...

And it was a whole new world unto itself, of mystery and history and magic. Silvery water in the distance gleamed around dark mounds of earth, sharp-edged under a sky crusted with diamond-like stars. It was like nothing I'd ever seen before and knew I would never see again. No question but this was where fairies had come to sit and look out over their domain.

I turned to call to Danny, joyous beyond belief, but I saw Tommy slip a stone away from the base of a nearby wall. Brian dove into it, and moments later, out popped a bottle of whiskey and a fat bag of tobacco.

"Still here," he said, happy.

He vanished back inside and brought out another bottle and laughed, "Irish!"

"Have a care, lads," said Danny. "If too much is gone, it'll be noticed and then it'll all vanish."

I started down, saying, "Danny, this isn't your stash, is it?"

He shook his head.

Tommy finished taking a swig of the whiskey and offered him the bottle, saying, "Finders keepers, y'know."

Danny downed some then handed it to me. I didn't want anyone to think I wasn't as much a man as them, so I took a swallow. And near choked on the sudden sharpness of it.

Brian Boru-to-yous smirked at me. "Can't hold his liquor."

"I'm holding it fine," I snapped back. "I just-I just don't drink out of a bottle."

Tommy winked at me and said, "You'll learn."

I noticed Connor and Shane were busy rolling fags, so I took the moment to ask Danny, "What is this?"

He shrugged. "I was up here lying on the top wall, just looking at the stars, and some men snuck in. I kept hid and watched them pull that stone away. After they left, I looked into it. They'd hollowed out part of the wall and used it to hide things. I guess it's stuff they're smuggling into Derry. Stolen. Not paying taxes on it. Making a fortune."

"But all this way, so far from everything. It doesn't make sense." I looked around the rocks, the whiskey building a nice warmth in my belly. "This place is kept up. Eventually someone's gonna find that loose rock and brick it over."

Danny shrugged in answer.

Brian Boru-to-yous fired up a fag and inhaled...but he didn't exhale. Tommy did the same thing, after him, then he offered it to me. It didn't smell like any cigarette I'd ever had, but I still took a puff and Tommy laughed at me.

"His first drink and his first smoke," he chuckled, smoke whispering from him like a spirit.

"I've smoked before," I said, irritated.

"Benson and Hedges?" Aidan sneered.

"Blues," I growled back.

Danny took the fag, saying, "Like this, Bren." Then he inhaled and held his breath. And held it and held it till I thought he'd pass out before he exhaled and choked out, "Here," as he handed it back to me.

I took the smoke in and held it as long as I could, handing the fag off to Tommy, who carted it over to Shane. When I finally let it explode from my lungs, I was starting to feel dizzy.

"It's best to lie back," said Danny. "Look at the stars. You'll not see the like of them, again."

I lay on the wet grass and gazed upwards. He was right. Suddenly, it was as if the heavens were fresh and new. Bright, gleaming pinpoints of light cutting through the black, black velvet and so-so-so gloriously brilliant. A billion, billion of them, it must be.

Then they moved.

I had to hold onto the earth as it spun.

"Christ, Danny," I whispered, "what is this?"

"Something to make the world a better place," he whispered

back, and I'd say he was only half talking to me.

The bottle came my way, again, so I sat up to sip...more carefully, this time. It was a smoother sort of whiskey, more flavorful. I offered it up to Danny but he waved me off, opting instead for another drag on the fag. I giggled at the rhyme, and then couldn't stop giggling.

Tommy sat beside me and took the bottle then offered me a fresh ciggie as he looked at the label.

"Bourbon," he said as I inhaled. His tone became too-properly-British as he continued with, "A good Protestant drink, I'd say."

"Naw, it's Scotch, that is," snapped Brian Boru-to-yous.

"Don't like Scotch," said Connor.

"Da says you have to build a taste for it," added Shane. "But why? If you don't like it to start with, why make yourself drink it?"

"'Cause you're an eejit," laughed Tommy.

"Bloody right about that," snapped an angry voice.

I calmly looked around to see—

Colm standing by the passageway, and he seemed so angry I had to laugh, "Howya, Colm, come to join the party?"

"I knew it!" Colm snarled. "I knew there was pilfering, but you, Bren? You're part of this?"

"Catch yourself on, Colm," said Danny, rousing himself as lazy as a cat from a nap. "It's his first time, here. I brung him."

Then he deliberately pulled out a lighter, put a Marlboro to his lips and fired it up all I could think to say was, "Christ, Danny, you looked like Steve McQueen, just then."

He half-smiled at me then exhaled and said, "I'm the one found the stash," smoke still drifting around him as he spoke.

I couldn't really control my giggles, anymore, made worse by Colm's growling face. I finally began to understand and carefully rose to face him, gasping, "Wait, you? You're part of this? This smugglers' row?"

"Didn't I tell you, Bren?" asked Danny. "He's the one crawls into the hole and stacks everything in its place." Then he offered me the fag.

I took it and looked at it. Said, "This is more than tobacco and—"

Brian Boru-to-yous was creeping around to jump Colm and I

pointed at him and snapped, "STOP!" just as he leapt.

Colm dropped to one side and Brian Boru-to-yous crashed to the grass and rolled as Shane and Connor scrambled to pile onto my mate. I didn't think but jumped up and grabbed Connor from behind and rolled over and pulled him away as Colm gave Shane a good smack in the teeth.

Brian's nose was bleeding something fierce (and the hell with *Boru-to-yous*). He still rose to his feet and was about to join Sean in fighting Colm as—

Danny whistled in this loud, piercing way that startled us all.

I looked around to see Tommy crouched to spring at Colm.

With a knife in his hand!

And his eyes—Christ, the look in them scared the piss out of me.

But what really shocked me was how cool and casual Danny was, strolling between us and him and saying, "What the fuck, Tommy? You gonna kill him? Kill 'em both? They're me Chinas, so you do that, I'll have to kill you, and that's fuckin' stupid. Use your fuckin' head! If Colm knows about us, so do the lads he's workin' with, and they'll come after all of us. This is over! We had a good run of it, but we'll have to find someplace else to meet up. Put together our own stash." Then he added with a wink at me, "And you know we can."

It wasn't so much what he'd said that made it spooky; it was how Tommy lost that animal look, straightened himself up and put away the knife, as if Danny were his trainer.

I let go of Connor, then he, Shane and Brian strolled over to Tommy. I helped Colm to his feet and asked him, "You right?"

He looked at me with near embarrassment and nodded then looked at Danny and the others. "Me mates'll be along, soon. If you're still here, you'll get a lashin' like you've never had. If you're gone, I can talk them into forgettin' about it. And you can come back if you want, later. We're sealin' that hole up and changin' locations."

"Someplace more convenient, I hope," I said, meaning it, but then dissolving into giggles, despite myself.

Colm swatted me, backhanded, and shoved me at the passageway. "You're stoned! Go home," he snarled, but I could see gratitude in his eyes, now.

I looked around to find the others had already snuck off.

Don't know how they did it so quick and quiet and easy, but I could just hear the whishing of the bikes as they raced away and wondered if Danny was sitting on Sean's lap, then decided Brian Boru-to-yous would be better suited and Danny could be on the back...and again, I could not stop giggling at the image of it.

I slipped out of the fort, cast a last look at Colm, who was pulling more items from the hole, then set down the long walk home alone.

Long walk? It was shorter than the walk there. Probably because it was mostly downhill. But I also had the newfound beauty of the stars to accompany me in a cloudless sky, and I knew I could never feel alone, with them. More than once, I stopped and held open my arms and whispered to the heavens, "This is how it should be. This is all I want."

It was well after midnight when I got in. All were a-bed. Even Eamonn. Smelling of roses. I wasn't sleepy. I wasn't weary. I sat on the floor beside the bed and listened to my brothers breathe. Held on to my sense of peace and comfort as best I could. Let the shadows be my company. When dawn finally crept up and Eamonn rose, I was still there, unmoved.

I told them nothing of where I'd been. I went with the family to Mass with no complaint, though not without a few yawns during Father Jack's sermon, as the weariness was beginning to sneak up on me.

Ma had been truly angry with me for sneaking out and her every word to me was a snarl, but I was still feeling the effects of the pot and bourbon, so ignored her. All that served to achieve was to increase her anger and dig her nails deeper into me, until Mai had started her talking about something else—I don't remember what—and Eamonn had dragged me out for a walk.

Like Ma used to do with us when Da went on a tear.

The memory of that set wrong, but I wasn't going to argue. I know Eamonn was talking to me, but I wasn't hearing a word. It was as if my ears had shut off. Very odd.

We'd walked across the waste land to Waterloo and up William to Little Diamond. By then I was feeling a bit more energetic and caught on that he was talking about the demonstrations and sit-ins and DACA and how the Civil Rights Association in Belfast had come *to assist us in our planning*, which also brought a light snort of derision from him since they knew little about Derry. I chatted with what little I knew about it all, but my head was still full of wool, so I don't remember much of what he was saying.

Then I saw Mrs. McKittrick's Cresta heading for us, down Creggan. She pulled to a stop, her eyes on Eamonn, and glanced at her watch. Out of the corner of my eye, I saw him shrug and motion to me.

Had I kept him from a meet-up with her?

Another one?

Tonight?

Jesus.

I just sighed, stopped walking and told Eamonn I was going to Colm's. I had no intention of going there, nor interest in being around anyone, especially her, and my feeling was they would like to have been alone together. I've no idea if they actually were.

I just went up on the walls and walked to the bastion overlooking Nailors Row. I sat in a crenel and smoked more Blues. The name seemed right for the moment. It was still bright day. I looked to the left out over the unending rows of cramped, ugly homes flowing up the hill, whisps of white smoke trailing from their chimneys and adding to the foulness of the air.

This was why I so liked the night; you couldn't see the details. The tired people walking along the vanishing streets or across the empty lots. The others on Nailors sweeping their stoops or smoking next to the doors or as they hung out windows, the bored air of desperation to them all.

Suddenly, I felt so very sad.

Was my life to be like theirs? Lost in despair and pain? Thought of as simple, as the odd one, from now till forever? Breaking the tedium with whiskey and fags? And pot? Was this the destination for my Chinas, too?

Danny had looked so cool without even a thought, the night before. And Colm, for all his anger he seemed more grown than the rest of us. The others? I didn't know them so had nothing to say—except now I would not have trusted Tommy a step. I finally understood just how bad things could have gone had Danny not been in control of him and the others. And it spooked me. The only way I could work with it was to just let myself be as it slowly drifted away from within.

I lasted till supper, after which I hit straight for my bed and slept for near ten hours, then hated having to get up for school. I paid attention to nothing the brothers taught and was handed the usual punishments for my lack, thereof.

But then Colm caught me as we let out and whispered, "You backed me up, me China. I won't forget that."

I grinned.

Never had I felt so proud, not before nor since.

Barking Dogs

After a lot of talk and agro between the CRA and DHAC and a dozen other groups, a civil rights march was set for the first Saturday in October, the Fifth, despite no one but a few feisty lads—who *everyone just knew for certain were communist agitators*—really wanting it. It wasn't going to be a long one, just from the train station across the bridge to the Diamond. But that last, alone, made it a major development. There was an unwritten rule that only Protestants were allowed to march in the Diamond. It was the center of Derry and held emotional meaning, so Catholics had never even tried to before.

The anticipation was enormous. I had to fight to keep concentrated on my coursework. Until I started work on finding out why the film wasn't advancing right Mr. Keenan's Rolleicord camera. It turned out one of the teeth in the advancer gear had snapped off and was trapped in a space in the body. I'd need to replace a full gear mechanism connecting to the turn knob, only none were to be found, not in Derry or the whole of Ireland. But he wanted it ready for the march so waiting for it to come by post was not acceptable.

I pulled it out, gave a long glare for half a night, then worked up a temporary fix by sanding the broken gear down, using Ma's scissors to cut a bit of tin in the exact same configuration and gluing the broken tooth to it before sanding it even more. It barely fit, but would do well enough until the replacement part arrived. From Munich. I asked for five pounds on the repair—which he paid! Bloody hell, I should've asked for a tenner.

I fixed it at his home after school, so Ma never knew, and I gave Mai three quid, which she kept quiet about. But then she'd been quiet about a lot, lately. Sometimes she'd be doing dishes and would just drift away in her thoughts and gaze off at nothing, a look of tenderness on her face. And she was wearing makeup and perfume as well as a new skirt and blouse from Mrs. Hobbs Ladies' Garments. It was weird.

Then a few days before the march I came straight home from school because I needed my grips and found a Ford Transit van parked in front, its sides painted with *Devlin's Fine Furniture Fashionably Fixed*. Then I heard Mairead squeak a little scream, inside, and bolted straight to the back—

To find her leaning against the basin as a tall, strong, ginger lad tried to grab a kiss.

"Oi!" snapped out of me faster than I could think, and they both jumped up and backed away from each other. "Mai, what's he doing?"

Not that I didn't *know* what he was doing; I just wanted to know what he *thought* he thought he was doing.

"God, Brendan, you gave me a start," she said, her face bright pink. Then the ginger lad cleared his throat and she looked at him with such big, painful eyes, I almost felt like I'd done something wrong. "Right," she continued, "Um, Brendan, this is Turlach Devlin. He lives up Creggan and-and..."

"It's Devlin's you got our table from, isn't it?" I said.

"Yes. Well, his Da and...well..."

Her voice trailed off, so he stuck his hand out and said, "Call me Tur, and it's good to finally meet you, Brendan."

I shook his hand, wary, but I'd seen him about and felt right about him from the first moment. His eyes spoke of kindness and certainty, so if he was a dog, as Mr. Geary put it, he was a joyous puppy, still.

"You-you-you related to Bernadette?" I asked, not knowing what else to say.

Mai cast me a startled look as she asked, "Our mother!?"

"No! No, this girl Eamonn talks about. Devlin. She's at Queens."

"No," he said, casting a smiling glance at Mairead. "None of my family's at university."

"He-uh-his father and him," Mairead stuttered, "uh, they repair furniture. And have a shop."

"I know," I said, irritated. "I've been there."

Now she gave me a wary look. "You have?"

"Yeah, right, right," he said. "You're the lad likes to fix things." I nodded. "Well, like, uh, like what?"

"Clocks, radios, lamps, cars," I said, then added, "Cameras."

"Wow. That's a wide range. Think you could do some for us?"

"I come by your shop. Your man told me there's nothing for me. Furniture, only."

"Not always."

"It's what he said."

"That'd be Mr. Cunningham," Tur smirked at Mai. "He thinks I know nothing, as well." He turned a smile to me. "Lamps, then? Come talk to me Da; maybe we'll send some work your way."

"If you want." I was casual on the outside, but deep inside I was thinking, *I'll be there tomorrow, after school.*

I started to back away but Mai rushed up and whispered, "Brendan, please don't tell Ma of this."

I rolled my eyes. "Where is she?"

"Down harassin' the mayor into findin' us better lodgin's. Again. She's got Rhuari, Maeve and Kieran with her and is in such rags, you'd think she's a tinker."

"It won't work with those hard-hearted bastards," I said.

Mai jolted. "Brendan Kinsella, your language!"

Then a thought hit me. "Mai, you're not gonna leave us?"

That made her pink, again. "I-I don't know what'll happen. Bren, you won't tell Ma anything, will you? Not till I know for sure, myself."

Now I had to snarl, "When have I ever touted anyone?"

She bit her lip, nodded and cast a quick glance at Turlach that was anything but wary, and that convinced me there was more afoot than just kisses, here, so just to be the cod I continued with, "I hope Ma's successful, for we'll need the room if you and he're to be married and move in with us."

"Whist that talk!" she hissed. "It'll bring bad luck."

I just sighed and got my grips and left. If after knowing me all my life Mairead didn't know first off, I never told tales, and second, I wasn't that much a fool about life, she'd obviously never paid much attention.

But it did make me a bit nervous about her and Tur, because the expression she'd cast him was the same as was on Mrs. McKittrick's face when she'd driven up in her Cresta and seen Eamonn.

Damn! I hated having that memory dragged back into my

head. Eamonn and Mrs. McKittrick, and how ugly it was. How Ma and Da were; sometimes loving, more times fighting. And the thought of our Mai and Tur doing the-the-the same thing?

I feared for my sister, if that happened in all marriages and relationships. Rutting like animals then being sick and hateful to each other, ending with fists to the face and nails kept sharp and mean. It hurt me, inside, because I did not want that for her.

As if I had any say in it.

Anyway, that Saturday was the march, and oh, did we go through some massive ups and downs. First, no one would support our request for it. Then it did get set. Then Craig banned it, even as he seemed ready to allow a Protestant parade that was announced after ours but for the same day. Which infuriated our side. Then at the last moment he decided to ban them all, which placated no one, of course. So the action committee took the attitude of *We'll have ours anyway*, upsetting a great number of people on our side as well as everybody on theirs.

Why? Well, some just did not want to cause trouble. *We've made our point, now let's go home like properly trained dogs and enjoy our scraps.* Others felt the push for rights was being used by communists to hurt the *one-true-church*. But worst of all and most important? They picked a day that Derry City had a home game.

Talk about misunderstanding priorities.

Still, not everyone cared about football, so those who were marching gathered over by the train station, on the Waterside in Duke Street and Bond's Hill. An odd area that seemed to be both crowded in and not with buildings as shabby as our side of the Foyle. Hundreds managed to make their appearance, and my brother wound up not far from Gerry Fitt and some Members of Parliament. I didn't know who those men were; a lady with a speaker horn identified them. People were dressed in nice overcoats and suits and dresses with hats on as kids scampered about in jeans and jackets. It was more like a fair or open market than a rally.

What I did notice as we milled about was well over a hundred RUC men and some odd-looking vehicles with curious snouts on them were setting themselves up on Duke Street, between the rail station and the bridge. Another cordon of constables was to the other side, close to Simpson's Brae.

I began to grow wary, and that bloody cough started up.

Then I saw Billy with his uncle, watching us from up Distillery. I don't think he noticed me and I tried to keep out of his line of sight, for it sat wrong with me.

There were speeches made, but with Colm, Danny, and wee Eammon at my side—Paidrig being off to the football game with his brother—it was all too busy and playful for me to remain wary or even take much notice, especially since the rumble of hundreds of voices gave the crowd the sound of a living beast. Danny's eyes were as bright as that night we'd gone to the fort while wee Eammon kept trying to find a better view.

Then I noticed Colm's glances were wary. We exchanged careful looks and he pointed out to me where the RUC had bunched up and how some were working their way around the crowd.

"They're up to no good," he said, under his breath.

"Like they're boxing us in," I muttered.

Danny heard me and chuckled. "And that's news?"

I wondered if the reporters and TV cameramen were catching that and tried to get a better view of them. That's when I saw Tommy and Aidan in the mix, not far from another group of constables. I nudged Danny. "Your mates're over there."

He just nodded. Looked like the peelers were not the only ones up to something.

People were noticing and growing difficult to hold in place, pushed as much by attitude as by fear. There was Miss Sinclair on a chair pleading for this to be a peaceful march, but some in the crowd were jeering her and howling back, Eamonn McCann followed her, and he was calling for-for *a vote on how to proceed*? My brother had told me he'd been sent down from Queens for being too radical, but that seemed the exact opposite of such a thing. There was more yelling and howls of anger and cries for being careful.

Then someone cried, "We're off."

Everyone slowly turned in the same direction and flowed away from the station towards the bridge, like a dam had give way. Voices were happy and proud and filled with expectation.

Until they ran straight into that line of constables. The lead man used a loudspeaker to tell us we were an illegal march and ordered us to disperse.

But there was laughter and jeers howled at him and the crowd kept flowing, like a flooded river smashing against a jam of logs and refuse, sending it in a different direction. Mostly back up Duke to Bond and Simpson's Brae.

Colm climbed up a lamppost and called out, "We can't go that way! There's a line of peelers coming!"

No one paid him any mind, not until the crowd began running up against those constables and started trying to turn back but couldn't, because the first line of peelers had moved closer to bunch us in.

Colm jumped down to grab me and wee Eammon as he growled, "Stay to the right."

I glanced around for my brother but couldn't find him, then looked back up Duke and saw one of the peelers whip a baton down on a man at the head who was trying to talk with him, and that's when the constables went mad with wailing on everybody, and the happy voices turned to shrieks of pain and terror!

News crews appeared, recording it all, and the bloody peelers went after them, as well! Mr. Keenan was one of them, and used his body to protect his camera! People scattered, some screaming and falling as the constables kept beating at them with wild abandon. Then the vehicles with the odd snouts rumbled to life and began shooting water at us, like from a fireman's hose!

Wee Eammon, Colm and I got hit with it and it felt like I'd been punched in the gut. I crashed to the pavement and rolled around the fence to the depot. Wee Eammon was gripping the ground, and it looked like he was hollering but couldn't be heard over the roar of the water. Colm had vanished.

Suddenly people were running about like trapped animals and those on the side were laughing and chucking stones at them, even as Tommy, Connor and others chucked stones at the RUC. It was chaos.

I scrambled back over to wee Eammon and pulled him to a train station wall, where we hid behind a refuse canister. I looked around it and saw the water cannon shooting at people running across the bridge, hitting not only them but families coming back from the city center and women with shopping bags and cars and lorries; the constables had become madmen, not caring who was smashed by their actions. People kept running. They kept howling and swinging and slamming against them, laughing like hyenas.

Whoever was supposed to be in control of those animals

finally made himself known and the chaos began to subside. People were lying about on the street, hurt and bleeding, like after a wartime gun battle. I saw my brother helping an older man limp back down Duke and cried out, "Eamonn!"

He couldn't hear me over the jangle of police lorries approaching. I almost started across for him, but wee Eammon was whimpering and had no one beside him, so I sat down and nudged him and made myself laugh as I said, "No need to bathe tonight, eh, me China?"

He looked at me, shivering, and sort of shook his head. I think.

I scanned the area to see if Colm and Danny were still about, and finally caught a glimpse of them heading up Simpson's into Protestant country with Tommy and Conner, and I think I saw Brian, as well. All soaked and huddled tight, together. My worry for them lessened; in fact, I almost hoped that Tommy had his knife and some Proddies would be dumb enough to have a go at them.

The constables were still running around, and some man with shaggy hair was yelling to a reporter about this travesty and how the RUC had deliberately attacked peaceful protesters, even as he was being dragged away by them. Some were looking around for more people to pummel while others tended to the injured, in the background. That's when I stood up and pulled wee Eammon to his feet, saying, "We'd better get to home, fast. Get some dry clothes on."

He nodded and we scurried away.

Of course, the wind was strong as we crossed the bridge, and being wet made me feel miserable even as I wondered at the madness of what had happened. And so quickly, too. One minute everyone's having a lovely time; the next, it's chaos, blood and terror.

"Bren," said Eammon, his teeth chattering, "d'you think this'll be on the telly?"

"Probably," I said, my stomach beginning to quake from the icy dampness. "Some of those reporters looked proper shocked and disgusted."

"So why'd they do it? Now there's pictures of how they are. The RUC. Now there's film. Why would they do it?"

"Because they're dogs, son," I said. "Snapping at something

they're scared of, hoping it'll keep its distance and not thinking beyond that."

"I never had a dog do that to me."

"Me neither," I said, remembering that pack of dogs and the cat.

"I like how you describe it."

"Arra, I-I-I overheard it at one of Eamonn's meetings and it makes sense." Not wanting to tell him about Mr. Quinn's comment and-and everything.

"He lets you join him, then?"

I shrugged at the wee lad, feeling very big and manly.

"That's a cutting wind, inn't it?" wee Eammon chattered. "Me mum'll be at me for this. *You'll catch your death*, she'll say."

"We'll go up to my place and have some tea. Give us a chance to warm up before you're to home."

"Sounds grand. You do make a nice cuppa."

I smiled and walked faster, making him run a little to keep up. I may still be on the small side, but I can leg it when I want to, and that helped warm us both.

Neither the tea nor the drying off by our hearth nor the cup of hot broth Ma give wee Eammon did any good. He continued to shiver until his mother roared in to grab him and take him away. How she knew he was there, I never found out. Nor did it matter. Two days later he was in hospital with pneumonia, fighting to live, his mother weeping non-stop at his side.

The one moment she left him was to come to our home and blame me for him being ill, her lips flecked with fury as she screamed, "Why'd you let them try to drown him? He's not strong as you and you led him into his death! Why'd you do that?"

Ma just shook her head, her arms around the woman, saying, "I know, I know. I told him not to be there, but he never does as I ask, not once."

"He's a trial for you, Bernadette. A bad influence to the others, with his quiet ways and-and-and..." She dissolved into tears, at that.

I had no idea what to say so just stood there, listening to them go on and on until Mairead came home. She heard what was happening and took over from Ma to guide wee Eammon's mother onto the divan for a cup of tea, promising her she'd say a special rosary for him. Then sent me a sign to leave.

I had already been edging to the door, but Ma was scowling at me, her hands twitching for a go at my face. If I'd moved an inch or even thought to look at her, she'd have sent me straight to hell, by her fury. It took Mai putting her hands on Ma's shoulders and making her turn, saying, "Won't you have a cuppa with us, Ma? Then we'll go back with herself to wee Eamonn's bed and pray with her, if you will."

"Which is more than some would do," Ma snarled as she settled into the chair.

I just went up to my room and sat on the bed and looked out over the Bogside, my thoughts silent, my heart heavy.

They were right. I shouldn't have let wee Eammon come along. He was the weakest of us. But it was only supposed to be a quiet march across the bridge, and he was well-dressed for that. Could he have gotten sick, anyway? I didn't know. I knew little about medicine or illness, and halfway thought I might ask Father Jack about it, but I wasn't so sure he wouldn't agree with Ma, just to agree with her. Or find some way to agree while not really agreeing, as I'd seen him do on other occasions. But I had no one else I knew who I could ask. None of the brothers or teachers. Maybe John Hume? Oh, but he's far too busy a man to pay attention to a lad of twelve. Maybe that doctor who'd fixed me in hospital, not so long ago? Perhaps. If he wasn't also too busy.

I decided that if I ever had occasion to go to hospital, again, I could seek him out.

At that, I took in a deep sigh and turned to fixing an old record player for Mrs. O'Canainn that wasn't running at proper speed.

Of course, when Eamonn got home after that march, his glorious sports coat had been stained with blood and one of his new boots was torn across the heel. But he hadn't cared, for his grin was as wide as could be on his face, and to Ma not even the destruction of his *far-too-expensive* clothing had mattered.

"It's over for them, Ma," he said. "We'll have new digs within three months."

"Do you really think so?" she had asked, in raptures.

"Without question. The world is watching, now, even in England. They'll see that civil rights is not just a problem in America, and the Loyalists'll have to provide the neediest, like you, with the next available unit of a decent size."

I hoped it was true, but after that march I started paying real attention to how stupid the people running the country were. Not just the Mayor's office or Stormount but also in London. And I started to wonder if we were being too optimistic. We were led by men who couldn't see or accept that the world had changed around them, and who honestly thought handing out middling words of understanding would quiet the building anger.

Mere promises that this incident would be thoroughly investigated were no longer sufficient. And swearing the attack was caused by the protesters flew in the face of film evidence and eyewitness accounts. But lies was all they had needed in the past to make it vanish into history. That they were shocked at how none of the old tricks worked anymore was only further proof of their stupidity. I was but twelve years old and could see it was blind lunacy.

Father Jack said it best, a week later, when he compared the Protestants to those in the Bible who ignored the warnings of the prophets and wound up in destruction, where if they'd but taken heed, all might have turned out well. "Only a fool ignores the writing on the wall," he said, to end his sermon.

His long, long sermon, for he did love the sound of his voice.

I took some of it to heart and began reading the papers in the school library. Of course, it being a Catholic school, all the papers there were the *Derry Journal*, from the Republic or through the Diocese with stories solely about Catholics. So on occasion I'd stop at Mr. Wynn's news agency and he'd let me read the first couple pages of the Belfast papers.

Those made me cringe.

It wasn't just how they were so casual about Protestants being the one true faith and Catholics being of the devil; the Catholic papers were just as adamant, in reverse. It was the letters published in them that insisted Catholics were dumber than Protestants, worth nothing but the boot to their neck, out to destroy them all with fealty to the Pope, and lazy at best. It angered me enough to where I thought it might be a good idea to ignore them, completely.

But then it looked as if Stormount might just have learned something from this. For the RUC's assault on the marchers had angered many who had thought the march stupid, so when another one took place, a month later, along the same basic route, this time led by many of those who had opposed the October March, including John Hume, there was no interference. Mainly because it was thousands taking part and not hundreds, and even the RUC wasn't fool enough to try their antics against them.

Sit-down protests of thousands of people in Waterloo and in the city center made the message even clearer. *We won't accept things as they are any longer. One man, one vote. Decent housing for all. A job for any who want it.* They sounded like simple, honest requests to me, something any man should expect for himself and his family. Why would it be acceptable for those to be given to a Protestant but refused to a Catholic? It was stupid.

Of course, Paisley preached loud and hard against it, calling us papists and communists and the like. His search for power and fame was doing him well. But while he was gaining followers, he lived in Belfast, not Derry. My hope was he'd stay there.

Well, Eamonn was right that we'd get new digs, but was wrong about how long it would take and how hard they would fight back. Still, as I said, who can sense history when it's coming at you from behind, like a silent wave a hundred feet tall? Nobody. All you can do is clean your coat and mend your boot and fix your things and keep on with your daily life and let the chaos explode when and where it will.

And it will always come as it pleases.

Adjustments

Eamonn came home from Queen's for Christmas *with news of great importance*, as he put it. He'd joined a group called People's Democracy and they planned to stage a long walk from Belfast to Derry over the course of four days.

"We leave on the first and arrive at Guildhall Square on the fourth. So I'm back to Belfast on the 30th."

"What's the reason for it?" Ma asked.

"Draw attention to how we're being treated," he said. "Calling for equal rights."

"And takin' a stroll from Belfast to here'll do a thing for it?"

"It's better'n nothin'."

I noticed he had some fresh scars above his eye and asked him about it, and he said, "Paisley's thugs smashed up one of our meetin's. The other lads needed sutures."

"And you're still going to do this?" I asked.

"We'll set up protection with the police," he grinned.

"How many are you?"

He hesitated then shrugged. "Forty, fifty..."

"You're trusting the peelers after what happened on the Fifth? And that was in Derry. This time you'll be in the middle of nowhere, alone and—"

"With the press, so they'd face even stronger condemnation for their actions than before. They're not that bloody stupid."

"They wouldn't protect the Queen if they didn't feel like it."

"Be still!" Ma snapped. "Eamonn knows far more about life's realities than you ever will, so keep a civil tongue. It's a glorious thing to be taking up the cause."

I rolled my eyes. Seems all it took for her to join his side was for me to question it.

"Aw, Ma," said Eamonn, "let him be. Truth is, others have said the same thing. But what good is it to live life afraid, Bren?

Sometimes, you have to take your chances."

"Like your father did, God rest him," said Ma. "Going to Liverpool to find work when none was to be had here. Sending his wages home for us to be fed and keepin' only enough to not starve. *He* knew the meanin' of sacrifice."

Now I looked at Ma, confused. Every one of us knew full well Da had gone to Belfast, and then only when driven to go, and he'd brought little enough home to live on since he lost most of it to gambling and drink. I was close to reminding her of this when Eamonn stood up and said, "Bren, I'm off to Austin's to buy a present for a friend. You comin'?"

"Austin's!?" Ma snapped. "And what you doin' for money, m'lord?"

"I ran an odd job or two durin' the term, Ma," was all he said.

I grabbed my parka and was halfway out the door before he'd finished talking. It being so fine and rich a store, I'd known from the beginning there was nothing in it I'd want to spend my money on, so why bother with it? I'd only ever gone in to watch the pay boxes whisk overhead as they sent money all about to the cashiers. Still, if Eamonn was going I was more than willing to join with him.

We walked along in a cold drizzle. Eamonn had pulled Da's old mac over his sports jacket so he was fine, and my parka kept me warm enough. It still had stains from when I'd helped Mr. O'Faelan with his cab; not even Mai had been able to remove them all. So Ma had told me it's all I was worth so left it as such, as if that were supposed to be a punishment. Which made no sense to me.

As we walked, I asked Eamonn, "What jobs you been doing?"

"Runnin' errands for a professor and things off the employment board," he said. "There's always occasional work available, and if I go dressed like this, they don't even think to ask what religion I am."

"They can't tell from your name?"

"Most of the time they don't even ask it," he said. "I don't think they care, and it's cash in hand. Something you'll learn, Bren, is the more you meet with others, the more you find they're just like you."

"Maybe. Two of me best mates were Billy and Gerry, from

the Fountain."

"*Were?*"

"Yeah."

"What happened between you?"

"Gerry's Waterside now, and Billy—he stopped meeting us for footie. It's too bad; he was good midfield."

"Once things calm down, I'm sure you'll be best mates, again."

"Maybe." But I knew we wouldn't, not with Billy, anyhow. Last time I'd seen him, his uncle all but spit at me and asked why a papist was allowed to smell up the parlor, and Billy'd said nothing. That's when he'd stopped joining up with us after school. "So you've got Protestant mates at university?"

"A few," he said, thinking. "We share the same values— fairness and respect for others. It's those vyin' for power and control, like Paisley and Bunting, who've screwed it all up."

"Will they be with you on this march?"

He didn't say anything for a moment then sighed. "No. They're some who think it's foolish to do."

"So it's all Catholics."

"As it should be." We passed through Butcher's Gate then he drew me close to him, whispering, "Why do you keep goin' up against Ma?"

"I-I-I dunno what you mean," I said, even though I did.

"Just before we left, you were about to remind her of Da goin' to Belfast, not Liverpool."

"Well, he did," I snapped.

"But he did go to Liverpool for work. Before you were born. He found it just as troubled, there, and more expensive to live so stuck with Belfast, after."

Which I did not know.

"But what if he did?" I growled. "Once! Or twice. It's wrong, the way she goes on about how great and glorious he was."

"What if she does?" he sing-songed back at me. "It's nothing but myth-building, to help her get along in this world. It's normal to focus on the good of the past and ignore the bad."

"Bollocks. She's rewriting what happened."

"Brendan, your memory's too sharp. Sometimes it's better to let the past be what it is."

I nearly snorted a laugh, thinking I knew what he meant.

"You can say that in a city that remembers horrors from three-hundred years ago?"

"It's what's made us what we are, today—angry and hateful and filled with distrust. If we're to have a better world, we need to drop the hurts, be they real or imagined, elevate the good and look towards the future. Looking backwards on those horrors only causes more and more pain and sufferin'."

"You talk like Father Jack."

"You're a cynical one for twelve."

"Near thirteen!" I snapped, then added, "And-and-and I'm not sure what you mean."

"We need to stop bein' distrustful," he said. "Wary. Knowin' it all. Seein' the worst and never the best, especially of the other side."

I huffed. "Eamonn, both Catholic and Protestant have cheated me. The last fight I was in was with some Catholic lads."

"Fight? You? With whom?"

Bugger, I hadn't meant to say a word about Tommy and his knife about to go after Colm. So I just shrugged and said, "Last summer. And it was a Protestant constable upbraided Ma for hitting me, once, so—"

I stopped myself short. I'd almost done what he does, again—let stories out without meaning to.

He stopped me and put his hands on my shoulders, concerned, asking, "When was that?"

I shrugged the question off with, "Ages ago. And you know how Ma can be."

Besides, it wasn't a pleasant thing to remember. I'd gone to Edmiston's to drop off a watch I'd repaired for a clerk. It had been a nice morning and the clerk had yet to show, so I'd looked over the Corgi Toys in their window. I was thinking I might exchange my fee on the watch for an Austin Cab they had when Ma'd appeared down Shipquay, sharp and sudden, grabbed me by the hair and smacked me three times before a Constable had roared up and yelled, "Here, enough of that!"

People had been looking at us, in horror and amusement. I'd felt brutally embarrassed, for none of them knew us.

What was worse? That was when the clerk had showed and simply entered the shop.

Ma had turned on the peeler and snapped, "He's my son, to

my shame, so I'll do as I want with the lyin', thievin' little snipe."

"Thieving? What's he done?"

"That is no concern of yours."

"When you accuse someone of thieving, madam, is most certainly is my concern."

"Well then, what do you make of this?" Ma'd snarled. "We're a poor family of six, with me a widow this past year and on the dole, but he's been makin' pounds and givin' me thruppence! Has been for months. I only found out because a lady in my group happened to mention the price he charged for to fix her telly was a bit high, and it was twice what he told me."

Meaning it was Mrs. Mellon who'd touted on me. Never more with her.

The constable had looked at me, gruff and demanding. "Is that true, lad?"

I'd just shrugged.

He'd then snapped, "Where did the money go? Why not help your mother?"

"I *do* help," I'd snapped back. "I fix things."

"You know what I mean. If you don't give money to your mother, were does it go? For toys?"

"No."

"Then what were you doing here? Planning to steal one?"

"No!"

"Well then?"

I had glared at Ma but dared not do the same with the constable, so I'd dug into my pocket and pulled out the watch.

"It's Mr. Collins'," I'd said.

"This is what you stole?"

At that, I did glare at him. "I *fixed* it! Ask him; he just arrived."

"And he would pay you for this?"

I'd nodded.

Ma had snarled, "How much?"

I was trapped so had been forced to tell them, "Shilling."

"Wait here." The constable had taken the watch inside Edmiston's as Ma had glared at me; I could tell from the side of my eye. I'd refused to look straight at her, for I'd been truly angry and she'd have seen it and everything would have been worse.

Moments later, the constable had came out. With a shilling.

"He's telling the truth," he'd said.

Ma had shot a growl at me. "And you'd not have given me a farthing of it."

I'd finally snapped out, "You don't use it right!"

She'd grabbed for me, screeching, "You ungrateful little devil, to suggest I don't—!"

"STOP THAT!" the constable had bellowed, and you could hear his voice over the whole of the walled city. Ma had stopped as he'd turned back to me and asked, "So you disapprove of how your mother handles money?"

I had shrugged.

"Then why not buy things for the family, if it's needed so much?"

I'd kept my silence.

"Young man, you'll answer me before we're done."

Then Ma's eyes had grown sharp as she whispered, "It's Mairead. She's in this with him."

"Who's that?"

"His sister. She's older and breaks her back tendin' to this one, and now I can see why."

"You give your sister the money?"

I had just shrugged.

"To make her your maid?"

"No!" I'd snapped. "When I give it to her, she uses it for us and don't give it all to the church for people ten thousand miles away."

Ma had gasped, and I'd kicked myself for revealing I knew about that. It was supposed to be a secret between her and Ma, still.

"You blasphemous child!" Ma had finally gasped. "I'll have Father Demian speak to you of this."

I hadn't moved.

The peeler had huffed, then laughed, handed me the shilling and ruffled my hair as he said to Ma, "Madam, I suggest you work *with* the lad, for he's a sly one. And if you can't, then keep your family squabbles at home. Now move away." Then he'd strode off, chuckling.

What had been good about it was, Ma'd glared at me, hard but curious, and had not tried to snatch the shilling from me. "So you give money to Mairead so it won't go to the church? After all the Fathers have done for us?"

"What little as they had to," I'd snapped back. "And Aunt Mari sends us money and you give them a part of that, as well. It's not right." I'd decided to let her know I knew it all.

She had grown tight and angry. "Who told you about that?!"

"Nobody." Then I'd looked her straight in the eye and said, "I was up top the stairs and saw you open a letter that come, and in it was what looked like fifty pounds. I found the envelope in the dust bin and it was from Aunt Mari, and that night you read us her letter."

"Spyin' on me?!" She had grown near a fury, again.

I hadn't moved, just said, "Maybe I should write her and tell her what you do with the money she sends. Ask her to send it to Mai, instead, for she cares for the family, first!"

Her fist had bunched but she held still. "That money is for-for-a-a pledge I made to the church."

"And they accept it, knowing how poor you are when Father Demian has gold threads on his cassock. Knows how many of us you have to care for and on how little. Strikes me as greedy of them. And with Father Jack coming in, will he let you continue this pledge? What are you buying from them, Ma?"

An odd expression had come over her face, like she was torn between being afraid of me and tearing me apart. I hadn't moved so people worked their way around us and on to the gate.

"It's not about *buyin'* anything," she'd said, but her voice wavered.

I sneered. "When it comes to money, that's all it's about."

She'd seemed to deflate, a little. "That's why you give Mairead the money, to use for us all," she'd finally said.

I'd nodded.

"You don't trust me with it."

I still hadn't moved. She had sighed. For the first time she had almost looked broken. It had startled me.

"Will you keep doin' it?" she'd asked, her voice soft.

"You'll take more from the dole to make up for it, won't you?"

"That money is for me to use. You have no say in it."

"It's not fair, Ma!"

"Will you keep doin' it?"

I'd sighed and nodded. I had finally admitted to myself this was a fight I couldn't win. With that, she'd walked away.

That flashed through my mind in a heartbeat, but all I did was look at Eamonn and say, "Money."

"What—did she find your hidey-holes?"

I shrugged and nodded. She had found the one in the garden, because the three pounds in it was gone when I went to add some to it, one night. But the board under the sink was untouched with its four pounds ten. The next night, I'd built a new one under a paving stone in front of the house, and thanks to the work I'd been doing, it now held five pounds.

Eamonn looked at me and smiled. "You haven't learned how to handle Ma, yet, have you?"

"How can anyone?"

"By lettin' her do and say what she wants, even when it makes no sense to you. Certainly not by pointin' out her little lies. That's guaranteed to make her angry and you will never win over her."

"Why would I let her go on like—?"

"She's your mother." Said in a way meant to end the discussion. I cast him a confused look and he smiled. "Think about it. Now come in with me, help me pick out a nice gift."

"Is this for your-for your married lady?"

His smile just widened.

We went in and found the perfume counter, where they had a nice one that smelled of roses, so he bought that. No surprise, there. And he took it over on Boxing Day after spending the whole of Christmas with us. I had a feeling Mrs. McKittrick would like anything he brought her, but I didn't say that, for he looked as bright and happy as a child, and I felt it only right to let him be.

A Deepening Dream

A few days later, Eamonn was off. He hadn't brought much home with him, so Ma sent him with a blanket wrapped in a sheet of plastic and bound by a rope at the two ends, a length of it still loose for a shoulder strap.

"We've got lodgin's set up along the way, Ma," he whined.

He got a gentle swat on the cheek, in answer. "In case you have to sleep outside," she said. "You never know with them Orange bastards."

He shook his head but accepted it and tossed me a wink.

I almost chuckled. *Push but don't shove.* Even as we were shoving against the Prods. It was madness, trying to make sense of it.

From the way he acted, you'd think he had no concern about the march, despite all the dire warnings and careful tut-tutting of tongues by those supposed to be on our side. Me, I flipped between a bad feeling about it all and the adventure of it, and desperately wished to join with him.

"That's foolishness, Bren," he'd said in a way that let me know I was still a child to him as he pulled on mittens he'd borrowed from Father Jack. "We'll be marchin' over seventy miles out in the damp and freezin' cold, and you're still healin'."

"Away on," I'd snapped back at him. "It's been near a year since I was in hospital, and all's fine. And the more folk you have around you, the less a chance of trouble. Colm's up for coming, too. We can be ready in two shakes."

"There'll be no trouble. We'll have police guards and news crews with us, and look what happened in October, when the bloody RUC went after people. They backed off, after, and wouldn't dare allow a repeat of that spectacle. Not when even Westminster has an eye on them."

"Oh, you're still on about that, and you call me a dreamer."

"What's this about? Is little Billy fillin' your head with fear?"

"They'll not let you cross the Foyle, RUC or no. That bastard, Bunting, has 'em all worked up. They're saying the IRA's behind it all."

He snorted. "The IRA's behind the price of milk, to that crowd. The only democracy they seem to understand is their heel on our neck, and the only way to get it removed is to make it known to one and all."

"And what of Paisley and his devils? They might not even let you leave Belfast."

"It's a peaceful march and we'll walk it all the way here, and on the fourth day of the New Year I'll see you on this side of the Foyle. You can trust me on that, and the devil with anyone's whimpers and fears."

Of course, Ma sent him off with great fanfare, making sure all the neighbors saw her eldest son was *taking part in history*. She'd wrapped the blanket around bricks of cheese and bread, with a spread knife to cut it all—any other knife could have brought about his arrest—even as he'd told her food was arranged along the way. And she'd pressed three pounds from the jar into his palm and made him promise he'd use it only for juice drinks or tea. As if she had reason to fear for him buying drink; he'd never even looked at a pint that I knew of.

"Make us all proud," she called as we walked away. "Show them Orange bastards what stuff a good Catholic lad is made of, especially one at University. And your family." I knew without looking she added that last with a sly nod at me, and she just had to add, "It's a pity we don't all have the will to press back against those who'd keep us slaves."

Eamonn sighed and turned to call back. "It's just a long walk, Ma. I'm not off to war."

"Whist your blather!" Her voice now echoing in the chill air, she was so loud. "We do what we must when we must, and you're showin' yourself willin' to do so instead of workin' with them what hate us."

That's when Eamonn caught her meaning and stopped. He cast a look at me, calling back, "Y'know, Brendan wishes to join me."

Ma actually laughed. "And have you worry about him rather than yourself, the whole way? He'll see you to the bus and not a foot farther. He's plenty enough to do around here now you're gone, and I'll not have it all put on Mairead. So off with you. And I'll see you next year."

He grinned, spun about, and led Colm and myself down the path to meet with Father Jack, at the base. Paidrig was at Butcher's Gate and Danny found us at Waterloo, but wee Eammon was kept home. His mother almost spit at me when I went up to see if he wanted to join us. She still held me responsible for his every illness, thanks to what happened at the march.

We cut around to Guildhall Square, where I'd sometimes stand to watch the busses come and go and wonder where they'd wind up, even if they did have their destinations in a placard behind the windscreen. I loved the manner in which they scurried about like little caterpillars.

Some folk we passed wished Eamonn well, but many more gave us their tut-tut expressions and shakes of the head. I was wearing a cap Aunt Mari sent me for Christmas, with an Apollo 7 Patch sewn on. America was back in the space race, after that horror of a fire, and I felt very worldly, wearing it. So just to be cheeky, I doffed it to them all, my smartest grin on my face.

Father Jack seemed as excited as Eamonn. "It's quite an adventure you're off on," he told him. "I only wish I hadn't such responsibilities so I could join you."

"Frank Downey's brought his camera, Father," Eamonn said. "And with all the reporters comin', we'll have snaps a-plenty to show."

"Excellent. Make our own document for the ages. Inform Master Downey I may post some in the rectory, if they turn out."

I felt a bit odd about Father Jack's wary enthusiasm. I'd heard too much from other fathers and the Bishop and on up the line that this was actually a communist undertaking and wrong. Could that be the real reason for his reticence about joining the march? I knew priests had long been part of the push back against Protestant rule, but from him it sounded like he felt he was doing what he shouldn't or wasn't proper or something of that nature, and it made him feel sneaky or the like.

I can't say what or why I believed that, it's just—well, he seemed to have caught up quick to the goings on in Derry. Probably thanks to so many of the ladies tending to him, daily, now he'd taken over. So I'm sure they'd let him know who needed a foot in the arse to remember his responsibilities, what lads were thieving from shops owned by good Catholics, and even which of the other ladies had the best craic going, so as to keep up with things. Of course, I liked him far more than Father Demian, but that isn't saying much.

Ma had dragged me to that man to explain where the money she gave the church went, after our set-to by Edmiston's, then left me alone in the office and sat just outside, at his request. He was on his feet before me, leaning back against his desk as he'd labored on and on about the good done by the church, saying all the right, proper and meaningful things that any middle-class Catholic might feel were important. On and on, he went.

I was standing before him, like I was in school about to be punished for some real or imagined crime, but I was paying more attention to his vestment with its gold thread, hanging from a hook in a corner. The sun was hitting it in a way that made it glitter and gleam, casting bright spots of light on the dark wood walls and half-enclosed shelves. I have to say, his words were gentle and full of grace as he told me of the missions in Africa and Asia and South America and on and on, but I'd felt I was being handed excuses, so a shrug had been my only response to his every comment.

When it had finally become obvious to him that he was not convincing me, he'd pulled up a chair and sat before me. Motioned me closer.

"You never have been much of one for the church, have you, Brendan?" he'd asked, his cold eyes locked on mine.

Another shrug.

"Never a choir boy. Nor an altar boy. Not even confession, not really. Always off to yourself. Apart, even from God. A simple lad, thinking himself an island—"

"I'm not simple," I'd snapped, cutting him off.

He'd hesitated, his cold eyes cutting into me. "I know. I can see that you aren't. I can see how carefully your thoughts were put together to disparage the church's good works. It's almost as if you feel you're better than us all."

That had angered me and I'd stiffened, but said nothing more.

He'd noticed and taken my hand. "How old are you now, Brendan? Ten?"

That *had* confused me. He knew I was past eleven.

"Do you not believe in what we do?" he'd continued. Then

he'd begun to stroke my hand with his thumb.

I'd yanked it away, suddenly confused, and muttered, "I-I-I just think Derry needs help more than Africa."

"And how would you know that?"

"I live here! I see what people have and don't."

"That is not the church's doing."

"And you're doing nothing to stop it. To make things better for us. You take our money and send it places I don't know and use it to put gold in your vestments and—"

He'd slapped me, then bolted to his feet and stormed over to a table with bottles of whiskey and wine, his voice a growl. "Your mother's waiting without. You may go. We needn't see each other, again."

I'd grown cold and anger took over. I very deliberately rubbed my cheek before asking, "So will you no longer help my family?"

He'd merely glanced over his shoulder at me as he poured a whiskey. Not a word.

So I'd snarled, "Do I have to be your altar boy for that? Like Danny Gallagher?"

This was not so long after I'd seen the set to between Danny and his Da, and I didn't really know what it had meant, but the wild fury that filled Father Demian's face had scared me. He'd started for me, but I'd quickly backed out of the room and let Ma lead me home, thinking she'd shown me I was wrong about the church.

I never put her right.

Now Father Jack had taken over, and it seemed everything was settled into its proper place. I was still upset at Ma's continued tithing, while the church continued to do little to nothing about the grinding poverty in the Bogside, but Father Jack was more attentive to the local needs and that soothed a little of my irritation.

So I think that was what troubled me, as we neared the bus stop. Surely a man as aware and smart as Father Jack had heard of the Loyalists' anger and words tossed at the People's Democracy, as well as that from his own superiors. *Communists* and *Fenians* and *IRA scum* and the like along with the usual *Papists* and *Taigs*. Surely he knew the potential of trouble against us should they choose to do it.

October 5th was still fresh in my mind. I'd already seen

enough times where the RUC would let their Loyalist mates do as they pleased to a Catholic, when they weren't doing it, themselves. I was sure there'd be something happen along the way and I feared for Eamonn. But Father Jack seemed set only on *the bright and shining path of the venture*, as he'd put it, while all but deliberately ignoring the dark shadows growing. It raised questions as to what he was truly up for.

The bus was waiting as we rounded the corner and then I saw Mrs. McKittrick across the road, leaning against a wall and smoking, a scarf covering her head and her coat fully buttoned against the cold and damp. But this time she was sad, even after my brother finally saw her and sent the slightest of nods in her direction. She just gazed at him, and the look on her face cut into me.

I'd seen Ma look at Da in the same way, a few times. Sad, like she wished things were different. If he could be closer to her than he was. Disappointed that his usual response was to almost pretend she wasn't there. Like she was an embarrassment. Or that he was lost to her. That is how Mrs. McKittrick was looking at Eamonn, as if she were embarrassed to be there but had no choice except to be.

She caught me looking at her and grew haughty, crushed her cigarette and walked away without a glance back.

I only turned to Eamonn and asked, "So-so are Jackie and Aidan joining you?" I asked, now waving to his mates.

He laughed. "They aren't part of the PD, Bren. The others will meet up at Queen's, on the first."

He ruffled his fingers through my hair and boarded the bus, and away it went.

I said a quick, quiet prayer to St. Brigit, then Colm, Danny, Paidrig and I said goodbye to Father Jack and bolted up Shipquay, aiming to check out the latest comics at wee Johnny's, laughing and chattering about where we'd be on the fourth, when the marchers arrived and—

I saw her, again.

Joanna.

Standing in front of Austin's. She was with a couple of mates, all dressed in mini-skirts, fur-trimmed coats and boots, chattering with each other as they looked in the store's Christmas windows. Again, her golden silk flowed down her back, this time in a ponytail from under a knit cap, and her cheeks were as rosy as fresh-picked apples. Her stockings were black and complimented both her outfit and her form. I thought I was seeing an angel, once more.

I stopped still. Could not move. I was at the corner of Shipquay and the Diamond as she and her friends headed down Ferryquay, chattering, oblivious to one and all about them. Oblivious to my heart no longer beating or my breath no longer part of me or my mind incapable of anything but the thought of how glorious it was to see her, once more.

My mates had gone across the square before they noticed.

"Oi, Bren, what's this?" Colm yelled at me, breaking my spell.

She turned at the sound of his voice and saw me and seemed to recognize me and offered me the tiniest of smiles and I near died from the joy of it.

She'd smiled at me.

She'd smiled at me.

I gave her a secret wave and a nod. She turned back to her friends and they continued on.

I headed over to join me mates.

Paidrig looked at me with a wariness while Colm lit up a Marlboro and offered me a pull on it. Both tried to act like men, but something about them struck me as foolish and childlike. Danny just smiled to himself, something he did less than usual but still far too often. I handed the fag off to him and as he smoked I said, "I'll join you later, lads. I've errands to run for me Ma."

"That's never kept you from wee Johnny's before," said Colm, his breath smoking as he spoke.

"I'm the man of the family with Eamonn at University. I've responsibilities. I'll be down with you, later."

Then I headed across the Diamond towards home before they could say another word. Only I doubled back once I knew they'd gone far enough, and rushed down Ferryquay and saw Joanna and her mates through the window, in Woolworth's. I slipped in, careful not to get too close or be too obvious. Their voices were musical in their happiness, and their attitudes spoke of pleasures too simple for me to understand. Just a group of girls out for some fun.

They wandered into the music section and flipped through

the rows of records, idle, chatting about nothing and everything, until Joanna pulled out a 45 with a squeal.

"They have it!" she cried, and her friends gathered around. They rushed over to a clerk and had him play the song, *Never Shall I Marry*, then laughed as they sang:

I never will marry, I'll be no man's wife.

I intend to stay single all the days of my life...

When the song began in earnest, they danced a sort of jig mixed with the Twist, giggling along with the words.

I acted like I was interested in some albums not far away, watching them with a side view. Then Joanna caught my eye, once, and looked away, smiling to herself.

She knew what I was doing.

A friend purchased the record, then she and the girls left.

I jumped over to where she'd been looking, found another copy, grabbed it up and paid for it, intending to give it to her when I caught up to her, outside—but they were gone, like ghosts.

I ran back to the Diamond and searched down Shipquay and a couple of side streets, but found nothing. I guess I'd scared them off with my clumsiness. So I went home.

When Ma saw the record, she was furious about the waste of money and her sharp fingers dug at me until I told her I'd pinched it. She eyed me for a moment, saying, "You stole this from that store?"

I nodded.

"Did you make off with a record player, as well?"

"You know full well I'm fixing one for Mrs. O'Neal."

"And what're you chargin'?"

"Same as Mrs. O'Canainn. A sovereign."

"She told me two pound."

I snorted. "She's mad! For a pound or two more, she could buy a new one, and my charge includes the cost of a new pulley."

"Hush," she snapped. "You've other things to do, first." And kept me busy with them, since Mai was not expected home until much later.

Again.

Though Ma said nothing, my bet was Tur was taking up my sister's time. More and more of late. I cleaned out the hearth and ran for a haddock down McCleary's and peeled the spuds and turned down Rhuari's and Kieran's bed as she fixed supper.

Mairead came in just as it was being served, her blissful expression on, again. Ma noticed but said nothing that I know of.

After we'd eaten and I'd finished the dishes and cleaned up and the wains were in bed, I recalled I'd told Mrs. McKay I'd have her transistor fixed by morning, so got onto that in my room. By this time, I was close to knackered, so listened to the record as a way to keep awake, the volume low. It was sung by The Johnstons, and *The Banks of Claudy* was on the reverse side. I liked that tune more. So kept going until near eleven, before I was done.

I fell onto my pillow, exhausted, but couldn't sleep. I was alone in the bed, again. I'd grown used to it, with Eamonn off to Queen's, and had looked forward to the solitude, once more. But rather than it feeling nice and luxurious as it had in hospital, it felt wrong. Empty. Frightening. And it was because Eamonn was gone on that walk and I knew, I knew, I knew something wrong would come of it.

There was too much anger boiling about in Derry. Belfast, as well; you could taste it in the air. Catholics weary of being kept down. Protestants wary of letting their control slip away from them. Paisley and his scum rutting for power through retaliation, though against what I still had no idea; seemed to me it was the Proddies needing to be retaliated against. And those like Father Jack hinting maybe it's good to fight back against those who oppress you since they'll never back down on their own. And then all but saying, *it's not for me to say.*

What bollocks.

Why Eamonn thought a simple march to bring attention to unfair housing in Derry would make a difference in it all was beyond my ability to understand. The whole of the city felt like a whirlpool of anger and hate swirling everything around and into this endless abyss, and the more I thought of it the more afraid I became.

And confused.

What was so horrible about a man wanting fair treatment? Or a decent home for his family? Or a job that paid enough to feed and clothe them? Or be allowed to worship God in his own manner? Was being Catholic really so very bad in the eyes of the world? Was that reason enough to treat us like rats? Was it like this everywhere? We'd been taught enough about how Catholics were slaughtered all around the world for some reason or other, half of which I thought they set themselves up for. But only suggesting that in Brother James' class had gotten me a massive walloping and a trip to the principal's office.

Father Jack had shown us images from the civil rights marches in America, but there it seemed to be the color of a man's skin that divided them, which also struck me as foolish but was at least a bit more understandable. *You're obviously not like me so you must be bad.* I'd heard enough comments from the nuns who'd been to Africa about how different life was there, so maybe the black culture was different, as well. And Father Jack had also mentioned people fear that what's different.

But how could they know of any difference between us? Stand me and Billy next to each other without our names and who could tell which is what? It was stupid to do that.

Questions rushed at me, crushed at me, kept my mind racing till well after midnight. It was a cold clear night, so I could look out to see the millions of stars gleaming in the black velvet. It reminded me of when I'd smoked with Danny and his mates, only this time it seemed the stars mocked me. To put them in their place I began to count them, stopping at one that seemed particularly bright and sparkly to make a wish or offer a prayer, each with a smile to show I knew how silly I was being while in my heart I knew I was not.

Finally, Joanna whispered back into my mind and I began to feel easy, once more. And felt a stirring in more than just my soul. I mean, I knew she was Protestant. But I didn't care. I wasn't looking at a religion in her. Nor was I even thinking about differences in station. I was thinking of how lovely those few words I'd heard her speak were. And how she didn't so much walk or stride as seem to float as she passed. And how simple and easy everything was about her.

I rolled over to lie face down on the bed and pulled the covers tight under my chest and face, trying to ignore what she was doing to me. But those covers became her, lying under me and smiling up at me and my dreams grew too powerful to ignore. And I began to shift up and down in the same manner I'd seen Eamonn do with Mrs. McKittrick. Pictured Joanna's legs around me in the same way. Planted gentle kisses where her face was in the covers as screams of happiness shot through me and the very feel of my pajamas against my skin drew me close to delirium.

Colm and Paidrig had called me liar when I'd told them of how it worked between a man and a woman. Of course, I couldn't tell them who provided the demonstration, so they'd insisted I was making it up.

"It's better to take a girl from behind," Paidrig had said, "with her on hands and knees like a dog, hi. That way she won't wind up preggers and it's easier for you both."

"I can't even picture that," I'd shot back.

"And you call Bren Looner," Colm had laughed. "You'll get her up the pole no matter what you do, unless it's in her mouth."

"Her mouth?!" That shocked me. Why would a girl even want to do such a thing?

"That's what my brother, Liam, told me. He's down to Sydney, and says the girls there take care of him well, and all he has to do is lie back. He's been to Paris, too, and got the same thing done."

Danny had been sitting there, just listening with this far too quiet smile, but then this cold look had taken over his eyes and he'd whispered, "It's all over the world, with all kinds of people."

I must have been the only one heard him, for Colm had turned to him and asked, "What's that?" And Paidrig had given him a look of confusion.

"Nothin'," Danny'd said and returned to his smile.

I'd put it in my mind to ask him, later, but that's the night Eamonn told Ma he was leaving early for Belfast to be with the PD march, and I didn't think about it till now. When I was on the bed alone and rubbing myself between my pajamas and the sheets, faster and faster.

His comment made me pause and try to picture Joanna doing such a thing, but that felt like a violation of her meaning to me. This was good enough for now and I got back to going and kept going and going and going until I felt something like a damn burst and my breath grow still and my heart gasp for joy and that stuff came out of my tadger. Then I froze and waited to see if I'd hurt myself, again—but all I did was grow peaceful and small and happy to wrap myself in the covers that had become my lover, even in the midst of this wet stickiness.

Now I knew why Eamonn kept returning to Mrs. McKittrick.

I drifted to sleep moments later.

1969

January

The Long Walk

New Year's Day, the march began. The celebrations seemed muted, this year, as opposed to previous ones. Sparklers were about, sure, and crackers leftover from Christmas, but there was hesitation in the air. We followed their progress on Radio Eire and, to my fears, there was more than mere taunting along the way. More than the occasional attack. With the RUC doing little more than making the marchers change course, and once near sending them into a group of Proddies waiting to attack. At the same time, Paisleyites swore to stop them at all costs, and did try to in Antrim.

Some fellow claiming to speak for Sinn Fein said it was ill-advised, this march; that *pushing Westminster for improvements in the lot of all working men in The North would help Protestants as well as Catholics, and it was necessary to educate those fighting us to show them they were being used by the landed gentry and fools on the councils*...and on and on and on. As Eamonn had once said to me. They must have read the same book.

I even heard Father Jack giving his usual double-speak on how our intentions were pure, but he could still understand how this would be seen as a provocation. And through it all, Stormount's attitude was that nothing was really happening. You had to stop listening to the silliness, after a bit, in order to keep your sanity.

Except I couldn't, really, not with Eamonn being a part of it. So I'd pop over to Danny's to watch the telly, since it was on the BBC, as well. His Ma didn't seem to mind. I got the impression all she cared about was that the telly was broadcasting something. During one news piece, I caught sight of Eamonn in the background, walking close beside this pretty girl. They were singing *We Shall Not Be Afraid*, and it looked like his arm was about her shoulders. She seemed upset and I could tell he was angry, but the newscaster would say no more than they had been refused access to Knockloughrim enroute to Maghera, which added some miles to their trek. Ma's blanket was around the girl and I'm sure he was glad she'd made him bring it, for it was horrible cold out.

I also hoped Mrs. McKittrick wasn't watching, that night.

The coverage was fair intense as each day documented more of the Loyalist's obstructions and taunts and sneaking attacks. Those around the Bogside who'd been unsure of the correctness of the march grew more and more to be on their side with every push by the bastards along the way. It was so obvious that would be the reaction, I wondered if that was the PD's true intention. Still, despite the RUC's and Proddy's best efforts, progress was being made and their schedule kept.

They were also greeted well, here and there, especially more to the west, and no one could say they'd done anything to provoke any sort of reprisal. Of course, they'd still have to cross the Foyle, but I'd slipped over to the bridge a few times to see if anyone was preparing for a fight, there, to find nothing in the way of stones being laid up for tossing. I'd have checked on Irish and Spencer to be sure, but there were too many peelers about for crossing to be easy. Also, if I was snatched the name Kinsella would draw attention to Eamonn, so I played it careful and hoped for the best.

Then on the third, I finished rewiring a lamp for Mrs. Clark, in The Fountain. I'd done other work for her and she'd always treated me fair and given me cookies and tea along with thruppence or sixpence for my work, but this time she offered no invite. Instead, she yanked open her door, took the lamp, shoved a half-crown in my palm with barely a *Thank you* then slammed the door. It took me aback. I glanced around to see if someone was watching and saw a couple of curtains move, just a hint.

Then it came to me.

The Fountain was quiet.

Too quiet.

No children's voices. No women having a craic. No men growling.

I slipped the coin in my pocket and walked away, trying to seem normal but shaking within. The moment I reached Wapping, I raced down to the bridge, but still there was nothing to see. No RUC checkpoints. No stones or garbage piled up. No one waiting to have a go at some foolish University kids who still had hopes and dreams of peace in their hearts. Nothing. If there was to be a set-to, then it would be on the Waterside, not here. But if that were the case, then why was the Fountain so quiet?

I ran back to it and this time slapped up to Billy's door. I knocked and knocked, and I could see shadows move inside. I cried out, "Billy, Billy, you home? You home, me China? Billy?!" But his Ma never answered. I scrambled around to Bishop's and onto the Derry Walls to run back and look into his garden.

Both his and his uncle's bikes were gone.

I wasn't cold till that moment and my mind started racing. Billy wouldn't join with his uncle on a tear against the marchers, would he? He couldn't. He knew Eamonn. Knew me.

Throughout, I'd heard murmuring noises from Guildhall Square, angry, dangerous shouts made the more nerve-wracking by the distance of them. I'd heard Paisley had come to town to speak there, so had avoided it; now, I ran towards Guildhall to find a crowd massed along the wall, seeming about to fire the cannons that lined it and faced the building.

I pushed between them to get a better view, and sure enough, the square was massed with men and women milling about, angry and calling curses at the tops of their voices. Lights were on in the Guildhall, where some from the Derry Housing Council were still occupying an office, but most of it was dark. I knew many in the swirling mob, and the only thing between them and the hall's doors was a line of very nervous constables.

This…it stunned me. Had the Orangemen come en masse to wreak havoc on Eamonn's march? Were they gathered inside? Had I been so lost in fixing Mrs. Clark's lamp I'd missed a call to arms?

I searched for Father Jack but could see him nowhere. I did see a neighbor of mine and called down, "Mrs. O'Canainn, up here! It's Brendan!"

She looked around and waved, actually smiling. "This is some show, wouldn't ya say?"

"Smashing!" I nodded to the Guildhall. "So how many Proddy bastards're in there, you think?" I was only guessing at this.

"I'm hearin' near five-hundred. And there's more than a few would gladly burn the damned hall around them."

"With the Housing Council still inside!?"

"That's what's holding us back."

"Have you seen Father Jack?"

"He was up by the hall, speakin' earlier, and—"

We heard a man start calling for the crowd to disperse. She turned back to the crush, to listen. He told people that the whole purpose of the march was to show non-violence and if they did attack the Orangemen in the hall, they would only prove the liars in Stormount right, that Catholics were out to do Protestants harm. Some still circled the hall, howling insults, and I could see smoke rising from the car park and the Christmas tree was waving oddly, like someone was climbing it, but the animal danger seemed to be dispersing.

Maybe half the crowd had melted away before I saw Mairead, Tur with her. Then I remembered Ma hadn't known I was off to Mrs. Clark's. In fact, the house had been quiet, with not a noise from the kitchen or in Ma's garden. Not a sound from Rhuari, Maeve or Kieran. Had Ma even been home? Were the wains? Or had I left Maeve and Kieran in the care of Rhuari, who had little enough attention to care for himself? Oh, God, would she be vexed with me for that.

I raced over to the steps and scurried down and around then screamed wildly, "Tur, Mai, here!"

Mairead spun about. "Brendan, what're you doin' in this crowd?"

I caught up to them. "Something's about to happen!"

"To them fuckin' Loyalists, is what," snapped Tur, heading us back home at a quick, angry pace. "They think they'll keep the marchers from reaching Guildhall, tomorrow. But if they think this is anger—"

"No, it's something more. There's nothing set up around the bridge. No stones or clubs."

"That's a good thing, ain't it?"

"No, I think they might attack on Waterside, like Irish Street or Spencer and—"

"Don't matter. A number of us're bussing up to join with the marchers in Claudy for the last leg."

"Claudy?"

"It's where they're stayin' the night," said Mairead.

"Where's that, again?"

"On the Dungiven Road, not so far. But it's narrow and tight, so we figure it's best to have more than just a few kids from Belfast walkin' by. Let the bastards pick on a fair-sized crowd willin' to fight back."

"Tur, you can't go with that attitude," Mairead said to him. "It's a peaceful march. You heard."

"We'll discuss it in the morning."

"I'm comin' with you," I piped in.

"Ma won't allow it," said Mairead. "If there is trouble, Eamonn'll have enough to worry about without you there."

"I'm telling you, it's something bad's about to happen. And not just to the march."

"Let the fucks try anything they want." And his tone warned me to be silent. So I was.

We were halfway up Waterloo when Colm and Danny whisked by not far from us, a bucket of stones carried between them. I waved and called, "Oi, me Chinas, where's that battle?"

"Howya, Bren, come help!" Colm cried back. "There's word the RUC's plannin' somethin' soon and we've decided not to let 'em dance away with it, this time."

"That's why Paisley's here," yelled Danny. "He's goading the constables to put us in our place, and we're after showing them what that place is like."

"I'm off to home, right now," I called back to them. "Maybe Ma'll let me join you."

No luck in that. Ma had been at church, lighting a candle, with the wains at Mrs. Keogh's—and I had left the door wide open. It brought me a couple good slaps and more than a few harsh words. Which I took; on this, she was right. Then Mai calmed her. But when I brought up how I wanted to go with Tur, Ma near struck me, again—and would have if I'd flinched even the slightest.

"There's important business here and you're still a boy. Nor will you go, Mairead. I'll need you to help with the wains. Master Devlin can handle himself, well enough, with folk a plenty to back up the marchers, right?"

He smiled and said, "There will, indeed."

"Staying for supper, then? It's stew and black bread, but you're more than welcome."

"Sounds grand," he said and sat with Mairead on the divan.

Ma yanked me into the kitchen and whispered, "So you're

done with that lamp and snuck it off. How much did you get off that Proddy bitch for it?"

"Why're you asking? I'm to give money I make to Mai."

Ma flicked me with her hard finger. "Answer me!"

"She took it and shoved the door in my face."

"Don't lie to me!"

"I'm *not*! All the things I fixed for her and she does this to me!? But that's how I knew something was happening, and I found the Guildhall and—"

She dug in my pockets. It wasn't there, of course; I'd hidden it in my y-fronts the moment I saw Mai and Tur were heading home. My plan was to change it out and give her half, still.

Ma shoved me away. "If I find out she paid you for this lamp and you didn't contribute to the family?"

"I *do* contribute, in the way we agreed to! A damn site more than Da ever did—"

She slapped me. This one truly stung and my left ear rang, but I took it and glared back at her.

"I told you not to talk of your father that way, do you understand me?" she snapped.

That's when Mai appeared at the door, her eyes wary as she said, "Ma, let me help you with our supper."

Ma shot a glance at her, saying, "I've this one, here, for that. You've done enough, today. Go sit with Tur."

"It's no trouble."

Ma's look went hard so she backed away. I was next to get Ma's glare. "As for you goin' to Claudy? You're not yet thirteen, and even then you're still my child. Don't get carried away thinkin' you're a man, as of yet."

"What do you want this *boy* to do, Ma?"

All she answered was, "Open the table and set the places."

I did.

And we ate.

And twice I slipped my hand in my y-fronts to feel the half-crown. And fought the smile on my face at knowing it still was mine. Then when the dishes were done, I sat on the stoop in the cold night air and listened as the old cows talked. Huddled in little groups throughout The Bogside, I'm sure, discussing the latest lies from Paisley and Bunting, and warning what they'd do about it if push came to shove. Irish newspapers were being passed about, with photos of how the marchers were being obstructed with the complicity of the RUC. I remembered Eamonn telling Ma he wasn't off to war, yet here we were acting like they were in a battle zone and we were looking over the casualty list. By this point even Ma had to agree things were not going as planned for the march.

"But my Eamonn'll be home, tomorrow," she said to Mrs. Haggerty, "and that will be that. And at least *he* will have something to be proud of." Accompanied by a cold glance at me.

Which settled it. Once everyone had gone to bed, I waited till long past midnight then quietly dressed, pulled on my old boots since they were the most comfortable, snuck from the house, shoved two pounds in my pocket from my hiding place under the stoop, and set out for Claudy.

Claudy

To say it was easy getting out of Derry would be a lie. Lads were everywhere in the Bogside, keeping watch, just daring the RUC to enter, while the constables were watching, right back. That they hadn't done anything, yet, only added to my concern, and a little voice inside me kept whispering, *Sunday was not going to be a holy day*. But I managed well-enough by keeping to shadows so I'd not be noticed.

The Craigavon was empty. I kept to the lower level and was sure any car that approached would be an RUC patrol, so I'd rush between lamp posts and scrunch to make sure none could see me. Near the Waterside I thought one had, but it simply passed by; it helps being small. Once across, I snuck along Spencer Road and climbed Fountain Hill up to Irish Street, but saw nothing to indicate there would be any problems along them. Next, I tried to find the Dungiven Road. All I knew was it ran in front of Altnagelvin Hospital, so that was my first point of destination. The lights around the place were bright, even this early in the morning, and I used them as my compass point.

I remained in shadow as much as I could, but I saw few on the Waterside. I kept walking down Irish and felt somehow I'd gone too far so cut left at the next road, which actually led straight up to the hospital. I walked down Glenshane for a piece then saw a sign for Dungiven and knew I was headed right.

Did it make me proud of myself.

Soon I was past the last of the housing and into meadows and farmland, and the quiet of it was different from that of the sleeping city. No, it wasn't quiet; it was peaceful, like when Danny and I had walked up to the fort. And when I'd walked home, alone. Just myself in the world and none other.

So tender, it was. Gentle. You could hear toads grunting and foxes yipping and owls calling, none of them screaming for attention to himself, and if you listened even the sound of your own breath mingled in. Water chuckled down the ditch beside the road to join with a pleasant little brook. A light breeze gave voice to the bushes and trees and leaves dancing about. It was cold and snow was spread here and there, so most farm animals were in their shelters, but you could still hear them offer a soft bleat or mew at the sudden footsteps of the unknown traveler. Even the mist from my breath seemed calm and amiable, in its own proper way.

It wasn't a clear night, and while I did feel it would have been nice to have the stars as companion to my wandering, I was hardly sorry for it. I made do with the shrubs and owls and cattle that still braved the chill.

The road would climb up to let me look around in wonder at the dark beauty of existence. Then would come shadowy glens as it dipped between mounds of earth and trees. No cars passed me for the first two hours of my trek, so my sense of one with the world remained intact. The first to finally thunder past was just a lorry ferrying winter produce to Derry's markets.

Oh, how I loved the smell of the breeze as I walked, even with the vague odor of manure mingled with it. It had a crispness that Derry's cloudy air lacked. Only a few miles separated this part of the world from the city, but they were on different planets to me. Different concepts of reality.

A tenderness settled over my heart, like a cozy blanket, and I began to hum *The Banks of Claudy*. I'd played it to Ma's near distraction, till I had to return the record player. Now the words flowed from me in a cracked voice:

"T'was on one pleasant evening, all in the month of May.
Down by yon flowery garden, I carelessly did stray.
I overheard a fair one most grievously complain.
T'was on the banks of Claudy where my darlin' do remain."

It was to heaven I was soaring, and all was well and good around me. There was nothing to fear. No worries to hold me down. I was myself and one alone, with naught to bind me and little but road before me. Money in my pocket. My parka tight but warm. A gentle push of a breeze at my back. It was life as how it should be lived—open and free from anything others might force upon you. I could have kept walking forever.

Joanna would've been on this walk, had I asked her. I knew

it for certain. Aye, she was Protestant, but that was an Irish jig she danced while singing to the other song on that record, and hadn't the two religions lived side by side for years without much trouble? Weren't there a number of Presbyterians as bad off as my family and wasn't Billy's family living in the Fountain as much of a disgrace as Nailors?

But she wouldn't have minded where I was from. She'd have seen the need for this march, the need to show those few bastards in control of our worlds that they should have that control no longer, since they'd done ill with it. I knew because when she'd looked at me, she'd not seen a boy who's poor or Catholic, but merely one she fancied. It was visible in her eyes, in how she looked at me, and I could picture her at my side as on we strolled, singing together while marching to our fates and—

Voices and the distant click of stones being tossed about cut through my sense of wonder. I stopped cold. Those were not the normal sounds for the area, of that I was certain. I was by some trees where the road climbed through another rise so could see little more than the dark pavement carrying on ahead of me. Without really thinking to, I carefully edged near the trees, to listen.

The words were indistinct, but they sounded happy and filled with fun as more stones clattered together. They weren't taking any care in maintaining secrecy about their whereabouts, so I couldn't make out the reason for it all. I was about to continue on to see what I could see when a car approached from the direction of Claudy.

I pressed closer to the tree trunks and was glad I did, for it was an RUC tender. A second car was right behind it. But they didn't pass me; they stopped about a hundred yards down and some men got out, two of whom wore constable uniforms. They crossed the road and were greeted by another man in naught but loose trousers, a jumper and cap, his face gleaming with sweat. They were too far away for me to know if I knew them and their voices still too indistinct, but without question they were much friendly with each other and quite happy with themselves. They turned away to look out at something so I scurried across the road to climb the rise to the hilltop.

I was halfway up when I heard a lorry roar to life, behind me. I froze. I carefully looked around but saw nothing, even as the sound of the lorry drew closer and closer. Then it appeared from a side road across from the two parked cars and I realized I'd been hearing its echo; that it was in front of me. It drove off to Claudy, smoke billowing from its exhaust, its tail empty of everything but dust.

I climbed higher and peeked over the summit to see a number of men, young and old, sorting out piles of stones as others laid up stacks of cudgels. And I knew one of the men ferrying stones to a pile further down the hill—Billy's uncle. Actually doing work! That was a shock.

But what was worse? A lad my age was handing out cups of hot steaming tea.

Billy.

To be honest about it, I was not surprised. After not finding him, yesterday, I'd felt he was going to be some part of a crowd out to harry the marchers. But to actually see him helping prepare stones and bricks and cudgels to use against them? That sent an icy dagger into my heart, laced both with fury and pain.

I dug my fingers into the cold earth. Pressed my forehead against the ground to keep from doing or saying anything to reveal myself for the anger in me was building and—

"You, boy, what you doin' up there?"

I jolted and half tumbled back down the embankment to find a constable walking up to me. The other constable was a few paces behind him.

"Off to home," popped out of me. "What's it to yous?"

"It's the back of my hand to your face if you don't take a proper tone with me," he snapped back. "Where's home?"

I thought I caught a Belfast accent off him, so chanced saying, "Claudy. And where the devil're you from?"

"What you doin' here?"

"Nothing. Just off for a wander."

The other constable snarled, "I think he's a fuckin' Taig come to join his mates!"

"Leave off me!" I snapped back at him. "Who the devil're you to say anything? You're not from here! I know everyone in my town and—"

"D'yer know me?" This tall man with a white armband strolled up the road. His clothes were too fine for labor's work and a quick glance at his one ungloved hand, even in the pale light, showed his nails were well-kept.

"Should I?" I asked him back, feeling a sickness in my stomach. This man's eyes were black and cold, like Father Demian's, and I had no interest in even thinking of going up against him.

"I'm in Claudy," his voice smooth and quiet.

For some reason it didn't sound right, him saying that. So I smirked and said, "Maybe on market day, and then only to buy, and then only when your man can't do it for you."

His eyes glistened with anger, then he laughed and clapped me round the back of my head in a friendly fashion. "He's too feisty to be a papist, lads. And too young to be a marcher. What's your name, lad?"

"Billy Corrie," was the first name that came to me, and the second I said it I thought, *That was stupid, Brendan, stupid, stupid.*

"Good Protestant name."

"So what's all this?" I asked, managing to keep my voice light.

"Don't ya know of them Fenian bastards from Belfast, little commie taigs? They're in Claudy, the night."

"Not sleepin', that's fer certain," laughed the big one.

"I thought they wasn't comin' till tomorrow," I said.

"May be comin' but they ain't goin'." Everyone laughed.

I just smirked. "So you're after stoppin' 'em here, then?"

"Givin' 'em a real welcome."

"Care to join us, Billy?" asked the man with the armband.

"Thanks but I've chores to do, now, and me Ma'll be seekin' me out. I-I'll take the back way home."

"Back way?" It was the man with the armband eyeing me, wary all of a sudden.

Oh, shite.

I laughed and said, "You're not from these parts, are ya?"

He grabbed my arm, tight and angry. "There's another lad here, name of Billy, and I think we might compare the two."

Yeah, Brendan. *Stupid!*

So I kicked him in the knee.

He howled and fell and I yanked myself away then ran back the way I came. No need to check to see if I was being chased; I could hear footsteps behind me laced with curses the like of which I'd never heard before. Then stones come whisking over my head to clatter down the road. One near clipped my ear. They were getting a better aim.

I heard that RUC tender roar close then grind to a crawl, I guess to let the fellow chasing me get in since I heard a door slam. I topped a hill and the ground dropped down to a gully on my left, so I tumbled over and grabbed some vines to hold me and lay still.

The tender drove on past, so I guess I'd been out of sight around when I hid. Soon as they were gone, I slipped across to the other side and through a wire fence and crept on back towards Derry, using a hedge to keep me hid. I heard the tender snarl past, again, then stop and someone cry, "Billy, fair Billy, come out to play!"

Oh, aye, I may be stupid but I'm not a bloody eejit. Bloody bastards.

I heard them coming up, again, so settled into a hedge to catch my breath and let them search as long as they wished. Then I heard them screech to a halt and my heart near jumped in my throat. Had they seen me? They backed up and skidded a bit, then drove off.

I peeked through a gap in the hedge to see headlamps approaching. I couldn't tell the car, but it was small—actually a van.

I scrambled over the hedge and tried to cut it off but I dared not yell to stop it; those bastards weren't so very far away and the sound of my voice would only bring them here.

The van zipped on past me without a thought. I just knew it would be showered in stones, in a moment. My immediate thought was to warn anyone else coming, so I backed down the road, aiming for a side lane I'd passed.

Only I heard no yelling. No sound of rocks hitting metal nor smashing glass nor curses hurled in either direction. It took only a moment for me to figure out why; they were saving their hoard of weapons for the marchers and wished them to be unknown. They were planning something far worse than a mere harassment.

They were planning a massacre.

I didn't know what to do. I was nowhere near a phone and even I had been, who'd I have rung? 999? The RUC was in on the planning of it. And I had no other phone numbers in my head— except for Mrs. Rafferty's. But somehow I needed to get warning to Eamonn or somebody with the march.

I was almost to the cross lane when a cab approached. This one I flagged down with no trouble, hoping it was Mr. O'Faelan's. It wasn't, but inside were a couple of older women—and one was Mrs. Rafferty, herself! Of course, she opened the door.

"Brendan Kinsella, what're you doin' here this time of the mornin'?" she shot at me before I could speak. "Your mother'll be frantic lookin' for you."

"Your pardon, Mrs. Rafferty, but're you passing to Claudy?"

"We're off to join with the marchers," said the woman beside her. Mrs. O'Fay? Or was it *Miss*? I didn't know her well enough.

"Well, have a care," I said. "There's Loyalists not a mile down the road piling up stones to cast at the march. Just over the top of a hill, where the road curves."

"Oh, don't be daft, they wouldn't dare," she said.

"Come ride with us, Brendan," said Mrs. Rafferty, "and you'll see for yourself. I'll ring Father Jack to tell Bernadette where you are."

"No, no, no, you don't understand. I've seen 'em," I said. "I've already had a set-to with 'em."

"D'you think it's possible?" asked a woman, seated next to her.

Mrs. Rafferty shook her head. "Brendan's a bit on the simple side. Probably saw some men workin' the fields and made a full war from it." Then she looked hard at me and added, "He should be at home, with his mother, not out here on his own. Get in; we'll keep you."

"No, if they see me with you, they'll stop you."

"As you wish. The meter's running. Let's be on our way."

She closed the door, the driver hit the pedal and off they went.

I couldn't believe it, but in the next half hour, I tried to flag down a couple more cars. None would stop for me. Then I heard the motor of an RUC tender approach and hid behind some shrubs massed around a fence and peeked through.

The tender pulled off to the side and two constables got out— one who'd chased me and one I'd not seen before.

My constable said, "It's here he was, the little bastard."

His companion nodded. "Not a cheerful spot, is it?"

"He'll find it less cheerful if I get me hands on his fuckin' arse."

They lit fags and leaned against the tender's bonnet. Shite, they were planning to stay.

I have no idea how long I sat there, hoping they'd leave, before a bus roared up the road from Derry. The constables straightened and looked as if they'd be stopping them, but they just waved it on past then got in the tender, turned around and followed. I caught only a bit of my constable saying, "Wish I could be part of it," before they were whipping back down the road.

I was at a loss what to do. I had no idea how to get to Claudy except by that road, so trying to circle around the bastards might do nothing more than get me lost or delayed till it was too late. Light was filtering through the clouds to the east, so the marchers were probably already on their way. My only hope was that Mrs. Rafferty was making sport of me with Eamonn and he would sense from her tales that I was not the fool she so happily thought me to be and would spread the alarm.

I was famished from the hunger as well as bloody tired. I had to laugh at myself; perhaps I was simple, not thinking to bring food with me. I couldn't have walked a hundred yards, right then, so I figured I'd rest a bit. See if I was being too lost in worry, and that the marchers did make it past. I could connect with them, here, and return to Derry, with Eamonn. See if he had any of that cheese and bread left. Or perhaps I should head back to Altnagelvin. They were sure to have a cafe where I could have some breakfast and not have to face my punishment hungry. Let my brother have his glory to himself. That sounded like a good plan. A better plan.

So I pulled my parka around me and closed my eyes and—

The jangling of an ambulance woke me. I bolted to my feet as it cried down the road then looked around. It was full daylight. I'd no idea of the exact time...then another car drove past and in this one I saw people in the back, holding bloody cloths to their heads. Panic hit me and I ran down the road for Claudy.

Another ambulance whisked past. I felt my heart in my throat.

My warnings had been for nothing.

It was happening.

They were killing everyone.

I knew it.

I knew it.

Altnagelvin

At the bottom of the hill, I saw an estate car run off the road. Its windscreen was smashed, and dents were on the bonnet I looked inside to find two blood-covered lads of Eamonn's age tending to an older man who was behind the wheel. He had only a bruise to his temple, from what I could tell, but he was unconscious.

"You need help?" I asked.

One looked at me wildly and snarled, "You with them?"

"No!" That he'd even think such a thing insulted me. "My brother, Eamonn Kinsella, he's with the march."

The other lad turned his face to me but his expression was a thousand yards away. "Eamonn? He got it good. He got it good."

His words jolted me. "He's hurt!?"

"He got it good," was all he'd say.

An ambulance topped the next hill and headed for us. I darted out into the road, waving at it, but the driver didn't even let off the pedal. An RUC tender whipped past, close behind it, more bloodied people in it. I hurried back.

"Can you drive?" I asked the lads.

"He got it good," was all the second one could say.

The first one shook his head. "I've no license."

That wasn't what I'd asked, but I took it for a *no*. I'd only driven Dr. McCurdy's Morris Minor a time or two, to check its brakes, but I figured that would be good enough practice, since it was open road to hospital. "Then get this man in the back."

"Somebody's back there."

I looked in the rear and saw a girl curled up in a pool of blood, her head gashed, her legs a mass of puncture wounds. It was good I'd had no breakfast, for I'd have lost it.

I opened the driver's door and took the man under his arms. "Then let's put him in the rear seat, with your mate."

He helped me as best he could, and between us we set him

beside the other lad, who muttered and stared at nothing. Then the first lad started to get in the passenger seat but I stopped him. "Get in the back with that girl. Keep her still, if you can." He nodded and climbed over the rear seat to kneel beside her.

I got behind the wheel and started praying I'd remember enough to get us going. It was only then I noticed the glass covering the seats and floor mats and in the middle of it all was a stone the size of a small ham. Jesus, if that was what hit the man, it's a miracle he wasn't dead.

I eased in the clutch, turned the ignition, put the shifter into where I thought reverse was—only we pushed deeper into the thicket. I hit the brakes, remembered how I found reverse on Dr. McCurdy's car, set the stick in there and let off easy—and we backed away. The wheels spun a bit and spewed mud, but somehow I was able to back onto the road—

To nearly get run down by another ambulance. It swerved around me, its driver cursing, madly, and continued on. I put the car into gear and raced after it, the engine whining. I knew if Eamonn had *got it good*, he'd be at Altnagelvin. And that bastard was going there, fast. So I stayed as tight on his tail as I could, and damn anybody who tried to stop me.

The ambulance led me straight to casualty. I screamed to a halt by its side, killing the engine before I could press the clutch. A security man started over to yell at me but then saw the lads piling out and called inside, "Here's more!"

Sisters and nurses rushed out to take the lads, the man and the girl away to be tended to. Then a sister stopped me and looked me over.

"How were you hit?" she asked.

"I-I-I wasn't there," I said, not understanding. Then I noticed I had blood covering me; apparently the man *had* been bleeding and I'd not realized. "It's not mine, this blood. It's the man in the back of the estate car."

"So you're well?"

I nodded.

"Then move that car out of the way." She started back for casualty.

"Sister, please!" I grabbed her arm. "My brother, he was with the march. Eamonn Kinsella. I'm told he—"

"Move that car then come inside and check at the intake desk.

They'll answer you." And she shook me off and hurried inside.

I could hear another ambulance coming, so I jumped back to the estate car, started it up and drove it down to the car park. I didn't position it the best, but I didn't care. I ran back up to casualty.

To say it was bedlam is to be mild. There were well over a dozen hurt just from what I could see. And they were from college, or retired, or working folk, or Ma's age—and they showed cuts and scrapes and bruises and puncture wounds enough to make you think they'd been caught between two factions in a war.

I went to the intake desk but no one was there. I tried to ask a couple of sisters passing by where I could go for an answer but no one paid me any mind, and I can't say I blame them. More injured were coming in, and that didn't help my panic.

Then I saw a doctor come out of a curtained area, his white smock coated with blood. Without a thought I bolted through the curtains to see a girl lying on her side, a nurse taping gauze over her sutures. The nurse turned a hard glare on me and snapped, "Get out."

"I'm looking for Eamonn Kinsella," I said, half to the girl as well as to the nurse. "Do you know if he's here?"

"Get out!"

"Is he all right?"

The girl chuckled. "None of us are. None of us."

The doctor came back in, asking, "What's the problem?" His voice had an accent that I almost recognized.

The nurse nodded to me and I turned to him and said, "My brother was with the march. I'm told he's hurt. Kinsella. Is he here?"

The doctor gave me the eye. "Do he look like ye?"

I shook my head. "He's after me Da; I'm more like our Ma."

He nodded then took my by the arm. "Come." He took me to a side wing where people had already been tended to but needed further attention. "We got a couple lads brought in without identification. Is one of 'em yers?"

He took me into a curtained area and I saw two fellows lying side by side on trolleys, each connected to an IV bottle, their heads bandaged and cuts plastered. Both sported massive black eyes and one's neck was locked in a brace of some sort with his left arm in a cast.

The other lad was Eamonn.

I couldn't speak, I was shaking so. I just nodded to him.

"What's his name, again?"

I croaked out, "Kinsella. Eamonn."

"Kinsella? Ye Brendan? Here back a year, weren't ye?"

I nodded.

"Well, Eamonn will be fine. He's unconscious, but we expect him to wake, soon. I'm having him kept overnight; just as a precaution."

My shaking was worse. He put a kind hand on my shoulder. "Ye got some blood on ye. Were ye there?"

I shook my head.

"Have ye ate?"

I shook my head.

"All right, come with me."

He tried to pull me away but I wouldn't budge. Couldn't. All I could do was cough.

"Brendan?" he asked.

I knew what he was saying, but I couldn't understand him.

"That's yer name, right?"

I still couldn't respond.

He finally turned my face to look at him. "Come now, master Kinsella, do ye not answer to yer Christian name?"

Somehow I found the ability to say, "Br-Br-Br-Brendan." And coughed. Then remembered he already knew who I was.

"Very good. Now, Brendan, we need to contact yer parents."

"Da's dead."

"Oh. Right. Sorry. Yer mam, then. She needs to know where ye be. So will ye let our registry clerk know to contact her? And we'll get ye some grub, as well."

"I (cough) I've only two pound on me," I said.

"Don't be daft. Come along. All right?"

I nodded and let him lead me back to the intake desk. This time a large woman sat behind it, and she eyed me with the purest malevolence. He seemed not to notice, just handed me off to her with the order to have me fed and went on his way. She found my old information and called Father Jack to go tell Ma, since Mrs. Rafferty wasn't to home, of course. Then she had me sit in the reception area to wait for them.

Things had begun to settle by this time. The worst casualties had long been brought by and those who straggled in, now, merely needed to be taped up or cleaned. I heard from some the march had continued on and was crossing to Irish Street. I still shook and coughed, but not steadily.

And I got nothing to eat.

Of course, my hunger was making itself known, thanks to aromas from the café. It finally overwhelmed me, so I got up and went looking for it. I heard the clerk yell after me, "You're to sit where I told you!"

I paid her no mind.

I bought fish and chips and a Coke to take away, doused them with vinegar and brown sauce, then dug into them as I returned to intake. The bitch clerk was gone from her desk, so I slipped back to Eamonn.

He still lay there, but now he was awake and, St. Brigit, but his skin was white and his eye looked the worse now he had his good one open. He smelled the food before he saw me, and his smile was the weakest I'd ever seen.

"Bren," he whispered.

I made myself casually stroll over and lean against the trolley to smile at him. "About bloody time you woke up, and you wait till I'm off for grub to do it. Chip?"

He took one and carefully nibbled at it, which scared holy Jesus out of me, for many's the time he'd have put the full handful in his mouth before I'd finished the question. Then he groaned and said, "Christ, Bren, you and the vinegar. Did you soak 'em enough in it?"

"I'll get you some red sauce if you like."

"Wouldn't help." Then he frowned and looked at me. "You spill some on you?"

I looked down. The blood had crusted and did look something like the sauce. "Naw, some people in an estate car were hurt."

"What're you sayin', Bren? That's blood?"

I nodded. "I-I was walking to Claudy to meet up with you and-and I didn't make it."

He looked away. "Be glad for that. They're animals. Fuckin' animals. The things they did to us. To girls. Ladies. Older men and—"

He started to breathe quick and hard and his face contorted in a pain from deep inside and it hurt so to see it that I nudged his arm and said, "Eamonn, you-you want another chip? I'll find one with no vinegar. Or I'll get you something else. I've still over a pound on me. This fish is shite, anyway. I think they give me the worst piece they had."

He looked back at me with his one good eye. "Pound?"

"I just brung a couple with me."

He almost smiled. "Our own little Jew in the family."

"Oh, it's just money! No great shakes to it."

"Listen at you. Mai should turn the finances over; you could make thruppence think it's a tenner."

"Mai does that, well enough."

"Right. But you'll do good in sixth form."

"I'm not for university."

"No? You're smarter 'n you let on."

"If I was so smart, I'd have got past them bastards on the Claudy Road. No, I-I fix things and I don't spend me money if I can help it. That's all there is to me."

"No, son. No. You knew this would happen. You knew and still you came. You knew."

He seemed about ready to weep, then pulled in a deep breath, patted my face and took another chip. He carefully slipped it into his mouth and painfully chewed it as he looked up at the ceiling. "Ma here?"

"Not yet."

"How long you been?"

"Couple hours is all."

"And just now eatin'." I shrugged. "Loyal as a dog."

"Bloody hell, what's that supposed to mean?"

"Nothin'. I'm glad you come." Then he drifted into silence and closed his eye.

I froze, half-afraid he'd died, but then his chest moved and his breath drew in harsh and deep and I knew he was just resting. I stood there for I don't know how long then finally backed up to sit on a chair, hidden by the curtain, and finished my chips. The fish really was horrible, even soaked in vinegar.

Finally, a sister came in to check on him and saw me. "You're not supposed to be here."

"He's my brother," was all I said, nor was I gentle about it.

She looked at his chart. "Kinsella? There's some people just arrived, looking for you. A woman and priest."

Oh, Christ, I thought. Let's get it done with. I rose from the chair, dropped the fish into a dustbin and started out. The sister came around to stop me.

"Is that blood?"

I drew a huge breath and looked her straight in the eye and said, "No. Brown sauce." Then I continued on to my fate.

Ma saw me the second I came through the curtain, stormed over without a moment's hesitation to slap me a good three or four times before Father Jack could stop her.

"I told you not to leave the house!" she yelled at me. "I've been frantic searchin' for you. Why do you always have to vex me, so? Why do you make my life such a hell?"

I said nothing; just accepted it all.

Father Jack backed her away and said, "Bernadette, why don't you go check on Eamonn?"

I looked around and noticed the sister standing behind us, looking very dour at Ma. I felt blood run from my nose. She noticed and smirked, "Is that red sauce?"

I glared at her, snapping, "What d'yous think we bleed— green?"

She sniffed. Turned to Ma. "He's awake now, Mrs. Kinsella."

"He was resting! You didn't need to wake him!"

"I know me duties, young man," she snapped back. Then she opened the curtain to let Ma pass.

"I'm sorry, sister," Ma said as she went into the room. "He's been a thorn in my side since the beginnin', but the quiet ones always are. You never know what they're thinkin' or doin' till they've done it."

"I understand perfectly," said the sister, and then they were gone.

Father Jack said not another word, just let out a sigh as this look of disapproval crossed him. He took me to a lavatory and helped me clean the blood off my face, and while we were in there, I found I needed to use the toilet. He stepped outside, saying, "When you're done I'll take you home."

I did my business and put my caked clothing back in order, and...

And...

And...

And I couldn't move.

I couldn't move.

Suddenly I fell back on the toilet, shaking and gasping and fighting the need to scream, and I began to sob, quiet and sharp, and pounded my head with my fists to keep from getting too loud.

He'd almost died. Eamonn. Those bloody, fucking bastards almost killed him. Over nothing. A walk. A simple fucking walk to say we were men, like them, and due the same consideration. And for that, they'd tried to fucking kill him!

Oh my God, the hate and horror and anger and fear I had boiling within was now spilled into the open and I could not stop it. I tore at my hair, my head resting against my hands. My eyes crushed shut. I rocked back and forth, keening softly like an old woman.

The rank stupidity of those fucking bastards. Did they honestly think there would be no response from us, over this? Did they truly believe we'd be so scared of their vicious bullying we'd creep back to our homes and cower in fear? Were they really that fucking stupid?

Yes.

They were.

I finally saw they were. For the same thing had happened when Da was killed. Others in the same year. Those clever men had achieved nothing except to strengthen our resolve. The same in October. Yet here they were, at it, again. They couldn't see. Couldn't accept that playing the part of a bully no longer worked. That we wouldn't stand for it. That we were done with letting them kick us. That we would kick back.

The stupid bloody bastards.

And Billy had been one of them!

Me China had helped hurt Eammon! A lad he'd known for years.

My brother!

And me he'd known for years.

Suddenly I was cold, again. My shirt freezing against me sending shivers cascading through my whole being. Shaking.

Fucking Billy.

I had no idea what I'd do should I ever see him, again, so honestly hoped I wouldn't. I honestly did not want to know what I was capable of, thanks to this deep, growling anger within me. I dared not move for fear I'd run mad and search the little bastard down and kill him. Fucking kill him.

I have no idea how long I sat there before Father Jack had to come back into the lavatory and ask, "Brendan, are you well?"

No, but at least that broke the chaos in my mind.

I managed to croak out, "Fine. Just took. Took me longer than I thought and-and I'll be out in a minute."

I heard the door close. My spiral into madness was broken. I could guide myself back to normal, now.

I slipped out of the stall and washed my face in the cold water of the basin, using soap and the rolling towel to scrub me. By the time I stepped out of the toilet, I was in complete control, again.

Father Jack drove me home in his Cortina, and it was difficult. RUC checkpoints had gone up throughout Derry and barricades had been built around the Bogside to keep the constables out. The march had continued on and been pummeled, again, on Irish Street, but they'd still managed to cross the Craigavon and made it to the Guildhall just as the RUC was breaking everything up. That's when people saw and heard of the horrors that had been inflicted, and their fury exploded.

The attack had happened at Burntollet Bridge, and the news crossed the globe. To say this set off riots would be a simple way of describing the insane anger and destruction that rolled across the North. And whether they chose to believe it or not, the Loyalists had done a serious damage to themselves. Not just in the eyes of Catholics in Ulster, but in London and even the world. Headlines and photographs of bleeding kids were splashed across the newspapers and the television news had footage of it all. That news cameras had been smashed in a foolish attempt to keep the attack undocumented only added to the shock.

Arrogance breeds a certain blindness in people and it was in full force now, with the idiots insisting nothing had happened and what had happened was the fault of the marchers and no one else, unable to recognize their claims were seen for what they truly were—lies. There was too much evidence of it to ignore. Even Father Jack could see it

"It's laughable," he said, as we drove. "It's the beginning of the end of their rule here, and the start of a new order. Westminster won't tolerate this, any longer. They'll be too embarrassed by it all." He kept on and on about it, almost as if he was pleased at what had happened.

Finally I had to ask, "Did you expect this?"

"No, nothing like this," he told me, absently.

"But something?"

He looked at me, finally taking note of the question. "What're you asking me, Brendan?"

"Did you know what would happen on the march?"

"Know? Of course not. Why would you ask such a thing?"

"But didn't you at least suspect?"

He grew so careful in his words. "I recall you being wary of some violence occurring, but I thought you had come around to understanding the importance of what they were doing. And that to back down in the face of possible threats was never a choice."

"That doesn't answer me."

He took in a deep breath. "The leaders of the People's Democracy expected there to be difficulty along the way. That is why they emphasized there was to be no retaliation. By anyone. They wanted the world to see we ask only for that which is guaranteed to all citizens in a democracy. However, the actions of those people at Burntollet was inexcusable and completely unexpected."

Was it? I don't know why, but something about the way he said that made it seem like all I was hearing were half-truths, and to me that was the same as lies. So I decided to ask for a lie about something else.

"Why was Father Demian sent off?"

He looked at me, taken aback. "What has that to do with the Loyalists?"

"Was it something to do with Danny that got him sent away?"

Father Jack looked ahead and slowed down for the next checkpoint. "I was under the impression you were happy he was gone. Father Demian is gone."

"I didn't say I wasn't. It was just sudden-like, and I'm wondering why. I hear he was sent to a place—well, is it because he drank so much? Was he getting Danny Gallagher drunk, too?"

His voice grew sharp and cold. "You have no right to ask such questions. None of that is your business."

He was right. It wasn't. But his refusal to answer me told me far more than just the rumors I'd heard—that Father Demian had been *sent away to make himself right*. Right about what? While I had my suspicions, that part was still uncertain. But it did tell me Father Jack was instrumental in handling it quietly, so no one could really know why Father Demian was gone. All so very much like a sneak.

"You knew," I said, not intending to actually speak the words. They simply came out of my mouth. "You expected what was going to happen at Burntollet and let Eamonn and his mates walk into a trap."

He grabbed my arm in the same way Da often had. "That is a horrible thing to say to me, Brendan Kinsella! Why would I even think of doing such a thing?"

I couldn't put it into words, yet. I felt it had something to do with the publicity of the attack and the world's reaction. It's like he wanted that, but I couldn't make the connection to understand why that would be such a good thing.

He knew what was happening in Derry and Belfast. Knew how close everyone was to betraying their neighbors and hurting each other and laughing about it in the worst ways. Knew that people could have been killed not just at the bridge but around the Guildhall the night before. With the mob close to anger enough to commit slaughter and the RUC ready to crush anyone who even so much as looked at them wrong. And knowing all of that, he hadn't expected something like the Loyalists putting deed to their loud threats? A man as smart as Father Jack? When even I saw what was coming and was afraid for it?

Add to that his finely worded answers to Father Demian's departure? I finally understood I could trust nothing he said to me.

Oh, I know I had suspicions and concerns before this, but it still was a shock to have it laid so bare. He's one of the holy fathers. The direct representative of the Pope, the man who spoke to God. I'd taken communion from him and he'd said prayers with us and seen to it I was well cared for when I'd been in hospital. He was known by all in my neighborhood and loved and tended to by married and unmarried ladies, alike, and knew the bible from cover-to-cover and-and-and he was lying to me. If Eamonn had been killed, the bastard would have seen it as bad for my family, true, but also a good thing for the Republican cause.

Or maybe a political one. Or the church. I don't know. I couldn't sort through it, yet.

So I didn't answer him. My mind went blank. I know we went

through another RUC checkpoint after this one and had to get past a barricade put up by the local lads. I think I heard Colm calling to me, once. And we might have caught the tail end of a confrontation between constables and a few rock-throwers. But I swear, I cannot remember another honest thought in my head until he'd pulled up in front of my home and Mairead was at the car's door, wiping her hands on her apron, her face white as a sheet.

"Brendan, are you all right?" she asked, her voice pitched high in near terror.

I smiled at her and said, "Why wouldn't I be?" Then I got out of the car, tossed a "Thanks, father," over my shoulder and headed into the house before he had a chance to respond.

Rhuari and Maeve met me, breathless. "Brendan, you're home and safe." Both of them saying the same thing, so much so you'd think them twins. "Ma was in a temper. She tore through your room, looking for something. What's this all over you?"

"I'll tell you all about it later, if you eat well."

Mairead followed me in, saying, "Just fish fingers and potato nuggets but..."

"Sounds brilliant," I said, still smiling. "Is Tur unhurt?"

"A few bruises on his legs and back is all, and he made it all the way to the Square, but not for lack of trying on their part. He says there were B-Specials there. Wore regular clothes but had white armbands. And the RUC helped the bastards. Some had cudgels with nails in them. Nails! And Irish Street was like an obstacle course."

I just nodded and started up the steps.

Mairead stopped me. "Bren, that's blood on you..."

I looked down at my shirt and parka and jeans. They were ruined, sure. But the coat was tight so I'd have needed a new one anyway.

"Bren?" I looked at her. "Is-is Eamonn bad hurt?"

I smiled at her. "He'll be fine. He got a nasty eye and his head'll be hurting for a fortnight, maybe, but he'll be fine."

She looked closer at me, wary.

It made me ask, "What?"

"There's something different about you."

"Is there?"

"I don't know. It's just—something's not the same."

"Let me wash up and into fresh duds, then I'll tell you

everything over our supper." Well, not everything. But enough to make you happy. "Maybe that'll explain it."

"Water's hot for you."

I smiled at her and went upstairs for a fresh shirt and trousers. And I cleaned myself from top to bottom. And as we ate, I told them of my adventure. Rhuari and Maeve were caught full in it, while Mai just shook her head and Kieran slept.

Then that night, just as we were preparing for bed, we heard the first can lids clamoring a warning. The RUC was on its way to reassert their domination of the Bogside, and without question would do so in the most violent manner possible.

Father Jack would be pleased.

Night of Broken Glass

Long Tower, Howard Street, Nailors Row, Walker's Place, Friel's
Terrace—all were hit the worst. I think because we already were
slated for demolition and redevelopment and housing *would soon
be made available*, so there would little condemnation for the
damage. Perhaps they even thought they'd be applauded for
saving the Corporation a bit of scratch.

But the peelers also poured through Butchers Gate and up
from Waterloo, and it was clear from the start they were out to
prove they were lord and master of us all in the harshest way
possible. Uniforms. Batons. Barricades torn apart. Windows
smashed. Homes rousted. People beaten for fighting back or even
just letting them do as they wanted. Their howling matched with
the faces of wild beasts let loose. Not a care that reporters and
photographers were pouring in to catch it all, like they had but
three months earlier. Yesterday, even.

Ma was still at Altnagelvin with Eamonn, so Mairead and I
grabbed coats and put them on the wains as we heard the crashing
getting closer and hurried them into our back yard. The girls and
Kieran hid in the toilet as I helped Rhuari over the back wall to
Mrs. Haggerty's.

"Toss stones over to me," I whispered. "Good ones."

He did so.

I closed the door to the toilet and waited as I heard the chaos
grow nearer. I quaked within, but not one cough. Mairead kept
Maeve and Kieran quiet with soft words and bites of hard candy,
earmuffs on each of them to muffle the noise. A smile on her,
steady and sure.

Every window in the front of our hovel was shattered before
they burst through the door. We heard them crashing through like
mad elephants, wrecking anything they could. Chairs. Curtains
ripped. Glass in picture frames. Pots and pans clattered. Dishes

smashed. Our table splintered. Each sound closer and closer and closer to the back door.

Now, I coughed but managed to keep it soft. Still I waited, fair-sized stones in each hand, another pile next to me. Rhuari kept tossing over all he could find, and I was letting them build behind me.

Then the back window smashed from within and one bastard stuck his head out and saw me, and I shied a stone straight into his face. Caught him in the eye. He howled like a hurt dog and fell back.

I laughed and hissed, like that tom had.

Another kicked at the door before deciding to open it from within, and the moment it was wide enough I shied rock after brick after stone at them, most missing, hitting some, causing them to back away in shock. I didn't let up. Made it seem like there were more than one of me.

Another fat bastard tried to come at me but I hit his knee with a brick and he crumbled, screaming like a child. The man behind him looked at me in horror, and behind him I could see two of them with blood on them, so I sent more stones and bricks and rocks their way. They roared like unfed beasts, but backed away from me. I'd have laughed if I had any breath left in me from it all.

My stockpile was dwindling fast, so I yanked the toilet door open and motioned to the side wall, saying, "Get over it, fast. They're past Mrs. Haggerty's, now. I'll drop the wains to you."

I must have had some look on my face for Mairead didn't even try to argue. Over the wall she went then I lifted Maeve and Kieran over to her.

She held up her arms to help me, last, saying, "C'mon, Bren."

I shook my head. "Go. I'm gonna have fun with these bastards."

Her eyes went wide with horror. "No, you can't!"

But I heard them storming back into the house and dropped down to sit on an upturned bucket and put on the most innocent face I could as they burst from within, ready to face a horror of men against them. They skidded to a halt upon seeing just little old me.

"Are yous done, yet?" I said, "I must get to cleaning before me Ma gets home. She'll toss a fit at the mess you've made."

One ugly bastard snarled up to me. "Where's the rest of 'em?"

"Rest of who?" I shot back. "It's only me here."

He yanked open the toilet, saw it was empty, then looked over the wall. But I'd heard Mrs. Haggerty's back door creak closed, so he'd find nothing. The ugly bastard growled as he hopped back down, grabbed my shirt and gave me the back of his hand. I felt my nose bleed, again.

"*You* shied those rocks at my men?"

I didn't try to wipe the blood, just glared at him and said, "I'm in me yard and suddenly there's smashing and breaking in my home and I'm here by meself and some bastard breaks the glass, so yes, I shied a rock at him. Shied more till I saw it's you peelers. Bunch of bloody cowards trying to—"

He slapped me, again.

"You assaulted a copper," he said, grinning ear to ear. "We're takin' you down Strand Road."

One of his mates come up and said, "Sir, there's reporters in front. Photographers."

"So fuckin' what?"

"He looks what—nine, ten year-old and he's got blood on him? I heard over the radio, BBC's already called the Executive asking what's goin' on. My girl at Malone's said reporters have been callin' in stories about this and weeping about the poor little Taigs. You want a photo of him, lookin' like that for the likes of them?"

A hideous growl whispered up from the ugly bastard, then he straightened himself and slapped me, twice more, before he slung me to the ground.

"I got my eye on you, you little cunt," he snarled, pointing his two main fingers at his eyes and then at mine.

I just glared at him. Blood smearing my face.

They stormed out, breaking the last of what wasn't broken.

I finally sat up, my ears still ringing. Gave a slight cough. And silence whispered in. It took a few moments, but step by step I rose to my feet to slowly, slowly go inside. I ached more than hurt. Felt oddly light-headed more than dizzy. And so very tired. But I made it inside.

Everything was shattered. Table. Chairs. Doors on cabinets. Ma's little Dresden figurine. I saw it wasn't beyond mending so found a torn cloth to put the bits into and held them. I could handle that, tomorrow.

I wandered back to the dish pail. Saw there was water still in it, so I dipped into it and cleaned my face. My nose had slowed its bleeding enough that I could push a torn bit of cloth up into it to hold. Finally, I sat on a half-broken stool and just looked around at the mess. I had no idea what to do or where to begin.

It felt I sat there for an hour before Mairead returned.

"Brendan?" I hear her calling, her voice shaking.

"Aye," I murmured, not really thinking about it.

"Oh, good," she said, getting closer. "I was afraid the peelers had snatched you."

I realized I was sitting in a shaft of soft moonlight whispering in through the broken window. And it was cold, but I didn't care. She picked her way into the back and saw me. The moonlight made everything but her face seem dark, still I couldn't tell the expression on her. Just that her voice went gentle. "It's quite the mess."

I shrugged and held up the cloth with the broken figurine. "I think I can mend this, well enough."

She nodded, came over, took the dishcloth from me and wetted a corner under the tap then squatted beside me and put it to the side of my face. Christ it was cold, but it felt so good I moaned in happiness and wondered at not thinking of doing that, myself.

"Did they hurt you much?"

I shrugged. "No more'n Da ever did."

"We're down at Mrs. O'Canainn's. I rang Ma, at hospital, and she said we're to stay there till the place is livable, again."

"Did they go upstairs? The peelers?"

"I haven't been up, but I don't think so..."

I smiled. "Then we'll be fine. I got five pound, seven."

She blinked then nodded. "I'll talk with Tur. We should be able to get a decent table and chairs, second hand. Or third. Some plates and such. I'll also ask about repairing the divan. It doesn't look so bad."

"We-we'll need glass for windows." My voice was beginning to break. "I can put them in if Tur'll lend me a cutter."

"I'm sure you can and he will."

I nodded. I dared not say anything more.

She checked my nose, murmuring, "I think it's stopped. So

let's go down and have some to eat. We'll face this in the mornin', once we're fresh."

I nodded and rose with her, feeling old and weary.

We walked out into a street filled with the remains of the chaos. Neighbors milled about, snarling curses on the peelers, every one of them. Boards and tin were already going up to replace the broken windows. Their voices went soft as they saw me pass with Mairead.

One little girl—I think it was Jenny Dougherty but can't be sure; I wasn't paying anything much mind—rushed up and said, "Bren, is it true you beat the peelers back?"

I know I looked at her, and she gasped and ran back to her mother.

Then we were at the O'Canainn's and going inside. Her home had just a broken window or two. I was sat at the table and given a bowl of the finest stew ever made on the face of the earth. It didn't seem so long since I'd had Mai's fish fingers, but I found I was starving and the smell of it overwhelmed any hesitation. Of course, I had to eat careful but I finished every bit, though all I could eat of the bread was the inner part; the crust was harsh and hurt to chew. And as I ate, Mrs. O'Canainn set a glass before me and poured a dark ale into it, saying, "I think you earned this, tonight."

I know I smiled my thanks. Tears may have been in my eyes but I didn't let them fall. I just sipped it. Afterwards I washed and slept on her divan till after morning's light.

And when I woke, it took me half an hour to recall that it had not been a dream.

*****

Turlach was good to Mairead's expectations and sold us a table of the same sort, with six chairs. He also saw to it we got a settee to replace the divan, and found me panes of colored glass for the windows.

"Not the best," he said, "since they'll soon be tore down. Just to keep out the wind."

Then he showed me how to fix it so them so they wouldn't rattle, using bits of chewing gum in the corners. I chose Spearmint to use, but still had to be careful which side I chewed on.

I got the figurine fixed well enough, though a couple bits got lost in the mess. Ma was kind enough to point out I could have done a better job searching the rubble, but at least she blamed the peelers for everything and not me. Took us three days to clean it all and have it collected by the junkman, then Tur and his helpers brought the table and chairs along with the settee. When he saw I'd also pasted paper to the walls to cover the torn spots, he jostled me, saying, "You'll be in new digs, soon, and wonder at how much effort you wasted."

I just laughed as best I could, still a bit sore, and said, "Since when is it a waste to live like a man instead of a pig?"

But to his credit, he was right; it took the Mayor only a bit more than two months to move us into a newer terrace home on Clíodhna Place off Abbey Street. A nice short street with no outlet and small, walled yards in front, walled yards in back pressed up to other houses of similar setup.

The family that was there before us were off to Brisbane and a new world...and to put it kindly, they'd had little concern for those following them into this hovel. However, it had a full kitchen and range, with a hot water tap over a basin, and three fine rooms, upstairs, two of them separated by an actual toilet and bath. It was like we'd finally joined the Twentieth Century.

The yard in back was small and tight because a fair-size hutch took up much of it, but to Mai's pleasure there was room enough for a small garden and the clothesline worked well strung between the hutch's roof and the opposite wall.

"I'll plant herbs," she said. "Give us a change for our meals."

"Can you grow tomatoes?" Maeve asked.

"I don't think they'll work in this thin soil."

"Bren could build a box. Sister Samuel had photos of tomatoes growing in boxes, and there's so much dirt available in the open lots."

Mairead looked at her, as did I. "Aren't you the forward one," I said, "deciding for me what I'll do for you?"

Maeve had looked straight at me and said, "Now, Brendan, don't be silly. You know it would be for all of us."

"But there's plenty to fix up in this house and—"

"And it would take you no time, at all."

Mai fought a smile and said, "Let me see what Mr. O'Connell says about that." He worked a small nursery up in Shantalow.

Maeve shrugged and wandered off, knowing she'd get her way.

Which she did.

It was three weeks work for Danny, Tur and myself to repair what was needed, thanks mainly to Tur's schedule. Mai, Rhuari and Maeve painted and cleaned as Ma kept Kieran out of the way, for the most part, and did the laundry. But by the end of March, it was so much like new Ma could find nothing to complain about. She just looked it over and only let us know she was pleased by leaning the wedding photo of her and Da atop the center of the fireplace mantle. It was still in its frame from the old place, just cleaned up and with only a crack in the left lower corner. Then she set her Dresden figurine to its right.

We were all standing about, watching as if it were a ritual, and that is when Mairead told us Tur had finally asked her to marry him. Then added they would be looking for new digs.

Without a thought, I asked, "Why can't you stay here?"

Mairead blushed a bit and said, "Well, we'd like to have some privacy, and if a wain comes along of our own..."

"Then we could make the hutch over into a room for you," I said. "It's filled with nothing but clutter and is near the size of Ma's room in the front. We could even expand it, some. That yard's no great shakes and-and look at the materials being wasted in redevelopment. I could build a full house with what I see them tossing out."

Ma glared at me. "Tur's enough to do without workin' on one of your schemes."

"It wouldn't take much," I snapped back.

Ma huffed and turned back to Mairead. "You can keep the room you have, now. I'll move Maeve in with me and Kieran."

Maeve jumped up and said, "Ma, the closet between your bedroom and Mai's is a nice size. I could sleep in that."

"Don't be ridiculous," Ma snapped. "No window? Your bed will be moved into my room, and that is that."

"My bed fits that closet," Maeve shot back. "I measured it. And that's what I want."

"I can hook you a lamp," I said, almost smiling.

"If it's such a chore for Mairead and Tur to live here, Turlach's parents have a fine terrace home in Creggan," Ma said, almost flustered. "And there's his brother up in Pennyburn."

"He's got a sister," Mai said, "with her two at that home, while her husband's in Toronto gettin' set up with their uncle. And he has two married brothers sharin' that flat in Pennyburn."

"Mai, the hutch would be perfect," I said. "Clean it up, put in boards for the walls, some paper or-or plaster and paint. It already has an electric bulb in it, so you've got that."

"And how will you heat it?" Ma snarled.

"Get a round stove for wood or coal, and it's nothing to add an exhaust."

"We could do a paraffin heater," Mai said.

I shook my head. "I've heard too much about them; they can smother you. Do it right, up front, Mai."

Mai smiled at me and nodded. "I'll talk to Tur."

"You'll do no such thing," Ma snapped. "As-as it is, you're too young to be married, and-and havin' my daughter live in a made-over garden hutch..."

Mairead cut her off with a strong look and smile as she said, "Ma, it's better if we're married sooner than later."

Ma jolted and looked at her for a long moment, more still than I'd ever seen her, then finally drew in a deep breath.

"We'll talk of this, tonight," she said, her voice low and scary.

Mairead nodded and said, "I'll speak to Tur this evenin'."

Well, to put it simply, it took Tur, me, Colm and Danny but a week and less than twenty pounds and, let's just say, a few *late trips* to some *piles of refuse*, so to speak, to make over the hutch into something more than merely livable. Of course, Paidrig cheered us on while helping himself to our tea. Wee Eammon was able to join us, a couple times, and made an excellent suggestion.

"What if you add a skylight to the roof, at one end?" he'd asked. "Or a gable window? Wouldn't that make it seem more like a home?"

Mairead was next to him and that tender expression came over her. "What a lovely idea, Eammon," she murmured, "but I fear it might be a lot of trouble and expense."

Tur saw her and smiled. "Let me look into it."

Well, with Colm being...um...especially good at *locating better materials* we could use—and never did we ask him from where—and wee Eammon and Rhuari working up a schematic, and Tur borrowing tools from his Da's shop, adding the window cost but an extra six pounds. Then after I showed him how to do it, Danny upgraded the electrical wiring so they now had an actual power outlet. When he was done, he all but danced from joy at how well it worked.

"Fine job, Danny," Tur told him. "I could set you up as apprentice with a man does work for me Da."

Danny beamed. "I think I'd like that."

I added, "I'd say you got the touch for it."

He all but strutted.

So three weeks after we completed the hutch, Mairead and Tur were wed at St. Eugene's. And not six months later, Michael Paul Devlin came along to make Ma into a grandmother, and me an uncle, and Mai and Tur still were living in it.

And in a mystery for the ages, somehow Mairead timed the birth so as to avoid the worst of the unpleasantness that was to come.

February – August

Semi-new World

Christmas and Boxing Day, last, had been simple affairs, with naught but little gifts between us all. Well, except for the package from Aunt Mari with something for each one. There had also been the light exchange of sweets and cakes and pies, most made by Mairead and much appreciated by our previous neighbors.

But now we had new neighbors, and Mairead thought the best way to become one with them all was to re-do the exchange. Which all of them jumped in on. Especially since the previous tenants had happily accepted gifts but were loathe to hand back anything more than a couple pieces from a Woolie's grab and mix.

Not even from Quality Street, was the quickest complaint.

Nine wains they had.

How they lived on the dole was beyond my ability to understand.

Not mine, considering the shops they were barred from.

Wasn't till their oldest was set up in Australia, they took after him.

Without a word to one.

My bet is they showed up on his doorstep before letting him know they were coming.

In Brisbane, no less, not even Melbourne or Sydney.

Well, they only had one brain between them, and it's more than certain he took it with him.

Usually followed by much cackling and giggly murmurs of, *You're wicked.*

Their name was Cassidy, and I'd had one of their sons in my class. A quiet lad who always seemed like he was lost in a thick fog. He never was close to anyone, so I'd never learned where he lived. But with that many brothers and sisters in a place the size of this? I wouldn't be surprised if it was lack of sleep that kept him dazed and confused, were comments about the family's *boisterousness* to be believed.

Leading the chatter about them was Mrs. Keogh, to our left. She was half of an older pair whose children were all off and married in London, Glasgow, Dublin and Paris. The mister ran a betting shop, which brought in enough wage to become the second owner of a Rover. I found out he and his wife had driven to Stormount in the caravan, a few years back, protesting the new university going to Coleraine instead of Derry, so they were on the right side, so far as all were concerned. Their home was neat, not overdone but comfortable, and they were owners of two cats that liked them and me, but no one else.

With her family gone and her home already in such order, the missus had far too little to keep her busy so was always available for a bit of nasty, nosy craic with those around her and behind the wall. Which Ma would participate in, even as she sniffed, "Cut crystal Irish. Better than us all," with our other new neighbors.

There was so much of this chattering going on, after but a week I kept to my room to work on my projects, with the window closed. I also wound up owner of a small transistor radio with a cracked body and no back but an earplug, so would listen to that to keep from paying them any mind.

To our other side was the Whites, whose three sons I knew too well from school, as noted earlier. Cold, thin and angry, that whole family was, and I had been hard put to slough off some of their sons' worst words sent my way. But never was I laid hand on, since I couldn't be bothered with their sad attempts at bullying. Then Colm was me China so they knew better, as good bullies will.

Past them, Mrs. Haggerty had joined our street, and across from us and behind were the Sellars, the Paynes, the Doghertys, McCorys, and the Mahons, all with children too old for me or too young. But Maeve and Rhuari knew enough of them to be invited into their midst. Playing in the street with happy cries so innocent.

I wasn't pleased with the lack of a decent view out my window, upstairs. Seeing only into the yards behind us and too much city light to get a good look at the stars. But the room stayed warm and relatively quiet, except when the Whites were having one of their set-tos. Also missing was the simple easiness that had been part of the old place, but I guess there's always a trade-off.

Of course, a lot of that easiness was gone, thanks to what was now normal practice in our spot of the world. A march in Newry. Fighting and RUC tenders burned and run into the canal. I saw a photo in the *Journal* of someone who looked like Tommy in a crowd pushing one onto its side. Word was Eamonn jumped atop another tender to cry, "This has nothing to do with civil rights! Come away from this horrible place!" But he never mentioned it in his letters home, and others said it was just some other lad who resembled him, for it was a photo from his left side and he came across much better in photos of his right.

Of course, it snowed over the winter, so despite moving house and repairing it, and little fix-it jobs that still came my way, Danny and I also had plenty of work clearing passageways and doorsteps. He seemed to be happiest when he was busy, so I even started to let him repair the easier things I had to work on—clocks wound too tight, wrist watches needing to be cleaned, that sort of thing.

Colm was rarely around, and I never asked after him, having a fair idea he was off with his mates from the fort. But he kept me in Blues, and Danny used him for Marlboros, pot and a bottle.

Mairead got Paidrig's sisters-in-law on as smoothers at Hogg and Mitchell's, so he was kept home to watch his nieces and nephews. And enough about that. Not much pay, each, but enough so they'd give Paidrig a schilling a week, putting him more well-off than he'd ever been. Of course, that changed nothing about him; he still claimed never to have any scratch on him when it came time to pay for the cigs, whiskey and pot. Don't know what he did with it.

Wee Eammon grew ill, again, and spent a month in care, and when he came home he was never let out since his mother was terrified he'd die in the street. On the few occasions when he did sneak off to be with us, she'd come screaming to my house first, looking for him, and would toss twice the fit if she caught us smoking around him. Rhuari kept watch for her and tried to give us fair warning, but any fool could tell she'd smell the smoke and turn into the purest harpy.

And at such moments, Ma'd be in her gentle agreement phase.

We got to where we would meet at an empty shell of a place to have our card play, smoke and drink—and there were more and more empty places to find. But that only worked if it wasn't raining or snowing or blowing hard. Which was rare, that time of year.

The marches, demonstrations, sit-ins and speeches were non-stop, especially once Paisley near toppled O'Neill in an election for Stormount. Faulkner resigned. John Hume took over for Eddie McAteer in the Parliament. People squatted in homes and caravans to protest housing conditions and marched on Guildhall, demanding better accommodations. It was something new, every day, and hard to keep score of them all. After a while the excitement of them dimmed, no matter how loud and wild the leaders were.

The RUC kept a low profile—well, for them, during this. It seemed the publicity of their actions in January had sent them to lie in a corner and lick their wounds. There is where they stayed, right up to the parade in remembrance of the 1916 Easter uprising.

I was there, as were all me Chinas; this was too important to be ignored. It was for when our side had risen up in full revolt, only to be put down by the British in so vicious and brutal a fashion, nearly every Catholic in the country turned on the bastards, and within 5 years Ireland was free. At least, that's how the brothers put it in class. I'm sure if I'd read more about that I'd have had a more nuanced view, but I was at a point I left all the reading of history to Rhuari; when I did read, my preference was science fiction. Something hopeful to look forward to.

On that day, we were grouped by the Guildhall when I noticed the RUC massing up Magazine Street, in their long black coats, helmets and shields, with their commanders laughing it up beside them. That did not set well with any who saw, and John Hume must have sensed it because he began speaking of keeping the calm, much of which was laughed off.

Christ, do people never learn?

I suppose their thought was that the Square was filled with people only out to have some enjoyment. We weren't marching and howling and pounding drums like the Apprentice Boys Marches, so there was no cause for concern. Of course, some Loyalists pushed in to make trouble, thanks to their sense of entitlement and condescension. Can't let the papists commemorate one of their own events. All glory must be reserved for King Billy's shite, only.

So the usual push and shove ignited between groups of

boisterous young men. Danny and his mates from Shantalow got into a shouting match with some the same age. I had to clip one lad with a half a brick before he could bring a cudgel down on me China's head. But it was nothing out of the ordinary.

Until the RUC came roaring in, yelling—no, howling and whooping like mad things. It was as if they'd been holding their hate in reserve so they could release it in the foulest way possible. All of us scattered as they wildly swung about...then smashed and looted shops!

They looted the bloody shops for drinks and food!

Then they roared into the Bogside to slam anyone who dared be caught by them. Even tore into houses and beat people who'd not been near the Square. One man in his own home, Mr. Devenny, who hadn't even been to the demonstration, was hurt so bad he died of his injuries a few months after. Oh, was there anger over that.

His funeral procession was ten times the size of the initial parade. Ma even let me walk along to the cemetery, with her and Eamonn. I didn't really know the man, nor could I say Ma did; being there was more to show respect and support for his family and himself than anything else. The bastards kept quiet with their snarling hate and batons, this time. Smart of them. This crowd would not have scattered in surprise or fear.

O'Neill resigned, to be replaced by Chichester-Clark, who was an even bigger fool, and a public order amendment was passed to slap the Catholics back into place. Which only meant more demonstrations against it. I wondered at how the Loyalists who ran the country honestly seemed to believe they could stop simple demands for justice and fairness with some ridiculous little laws that no one had the real power to enforce. By this point, even the RUC's violence was no longer acceptable to any but the most rabid of Paisleyites. Of course, Unionists grew crazier when Bernadette Devlin stood for UK Parliament. And won! Made us all the more proud and sure of our cause.

Our cause.

The cause Ma had let herself get wrapped up in, complete, and had tried since Da's death to catch me up in, as well. Eamonn had listened to her go on about the righteousness and honor of reuniting Ireland once the ludicrous border forced on us by the British was erased. And stories of Wolf Tone and Patrick Pearse and Michael Connolly and a hundred others were drilled into our brains as if they were part of our catechism by her as well as the brothers. More than once, thanks to my Da having been killed by the bastards, I was held up in class as an example of how vile the Protestants could be. But I fair certain the Brothers knew—or, at least, suspected—that none of this took deep root, in me. I found it all rather shrill, and my repeating of the stories told was too much by rote to be believed by any but the most faithful.

Me Da'd once said about the brothers, "Those bastards would make a saint out of a snake, if it had been the side of the Irish." And the more I learned, the more I came to believe him.

But Eamonn was getting caught up in the nationalism, starting after the attack at Burntollet. More and more blather about how our rights had been trampled for decades and it was our duty to push back and gain what was rightfully ours to begin with.

"It's obvious the Loyalists won't give us a thing without our fighting for it," he told me, once. "We've tried words and reason and appeals to decency, but all they do is talk and refuse to take real action."

He was trying his best to convince me the Protestants were scum and not to be trusted, and while I wasn't in complete disagreement, he soon noticed I was doing with him like I had with Ma. Let them talk, nod your head now and then, and focus on the job you have before you. He finally gave up on me.

So in truth, what little I had to do with anything, other than be one with the demonstrations and marches, was to fix things for those whose wages had been cut by the chaos. If you're on the dole with no steady income, you can't afford to buy new stuff. And since my prices were better than even the tinkers, I had quite a backlog of work to do.

Of course, Ma would then come nosing about, asking me what I'd made. I would simply tell her, "I give it to Mai. Ask her."

This usually set her off and I'd get her nails in my neck as she growled, "You will answer my question, you little—"

But my only response would be, "I'm doing what I said I would!"

Then she'd huff, shove me and storm off to complain about me to Mrs. White or Mrs. Keogh, both of whom would listen in tight agreement.

Gossipy old cows.

But sometimes their gossip was impossible to ignore, try as I might. And I must admit, not all of it was bad, for me. On one occasion I was in the hutch trying to sort out a leak in that bloody gable window, and heard Mrs. Haggerty was over to Mrs. Keogh's, and Mrs. O'Canainn was with them, on a visit. Though their voices were soft, I could make out that Mrs. O'Canainn had just received notice of what was to be her new home, across from the Market Flats, and she was hesitant about agreeing.

"Those who lived there before," she nattered, "weren't as house-trained as a dog. I'm fearful of going to even look at it."

To my shock, Mrs. Keogh told her, "Ask Brendan to go with you. He can see what may need repairs and give you a list."

"But be sure to pay him some," laughed Mrs. Haggerty. "He's our little Jew boy, does nothing for free."

"You're so hard on the lad," said Mrs. O'Cainnan. "Why is that? He's been nothing but kind to me. And look how he fought back the peelers, that night."

"Is that story really true?"

"You think I'm after making it up? I was there! I saw the damage done him by those bastards."

"It's not the boy is the problem; it's that trial of a mother he's got," said Mrs. Keogh. "It amazes me any of them are at all decent."

"I'll give you that," said Mrs. Haggerty, sighing. "She'd worry the patience of a saint. That poor man that married her, God rest him."

"Oh, I avoided him as well as her," said Mrs. O'Canainn. "Even when first they came, you could see there was a darkness in him. Made itself known, more and more, but Bernadette was solid for him. It's as if they were meant for each other."

"I hear he *had* to marry her."

"No idea, on that," said Mrs. O'Canainn. "She was well along with Brendan when they took up residence near me."

"That sort of thing carries through to the daughter," said Mrs. Keogh, and I would swear she was snickering.

"At least she didn't wind up as Mrs. Breen," said Mrs. O'Cainann. "Poor wee Eammon, having to live with that."

"*Mrs.* Breen," Mrs. Haggerty chuckled, and not in a kind way.

"Yes, well, enough said about her."

And off they went to tear apart every other woman they knew, laughing and clinking their teacups. The old cows.

But when Mrs. O'Canainn stopped me on Fahan, the following day, to ask what I'd charge to look over her new place, I told her, "Nothing. You let us stay with you when our home was smashed."

I almost asked her to tell me more about Da, but I knew she'd not keep my asking from Ma. Instead, I let her dither and blush and make herself say, "Now, Brendan, I can't expect you to be doing that."

"Then bring us another pot of that fine stew you made," I said. "Mai's working up some colcannon, tonight, so..."

She beamed and did so. Had some already in the pot. She even gave Mai her recipe, which included a bit of wine. No wonder it carried such a lovely aroma.

It was a relatively new terrace home she was set for, closer to Rossville, and I looked it over, the next day. She was right about it not being kept up; it was worse than ours had been. I'll never understand how people can live like animals. I gave her a list of sockets not working and pipes to be fixed, and suggested the toilet and tub be replaced. She gave it over to the powers that be and said she'd be happy to move if these were done. To my surprise, they did every bit, and soon she was in. I almost thought I should have asked them to do the work on our home. But in truth, between Tur, Colm, Danny and myself, with Rhauri's and Maeve's quiet assistance, we'd upgraded a great deal more than they would have, and I had no intention of letting those bastards know of it. Might bump up our rent.

It seemed Eamonn was home every weekend, now. He still had trouble remembering where we lived and wound up being brought home half the time by Colm.

"Whole streets gone," my brother usually snarled, hurt. "Bogside's been wiped away by the bastards."

I hadn't understood exactly what he meant, at the time, so responded with, "I doubt our old house could have been fixed up to be this fine."

But once I let my head stop thinking about the material and consider the ethereal, I could see he meant it was his past gone. His home was not just a house to live in, but the neighbors and streets and shops that were now becoming naught but memory.

There was even talk of a flyover taking off from Fahan *to speed traffic*, which meant more homes gone. Another neighborhood to be no more. No surprise it added to the sense of dislocation we all felt.

I realized that's what I'd been feeling, too, but had become too caught in making the place more than livable. So I'd let the thought drift away. Now I could understand how our old place, as awful as it was, had been his home. The new place hadn't settled in with him, yet.

Eamonn was often out consorting with Jackie, Aidan and others. He'd joined with a few other committees and now spoke of the planning for more demands and demonstrations that were to come. It was like that till the end of term and he was home, seeking work. We were back to sharing a bed, and I found I preferred being alone in it. Took me a week to become used to him there, every night, again. I almost shifted to Rhuari's and Kieran's bed, but that would have been even worse, with Kieran's restlessness.

I still snuck along with Eamonn to the meetings, whenever I could without Ma noticing. On one occasion, I saw Mrs. McKittrick trying to catch his eye, but he seemed not to realize. I found it hard to believe he hadn't.

Then the day before another meeting, she caught me on Abbey Street and pulled me to a corner, saying, "I-I'd like you to fix this." She unstrapped her wristwatch. "It's been sticking and slowing down, at times. What would you charge?"

"Won't know till I've seen it," I replied, glancing between her and the watch. I noticed she was barely paying me any mind, but was looking down Clíodhna at my house.

"Here's a crown," she said, pressing the coin into my hand. "If it's more, let me know. And when it's fixed, have your brother bring it to me."

"Mrs. McKittrick..."

She looked at me. "If he does, there's five pound in it, for you."

I didn't feel right about it, but I shrugged and she hurried away.

The watch was an old one, and the back was hard to get off, but all the inside needed was a touch of clearing up from corrosion. When I was done with it, I caught Eamonn just before he headed out and said, "If Mrs. McKittrick is with you, tonight, would you give her this? It's fixed, and she owes me nothing more."

He took it and eyed me, asking, "How so?"

"She paid me, and all it needed was some scraping, not much."

"She-she hasn't been coming, of late. You should take it to her. You know where she lives?"

I hesitated then shrugged. "Creggan? Somewhere?"

Then I coughed.

He noticed. Smiled to himself and nodded. "Yeah. If she comes, I'll give it to her." Then he took the watch and was gone.

I didn't follow him, this time. I had three things needing work, and my feeling was he'd not be coming straight home, anyway.

I heard him enter at near midnight and cross into the kitchen. Then silence. After what seemed like an hour, I slipped partway downstairs and looked over the banister to see him seated at the table. Smoking. A beer before him. Looking at nothing. His expression loose and unreadable. Almost like Da's had been, a few times. Lost in memories. Or maybe it was sad thoughts. I left him to himself. In the morning, a five-pound note was on my tools and Eamonn off already to whatever his plans were for the day.

Not a week later, Mrs. McKittrick left for London. The little information bandied about said she had both a sister there and a married son, to my surprise. But this is what happens when you don't listen to gossip; you miss out on other people's lives.

It's good she was gone before marching season started, for the air was thick with threats and anger, not only in Derry but in Belfast and a dozen other places, that I knew of. Paisley was stirring up his crowd, with the quiet backing of Chichester-Clark. Politicians always think they can manipulate people like pieces on a chess board and maintain control of them, but it never works that way. Paisley's crowd behaved like animals, thinking they could scare us, but all it did was inflame our side. We were finally at the point we would fight instead of talk.

The first explosion proving that was on 12 July, which wound up in riots in Belfast and elsewhere. People burned out of homes they'd lived in for generations. Lives ended for no gain. In Derry, Rossville Hall burned down, complete. I'm not ashamed to say I was part of this, along with Colm and Danny. Even Paidrig, who brought his nieces and nephews out to watch the fighting, tossed a few stones as he cried slogans to back us up. I caught a glimpse of wee Eammon looking out in wonder at it all as he took a shot of his inhaler. Then his mother's hand yanked him back from the window. I felt sorry for the lad.

Following that were weeks of blame assigned against the Catholics by the Protestants, and against the Protestants by Catholics, and against Paisley and his screeching against the Church, and against Chichester-Clark, and against the RUC, and against London, and each and every bit was warranted to some degree, in my eyes.

Still, all of this was naught but the lead-up to the hell on earth that was to wash over us all.

The Battle of Bogside

You always hear the drums first. Meant not only to announce the presence of our overlords but to laugh and intimidate. They echo through the whole town. Then come the fifes and bagpipes. Then you see the banners and flags held high and proud as they stride down Shipquay to Waterloo. With them, the Apprentice *Boys*— ugly men in their dark, plain, too-pressed suits, shirts starched to the strength of boxboard, most sporting bowlers atop their heads and brightly fringed sashes crossing their breasts, marching along in a manner that confused military precision with a Sunday stroll in the park. Many even held closed umbrellas, as if to add to the casual, condescending attitude they were trying so hard to show, all but screaming, *We may have jobs as poor as yours and may have homes as rotten as yours, but we are your masters, still.* And with the intent of proving that true, the RUC was out in force to keep an eye on the rabble surrounding the marching zone, rabble who'd always let the bastards pass with little more than an exchange of words.

Until this time.

This time would not be smooth, and they bloody well knew it. Anybody with a brain bloody well knew it. Oh, they made themselves jaunt, still, but with wary eyes darting about and movements that jerked and reeked of fear. Constantly so. And they held their heads high, of course, but there was such a tension to it, I thought a few of them would snap their necks if touched wrong. It was almost pathetic, how intent they were on showing us Papists they'd not be the least bit intimidated, even after almost a year's worth of back and forth.

I hadn't intended to be on Waterloo to heckle them, this year. I wanted to return a radio to Preston's and be paid before it began then back to home to finish readying Clíodhna Place for what was sure to be the evening's riot by the RUC. I'd also let the Keoghs and Haggertys know I'd do what I could for them; the Whites had sons enough to take care of themselves. But the crowds were thick and hard to pass, so I only barely made it to the Preston's shop before the rumble of the drums began drifting across the cool breeze.

I'd still have been done and out and back to Ma's except the Mrs. insisted on checking every channel on the radio to make sure I'd truly fixed it. As if I'd never done good work for them before. This wasn't the first time she'd felt the need to gently suggest I wasn't to be trusted, me being Catholic, but I'd let it pass, before. This time it rankled me, so I deliberately watched her do it.

Which she noticed because she then said, "Good job, as always," as she handed me a pound, like that would lessen the latest insult she'd so casually offered. So I decided right then to let her have Tully Gorman fix whatever next needed it and find out how much he charged for half the quality as me.

But with that taking twice the time it should have, I wound up caught on Waterloo behind crush barriers as the march came along. In truth, I could have worked around it all to get home, but I made little effort. After what had happened to Eamonn and Tur on the PD march and the vicious politeness I was being handed by people I'd been doing work for since I could first hold a set of grips, I felt an anger pouring out of my heart at this insult of a march, touched with an unwillingness to just send words the way of those bastards, this year. That their wives were gathered across the way, their own voices loud against ours, only added to the insult.

So jeers came from both sides, and I could feel the fury building. The constables who were there felt it, as well. Scuffles broke out as the black uniformed bastards jolted over to beat any Catholic who dared used too forceful of language to breach this public insult against human order. And some swung their batons for no more reason than to hit other lads.

But this time the crowd surged, in response, like some furious beast lunging at its tormentor. Many swore horrible things at them and stones flew across at their ranks. I'm not ashamed to say that some of them came from my hand. The release I felt as each flew into the air was exquisite. Like I'd been lifted to heaven, for a moment. I was that tom, howling and spitting and hissing against those dogs, and God help anybody once I decided to prove who really owned this fight.

Which was madness, for me! I'd never thought to physically strike back against the bloody Loyalists before this; but without a single thought I was grabbing for bricks like it's a part of my nature.

This one fat bastard struck an older man across the back a few times with his baton so I lugged half a brick at him. Hit him in his fat arse, meaning for sure I didn't hurt him, but he swung around and roared like a bull that's about to have a run at you and I danced back. Others in the crowd backed up, too. And that's when I looked about and saw the RUC was charging us, sticks waving in the air, and I was reminded of when they crashed into the October march.

But this time?

This time it's like we took the form of water and flowed off Waterloo past William and back into the Bogside, grabbing pieces of bricks and anything else we could find to toss. *Redevelopment* left us plenty to work with and we made full use of it. Older lads raced to the front of me and let fly with a thunderstorm of stones. I caught a glimpse of Eamonn with them. I called out to him but the howling and the yelling and the clattering of the bricks and rocks and clumps of metal raining down drowned out my voice.

To my shock, some Constables used their shields to gather rocks and bricks to ferry back to a pack of Paisleyites behind them, and they began firing at us, using catapults and smashing windows in the Flats. Those bastards thought to let those animals in to attack us? Not on your life.

That's when Jackie grabbed me and said, "Stay to the back of us. Build up piles of stones for us to use."

I roared back, "I can throw as well as—"

"You can't throw as far as us. We need ammunition to help us keep 'em out of the Bogside! And we're bloody keeping 'em out, this time!"

Jesus, the thrill I felt at his words. He was right; better to keep the bastards away from us than try to lessen the damage, so I yanked off my jacket and ran to a nearby lot and piled as many stones and bricks and bits of metal as I could carry in it then ran it back to where other lads were making piles, and saw Paidrig running up from another direction with more.

Paidrig! Actually doing something!

"Oi, me China!" I cried to him. He looked around, grinning like a madman. "Danny and Colm about?"

"Tossin' stones off William," he yelled back.

That was perfect. Both had the best arm of us and I was happy Danny was busy, for I'd had too little to send his way, of late and his moods had been returning.

People were running about, now. Some came to help. Some scurried home. Some dragged off their wains to be out of harm's way. I knew Ma and Mairead were with Rhuari, Maeve and Kieran so had no fear for them.

I kept piling up any-and-everything I could find to fire at the peelers. Wee Eammon appeared and helped me; when he started I've no idea, he just suddenly was there and we worked with nothing more than a grin between us, and only once did I see him use his inhaler.

But the rushing about seemed like chaos, or must have looked so to the constables since they came roaring in, again, arrogant in the certainty they were dealing with cowards and fools simply because they were chasing a few lads. And they were backed up by more of the Paisley bastards. But his time they found themselves met by yet another hail of stones and bricks from some of our side.

And petrol bombs!

They came down off the top of the Rossville Flats! Like glorious artwork, the trails of flame and smoke dancing through the air from on high them exploding in bright beauty on the broken pavement. More came at them from the sides and I think I howled for joy each time one burst alight near the peelers.

The bastards finally realized they'd been led into an ambush and hesitated, almost seeming lost. During this phase, I tossed more than a few stones, myself, and constables were suddenly scurrying back and helping mates away who'd been hurt, and acting like sheep caught in a storm even as they began tossing some of the stones right back at us, calling all of God's curses down on us as they did. I knew I was screaming for joy.

Then whispering over my head from behind me came another petrol bomb blazing in a milk bottle. It smashed to the ground a few feet from the nearest constable and he scrambled back with a scream, his pants leg ablaze. His mates quickly put it out and he ran back down William, his burned trousers flapping about his ankles. It was so comical, I laughed.

More bombs flew from our side and I howled even greater at the sight of it, because it meant for once the bloody bastards were outgunned! They were bloody outgunned! A thrill ran down me from head to toe and every moving part of my body. I truly shrieked to heaven from the pleasure of seeing it. For the first time, we were making them run and not the other way around.

Jackie rushed up with a basket of bottles, Aidan right behind him with canister of petrol, saying, "Can ya make more of these? D'ya know how?"

"Catch yourself on," I said back. Not know how to do it? Half petrol, a knotted rag inside, what more was needed doing to make it work? I found some old sheets in the bottom of the basket, so wee Eammon began tearing them into strips then knotting them. I poured petrol into the bottles and used a stick to shove the knotted end of a strip into each one and set them back in the basket. Other lads saw us doing it and sent the word around, and soon we had more raw materials to work from and more wee helpers. It was like an assembly line, for those we made vanished as soon as they were done, and a quick glance around showed there were other groups of wains making them. Some younger than Maeve; some with the help of their mothers.

Colm and Danny appeared. Dirty and near exhausted, they looked, as Danny said, breathless, "We're taking more up the Flats."

"They should be careful where they throw," I said, looking down William Street. "Some buildings're goin' up."

"Owned by Protestants," Colm snapped as they each grabbed a near full bucket of them.

"We don't know that!" I cried, but they were gone.

What could I do but get back to work?

Through the day, barricades were thrown together on the main streets, using wooden planks and wire and piles of dirt and massive slabs of stone that had to be carried by multiple lads. Soon after, cars and buses and lorries joined the piles, some set ablaze. The stench of burning rubber filled the air. Bands of both boys and girls kept up the barrage of rocks and bricks at the constables, taking turns to stay fresh and never letting up, even using our own catapults, at times. I never thought I'd bless the powers that be for their arrogance in redevelopment, but they provided us a never-ending supply of all we needed to keep the bastards back.

It went on and on like this, for hours and hours—back and forth and back and forth, like waves on the beach. The RUC flowing up only to be forced out. Again and again.

Then canisters flew at us, trailing evil smoke behind them. Smoke that set your eyes to screaming and tore into your lungs and made your stomach heave. CS gas! They thought this would show us, and it did take us by surprise. But some of the lads wrapped handkerchiefs over their nose and mouth and grabbed the spitting canisters and slung them back! And on top the Rossville Flats came more firebombs and stones and various other objects to crash down on the black-suited bastards, for try as they might their smoke bombs couldn't be shot that high.

But it did waft into homes and choke people on the ground, whether they were part of the fray or not. The sounds of coughing and crying of women and children mingled in with our shouts of fury as those at home closed their windows and stuffed rags under their doors to keep the smoke out. That didn't really work. The air filled with it, like a vile fog drifting slowly around, evil as black death. Trails of more canisters came at us and more canisters were slung back so the trails crisscrossed and smoke from our firebombs combined in it all to make it denser and more hideous.

I put a wet cloth over my nose and that helped my lungs and belly, but wee Eammon was caught up in a sharp asthma attack and had lost his inhaler, so I shoved him over to some women who were wetting more rags and raced up to his flat. I knew he had a spare.

His mother was in hysterics demanding to know where he was but I had no time for that; I bolted into his room, grabbed it and raced back down to him just as he was beginning to turn a soft shade of blue and the women around him were beginning to panic. He shot in a puff and began to grow better, so when he had some color back I guided him away from the worst of it, back into the clear, clean air up Creggan. After making sure, first, that the assembly line I'd set up was still hard at work.

I had to get him all the way to Demesne to be off from that stench and smoke. Then I saw Mairead waving to me from Tur's folks' place, Maeve and Rhuari with her. So there we went and I left him with them. He was doing better but not by much. Ma was at an upstairs window watching it all, Kieran in her arms. I looked around and could see down the hill to where the smoke was rising from the Rossville Flats, as if they were ablaze, and it was drifting this way. It had the look of the battlefields I'd seen painted in museums we'd visited. There was a Russian one—the Battle of Boro...something or other that seemed closest.

Mairead told me, "It's CS gas being used against us."

"Have you been hit by it?" I asked. She looked close to her time to deliver, and I wondered if it might affect the wain.

"No, we come up here 'fore that started. There's a report on the radio the Irish Army's settin' up a hospital camp across the border. If it comes to be, Ma and I'll take all of the wains over to be checked, and myself, as well."

"Aren't they coming to help us?" I cried.

"No one knows," she said, looking down the hill. "They keep sayin' one thing then the opposite."

"Blood fucking cowards," shot out of me.

"Brendan!" Mai was shocked at my words. "Does Eammon's mother know where he is?"

I shook my head, too angry to respond.

"She needs to," she said.

"Well, there's no time to tell her, now," I said the moment I finished a glass of water. I also grabbed a hunk of bread.

"How're you doin'?"

I huffed. "I'm well enough. I'll put a mask on when I'm back. I heard one soaked in vinegar is good against it."

"That won't work."

"Better'n nothing." Then I raced down the hill back into the fray.

It kept on like this for the whole night and the next day. More CS gas. Rubber bullets fired. Charges by the RUC beaten back. Sometimes supported by more Loyalists. Probably B-Specials. But they were looking more and more ragged and weary.

Again and again and again, we held the line. Catapults were built and passed about to use to fire stones. I kept building firebombs with a pack of women who were gossiping about reinforcements coming for the RUC from Antrim and Belfast. Others said fresh packs of B-Specials were massing down by Guildhall to come in with guns holding real bullets even as Protestant paramilitaries planned to sneak in behind us and attack the rear. And there was no more word of the Irish Army coming to save us. This added fear, yes, but also fueled our anger.

A radio broadcast coming from somewhere in the Flats filled us in on the news reports from Ireland and England and Europe and the States. Reports of riots in other cities across the North. Information on how to handle the CS. Where we could find tea and sandwiches and water to keep us sustained. And music. Sharp and tinny and mainly Irish fight songs, and sounding so lovely. It swelled my heart to hear it.

One set of rabble did think to use the walls to get better leverage at firing onto the roof of the Flats but found that only opened them to greater attack. Same for other packs who thought they could score some fun off us by slinging stones at us from the walls only to find the dilapidated roofs of Nailors Row were just as tall and had lads atop them to fire back, slinging slates and tiles like deadly cutting boomerangs. That sent them scampering. It was the chaos of a true battle. Civil war begun in earnest. And while we might not be winning, by keeping those bastards out we sure as hell weren't losing.

Several people showed up to help strategize the resistance, the only one I recognized for sure being Bernadette Devlin because she had been in the papers. They pulled together proper barricades and spread even better information about how best to combat the CS and saw to it the elderly and young were taken across the border to get away from it all and better protect their frail health. By the beginning of the third day we were better set up than the RUC, who'd taken only to slinging our rocks back at us as if they were out of ammunition.

I'd been able to get home despite the clouds of gas and smoke and pull what I had in my stash and give it over to the organizers for more petrol. Then I showed Paidrig how I'd been building firebombs as more and more bottles appeared for us to use. Paidrig had grown weary so reverted to his usual self, slow and steady, putting me behind as I shifted from filling bottles to tearing cloth to knot. Until Danny appeared, looking exhausted but happy, a soft cackle coming from him that was spooky. As was his focus on making the bombs, for he did three in the time it took me for one, and six in place of Paidrig.

"Have a care, Danny," I said. "They need to hold till they land."

He flashed me a grin of—well, what I can only call diabolical joy and said, "They'll hold well enough."

Then he and Paidrig had carted off our latest basket full.

Rumors continued to race about that the B-Specials had massed for a final assault with backing from the UVF, in full force. I doubted that; our own little radio station was saying there had been nothing confirmed or evidence provided of it. It also confirmed the riots in Belfast and other towns, begun in sympathy, were also out of control. Glorious news backed up by the BBC and Radio Ireland. That would keep the bastards busy. As for breathless claims by Stormount and London of assistance from the IRA, no one knew anything about help from them. Christ, we had even given up on the Irish Republic. At least the latter had set up that hospital camp, and when I finally saw Tur he told me Ma, Mairead and the wains were over there with wee Eammon.

That is when I headed up to let his mother know where he was. She screamed and slapped me for keeping it from her for so long then stormed out in her robe and slippers, but not without her purse, leaving her door open.

I shut it for her.

Then I looked down at Waterloo. What I could see past the side tower block. I heard distant shouting echo up through the courtyard. Cries of anger. Cries of pain. Cries of laughter. The pop of petrol bombs. The clatter of bricks and CS cannisters. From up here, it was like a living photo of some lost city in some lost civilization being sacked, emphasized by the drifts of smoke whispering around. Some came off the burning vehicles; some from now ruined buildings; some from petrol bombs being thrown and gas being shot at us, still; some from God only knows where.

I was the only one on the walkways. I caught bits of movement atop the tower to my left. Caught hands whipping stones and petrol bombs over the side and down as the RUC, even though they were hardly about, by now. It was too unreal for me. The space we'd fought so hard to preserve for ourselves suddenly looked tiny and meaningless, almost empty. I had not a clue as to how we could keep it, and a moment of despair washed over me.

At the end of this, nothing would have been achieved. Nothing changed. Nothing ended. It was only a momentary respite, where we finally demanded our right not to be treated as slaves and beasts but as human beings. And if it took bringing hell to those around us, so be it. Until hell died down and we saw what remained. And finally let our minds wonder if it had been worth it.

Yes, we'd proven we could be strong. We'd heard snippets of how tight the RUC was stretched and shown that if we truly wanted things to change, we could force it. Even if only by burning it to the ground to rebuild, like a phoenix. But there was also word of people being burned out of house and home in Belfast, again, by Protestant mobs in a sort of pogrom. Driven away by those they'd lived around for generations. That was how one broadcaster put it, but I'd need to look it up; I had no real understanding of the word.

No. No, Aidan had told me it was what was done to Jews in Russia, forcing them to leave their homes for new places. Run them off, like vermin. Yes, I remembered, now. And here, it was clear to me that one good push by fresh constables and we would be done the same, lose that little toehold we'd kept in our own city.

I wandered along the walkway. The elevators weren't working, of course. Part of the fight against us to lower our will. Electricity was occasional, at best. There had also been threats to cut off our water, but we met that with a promise if it was done then we would cut off the gas to the whole of Derry. The idiots had positioned its works within the Bogside. But wasn't that was the true basis of negotiation? Don't threaten me for I'll threaten right back.

Which only worked if you had the ability to do so.

It was seven flights down to the courtyard. Or eight. I couldn't remember, just then. I was too tired. Too unfocused to even think about it.

Till I reached the group I was part of.

The stories had changed.

Westminster was sending troops. Sending the bloody army! Soon verified by radio reports. None of us liked the sound of that. Not a one. Too many of us knew how the British had been when dealing with the Irish far too often in the last three-hundred years, so we didn't trust they were coming to keep the peace. But did we have strength enough left to fight them? No one wished to state the obvious, aloud.

I found Colm and Danny by Rossville, just looking around. Exhausted into a sort of stupor. Tommy, Connor and Brian Boru-to-yous had made it in to help, along with others from Shantalow I only vaguely knew. Jackie and Aidan were talking with them. Eamonn was seated on a barricade, half asleep from exhaustion.

So it was nearly over.

It was nearly done.

We had fought well.

And I felt nothing about it, now. Not even despair. Just blank and those thoughts in my head.

Then suddenly.

Suddenly.

Suddenly there was silence.

Complete stillness.

Too much so.

I started to cough, nervous for the first time.

The smoke whispered away, like a ghost, and I could see all the way to Waterloo Place. From down here the street looked like a country road there were so many rocks and stones across it. But the barricades were holding. Buildings that had been ablaze were now carcasses, still smoking. The air stank from the gas and lorries and busses destroyed by flames, some with still-burning tires. Why hadn't I understood much of the smoke I'd seen from above was due to them?

Or had I? My mind…

I couldn't speak, my throat was so caught by the foul air. I found even the thought of food made my stomach quiver in refusal. My fingers were torn and bloody. I'd not changed clothes since the beginning, so my trousers were rags and my shirt and jacket were ruined. I was bloody exhausted, having caught only bits of sleep and a bite of cheese and bread here and there, between battles. And a sup of milk? Or tea? I wasn't sure, but I doubted the latter; they'd make it too strong for me. I thought for a moment maybe, just maybe, I should go home and wash and dress in clean clothes to greet the end looking like a man and not vermin.

But I dared not leave. That would be desertion. It was like the calm before a storm, with such a sudden terrifying silence. Not a word from the constables. No curses from the Prods. Not even calls from lads on our side. Not a whisper.

We were down on the number of bottles and petrol to be used. There were still rocks a-plenty and our own homemade cudgels and bats. We had built a fine number of catapults from wood scrap, so we could still mount a decent fight. But the truth was, a fair portion of the silence was from our side, with people not sure what would come next.

Finally, we heard the rumble of lorries approaching.

And stopping.

Finally followed by marching feet.

Growing closer.

Closer.

Closer.

We held ready. Waiting. Fearing this might be the end. Fresh reinforcements against our ragged lot? We stood not a chance.

Then we saw the Army stride in, proud and sure. Rifles on their shoulders and in formation. So here it came. God only knew what would happen.

Except...

Except they had caps on their heads and not helmets.

And some carried bundles of razor wire.

And they stopped and calmly used that wire to make barricades between us and the RUC.

And stayed there.

They stayed there.

They bloody stayed there!

Facing the RUC!

Keeping us apart!

They were bloody keeping us apart!

Some began to howl for joy. Some wept from relief. Colm and Danny were pounding on each other, screaming and laughing. I was frozen. Couldn't believe it. Just stood where I was and stared at the soldiers for I don't know how long, letting it settle slowly into my brain that I could finally take a good long wash, have a decent sleep—and now get around to working on Mrs. O'Connor's wall clock. I'd promised it to her for yesterday.

I wandered through all of those thoughts before I could let myself understand and accept that, by all the saints that are holy, we had won.

The army had made itself a barrier between us and the Loyalists, they really had!

They were saying our right to Derry was now established.

They would keep the Proddys from our homes and families and hold back the worst of their threats.

We.
Had.
Beaten.
The.
Fucking.
Loyalists.
We had fucking won!

Fleadh

I staggered home, had another bite of cheese and bread with a glass of milk from Mrs. McCrory, took a lovely bath that I near dozed off in, and fell into the best sleep of my life. I woke to find Eamonn deep in slumber, beside me, half undressed. It was obvious he had not made it to the bath, first, but his face had such a peaceful glow to it, despite the grime and days of growth to his beard, I could only smile.

I carefully slipped over him, dressed and went downstairs, where Aidan was curled up on the settee, draped in a sheet and what looked like, from the bare leg sticking out with its foot on the floor and a still wet towel caught partly around it, not a touch of clothing. A vague snore whispered from him. Too bad we didn't still have the divan.

I heard noises from the kitchen so slipped in to find Ma and Mairead quietly working up our supper, and despite Mairead's belly they didn't knock into each other.

Ma eyed me. "So his majesty's finally up."

"Where'd you get all this?" I asked.

"Brought it back with us," said Mairead.

"Was it you left that ring in the tub?" Ma snapped.

"No, Ma, it was Tur and Aidan. And I've cleaned it, already, so no worries when Eamonn comes back to life."

"You? In your condition?"

"I'm not cripple yet."

"So how's wee Eammon?" I asked, quick and a bit sharp, casting a hard glance at Ma.

Mairead smiled at me. "The doctors gave him a shot of adrenalin and a fresh inhaler, so he's well and good." Then she sighed. "His mother, however..."

"Yes," Ma nodded. "The less said about her, the better."

"And Tur?" I asked.

"Asleep in the hutch. I'll wake him when we're ready. Like a cuppa?"

It took me a moment to understand what she asked, it was so calm and normal, like before the battle. All I could do was nod and sit at the table, silent, and watch my mother and sister prepare a feast fit for a king.

This was like the world should be. Simple and warm and peaceful and filled with lovely aromas and-and home. When Mairead put a cup of tea next to me—steaming hot, light and with a splash of milk—I knew there'd be sugar in it. She was good about that. And-and-and suddenly everything welled up inside me and I took it and got up and headed into the garden.

I was at the door when Ma snapped, "Where d'ya think—?"

Mairead cut her off with, "Bren, I think the containers of herbs could use tending. They've not been checked for days."

The other side of the hutch. Bless Mairead. I nodded and slipped out to the sound of Ma snarling, "Don't ruin more of your clothes or—!"

"Bring us some thyme, Bren. And some parsley, for garnish. We'll do it up as a celebration dinner."

I made it 'round to hide behind the hutch and crouch, and held the hot cup in my hands as my breath rushed in and out of me, short and sharp. I was able to keep quiet, though I shook from everything inside me. It took a few moments but it finally passed and-and I felt—I dunno—happy. Hopeful and at ease. The warmth of the cup in my hands. The soft steam drifting up to my face. I did not want to move for fear I'd lose this sense of—sense of calm. Finally, I managed to sip some tea and it brought me back to the moment. I drank more then pulled up a few small weeds, found the soil was wet so needed no more water and pulled off some herbs for Mairead.

And I got not a spot on me.

By the time grub was up, Eamonn was awake and washed, and Aidan was dressed, and we crowded ourselves around the expanded table, Rhuari on Eamonn's lap, Maeve on Tur's and Kieran on Ma's. I finally learned Aidan was of the Dunns down Lecky Road. I knew his oldest nephew, so it was right he was with us. We spoke little, for words were unnecessary, at the moment, but we did feast better than ever we had.

What was best?

Throughout our meal, the Bogside was in silence. You still could smell the smoke from fires, touched with the CS gas, but the breeze was slowly pushing it away and the quiet was so heavenly I cared not for anything but just to sit and let it be.

It remained so for days. The RUC skulked away with their tails between their legs, not only here but in Belfast and Antrim and a dozen other spots around the country. The army remained in place, setting up checkpoints to counterpoint our own, still without word one from the IRA. The soldiers even walked about, casual and sure, happy to accept tea and cakes from the ladies as they passed. It was all so pleasant and unreal.

Ma and the wains were excited by the new sense of control in our spot of the world, but Jackie still felt wary. Of course we only talked of this with Eamonn, Aidan and Tur, in the hutch. I said little, proud enough that I was allowed to be part of the discussion.

Jackie had a cousin who was a solicitor in Belfast and who had connections at Stormount, so he was a font of awareness.

"There's still fighting in Belfast and Armagh," he said, "and families are still being driven from their homes, there."

"Now the Army's seein' what we've had to deal with all our lives," Eamonn said.

"A poetic sort of justice, that," Aidan laughed.

"But aren't people still being killed?" I asked. I'd heard Tommy telling this to Colm, and both were livid.

Eamonn just nodded as Aidan said, "More proof Paisley's thugs are of the devil, and always will be."

And enough said about that.

Then a communiqué was put out after a meeting between the British Government and Stormount swearing there'd be no change in our Constitution without the consent of our Parliament, which we knew would never come. Wilson was interviewed everywhere and said the same nonsense to all. *Still more to discuss. No end to partition. The B-Specials are not under our jurisdiction so will be dealt with by others. This is a temporary deployment of troops to guarantee peace and security. Chichester-Clark warmly agreed to the changes requested by our side.* On and on so much, even the most tolerant of us suspected this was merely a gargle of words meaning nothing. As it always was. So our wariness was not lowered and our guard remained up.

It was Mairead who first brought us talk of a celebration, a Fleadh being worked up by Eamonn McCann and Mary Holland. "Like a victory dance," she said.

"We're not victors, yet," Jackie snapped.

"Arra, it's good to have fun and relax," Tur replied. "Let people see some fruits of their labor, and what could be better than that?"

"But my cousin says Stormount is already workin' to turn the Army against us."

"I'm not saying we shouldn't prepare for that," said Eamonn, "but no need to start trouble before we must. People are weary, and time to rebuild would be nice."

That's when I piped in with, "Won't this help make us more of a community, again?"

"We are a community," Aidan laughed.

"Even with redevelopment breaking us up, all over?"

Jackie nudged my shoulder, smiling. "Bren's got a point. Those in the Guildhall did all they could to separate us as friends and neighbors, thinking it would weaken us. Sending some off to Shantalow, others went to Creggan and even more up Springtown Road."

"And those damned flats," Aidan nodded with a growl.

"We showed them it didn't work; we can still fight back. But a fleadh does help us reconnect in ways pleasant and not from shared anger."

Jackie leaned back. "I like the idea. I know some lads're quite put out at the IRA's lack of show during this. Might give us time and cover to make plans, anew. Let the Prods think we're silly and childish still. Then he added with a wicked smile, "Even as we do prepare for the future."

Which even brought a smile to Aidan's face.

So the committee arranging the fleadh set its date for the last weekend of the month. Our new slogan was *Derry Merry, Derry Free*, and a gable wall by a wide, open area off Lecky was fresh-painted with *You are now entering Free Derry*. Our own declaration of independence.

A number of bands came in from the Republic. Irish dances were set up of girls in costume and perfect harmony. Music flowed not only from about every corner but from within some homes. The Dubliners. Tommy Makem to beautifully sing *Four Green*

Fields. Toffee apples off Wellington Street, though I never partook, in those; I liked apples and toffee, but not together. Donkey rides. Balloons. Pots of steaming food. Grills ablaze. It was a true fest...including how some Protestant lads tried to sneak in, possibly just to enjoy themselves but more likely just to disrupt the fun, so roving bands of lads were set up to keep an eye out for anyone unknown.

I wore my finest trousers, jumper, sports jacket and tie topped by my Apollo 7 cap, and me Chinas and I just wandered through it all, taking it all in. Even wee Eammon and his Ma came down to partake of the joyousness. Crowds flowing here and there. Some stopping to listen to the music or speakers or people just telling tales of old, like Da used to.

An odd emotion filled me, over them, for I knew without question if he had been here, still, he'd have been swilling a pint and weaving his magic with words. Telling his stories from atop a platform. Mesmerizing those who listened as completely as he had the men in the pub, no matter how jumbled they were. For the first time, I almost felt sorry he wasn't around.

Almost.

*****

Just past one on the second day of the fleadh, I was leaning against the *Free Derry* gable, my eyes closed and listening to a piper play *Dreams of Galway*, feeling so real. Colm, Paidrig and Danny had partaken of the toffee apples and were not doing well, and I hadn't seen wee Eammon all day, so I was all to myself and loving it. Catching glimpses of people I knew milling about. Hearing craic that was happy and quick. It was like a bright new world for us all. As if we all were to ourselves, alone, apart from the rest of Ireland, with prayers and dreams and hopes and promises aplenty, building our world anew. I was thinking, *This is how it should always be* and—

"I know this hat!" jolted me as my cap was grabbed off my head.

I spun around.

It was Joanna!

Laughing with those friends of hers, showing them my cap! She wore bellbottoms and a light jacket, and her hair danced in the breeze as she spun about and set it on her head and looked so much like an angel it hurt me.

"I've never seen it before," said the girl closest to her, a round pale thing that looked like a marshmallow in her white dress, stockings and shoes.

"In Woolworth's," she said. "Caught him sneaking a look at us. Shy and sweet."

She pinched my cheek. I was still so shocked, I could think of nothing to say.

"You're not one for words, are you?" she continued, smiling.

I glanced around. A couple people were eyeing her, curious looks on their faces. She wasn't known and could soon be asked to verify her right to be here.

I finally found enough voice to ask, "How'd you get here?"

"On the bus," she said, then they dissolved into giggles.

I kept my words soft. "But the checkpoints..."

The marshmallow said, "I've a cousin lives in Ballymena so said we all lived there, and no one stopped us."

"Helps to bat your eyes at the soldiers, it does," said the other friend, who resembled the pop star, Lulu, made more-so by how her face was made up. I realized Joanna wore only lip-gloss and a dash of powder, her skin was so clear and bright, and she had the air of mint about her. Spearmint. Yes, spearmint.

Like I'd chewed to hold the glass in our old home's windows!

I grinned, stupidly, at the thought.

But then I saw Jackie, Aidan, and a couple other lads from Creggan moving toward us. I feared they'd be unhappy some Protestant girls had snuck into our fleadh, so I waved to them and said as loud as I could, "Here, Jackie, some birds I met in Claudy!"

The Lulu said, "I've never been—"

I turned, smiling, and shot a quiet, "Whist," at her.

Joanna caught on and turned her smile on Jackie. "We heard there's a fleadh and came to see. It's lovely."

Marshmallow had a bit of fear in her eyes as she nodded, unable to speak.

Jackie wasn't ready to accept it, yet. "What's your name?"

"McGillicuty," shot out of me. "Jo, Mary and Lulu. They're cousins—nieces of Mrs. McKenna on Little James."

"The army let ya pass?" snarled one of Jackie's mates, a big bruiser of a thick lad with a voice like a growling wolf.

Joanna stepped around me and went straight to him, her smile growing near wicked as she touched his chin and said, "Why wouldn't they? The soldiers are boys, just like you, and how does any girl get around them?"

He blushed. The big bastard actually blushed.

I huffed and put some bite into my voice. "Jo, you said you'd not do that around me."

She stepped back and adjusted my cap further back on her head, still smiling. "Now, don't be such a baby."

Lulu giggled, despite herself.

Jackie took a look at her and his face softened. "So you're enjoyin' yourself, then?"

Lulu took on an attitude I couldn't quite make out as she said, "I've seen no reason not to, yet."

Jackie made a move towards her but I put myself between them, without a thought, and said, "Now Jackie, these girls aren't of age, and I promised to keep watch over them."

"You?" said Thick.

"Aye. It's not like we need worry about the peelers or lads from Waterside trying to make trouble with our lasses, is it? I'm here as their-their—"

Joanna wrapped her arm around mine and sighed, "I told my aunt we didn't need a chaperone, but she didn't believe us."

"You must be someone special," said Aidan, "for our Bren to let you wear his cap."

"She is," popped out of me before I could think to stop it.

She beamed at me, placed the cap back on my head, and it was my turn to blush.

Jackie laughed. "Keep a good watch on 'em, Bren. Show 'em the kind of man you are."

Then with a wink, he and his mates wandered off.

I turned to Joanna and her friends and said, "He might well check with Mrs. McKenna and be sore pissed when he finds out we lied to him. C'mon, I'll get you to home."

"But we only just arrived," said Lulu.

"Yeah, you're right, we should wander around a bit, first. Not leave too quick."

"What about you?" Joanna asked. "Won't he come for you?"

"I'll worry about that when it happens."

I didn't really think Jackie would care enough to do it. Even if he did, I'd be able to explain it away as my mistake, so he'd not be hard with me. But it did make me feel quite the man about town by acting all concerned for their safety. What's best is, I saw what I'm sure was a hint of respect in Joanna's eyes.

So we listened to more music. During one bit, they danced their jig and many around us clapped at how good they were. We had a bite to eat and orange crush, and Lulu was after having a toffee apple, but they were in the middle of preparing a new batch so it was forgotten. Just as it was starting to grow chill we headed for the bus depot.

I said little as the girls chattered about Aiden. Lulu was quite taken with him while Marshmallow thought them all crude and in need of a shave. Joanna just cast me a knowing smile.

It's funny, but me having on my NASA cap, wearing my finer clothes and escorting three girls out of the Bogside apparently gave us *an aura of respectability*, as Marshmallow, put it. We were asked a few short questions at the Waterloo checkpoint then allowed past. We caught a bus across from the Guildhall, grandly paid for by me, and headed back to the Waterside.

We hopped off on Irish Street and headed up through an area of nice semi-detached homes with gardens and flowers and nearly new cars parked in front. Some lads the girls knew were milling about in an open space and called to them in ways I found unpleasant, but they got ignored. We turned down a lane with no outlet and went straight to the house at the head, where I recognized the estate car in the drive. Joanna's mum and brother came out the door to watch us approach.

"Where have you girls been?" she asked, her voice sounding far too much like wee Eammon's mother's. "We've been looking all over for you. Who's this with you?"

Before any of them could speak I said, "I'm Billy Corrie of the Fountain, ma'am. I saw the ladies as I was coming off the train and thought it best to escort them home." And I made myself sound very grand as I said it.

Her mother smiled, wary. "Do you know each other?"

"We met in Woolworth's, not long ago. In the music department."

"Looking at albums, he was," said Joanna.

Her mother's smile turned indulgent, and she nodded.

"Thank you, Billy. How kind."

Lulu and Marshmallow cast a giggle at each other, said their bye's and scurried off to nearby houses, leaving me and Joanna alone.

She smiled at her mother in all innocence, asking, "Mum, have you done supper yet?"

"We were about to start without you," was her reply, a bit of irritation behind it. Then Joanna gave her a questioning look. The woman hesitated then nodded and turned to me. "Would you care to join us, Billy?"

Eat with them? That, I was not so certain about. But Joanna was now looking at me, waiting for me to give an answer, so I said, "That'd be-that'd be smashin'." Copying a saying from a program on the telly.

So in I was invited into a home that looked like an advert for fine furnishings, it was so neat and clean and properly placed. I was given a quick introduction to her father, then Joanna took me down a hall to the toilet, her eyes dancing with laughter. At the basin, she made a motion of washing her hands. I grinned, pleased beyond anything that she'd remembered when first I saw her.

As we came out, I noticed her brother was watching us, wary and cool in manner. That made me uncomfortable, but I did my best to ignore it.

Well, we had roasted chicken, potatoes and string beans. On real China. So just to show off, I accepted a leg and ate it with a knife and fork. Much to the delight of her parents.

Their last name was Martin, with her brother a Charles. Her mother had changed little since the one time I'd seen her, and her father was the lady's compliment. He owned a menswear shop off Irish Street and he was doing quite well, from all appearances. Her friends' real names were Angela, for Marshmallow, and Louisa, for Lulu. They went to the same school and had been friends since forever.

I told them I'd just *been coming back from spending the day with my aunt in Castlerock and her four orange cats.* A lie like that is best if based on someone you knew. I also told of how I fixed things. Of course, that's when Mrs. Martin mentioned a toaster she'd had forever but now didn't work on one side.

I asked to see it, and it took me but a minute to see a connector had broken its solder. Of course, I had my grips and turnscrew on me, and Mr. Martin had a soldering stick in his shed, so I put it back together, right there and at no charge. They were well-impressed, and I was so very proud of myself.

The one worrisome thing during this was Charles. As I was taking the toaster apart, he mentioned, "I know a Ronald Corrie in the Fountain."

Shite.

I just grinned and said, "That's me uncle, and a lazier man you'll never meet. If he even sees a speck of work to be done, he's off the other direction."

Which brought a laugh from all and a near smile from himself. Still, he did not stop looking at me.

Which I continued to ignore.

It was twilight when I took my leave. Her Da offered to run me home, but I insisted on taking the bus, so Joanna walked me to the curb, her Da watching.

She quietly asked, "How did you learn to eat like that?"

"Just something I picked up," said with full bravado.

"You pick up a lot of things, *Brendan*. Like girls at a Fleadh." Then she winked at me.

I felt so happy, I asked, "May I write you?"

"I don't see why not. So long as you don't lie to *me*."

"Never will," I grinned, then I nodded and headed off with my hands in my pockets, strutting like I had not a care in the world, even as I kept a soft watch on the lads who were still milling about. They let me pass, their eyes wary on me, but I guess I seemed too sure of myself to be thought of as a Catholic in the Protestant area.

I was almost to Irish when I heard a car race up behind me. I spun to look and it was that bloody estate car, with Charles driving, some of the lads from the street with him. He near hit me with the damn thing, trying to block me against a hedge, then they burst from the car. I was grabbed and slung against a back door and a body pressed hard against me.

It was Charles's voice that snarled, "The bus depot. I knew I'd seen you before. You're a bloody taig."

"You sure of this, Charlie?" came the other's voice. "Fountain's in the Bogside."

"He's neat, for a paddy," came as I heard more feet run up.

"And the hat," said the first. "Since when do papists have money enough to go to NASA?"

"He's a dirty fuckin' taig, I tell yous!" he howled as he punched me in the side, near knocking the breath from me. "Playin' in the gutter and now sniffin' after my sister!"

Charles's mates were crowding in. I had to do something to stop them, now, now, now.

My turnscrew was in my jacket pocket. I managed to pull it out just as Charlie punched me in the side, again, and the other one took me by the chin. Then I jammed it back into Charlie's groin.

He howled more from shock than pain. That startled them all, but gave me the chance to slip out from under their grip.

And run.

Two of the lads chased me as Charlie howled in anger and I heard him get back in the car. I raced down Irish and saw there was a bus just ahead, about to pull away but going the wrong direction. Still, I ran faster and jumped aboard. I doffed my cap as it pulled away, crouched down in a seat and saw the estate wagon race by. Seemed they'd not seen me board the bus.

It was headed for Altnagelvin, very much the wrong direction, but I didn't care. I jumped off at the hospital then hid behind a bench to watch if they'd followed me. I think I saw them drive past but not pull in, so I caught the next bus back to Guildhall. By then it was dark and I was calm, again.

My cap back on my head, I went through the checkpoints, the Army's and our own, with little trouble. Just name and address. Then I went straight home.

Everything was quiet. I got the feeling Ma and the others were still down at the Fleadh. So I took a chair into the back and sat by the herbs behind the hutch and gazed up at the stars.

And let it all settle in on me.

My side ached; I'd been lucky to get away only that. And I noticed that not once had I coughed during any of it. Nor had I cried from fear or pain or begged to be left alone. I had worked my way out of a hideous situation, all on my own. After strutting into the middle of Protestant territory. Into the middle of the Waterside. Surrounded by my enemies. And I'd come out in one piece. Of course, Charlie would tell everyone who and what I was, so I'd be a fool to consider going back to see Joanna, ever again.

But bloody hell, wasn't she worth being a fool over?

Joanna

It wasn't long after that the No-Go areas of Derry and Belfast were recognized by Stormount, so the British Army dismantled the last of our barricades and used stripes of paint in their place. Callaghan came to visit, a couple times, and Jack Lynch, Taoiseach of the Republic, made a long speech that meant nothing and said less. Through this, it was the Loyalists giving the government trouble, including setting bombs, being the first to kill a constable and getting killed by British troops. It was as if the world were upside down.

But in Derry, life continued as ever. Redevelopment never stopped. People went to work, including Paidrig's sisters-in-law to Hogg and Mitchell's. Food and merchandise came in and was bought by those who could afford it. The dole continued. The post office and credit union kept on. There were plays at school, and competitions and sporting events. Weddings were had and families begun.

Mairead's first, Michael Paul, arrived mid-October. We were banished to the Devlins' during the birth, as Mai was set up in Ma's room and the midwife brooked no curious children. Once he came forth and was wrapped, he was shown to us all in the parlor as Mai slept, upstairs. Tiny, wrinkled and pink, with ginger hair like his Da. Moaning like a kitten.

"You was this size once," the midwife told us. "Look at yous now. Little monsters, all."

Ma took over the baby and seemed like a child, herself, around the wee lad, wistful and kind and caring like I'd never seen her, even with Kieran. Tending to him as if he were her own, and only passing him off to Mai when time to nurse. It was a bit unsettling.

I still had my steady customers in the No-Go area, but passing the checkpoints, even as minimal as they were, made it much harder to get on with people down around Waterloo and up the

Strand Road. But Tur and his father sent enough work my way, and a kind word to Mr. McClosky at his auto repair got me on part time to clean the shop, pump petrol, and make an occasional fix-it, after classes; I was considered too young to be trusted enough with more, but it brought in a few quid, a week.

The problem with that was how Ma knew Mrs. McClosky and knew exactly how much my pay was, so she'd query Mairead on what I'd given over to her, that week. I let Mai know I was fine with her handling Ma's nosiness with the truth, because I'd keep most of what other money I brought in, and I built two more hiding spots for it, to the point I was back to having near thirty pounds by the end of the year.

Of course, one and all complained about the checkpoints, saying over and over that it was *like going to another country*, as I heard Mrs. Rafferty put it to Ma.

"What can you expect from the British," Ma half chuckled, in response. "Simplicity? Making life easier?"

"But they're such lovely lads," Mrs. McCrory had added. "So polite and kind and willin' to help. I find it so nice they're here and keepin' us safe from the peelers."

All had to agree it was far better than dealing with the whims of the RUC, so they continued to hand out tea and cakes to soldiers passing by, almost like they were after something more.

Father Jack had been in America through much of the trouble, handling a family illness that became a death. His father. Until this, I hadn't known he was American. He seemed unchanged, except for a bit of gray around his ears, and he was sorry that he's missed the Battle of Bogside, as it was now called, and the Fleadh.

"I watched some of it on the nightly news," he told us during his first sermon back. "As I sat next to my father's bed. Saw people I know fighting for their freedom with little more than sticks, stones and fire. It was very inspiring."

Of course, later in the sermon while still praising the chance for peace he warned we should be prepared, in case more troubles were ahead. He seemed very careful in his words, almost like he wasn't completely happy violence didn't erupt on a daily basis in Derry, now he was back.

That's not to say there was none, but it was not enough for his liking, was my thought. I'd have stopped attending but Ma was still in her *Look at all my responsibilities as I march them off to mass* attitude, and even dragged Mairead along, more often than not, wee Michael wrapped tight against the cold. So it was a full requirement.

Eamonn, Jackie and Aidan were all back to Queens and not home so much, till Christmas. Then they spent most of their time with other lads and some scurvy characters from Belfast and Newry, whom I did not want to know. What bothered me was how Colm seemed a natural part of their pack now but never once offered me an introduction. I knew a couple were from what he referred to as his *old days* of smuggling. As if that were not still happening. The border was open and easy, despite the Brits, and Colm never forgot me when he had Blues available.

For a price, China or no.

As for Paidrig, he always seemed to know when Colm was back with his treasure trove, but still never put in a penny, that I could tell.

At the same time, Danny was all but *my* apprentice in fixing things. His fair looks and innocent eyes made it easier for him to slip over to the Waterside, so I showed him a few simple repairs and let him keep all but ten percent of what he made. He also helped me start preparing shopkeepers for decimalization. The change-over was beginning and some shopkeepers were having trouble understanding how the new coins and values equaled the old, despite the government's letters and pamphlets. I worked with the older men, for Danny refused to even talk with them, but he seemed to melt the older ladies' hearts and they took in every word he said. For that, I let him keep all of what service rate he got. It was never much, but he seemed quite happy to have coin he'd earned in his pocket. His father was doing better in his job and his moods, while they still could get dark and silent, were fewer than usual.

Of course, Charlie reported to his parents who and what I was, so no question I'd not be welcome coming to their door to ask Joanna out. And I did not see her around town, after that. I found out her number and called a couple of times, but every time it was her mother who answered and I had to bark a gruff, "Sorry." Then ring off.

I did write her a letter and put it in an early Christmas card. Only I didn't dare use my return address; that could cause all manner of trouble. For the first time in my life, I wished I had someone I could talk to and confide in, but I knew better than to ask Eamonn, for he could not keep a secret, and none of me Chinas were adult enough to help. They would make a full riot over me being after a girl, let alone if they suspected she was Protestant. Which would only be fair, since we'd all mocked Colm for having a different girl every weekend. And I could carry her being a Catholic from Claudy only so far, should anyone ask.

But then I overheard Mr. Curran from up the road telling a mate, "I use my work address for the return, never home."

"I don't even put one," was the reply. "And I have me sister post it, from Newry. No tracin' me that way."

Well. That was the answer, dropped down to me from heaven above. I hurried up to my room and spent the rest of the day writing the letter. Over and over and over, must have been a hundred times before I settled on:

Hi, it's Billy Corrie, "as known." I know I have no right to ask this, but I wonder if you'd like to have tea with me, sometime? Like at the Diplomat? Just to chat. Nothing special. But I did enjoy the day we had, and hope you did, too. Sincerely, Brendan— Kinsella (my real name) PS Here's my real address if you want to reply.

And I used McClosky's as the return address, on the envelope.

I'd met a couple of lorry drivers so asked one if he'd post the card from Belfast. He agreed, but first wanted his fluids checked.

"She's been runnin' warm," he growled.

I looked at his engine, right there, and saw he was low on both oil and coolant.

"I think there's a leak," I said. "These shouldn't be so far gone, not if you've been checking them."

He merely nodded, meaning he hadn't, then bought me the oil and coolant and I refilled them. I didn't see any other issues, but that doesn't mean anything. Not really.

Two weeks later, I was all but certain she'd laughed off my letter and tossed it in the bin when I got a card from her! It's good I was home when the post came and got it. Though Ma still noticed and huffed, "Who's writin' to you?"

"It-it's just a card, Ma," I said. "Might be from one of the drivers I helped. With his lorry. You know."

She gave me a scowl that said she didn't believe me, but before she could say or do another thing, I'd raced up to my room and opened it.

The card was a lovely winter scene in an English village, with sparkling sprinkles on it, and inside was a little note.

Dear Brendan, I enjoyed our day, as well, and thought you handled what I now see could have become a difficult situation with maturity and grace. Meeting for tea at The Diplomat sounds lovely. I usually shop in Waterloo the evenings of Tuesdays and Fridays, often with Mother. Saturdays are with Angela and Louise, so I don't think that would be a good day. I hope to see you, soon. Sincerely, Joanna. P.S. Thanks to my childish brother, Charlie, it may be best not to be seen with each other, just yet, because while my father accepts you're Catholic, my mother just cannot see it. She thinks your manners are too fine. Best not to give her the opportunity to ask you."

Maturity! Grace! I was beyond ecstatic.

So after school was done, that Tuesday, I made my way past the checkpoint to hang around Wellies, making sure all knew I was merely out to see if I could get a couple repair jobs from a local shopkeeper.

When I told them of my abilities, the soldiers tried to slag me off, with one joking, "Here, me radio keeps dyin' off."

I took a look the battery first, and quickly saw it was old and had been wet and was corroded. One of the lads had a toothpick, so I used that to clean much of it and told him, "Get a new battery, and don't get it wet, again."

His mate laughed and said, "Tol' yer it's cuz yer took it in the shower, ye nutter."

But it was me choosing to have Marlboros on me that helped most. Danny had mentioned there's nothing like a quality smoke to make you mates with a lad but a few years older than yourself. Of course, Colm held the damn things dear, but I have to admit, they were of a fine quality.

Once I'd passed a few around, there was almost a problem when another squaddie asked me, "Ger lihke?"

I didn't understand him. He was getting angry. It wasn't till he waved the fag in front of me that I realized he wanted a light. I handed him a book of matches. That brought a "Coor, t'angs," from him. I scurried off before he could say anything more.

I did my rounds, keeping a close eye for Joanna and her mother. It was on five when I saw her crossing, other side of the toilet. I rushed over to it and pretended to look straight ahead as I waved my hand by my head, watching her from the corner of my eye. Some people looked at me as if I were off, but then she smiled her smile for me, not looking my way but obvious enough, so I rushed to the Diplomat and ordered tea and cakes for a table well away from the window.

"A lady will soon be joining me," I said, grandly.

A few minutes after I was served, there she came, looking so much like the first day I'd seen her, I took in a sharp breath.

"I haven't much time," she said as she sat, breathless. "Mum thinks I'm looking at new shoes. She'll be coming for me, soon."

"I'm glad you could make it," I replied, just as breathless.

She fixed her tea with milk, only, and took but a single bite of cake in so fine and delicate a manner, I felt like a lumbering fool.

"Was-was there much trouble for you, when I was-after I was at your house?"

She giggled. "Charles tried, but in no way could he cause trouble for me. I just told my parents you were a fine young man who escorted me home, and I'd hear nothing more about it. Then I made certain Charles learned what real trouble was." She took a sip then added, "He'll never bother me, again."

I chuckled. "I have a feeling it's best I not know the trouble you caused him."

"It's better that way." And her eyes twinkled of mischief.

"Is he your only one?"

"Oh, no. There's Robert, working in Westminster, and John, at some government office in Sheffield. Mum's from Liverpool and wrote a book about workhouses in the UK."

"It's published?" She nodded. "You're the daughter of an author."

"Such as it is."

"Is that what you're going to be?"

"Oh, no. I'm aiming for university. I want to be a doctor."

It was like her entire world was a galaxy apart from mine.

"So what family do you have?" she asked. "A dozen brothers and sisters?"

"No, not half that many."

"You're not living up to that silly stereotype."

"Well…me Da's not around."

"Oh?" Another sip of tea.

"He's-he's dead."

"Oh, I'm sorry." And she placed her hand on mine.

I had to fight a giggle, of all things, and say, "Thanks. But it's been near four years so..."

"Still, it must be hard for you and your mother." The concern in her voice told me she really meant it, and I near melted.

"We-we're doing well enough."

"You seem like you're strong enough to." Then she gasped and said, "Just saw Mum cross the street. She's looking for me." She bolted to her feet and started away then spun back and gripped my hand. "Till next time? Here?"

All I could do was nod before she grinned and was gone.

We were able to see each other once a week, that way, if only for a few minutes. I would do my rounds. Return items I'd fixed or pick up new ones. Keep a close eye for her and her Mother. Then make sure I did my wave so as she'd notice before her Mother could see me and rush to the Diplomat to order tea and cakes, always as far from the windows as possible. And I left a tip. I'd heard that makes the hostesses much happier with you. She would give her Ma some excuse and sneak over to where I'd be waiting, and I never stopped taking in a sharp breath at seeing her bolt through the entrance to join me.

I know I sounded a proper fool to her, talking about my mates in careful ways. And telling her how I'd repaired an air nozzle at McClosky's shop then complaining because his son, Diarmaid, took credit. How Eamonn was at Queens and doing well. How Mairead was back to her job and doing well, since Ma was keeping an eye on Michael Paul and doing well. How my brothers and sisters were doing well. How our new home was doing us well. How I was doing well. How helping shopkeepers with that crazy decimalization was doing well. I didn't notice my constant repetition of how *well* we were *doing* till she made sport of me by repeating it back. I'd laughed, in response, and said I'd take a course in public speaking.

What we never spoke of was how we felt about each other. I'd compliment her clothes, always different, always lovely. She'd say I looked smart, even though I was in the same uniform, every time—sports jacket, shirt and bell-bottom trousers, a jumper. She liked the curls in my hair, now I was letting it grow. I loved the light braid she'd sometimes put hers into. It all felt so very right and wonderful.

At Christmas, I searched for days to get the right present for her and found it at Sproule's on Carlisle. A gold heart pendant on a light chain. Cost me eight quid, but when I slipped the box to her and saw her eyes light up when she opened it, I knew I'd have been happy to have spent a hundred.

She slipped it around her neck and under her jumper, whispering, "Oh, Brendan, I haven't anything nearly so fine to give you."

"You like it, then?" I asked, as if I needed to.

Her smile both chided me and told me without question she did. She dipped into her bag and pulled out a small package.

"I had no end of trouble buying this when I saw it," she said. "Charlie would've made a scene, he's such a brat. I'll be so glad when he's off to RAM."

"Ram?"

"Royal Academy of Music. Fancies himself the next Bach. Beethoven. Brahms. Mozart. Never. I've heard his compositions."

I laughed and opened my present to find a lovely set of wee turnscrews within a small flap. I burst into a grin to hide how much it overwhelmed me.

She watched me, actually wary. "When you were at dinner, you mentioned some trouble you were having with some smaller things you were repairing."

"This is perfect," I managed to whisper. "Exactly what I needed. Thank you."

"Mum'll be looking for me," she said as she finished her tea, then added with a wink, "I'd best be in Preston's when she finds me, this time."

I nodded and rose with her, and she smiled and hesitated then leaned over to let her lips give me the lightest of kisses on my nose before she rushed out, crying "Happy Christmas" as she went.

Oh, yes, it was. It was. The happiest of my life.

1970-71

Danny

We were at the beginning of a new decade, one of promise and peace, we were sure, so fourteen came to me with great celebration. I had cake. Orange Fanta. Snappers left from Christmas. Festival ribbon. And best of all? Another NASA cap from Aunt Mari! Apollo 11! The moon landing! Mai held it back from the Christmas presents, and it made me joyous to receive it, then. With a grand flourish, I passed my Apollo 7 cap down to Rhuari, who actually smiled, he was so pleased. Maeve was miffed and whined that her birthdays were never as grand, and Kieran joined with her, but they got to feast on milk and chocolate cake with cream frosting, so quickly forgot the imagined slight.

Another gift was Ma going the day without complaint against me! But then her focus was still on young Michael Paul. With him around she was charming and calm and sweet. It made me a great deal more than nervous.

Eamonn was in Belfast, still, but sent a card of Scrooge McDuck signed *From one to another (joke)*. I didn't laugh.

Of course, all of this actually happened the day before, after mass, because the 2nd was a Monday and I had not only school but a few hours set for McClosky's. I could have begged the day off but I didn't want to lose the money he'd promised. I also knew Diarmaid would have left the shop in chaos, and I did not want to have to spend twice as much effort to get it cleaned on Tuesday.

I'd seen more than once his mind was elsewhere, but I knew nothing of him seeing any particular girl. Nor was he of a mind to keep himself fresh and right for one, should he want to go out. I finally got a hint of what he was up for when I saw him skulking off down an alley with Aidan and Jackie and a couple of lads best left nameless, followed by Colm. Then I caught a sniff of what they were smoking, and it wasn't Marlboros. So I made double sure I checked everything Diarmaid fixed and reworked a couple that were done poorly, at best.

I had to go hard at it but got the place cleaned and ready for Tuesday with little trouble and, since there was nothing left in the shop to do, Mr. McClosky let me off to run some errands for Ma. At least, that was the excuse I gave him. In truth, I'd been promised a quid if I could fix Mrs. Farrell's telly, and I wanted to stop off at her place to give it a look. From the sound of it the picture tube was gone and she'd not like the cost of replacing it.

"Dr. Wells is the only one set to collect his car by closing, sir," I said to Mr. McClosky as I washed up. Then I added with a quiet voice, "And you might mention to him, if he wouldn't ride the brake with his left foot, the pads would last much longer."

"It's that or the clutch," he shrugged back, meaning he'd not say a word and in a year we'd be working on the brakes, again. I made a note to speak to the doctor, myself.

Then I ran up the Flats to Mrs. Farrell's. As I came out the lift, I noticed Father Jack's Cortina in front of St. Agnes, down the way, and thought it odd, since he was supposed to be in Dublin. At least, that's what he'd told me when I'd prepared his car for the drive down; changed the oil, tested the brakes and all the lamps, made sure the tires were at their proper pressure. It may have been old but it was well-kept, and no need to give anyone cause to pull it over. Anyway, I shrugged it off and headed on.

Mrs. Farrell is one of those older ladies who smells of flowers and has seven cats, only one of which liked me—this little black tom with a white patch under his left eye. As I sat in the back of the telly, checking everything, he curled himself in my lap and watched with rapt attention, purring happily in exchange for the occasional scratch behind an ear. The others just glared at me from under the settee.

I'd once asked Ma about having a dog or a cat, and she'd laughed.

"Can barely feed ourselves and you want to bring in another mouth?" Then she'd said no more.

I'd been old enough to understand that meant, *No.*

Mrs. Farrell gave me tea and a couple biscuits that were hard as brick, they were so old. But dipping them in the tea made 'em soft enough to eat and they turned out to be quite tasty. I still made a note to have Mai bring her some fresh ones when next she made them.

That's all she did was cook, now she'd been let go from Hogg and Mitchell's and was expecting, again, and I smiled at the thought that Tur'd had to have his pants let out a bit.

I had a bit of luck with that telly; all it needed was a couple new tubes and a touch of solder to reattach a connector.

"Are you certain, Brendan?" she asked in her slightly shaky voice. "I won't have to buy a new one, will I?"

"I doubt it, Mrs. Farrell," I said, the little tom climbing across my shoulders, his nails digging in just enough to hang on while not enough to hurt. "Fixed, it's good for another year, maybe two."

"Excellent. That will give me time to save up. Perhaps you'll be able to find me a good one, second hand?"

"Tur's Da might know of one."

"Those bandits? It's highway robbery, what they charge. You'll do me much better."

I shrugged as I said, "I'll start keeping an watch." Knowing full well I'd ask Tur and he'd ask his Da and they'd find me one and it would cost more than if she'd gone to them, herself. But if that's what you choose?

She smiled and then trusted me with a ten-pound note to buy the tubes, so I told her if McClatchey's had them, I'd come back straight off to replace them.

But the McClatchey's being themselves, they said they'd have to order the tubes and it would be a week. I considered hopping over to Sander's on Irish Street since I knew they'd be in stock there and it would give me excuse to see if Joanna was available for a meet up. I could call her from the depot before grabbing the bus and we could share something at Marianne's Tea Shop, near her Da's store.

But I wasn't as clean as I wanted and the sun was near gone and a mist was coming in and I had but a couple of Marlboros left to exchange with the squaddies, so I put it off till the next day and headed home. I had no interest in dealing with the checkpoints in the middle of a fog or rain. Besides, there was a strong possibility if any of them found that tenner on me, it'd vanish into their pocket; I didn't want the responsibility of having to replace it. Tomorrow, I'd have my rucksack and could hide it in there.

Coming down Rossville, I saw Colm, Paidrig and wee Eammon turning up Howard, with a football.

"Oi, me China," wee Eammon called, and I grinned and

waved. It amazed me his mother had let him out, though lately I'd begun to wonder if he even bothered telling he was joining us. "We're off to Long Tower. Ya comin'?"

"Got your inhaler?" I yelled back.

He patted his jeans pocket so I shrugged, nodded and jogged over to them. Ma was funny about washing my clothes, of late. If I came home filthy from working a car, she'd go on and on to no end about how much of a bother I was to her, though she'd not demand Mairead turn down the money. But muddy from football or hurling? She'd query me on how the game went. Yet she wouldn't listen to any of the football games on my transistor.

"They talk too fast and I can't picture what they're doin'," she'd snapped at me when I'd bothered her about it.

"Then let's see a match at Brandywell, Ma," I'd said in answer.

"And who's gonna pay for it?" she'd huffed back. "You can't get in for free, and I won't go into someone's house to watch, like a beggar." Then she'd looked at me. "Or have you been sneakin' in?"

I'd kept silent, for I'd suddenly realized I was close to offering to buy her a ticket when I wasn't supposed to have any scratch on me.

What had surprised me was, she'd smiled. Oh, she tried to keep it hid but I saw it, clear as day, and then she'd said, "Well, nice to know you've some of me in you, after all."

Of course, that set my mind to wondering, so I'd written Aunt Mari asking about it, first swearing both her and myself to secrecy, forever. I didn't want Ma to think I was off finding stories to tell about her; that would really kill her momentary quiet with me. Didn't matter; all Aunt Mari wrote back was, "Let's just say neither of us was a perfect angel, unlike you."

Bugger.

But since Ma was easiest with me when I'd done no good, I never let on different.

So my mates and I headed for Bishop. As we reached the top, I saw Father Jack drive past, heading for Abercorn Road and looking grim. I caught a glimpse of the man with him and it looked like Father Demian. But I'd heard he was in America, though some also said he'd gone to England. I decided the mist and the early dark were playing tricks on me, and it was someone merely similar to him. I mean, don't all priests look alike, after a certain age?

Then I saw Danny standing by Bishop's Gate, smoking in deep shaky puffs, and the first thought that hit me was, *Christ, he's seen a ghost.*

We headed for him, and Paidrig being Paidrig couldn't see the warning in Danny's stance or expression so popped off with, "Well, here we have Father Danny, hi. Back from his holy orders—"

Danny roared and charged him, bashing at him like a madman! It took both Colm and myself to pull him back, then he kicked at us and spit and twisted away to storm up onto the walls.

Wee Eammon, Colm and I exchanged looks, then I chased after Danny as they tended to a now-bloody Paidrig.

It had started misting and even under my coat I was chilled while Danny wore neither coat nor jacket; he just had his hands shoved in his pockets and was cutting through it. His hair was longer and shined from being wet. I managed to catch him only because he slowed his walk at the double bastion.

"What the devil was that?" I asked him, a bit out of breath. "Paidrig's just saying the same thing he thinks sounds clever, all the time. Can't you see that?"

"Then let him be clever with you!" he snapped, glaring at me. His skin gleamed, thanks to the mist, which almost softened the hard look on his face. "But he don't talk to *you* like that, does he? Never says a fucking word to you about anything, not even about how tight you are with a penny or that little Proddy tart you're seeing and maybe're even—"

Ice cut deep into my heart and all other concerns vanished from me. I shoved him, shaken and suddenly afraid. "What d'you mean?!"

He shoved me, back, scowling, "I saw the two of you having tea and cake in the Diplomat, like she's the fucking queen!"

"Why-why d'you think she's Protestant?"

"Don't play me innocent. I saw her and her Ma get in an estate car, on Waterloo, and the bastard driving's been on the Orange marches."

I grabbed him by his collar, both hands, truly scared. "Who've you told!? Have you told anybody? Her family don't know about me and I don't want her hurt or-or—"

His face shifted into shock so quick, it cut me off.

"Oh, Bren," he murmured, his voice soft and quivering. "Bren. A girl from Waterside and-and her Da UVF and-and..."

I was shaking, but not from the cold. The hurt and reproach in Danny's eyes was near accusing me of betraying him, and the things he was saying about her Da. About her. I tried to say something but all that came out was, "No. She-no. How do you know that!? How do you know any of that?"

"I-I was with Jackie and your brother, and they knew the woman. Talked of her and-and, Jesus, Bren—her?"

Oh, Christ, if my brother suspected I was seeing Joanna, that would be the end of it. Ma wouldn't be the only one to go at me over this. And that's not to mention how mad the Provos would go and-and oh, God, they might go so far as to attack her and I couldn't have that.

"Did they see me with her?" I asked, now terrified of the answer. "Or you tell 'em?"

He shook his head, his voice a near whisper. "I didn't want to believe it."

His expression grew so deep with sadness, I felt the bastard for being angry with him. "She's a-she's a decent girl, Danny. And she-she likes me. She-she sees me as just another lad and I-I just don't want her to get hurt. Eamonn I'm not worried over, or Jackie, but Aidan? Tommy? They do first and think later. Jesus, even Brian. Boru-to-yous." I tried to make that last a joke but it didn't work.

He looked at me for a long moment then nodded and turned away. "So that's how you feel about her."

I didn't know what to say, in return. Yeah, her parents were Loyalists, and I'm not surprised Charles was an Apprentice Boy, but was her Da really UVF? They were the worst bastards. And was Charlie part of that, too? He'd already proven his hate for me. I could see catastrophe building.

It's just, she had never looked at me as being anyone but Brendan. Never treated me as something different or worthless. I had no idea how to let Danny know she wasn't like the rest of them.

Finally, I managed to ask, "How long've you known?"

Danny shrugged. "Two months. Three."

And here I thought myself so clever at keeping it low-key.

Yeah, the Diplomat's not the secretest place ever was, and my only concern had been to keep Joanna's mother from seeing us, but I'd thought for certain we looked like just a couple kids having a bit of craic. Away from the windows and only once a week. Was even that too much? Was my love for her that bloody obvious? And was it all that wrong?

Then I remembered I'd told Jackie she was from Claudy, and never actually said she was Catholic. Had he recognized her? Could that now be a problem?

"Danny," I whispered, "it's true east of the Foyle's filled with arseholes and fools but..."

His sigh was so deep and painful, my voice drifted to nothing.

"So now you defend her." It took him a moment to continue with, "It's not just Protestants who're arseholes, Bren. I know that. Christ, do I know it." He shook his head. "They didn't care about her or her Ma, Jackie and Eamonn. Barely paid attention to them. It's her Da they were on about." He looked at me. "I-I promise you, I didn't say anything. You-you're me China and..."

"I know, Danny. You're no tout. I shouldn't have gone at you, like that. I just—it startled me. Finding you knew."

"How did you think you could keep it secret?"

"I dunno. I-I just didn't think it was anybody's business but mine."

He just snorted and looked away.

He was right, of course. Everybody's business was everybody's business in Derry.

I had to do something to shift my mind away from my fears, so I nudged him, saying, "Y'know, Paidrig's a China, too, and you know what he's like as well as me. Acting the cod much as he can. What was you jumping him all about?"

He lit a Marlboro in his too-cool fashion, took a long drag and held it in. Meaning it was not regular tobacco. Smoking in the open? Bloody hell. Finally, he let the smoke whisper from him to join with the growing mist before he said, "Nothing. Nothing. Just hit me wrong, is all."

He sat in a cutout on the wall and looked across the Bogside. Past the housetops on Walker's and Howard to the rolling hills of tight, rotting homes where smoke curled from ageing chimneys and silence was like a blanket over it all. His eyes seemed focused on something that was a thousand miles away, and it made me uneasy. But he didn't seem ready to speak, so I leaned against the wall and glanced back toward Bishop.

I caught a glimpse of our Chinas heading down the hill, back to the Flats; Paidrig's family now lived in the newest of them. He was a bit hunched over, and none of them looked up at us.

Here's Father Danny. Words Paidrig had said hundreds of times to him, with never more than a huff, in answer. But this time?

This time?

After having seen Father Jack and Father Demian pass? Now I knew it *was* him. And Father Jack wasn't trying to hide that he was here; it was open and almost daring in how casual how they were being. Like they were saying, *Just a simple visit.* Like he was trying to minimize it. Which made me think it was anything but. Especially with Danny's reaction, now.

Could there be a connection? Could he have seen them, too? Could that have sent him into his old spiral of temperament?

"Danny," I murmured, "I'm sorry for going at you, like I did. If I'd stopped to think—even just a second—I'd have remembered you-you're one of me best mates. You and Colm. I got no one else I feel comfortable with. I feel like I can just be me. You're right; Paidrig doesn't go at me like he does you. He's afraid I won't pay for his sweets. It's Colm who rags me about being tight with a penny and-and-well, I hope you feel the same about me. About us. Have the same kind of trust with us. With me."

He took another drag off the Marlboro and let the smoke out, slow and easy, then let me have a gentle nod.

Which should've settled it. But did big, bad, benevolent Brendan leave it at that? Oh, no. I just had to ask, "So has any of this something to do with Father Jack?"

Danny's chuckle was so sad, it brought back my unease. "Since when is anything *not* about Father Jack, with us?" Then he frowned and turned a glare on me. "Why you asking?"

"I-I saw them pass by, on Bishop, earlier. Looked like they were headed for the bridge."

"So what if he was? He's a right to go where he chooses, hasn't he?" he snapped, then he smirked. "He's let it be known enough."

"He was supposed to be in Dublin."

He shrugged. "Maybe he just got back." Then his frown grew

deeper. "You said *them*. You saw who was with him?"

"Looked like Father Demian."

Oh, dear God, was I sorry I said that the moment I did. You'd have thought I shot Danny. He gave me the flash of a look, the same wild look as I'd seen on that tom that'd been cornered by those dogs, wild, terrified and ready to spin into madness if it'd save itself. Or at least would take a couple of the damned growlers with him. It stabbed into me, deep. Then it was gone and covered with a sullen glare.

"He has nothing to do with me, now," he muttered, looking away from me. "Best he stays in America."

"Is that where he is?"

A growl filled his voice. "What've you heard?"

"Nothing. I-I just wondered."

Danny jolted to his feet, almost like he had just before jumping Paidrig. That wild look flashed over him, again, this time so strong it caused me to catch my breath and step back.

"The ferry from Holyhead," whispered from him.

"What?"

"Nothing. Nothing." His voice now soft and rambling in tone.

I whispered, soft and easy, "Danny, what is it?"

A quiet sort of laugh came from him as he said, "Father Jack said it. Too late for Dun Laoghaire. Not Shannon. Not Dublin. Dun Laoghaire. Ferry to Holyhead. He's in England. He's in fucking England."

He sat against the wall and lit another Marlboro, and I would swear I heard, "Fuckin' liars," whisper from him.

For the first time since I'd known him, I was afraid for him.

Danny finally shifted his gaze to me and said, "You didn't like him, did you? Father Demian."

I shrugged.

He looked away. "I can't tell if you like Father Jack or not. You never say anything against him. About him. Nothing."

"I never say anything about anybody." But I noticed Danny still was looking at me. And I thought, *He's me China. Let's be honest with him.* "He's all right. I just—well, it hits me at times his actions don't match his words."

"They don't. But you're one of the few willing to see him for what he truly is."

He offered me the joint, and I saw it was a Marlboro paper

repacked with weed. Seemed like a lot of trouble, but I took a drag.

"That—neat trick," I choked out.

"Colm showed me. Does it for some soldiers he—well..."

I nodded. No need to say it. Their money's as good as ours, though knowing Colm his dealings were in a dark alley and not like the lads in the front of the barracks asking the soldiers if they wanted errands run. He'd never be a silly bugger, like that.

I handed the smoke back and Danny almost smiled. "You ever gonna buy your own?"

"That's Paidrig's way," I smirked, smoke whispering from me. "All I ever want's a hit, now and again. And it's you offered. And I usually pay for the whiskey and—"

He waved a hand at me, almost smiling as he said, "All right. All right. I'm only keepin' you goin'." He took another drag and sent a harsh glare down at Lecky Road to watch a Saracen pass towards Brandiwell. "It's getting harder to bring in, though, thanks to those bastards. They like having it; they just don't like us being the supplier. Fucking eejits."

"Careful, lad," I said, trying to joke. "They're the only thing standin' between Free Derry and the Protestant hoards."

"They won't, for long," he sighed. "We don't have their ear; the *Loyalists* do."

"Who's telling you that?"

Now he gave a look of the purest condescension. "Bren..."

I shrugged and nodded. Better I not know. We learned early to trust only some people, and even then only as much as you needed to. Which was why having Colm and Danny as those I could trust meant so much to me. But even with them it extended only so far.

Besides, something about the attitude of the British Army was hinting that they weren't happy to be pushing against their *fellow Englishmen*, and never mind how the Paisleyites had treated them the first months they were here. Lately there'd been incidents of lads being roughed up while being searched and word of good long chats between British commanders and upper-level constables in the RUC. Some lads said it looked too much like they were turning ear to the Unionists whilst ignoring those they'd come to protect, and only a fool wouldn't see the point as valid.

Jackie put it best. *They're here to protect British interests, not us.*

Danny took in another long drag, held it for what seemed like an hour, then let it out as he whispered, "I think they're just waiting for an excuse to show the world a bunch of Paddies can't shove 'em around."

I had a vague buzz off the pot, making me feel a lot better about everything. I'd heard nothing new about the situation through Eamonn, but he was in Belfast. And thinking about it, I could just imagine him, Jackie, Aidan, Colm and a host of other lads sitting around with beers and crisps having their own little craic. I had to fight back a laugh.

I finally sighed, "Well, I hope the excuse doesn't come."

"You would. Hopes and dreams and prayers."

"If we don't have them, the world is of the devil."

"Quoting Father Jack, now?"

I hesitated, but had to say, "I don't recall him ever saying it."

"Yeah, it's too definite for him. But it makes you clearer in my head. Explains why you play both sides of the fence."

"Here! I wouldn't go so far as that."

His voice went singsong. "You're the one after a Proddy lass."

"You think I'm using her to help me make money and—?"

He rolled his eyes. "No, Bren, I don't mean anything by it, but you-you know as well as me that Father Jack's a two-faced bastard, yet you still coach your opinion to allow him some benefit of the doubt. You can see the divide between us and them but still you're off to their side for a girl and-and it's hard to keep track of what's right and wrong and who's on whose side, anymore. Who can be trusted and..." His voice trailed off.

"Christ, Danny, what happened with you?"

He gave a long terrible sigh and said, "If I told you, you'd not believe me. There's nights I think, maybe even *I* don't believe me. Maybe it *was* all just a bad dream. A child's fantasy." He sighed, took another drag and let me finish it. There was a long silence between us before he said, "So. England."

"What?"

"I wouldn't be surprised. Just move him to another parish and..." His voice trailed off, again, and he sat in silence.

Again, I had no idea what to say, so I just stood there by him, waiting. He started up his third joint and gave me a drag, then looked at me, almost sad, whispering, "You never were his."

"His what? Whose?"

He just looked at me. A thought was building in my head.

"Altar boy for-for Father Demian?" I managed to ask. He smirked and nodded, smoke drifting from him catching the barest of lights from a nearby lamp. Making his face look even more innocent than usual. "Never wanted to be. I-I-I wasn't comfortable with him."

"Good to see you have some wariness about you. Believe me, no one cares for the other, not truly, not when it means something more than words."

I finally had enough of evasions and hints and suggestions, so asked, "Danny, can you not tell me what happened between you and Father Demian?"

His voice was almost hollow as he whispered, "Father Devil's more like it."

And the sneer on his lips let the thought explode inside me, telling me far more than I wanted to know. I wasn't so poorly informed that I hadn't heard about men like that, who go for boys. Who take advantage. But Father Demian? A priest?

Danny saw it in my eyes. Shock. Disbelief. Anger. Concern for me China. He wrapped his arms tighter around himself and looked away from me. "I didn't tell ya. You know that. I didn't tell ya."

I nodded. "Who else was there? Father Jack and...?"

He whispered so soft, I could barely hear, "I can't say."

"Your Ma and Da, surely?"

He nodded his head, the sneer back on his lips.

"Didn't they back you?"

The words burst from him. "They called me a liar! That fucking devil stood there, hand on a bible, and spit in the face of God to swear his innocence. Father Jack backed him up. And-and me Da. Said he just knew a priest would never do that-do that to a child." His voice was hollow. Soft. As if he didn't know he was speaking. "Told them I was-I was always troubled..."

Danny? Troubled? *Always* troubled? When any who knew him knew better? His parents agreed with this? They fucking agreed?!

Suddenly, he glared at me, and the anguish in his face cut me to the core. He almost snarled in a voice filled with tears, "You're not to tell anyone of this."

All I could do was shake my head in agreement and swear to myself I would never carry tales, ever again, no matter what reason I might have. It only added pain to others, never ease, and what little you might learn from it was worthless.

He nodded and his thousand-yard stare shot across the Bogside. "I know. I know. I don't have to say that, with you."

"Danny..."

He waved a hand to quiet me. We stood there in the chill, saying nothing for several minutes. I didn't look straight at him, again. I felt he'd have shattered if I had. But it was a horrible silence between us and it tore even deeper into me. The thoughts that must have been going through his head. The ideas in his mind caught between anger and hate, and not just at the priest.

No.

Priests. For if Father Jack had taken sides against him then he was just as guilty of anything that man had done. As if he'd done it, himself.

Father fucking Devil. And make that plural. Make that all of them. Jesus, this was a betrayal of the worst sort. Just the thought of it made me near ill, for I knew Danny wasn't one to tell tales, ever, and I remembered that day his Da had slapped him.

It seemed like neither Colm nor Paidrig or wee Eammon, even, noticed Danny'd begun to change, from that day. I'd thought on more than one occasion I should ask him what was wrong. But then Father Jack had taken over the parish, and Danny'd become my helper and finally an electrical apprentice so his moods had grown less frequent and his focus sharper. And there was also that night at the fort, how in control he'd been when he faced down Tommy. I'd thought he was back to being our Danny, so never a need to ask about it.

Until now.

I knew his Da had always been demanding and mealy about the difficulties of his employment. A job which had started around the time Father Demian had taken Danny under his wing and...

And...

Wait...

No...

Was Danny why he'd got the job?

No!

I forgot to breathe.

Could he have let Father Demian have Danny? Bargained with him? Or learned about it and used it...used it to make him give over a better position? And when Danny'd told his Da he didn't want to do it, was that why his Da'd hit him? And-and-and why he'd been kept on at the parish, even after Father Demian was gone?

Could a father do that to his son? Could he be desperate enough? Deep in need enough?

Jesus, would my Da have done it? He'd let us near starve and wander in rags so he could drink. Would he have offered Eamonn, Mairead or myself up in exchange for a pint?

No.

No, no, no, I couldn't see that in him. Not in my memory of him, as sharp as it still was with anger and pain. As for Ma, I knew she'd never have stood for that if she found out it had been done to me. Or Eamonn. I-I mean, I don't think she would have. But suddenly I wasn't so sure.

Now I understood what a blunder I'd made that day, at Woolie's, reminding Danny of something horrible. Something his Da might have arranged. I suddenly felt as if I'd not been good enough a mate to him. But then, what was there I could have said or done about it? I didn't know, even now, if it was true, and I didn't dare *ask*. All I could do was stand beside me China, as if keeping watch, and let him wrestle with his demons in the privacy of his own mind.

And then another memory drifted up.

Da staring at the door as it closed behind Father Demian. Words soft, muttering, "Bloody bastards come at ya. Come at ya from nowheres. Call ya in and come at ya. And naught ya can do to stop it. Bastards. Bloody fuckin' bastards."

Come at you from nowheres.

Call you in and...

And...

Oh, God, could my Da have been done to like Danny was?

By another priest?

Well, Brendan, it would have to have been another one, wouldn't it, because he and Father Demian were of the same age.

But Da's moods, suddenly I could see they had almost the same rhythm as Danny's. I'd only seen flashes of him when he was as cool and in control as Danny, but their fury and pain looked too similar, now. And Da having no family. Weren't orphanages run by the Church in Belfast? We'd learned of it in a religion course, presented as something wonderful the Church was doing. Headed by either priests or nuns. Where you'd be kept and fed and taught God's word and trained till you were of age and able to make your own way as a man or woman. What benevolence.

Only word was spreading about a local orphanage. That it was beyond hellish. And in one of those things a priest who wanted you could get to you at any time he chose.

I coughed.

Jesus, Mary and holy St. Joseph, could that be why Da drank? Why he was so filled with anger? Had I hated a man who'd been brutalized by those supposed to protect him? A man broken as a child, through no fault of his own? A man with no way of explaining or understanding how to tell others of what was tearing him up, inside? No one to support him? No one to believe him?

Was that what Danny was to become?

I coughed, again. I felt my whole world turning upside down. I couldn't have spoken if I'd wanted to, right then. I fired up my next to last Marlboro, a real one, and tried to calm myself, but I was shaking within and my hands were not hiding it.

Had Ma known? Was that part of the reason she was so hard on his side? And was that why she'd never pushed Eamonn or myself to help services at the church, but gave it money, instead?

Almost as if-as if buying our safety?

Oh, my God, oh, my God, oh, my God, oh, my God, I could not keep up with the thoughts and questions crashing into me. I needed another hit of that special Marlboro, but Danny was still locked in his own little world.

Holding the joint, loose and easy.

I carefully maneuvered it from between his fingers, without him seeming to notice, and drew it in, long and deep. Held it in. Again. Again. Let it wash over me. Let it calm me. It was only about half gone. I debated keeping it, but finally slipped it back between his fingers. This time he did notice but said nothing.

Then I fired up the last of my Marlboros and-and when had I finished the other one? Had I put it somewhere? No matter, I kept smoking and that little cough kept popping in, but everything was beginning to settle in my head.

Fortunately, it seemed the silence was exactly what Danny

wanted. Or needed. For after some minutes he slid his hands in his pockets and looked around, in wonder, and said, "It's cold."

The sound of his voice jolted me. The quiet had been so nice. So easy. I tried to smile. "You-you want to wear my coat? I got a jumper on."

"No. Thanks. I like the cold. Feels real."

I nodded. "When Derry's caught in such a mist, as this, she takes on a whole new life, doesn't she? Hides all the ugly parts. Makes herself lovely and mysterious."

He finished the joint then sighed, "You're right. She's almost beautiful."

I hesitated. "Are you doing well, again?"

"Fine." He nodded, softly chucking. Then he stopped and took in a deep breath. "Don't blame me, Bren."

The tone of his voice jolted me. I cast him a glance. "Blame you? For what?"

He shrugged.

I finally put an arm over his shoulders, making myself smile as I said, "Never, Danny. Like I said, you're me China."

When he fixed his eyes on me, this time, his face was calm and gentle, almost. He offered me a weak smile, almost sad, and whispered, "Always?"

"Always."

Then his smile widened and he pulled away. "Cheers."

Suddenly, fear gripped my throat. I followed him. "Danny, wait-wait-you're not gonna-gonna *do* anything...?"

"Like what?"

"Well, like-like what Cormac Dean. You know..."

He nodded. "Length of rope and a crossbar?" He nearly spit. "And give those fat bastards the satisfaction? No, no bloody chance of that."

"Then-then let's go for a wander. Cross to the fort."

"Through the checkpoints?"

"On Groarty? Is it important enough?"

"Can't tell with those bastards."

"Well, if it's a trouble, we'll come back and—"

"I can't."

"Come along, Danny. It's me birthday and I don't want to be home. I-I think there's still a fifth of whiskey hid behind one of the stones, there, and-and maybe some smoke and I think I left a box of Clubs. They ain't Marlboros but we can sit up all night and talk and look at the stars, again. The devil with school or anything else till we're ready for it."

He just looked at me, as if his heart was broken.

I kept on with, "It's gonna be a fair night, Danny. You can already see the mist lifting. By the time we're there, it'll be gone and no moon. Just the stars, Danny. The stars."

"Thank you for that," he whispered, then cleared his throat. "But some other time. I-I'm meetin' people at half seven."

I didn't believe him, but what could I say? "Oh. Right, then. Your Tommy and them?"

"No. Others."

"Tomorrow, then. Even if it's fog or clouds."

"We'll see." He was backing away, but then he stopped. "Be careful, Bren. It's those you most trust who'll damage you the worst."

Then he spun about and walked back to Bishop's steps.

And I let him.

Even though his words terrified me.

I had no idea what more to do or say, and there was no question in my mind he did not want me to know who his new friends were. So I let the mist welcome him. Whisper around him in gentle ways as he vanished into it.

We never got to the fort to see if my claims of whiskey and pot were accurate. The next day I heard Danny's father had been given a promotion and transferred to the Archdiocese, in Armagh, and he and his mother were gone in a day.

Not even twenty-four hours.

Not a word of farewell.

Couldn't get out of Derry fast enough, it seemed.

Of course, had I been home instead of with my mates, I'd have learned of it. For Mairead knew Mrs. Gallagher through Danny's sister and had heard of the possibility.

Which meant they'd been expecting it even before meeting with Fathers Jack and Demian. Which added another layer to my worry for my China.

Of course, Mairead had no idea of what was happening. She'd just made Danny's parents swear they would let her know the second they were certain.

Which they did.

His Da let her move some of her things into the place. Tur even bought most of their furniture off him, so the moment he was gone, the two of them were set up.

Of course, when rent came due the Housing Authority tried to make an issue of it. But Mairead went down to their office, sweeter than sugar, three months on and with Michael Paul still in swaddling, sat herself down and said, "We've been set up with the Gallaghers for nearly a year, so they let me keep the place when they were done."

"We've nothing in our records to show you've been living there," they'd responded.

"And where else could I have been livin'?" she'd shot back.

Which proved the HA knew nothing of what I'd done to the hutch.

She'd continued with, "Come look and see how we've taken fine care of it."

Which we had, Tur and I. Painting and fixing small bits here and there. One good thing about the Gallaghers was, the Mrs. had kept the place in decent shape, despite the valium. Though not as harsh about it as Ma, also probably thanks to the valium. Once the council saw how nice everything looked they shrugged and left my sister and brother-in-law alone.

Of course, there were howls at how she'd jumped the queue, but for once the HA's stubborn lack of concern worked in our favor.

So Eamonn took over the hutch when next he came home, and felt quite the man in it. Putting up posters and bringing in a black-light that made them glow in the dark and becoming a full young lad on his own. That left me, Rhuari and Kieran in the back room. They wanted my larger bed, which I was happy to swap them, my one condition being I keep by the window.

There was a reason for this. I wanted to see the stars on a clear night. Looking at them helped me think. Helped me settle. For my brain was still shaken by the thoughts about Da and my mother and Danny and Father Demian, and even Mr. Gallagher's and Father Jack's possible involvement in it all, and some nights I just couldn't sleep.

Of course, it was silly to involve Father Jack in thoughts about Da. But if he was helping Father Demian continue with his—with his ways and the church was covering for them, then he was just as guilty. Of it all.

But how could I find out if what I was thinking was true? How could I know, for certain, that I wasn't reading more into a situation than was really there? I knew nothing about Da except from when he was with us. I didn't even know if he actually was an orphan or if he'd even been a part of the church. He never went to mass, from what I could tell, so for all I knew he might have been Protestant.

And wouldn't that have been a kick?

Well, there was his one comment about priests. But protestants have reverends. Like Paisley. I'd hardly think him a man of God, the hideous things he says and does. He was one of the few Father Jack had nothing halfway good to say about; just called him spawn of the devil. And while I agreed with him without hesitation, I couldn't see him doing the same as Father Demian, to a child.

In truth, that one comment was the only reason I wondered if he'd suffered the same as Danny.

I remembered Mrs. O'Canainn's comment about us moving close to her when Ma was with me. I'd thought we always lived there, and no one ever bothered to say otherwise. But if that were so, then where did we come from?

I found Mrs. O'Canainn and asked her, straight out, but she had no idea and said it didn't matter. It did, to me, so I sought out another lady who was living up the street at the time of my birth, Mrs. Keenan, the midwife. She was in a new flat in the third tower.

But all I caught from her was a lot of huff and, "Why you askin'?" Though I did gain one snippet of information. When my parents had taken over that hovel, it was already considered unlivable and Da had made it livable before moving house. By himself.

"Like he was building a hideaway," she'd said.

Of course, she also let Ma know I was asking around. So when I came home from school, a couple days after, Ma burst from the kitchen, her eyes blazing with anger. I was quick enough to put my rucksack on the settee before she lashed at me with a fist.

A full fist, curled tight.

Knocked me to the floor, it was so strong. The only thing that kept me from being struck, again, was Maeve and Rhuari coming in, behind me, and letting out horrified gasps and near wails.

I was half-lying on the floor, blood dripping into the woven rug from my mouth or nose, I couldn't say which. It didn't hurt, at that moment; it was too much of a shock.

My ears were ringing but I still could hear Ma snarling, "You will never, never, ever nose around asking questions about your father, you little beast. Do you understand me?"

I could not think of what to say, not until she grabbed me by the hair and hissed, "Do you understand me?"

I managed to nod, then.

She yanked me to my feet and shoved me to the stairs, snarling, "Your room."

I went up, quickly. Cleaned myself in the bathroom, shaking and confused and angry. Once done, I returned to my bed and sat there, shivering in the chill air, darkness drifting down around me. I was meant to have no dinner, but Rhuari snuck up some bread and cheese for me, and a mug of water. Quiet, plain and direct as always.

"You all right?" he asked as he slipped into my room.

I accepted the food with a smile. He hesitated.

"What'd you do to Ma, this time?" he asked as he sat on the bed, next to me.

I just shrugged. No need to drag him in the middle of it.

"So why's it only you she hits?" I had no answer, but he wasn't going to put aside, like that. "Eamonn she chatters at. Mai she works with. Me and Maeve, she scolds, but you she hits. Why?"

I sighed, "You're better than me."

"No, we're not."

"Ma thinks so. She thinks me a sneak. Thinks me simple." I cast him a crooked look. "I can't be both, can I?"

"Why would she think you're simple?"

"Ask her."

He rolled his eyes, at that. "If Mai had been here, she wouldn't have let her hit you."

"But she wasn't, was she?"

He just looked at me, for a moment, then rose, sighing. "She is, now. She brought Michael Paul over. Ma seems happy, if you want to join us."

I shook my head. "Thanks for the grub."

He nodded and left.

Why did Ma never hit Eamonn? I think it's because he accepted her ways. I couldn't see him asking around about Da; the man was gone, and he had his own life to lead and other interests that were more important. Plain and simple. No need to complicate things, while that's all I did.

Of course, I couldn't ask him about where we'd lived before Nailors. He'd have let it slip to Ma and I'd have gotten plenty more like today.

As for Mai, she knew how to dance around Ma, like Eamonn had suggested I do. Redirect her attention, like you do with a child. But I didn't have the interest in playing games, like that. To me, when something needs to be repaired, you look into it and find out what the problem is and how to fix it, then do so. To me, it had always been simple and direct.

But now I could now see that it was anything but. You cannot work with people like you do clocks and toasters and radios. They're too difficult. Also, I had no willingness to just let things be or to bend, if I did not want to, but I would always wonder and question and put my full energy into all of it. Thinking I could fix whatever I wanted if I had the right tools.

Or information.

Maybe it was a form of madness in me to think that if I knew more then I could make sense of the world. Sense of my life. Maybe that's all there was to it—I was just too stubborn to back down. Or arrogant.

There were many nights, after this where, even when I had nothing that needed repair to keep me awake, I would simply lie next to the sill and gaze out at those tiny sparkling lights in the black velvet. Let them take my questions into the ether and decide when or how or even whether or not I was to be allowed to share in the vast knowledge they held.

What a silly thing to wonder.

Hidey-holes

Spring brought the usual political nonsense, starting with a reorganization of the RUC into the *new and improved* version of the RUC, now called the Police Authority. Big change. At least those bastard B Specials were disbanded, and probably incorporated into the PA. The Alliance Party came along, blissfully saying they could bridge the gap between Catholics and Protestants. Or ignorantly. Unaware no one really wanted to, at this point.

And a report came out to recommend a new political order that managed to change nothing. Demonstrations still devolved into rock-throwing by lads with nothing better to do, which on an occasion or two included me. They were always labeled riots, and the Army began hinting at their *growing impatience* with it all. Meaning not with Protestant intransigence regarding change but with Catholics still having the audacity to demand it.

Ma was drawn deeper into working with various organizations to push the Catholic cause because, as she put it, that's what history demanded. She was back to bragging on seeing De Valera when he came to Derry nearly twenty years ago, and how he'd smiled at Eamonn as she held him up to for the man to witness, even though he was but a toddler.

I also heard through Paidrig that Ma was telling people she once planned to be a dancer. His sisters-in law, who no longer had work at Hogg and Mitchell's, had been at a committee action meeting and overheard her talking with Father Jack.

"They say she claimed she had beauty and grace," Paidrig told me, once, "and still could do it until you come along, hi. A couple other ladies who were there agreed with her."

"What would I have to do with that?" I'd asked, not really expecting him to answer.

But he said, "Saoroise says it's because you took so long to get birthed. You stopped her."

"I did not," I'd snapped, knowing full well that idea might have some truth to it. But I was not going to ask, one way or the other. That would set Ma on a tear, again.

We'd begun our second summer at Clíodhna Place when Eamonn returned from Belfast, his clothes bearing the scent of burned wood and rubber, and announced he was not returning to Queens.

"Everything's mad, there," he said, his voice holding a quiver in it I'd never heard before. "It's naught but abuse and anger from all in control, and the Army listens only to them. I can't get to me classes without being rousted five times, each way, and all but spat upon for being Catholic. I'm a man like them, but the religion I'm born into is cause to hate me?"

Mairead was over with Michael Paul, looking ready to bring twins into the world, and she asked, "Could you go to Trinity?"

"Be run off from my own country?" he snapped at her.

"It's Ireland," said Rhuari, "not America."

Eamonn took on a very superior attitude, saying, "I still think not."

"True," Ma said. "You're like your father—never the sort to back down from or work with those who hate us." Then she shot me a glance. I was the only one to see it, but I refused to react.

Rhuari asked him, "Then what're you gonna do?"

"I have—I have some possibilities," he said, then ended the discussion by wondering about supper.

Which set off alarms in my head, but I made no comment.

Maeve hopped down to McCleary's for fish as I peeled potatoes to boil. Rhuari buried himself in his book and Mairead serve tea.

"You'll have some, Bren?" she asked.

"He'll wait till his chores're done," Ma snapped.

Eamonn hopped in with, "I can help, Ma."

"No, sit and tell us more," she said as she positioned him at the table with a cup of tea, as if he were man of the house. They chatted back and forth, Michael Paul in his chair and Mai next to him. Nothing of importance was said, just gossip of who's moved where and who's been made redundant and who's been arrested without justification and who's Ma's new best friends and how she's visited others spread up to Pennyburn and how nice Creggan seems to be, now she has in-laws in the area, and never-you-mind she thought it cut-crystal, before. The usual nattering, to which I paid even less attention.

Finally, Eamonn noticed I'd said not a word to him beyond hello.

"You're quiet, Bren," he murmured to me, smiling.

I gave him a shrug, and for some reason, my bloody cough started up. Not major, just occasional, but enough to irritate me. I finished the spuds and set them to cooking on the range, then went to the stairs to work on an ancient Royal typewriter Mr. Carlysle had brought to me. The keys were sticking thanks to him not removing the oil-dabbled dust between the levers, over the years. As a courtesy, I had also checked the teeth on the tab key and now was cleaning the ink tape fibers from the letters. For this, I'd make a pound—and it would go to Ma, since she knew of it from the start and Mai no longer lived with us.

"Would you have her handling two households?" Ma had snapped when I'd tried to argue about it.

Nothing to say against that logic. Dammit.

Besides, now that I wondered if that which she passed on to the church—to Father Jack, now—if it was nothing more than some form of protection money, I feared that thought might come out were we to have a set-to, again. I wanted no anger from her about anything, at the moment. Not till I knew. So I kept myself happy with the few jobs I could do without her knowing.

I had myself set up on a cloth laid over the two bottom steps of the staircase, giving me level spots to both work and sit. Eamonn brought his tea and another cup in and sat on the floor next to me, his eyes soft and careful. We could hear Ma jostling about in the kitchen.

"Wee Michael's feasting on some toast," he whispered as he put the second cup on the step. "You didn't get any."

I shrugged. My fingers were black from the typewriter's ink, but I had a clean cloth to use to pick up the cup; no need to get ink on Ma's *new* China, thanks to Tur (that was in its third household). It was done as I like it. I smiled at him. He smiled back, and struck me so much as someone years older, it suddenly felt that everyone I knew was becoming an adult while I was still stuck as a child.

"Don't you agree with my decision?" he finally asked.

I hesitated, but I'd always been honest with him so sighed.

"There's more 'n what you're telling us," I whispered back.

He frowned and was about to say something, but Maeve bolted in the front door and nearly knocked him aside.

"Jesus, Eamonn, what're you sittin' there, for?" she snapped.

"Sharing a cuppa with Bren."

"You could put yourself up three steps to do that and be out of the way, if you gave it a moment's thought!" Then she headed on to the kitchen.

He chuckled, rose, and followed her, saying, "Ain't you a bit small to be in such a rush?"

I just sat there, holding the cup, the warmth seeping through the cloth to bring a sense of coziness to my fingers. The steam drifting up into my face. The taste of it so fine, as I sipped. I wanted to stay like this, forever, unmoving, letting the world just whisper by. That would be perfection.

Eamonn and I didn't have a chance to speak again till I was in bed and he came in the room, freshly washed.

"What a joy to have hot water in the tap, eh? And a toilet inside," he murmured as he sat beside me in the bed.

"You act like we only just moved here," I said.

He nodded then cast me a glance, sideways. "My digs in Belfast weren't as modern as this." He cast me a wink then sat beside me. "You mind havin' the smaller bed?"

"It's by the window," I said, shaking my head. Then I looked out at the back of Mr. Payne's. "The view was better in the old place."

He sing-songed as he asked, "Bren-dan, what's the trou-ble?"

I looked at him. In the dark, he was back to seeming like good old Eamonn, again, and he was one of the few who ever tried to find out what I was truly thinking, so I took in a deep breath and asked, "Didn't your term end a fortnight ago?"

He grew still. "What if it did?"

"I read the papers," I said, soft and easy so as not to wake Rhuari and Kieran. "Mr. Hennessey clerks at Carroway's and he lets me for having fixed his bicycle. The bloody thing's older than me and..." My voice trailed off. I coughed.

"And?" whispered from Eamonn.

I took a deep breath. "And sometimes at Colm's I'll see the news. There were fires in the Ardoyne and Short Strand, in Belfast. Catholics burned out. People on both sides shot. Both miles from Queens, but I can smell it deep in your coat. And word is Provos split from the IRA and fought back, killing people, and—"

He held up his hand to stop me. Did not look at me. His voice was tight as he said, "I have never known you to be one who spreads gossip or rumor."

"News is not gossip," I snapped, "and I say this, 'cause-'cause..."

My voice trailed off, but he had noticed my words quivered so turned his gaze upon me, wary. I coughed, then kept on with, "I feel like I did when you were going on that long walk and-and I don't want you hurt, again. Seeing you in hospital, like that. Like you were that time. I'm scared for you."

He cast me an odd look, like surprise and confusion, then leaned on one arm and put his hand on my shoulder. "I've always wondered what you really think of the rest of us. You're so quiet. So focused on what you do. Sometimes it felt as if you were lookin' down on us all."

"Eamonn!" It jolted me that he said such a thing.

"I know better, now. I'm sorry for havin' ever thought it. I can't tell you anything more than-than I did *not* return to Queens in January. The IRA's cowardice in the face of what's happenin', it had to be remedied. And so it will be."

Oh, God. "You're with the Provos?"

"I didn't say that." But his expression confirmed it.

Oh, Jesus.

"Can-can I help you in some way?"

He looked at me, deep in thought. His face took back the expression of someone far older, then he said, "Do you—have you built yourself some hidin' spaces? For to keep your money?"

So that's why he was talking to me. I almost felt hurt.

I nodded. "It wasn't easy, believe me. Ma kept a sharp eye on me, expecting it. She's been picking everywhere, now Mai's gone." Then I smiled. "But I can be clever, now and then."

"Hang on."

He slipped back down the stairs, silent as a cat. I looked out to see him enter the hutch, for a moment, then come back out holding something. Moments later, he was up in my room, his back to Rhuari and Kieran, blocking their view, and he showed me a felt bag.

"Is one of your hideaways big enough for this?"

He opened the felt wrapper.

Inside was a pistol.

I gulped in air and coughed and slapped my hand over my mouth to keep from saying anything. He knelt by the bed and set it on the covers, his eyes locked on me.

I couldn't look at him as I whispered, "How'd you get it past the checkpoints?" He said nothing, for a moment, so I turned to him. "How?"

A crooked smile crossed his face. "I didn't come home the usual route. And it's not mine; I'm keepin' it for a friend."

"Don't lie to me," I snapped, picking up the pistol and turning it over. "It's too big for any of my spaces. Have you a match?"

He pulled a lighter from his pocket. I fired it up and inspected the pistol, carefully.

"It'll come apart, easy enough," I sighed. "I could spread it about."

"Could you?"

In answer, I slipped off the bed to get my tools, but Eamonn stopped me and moved the pistol to the window for better light then he ejected the bullet clip, and don't you think for two seconds I didn't notice it was filled. Then he pulled the slide to the rear to make sure the chamber was empty, cocked it, pushed a tiny button on the right side of it, shifted the sliding part back to release a lever. A slide-stop. When he removed that, half the pistol nearly exploded apart across my bed and the noise of it was startling.

He grimaced. "Forgot you have to hold it tight for the spring."

I stared at the pieces, unable to move. This was what the Provos were rumored to be heading for—armed resistance. I now knew why he hadn't returned to Queens.

He continued with, "You're not supposed to carry it loaded, but there was no time and-well-no place I could do it, till now." He removed the bullets from the clip, slow and careful. At least there wasn't one in the chamber.

"Jesus, Eamonn, if you'd been caught..."

I noticed his hands were quivering. He knew full well he'd risked years at Long Kesh, and now was risking me, for that, as well.

"Would you rather I take it away?" he asked.

"No. No."

He took a section off the main grip then removed the barrel and bushings. In moments, the pistol was in nothing but pieces. The grip was still on the large side, so I removed the wood panels on each side, my stomach shaking but my hands steady as granite.

I sorted them by size then checked at Ma's door to make sure she was sleeping. I heard her breathe, like a purr, so knew it was safe. I snuck half the pieces downstairs and used paper from the fish to wrap the slide and stop, coating it with oil from the larder to avoid the juices.

The felt bag held the panels, so I put it and the recoil bits in separate spaces behind the top frame of the pantry door. Then I slipped under the sink and pulled away a fake slat by the water pipe to hide the slide and stop. By the time I was done, you couldn't tell any of them had been tampered with.

I kept the pistol grip, magazine and sear until the morning, when Ma was downstairs fixing a fry-up in honor of *the man in the family*. I snuck into her room, found a small groove I'd made, and pulled at it. A corner of the sill dropped down to reveal a hole in the wall. I hid the last of the pistol in there.

Aidan and Jackie came up for Eamonn just before noon and they headed out, being quiet as to where they were going. I used that time to sneak into the hutch and make sure there wasn't a companion to the pistol—

And found half a box of bullets!

"Jesus, Eamonn," spit out of me before I could control myself.

Those, I hid inside a brace under the settee.

When he returned home, Eamonn took me aside and asked for me to show him where everything was, but I wouldn't.

"Better if you don't know," I said. "Then if you're lifted, you can't tell anyone of it."

"I never would," he huffed.

Says the man who can't keep a secret.

"It's still safer this way," I snapped back. "And if things do explode and you need it, I-I'll put it back together for you." Of course, my true intention was never to let him near that thing, again.

So he continued to his meetings and grew more and more secretive as to what he was doing, not only with his time but for money to live on. PIRA and OIRA were fighting over what best to do while one of them, no idea which, supposedly met with O'Neill to try and hammer out a peace deal. At the same time, they were blaming what happened in the Ardoyne and Short Strand on the Army's unwillingness to protect Catholics, and it worked better than anything else they'd howled over. This time people knew families who'd been burned out and tossed aside like trash, and we were all furious over it.

Of course, no one believed O'Neill truly planned to implement the reforms he was professing, but as many in the middle condescendingly tut-tutted, *at least people were talking.* Supposedly, the leaders of PIRA and the British Army even held talks, but they amounted to nothing, especially since Paisley was now elected to Stormount and doing all he could to crush any chance of peace with his howling hate.

Jesus would not have approved.

Next came a ban on all parades, which more than angered Paisley and his Loyalists; they felt it their right to lord it over the rest of us. Then John Hume and Gerry Fitt formed the Social and Democratic Labor Party and put out ideas for reforms of their own.

Of course, there were actual riots, now, especially when Bernadette Devlin was sentenced to jail for helping in the Battle of Bogside. They became like a weekly get-together of us all. Sure, stones were thrown and lads were snatched by the peelers, but weren't all parties like this?

At which the Army would huff and puff and threaten to blow our houses down as they did their own snatching. By this point, none were shocked they were doing the peelers' job for them.

Of course, more families were burned out of house and home, throughout the six counties, and there was even more push and shove between the Army and both Catholics and Protestants, with our area of William and Waterloo soon being referred to as Agro Corner. Hundreds of Catholics were pushed from their jobs by Loyalists, at Harlan and Wolff. Provos supposedly set off bombs at a number of targets, but there were questions about that; the choices seemed a bit too carefully chosen to make Catholics look bad. There were also full riots in Ballymurphy. It was at this point some idiot British politician began speaking of an *acceptable level of violence.*

Only a man who's never been in a situation like ours could ever think that was allowable.

But still the dole was always there and food was available to be bought. We had Christmas and Boxing Day and packages from Aunt Mari and Uncle Sean. I kept working my repairs and was brought in more at McClosky's, now Diarmaid was training with the Provos. Marching around in their jeans and jumpers and balaclavas as if they were an army. I know many were proud of them, but they struck me as little boys playing at war. What added to my belief was when they began to hold target practice in the fields outside the city, after which boys would scramble about to gather spent cartridges to collect and trade like football cards.

Joanna couldn't come to Waterloo, anymore, so it was me sneaking across to Waterside and meeting with her at Marianne's whenever I could. She worked for her Da three evenings a week, and Saturdays. I'd appear at the window, for a moment, dressed as sharp and Protestant as I could be, and she'd see me then slip away for her break to join me. Then we'd chat and touch hands and sip our tea and nibble our cakes then kiss goodbye, always-always too soon. She even remembered my birthday with a nicely bound notebook and pencil; I'd given her a pin in the shape of a car with green stones for eyes. It was difficult to manage, at times, but we made it work.

Until a few days after I was fifteen.

The first British soldier was killed, in Belfast, and the IRA blamed. Of course. Now the Army paid full attention to the Protestant leaders, and the deaths grew even as the bombings became more harsh and cruel. Three Scottish soldiers were murdered and Faulkner, who's the worst of the worst, became Prime Minister for Northern Ireland and everything spiraled closer and closer to chaos, so naturally the stupid Brits decided to make sure it came about by choosing sides and blaming it all on Catholics and the IRA.

Our world was out of control, with bombs going off so steadily they became no more noticeable than a car horn. Catholic men and boys were being arrested or killed, followed by retaliations against the Army, RUC and Protestants. All but daily. Back and forth and back and forth, each side certain this bit of viciousness would make the other side back down instead of increasing their own cruelty. Even Father Jack was shaken by the consistency of it and began to speak of it as being worse than mere fighting.

"As Albert Einstein once said," he quoted in one of his latest sermons, *"Insanity is to commit the same action, over and over, each time expecting a different result but only achieving the same one. Every time.* But rather than learn from it, you repeat the action, exactly the same. Again, and again, and again. We need to break this cycle of violence and listen to one another with ears open wide as well as hearts. For only in that way can true peace be found."

Nobody listened.

More cars were hijacked. People were forced to donate money, rooms, even clothing to one side or the other. And I knew it was happening with both because I overheard Jackie and Aidan in Eamonn's hutch talking of Joanna's Da and how was, indeed, high in the UVF so might be one of the main collectors of money for that side. Aidan spoke of hijacking him, but Jackie called that idea stupid, since they didn't really know. From what I could tell, no more was said.

Further proof came during one of my now rare meetups with Joanna. Louisa had cut her off as a friend because money for a new dress was given to her Da, instead.

"As if it's my fault her parents chose to do it," Joanna had whined.

"Chose to?" I asked, grinning.

She shrugged and sighed. "Everyone's doing it. So silly."

"She should learn how to make her own dresses," I said, very sagely. "That way anything she wears is like no one else's, and I bet she'd like that."

"Please. She couldn't boil water for tea."

I laughed. "I thought it was the law, in Ireland, that all children at least know how to make that."

"We're not in Ireland," she said, smiling. "We're in the North."

"Part and parcel," I said, in response as I took a bite from our cake.

"And you think I know how to do that, do you?"

I looked straight at her to say, "I think you'd know how to do anything you want."

Her smile went ear to ear and she'd reached over to kiss me

then then run back to her Da's shop. And I didn't care I had to pass through seven checkpoints and be manhandled by twelve different soldiers to get home.

But I finally had to admit the darkness was growing far too thick when Willie Pringle's old A4 vanished only to be discovered laden with C-4 by a customs hutch and deliberately exploded by Army Bomb Experts. It destroyed Willie, because he could not afford a new one and his insurance had been dropped, so his business died. As did he, soon after.

Then McClosky's was burned out during one of the riots, so I was back to making do on whatever repair jobs I could get from the Bogside and Creggan Estates, which were fewer and fewer, there being less money available to one and all. My sole joy about the hideous situation was that I had enough set aside to help subsidize the dole. Even a crown a week kept us going along, now that Aunt Mari had to stop enclosing money in her letters. One had been opened and the twenty pounds within taken. She offered to help set up an account through the Post Office, but that money would have been reported to the Housing Authority so Ma asked her not to.

Back and forth and back and forth it went, neither side gaining the upper hand, no matter how hard they pushed, for there were atrocities enough by the UVF to keep the British Army too off-balance to be able to blame one side for everything.

Over and over and over.

Dear God, why is it always stupid people in charge of us?

Dublin

I quit school at the end of term. I was near fifteen and a half now and could work, if I chose, so I helped McClosky get back in business. He'd found himself a temporary slot in Brandywell; not the best place ever in a building sure to be torn down the second the Housing Authority could return to paying attention, but it did well, for now. My only true issue was the checkpoint maneuvering that was required, going and coming.

Diarmaid had become tight with Jackie and Aidan and the rest, taking him away more and more, so it left me plenty to do, during the day. But at 5:30 sharp I was pushed off, no matter what I was in the middle of, and Diarmaid would take over. I know it was him behind it because I once left without my jacket and went back to get it, and there he was with some men who had Belfast accents and ice-cold eyes that never left me as I grabbed it and hurried away.

I also learned they were taking a part of the day's till, since Mr. McClosky was spitting anger at Diarmaid over it being too high a percentage and his own son shrugging at him.

"This way, you won't get burned out, again," Diarmaid told him.

"Was my old shop targeted?"

"No, Da; this is somethin' we come up with to better control those who get out of hand."

"How does me givin' you money control the mob?"

"Try not givin' it and see what happens."

Mr. McClosky had looked at Diarmaid for a long, long moment, as if he'd frozen in place, then turned, gone to his desk, pulled out a bottle of whiskey and poured himself a full glass, then sat there looking at nothing. Neither of them had noticed me watching, and I kept it that way.

The Devlins had been spared and were, in fact, doing well

fixing what furniture that could be fixed after each riot's destruction and using the rest for scrap supplies. They even continued to toss a few jobs my way. Paid me little, but that was better than none. I kept it secret from Ma because I had the feeling McClosky might have to make me redundant and wanted a nice bit set aside, in case.

We still had demonstrations, but everything was different. There was anger with the Army and its roughness, yes, but many were also shocked and numb and unsure and even apathetic. We were no longer in Free Derry, no matter what we said; Father Jack, in one of his rare displays of honest emotion, compared it to the Warsaw Ghetto of thirty years earlier, during a sermon, and I had to agree. We were self-policing, self-sustaining, with only the barest minimum of goods allowed us and no easy movement allowed.

PIRA, OIRA and the IRA each acted like they, alone, were our protectors and police even as they behaved more and more like thugs and criminal gangs. Sometimes lads who even looked at them wrong were beaten and put up for display as *miscreants* (I had to dig into Father Jack's dictionary to look that word up). To me, they were no better than the RUC had been.

I got to where I rarely left the Bogside, the checkpoints being so difficult. If I wanted to see Joanna, it could easily take me half the day just to get through the queues, then being rousted and felt up at every one, and I do mean felt up. Fondled. Groped. Grabbed. All of it done in the roughest of manner while being verbally abused in every dialect and by every color England had in her. It was like some game with them to see how vile they would become in hopes of getting me worked up. The first couple times it did start an anger in me, but then I caught on how they were just being childish little brats out to remain the big bad bully of secondary school, in their own head, and I had to fight to keep from laughing.

The only one who did come close to making me react violent was this one thick soldier who was twice my size, all of it beefy and tattooed, had a Belfast accent and hands as large as my head. It amazed me the Army had a uniform big enough for him. He asked the usual questions. *Where did I live? Where was I going? When was I returning? Why would I need to cross to the Waterside? What was I really up to? Was I part of the IRA? Did I support them?*

To which I gave my usual nothing answers: *Off Cliodhna Place. Across the Foyle. When I'm done. Work. Work. Who? Who?*

But then he ran those fat fingers over me arse and poked one at my hole while *checking for anything that might be considered illegal.* It made me jolt away from him, so he grabbed me by the back of my neck and snarled a whisper of, "You ever try to get away from me, again, I'll take you off someplace private to *interrogate* you." And the way he said that word meant a thousand times more than just asking questions. Then he smacked me arse and let me go.

I was so shaken by it, I couldn't keep myself from looking directly at him, as I left. He had the stance of a man ready to fight, but also cast me a wink. I'm sure I looked the proper fool as I backed away from him, my mouth open and eyes big. Then one young soldier caught my attention, sneered in the bastard's direction, and rolled his eyes at me. I guess he saw what had happened and wanted me to know I wasn't the only one he'd pulled this on. Nice of him, I suppose, but why not just put an end to it?

One of Colm's girls also saw what happened and walked with me a bit, telling me, "Same treatment other Brits give us girls. Grabbin' boobs an' arses. All but rape. No matrons 'round."

"Do you tell anybody?" I asked.

"Does no good."

"How do you handle it, then?"

"I hold me farts in till one goes down there, then let 'em out." Said with a wink. "Gets me called a dirty cow, but it also ends their interest."

That made me smile, and I said, "The way that fat bastard stank, I think he'd like it."

"Aye, they are sick cunts, ain't they?"

Joanna understood how hard it could be. While she wasn't treated as rough, the few times she tried to cross to my side of the Foyle, she always had to tell them a lie about it. Like, *I'm visiting my granny in The Fountain*, or, *I've something to buy at Wellworth's or Corner Boots.* Or whatever shop was left unburnt. Of course, the soldiers hated the thought of her going alone into the wilds of Bogside so would accompany her, at times, making like such big strong men protecting a wee slip of a girl against the savage and insane Papists. So after three occasions in a row where I'd be standing about and all she and I could do was wave to each other, in secret, it fell to me to go see her.

What wound up helping me most was McCloskey's. I met any number of lorry drivers still running between Derry and Belfast, and even Dublin. I found whenever I showed them ways to keep their lorries up to snuff and use less petrol on their runs, I could hop a ride across the Foyle. If I mentioned it was for a fix-it job, of course. I was never refused.

I'd be up before at cock's crow and down to McCloskey's, where the driver would swing up and I'd hop in. We'd head for the first checkpoint and he'd hand over his papers and present me as his helper. I'd get searched for weapons and they'd find none. They'd also see I had a few quid on me and a change of clothes, so I must be working for the man. After a bit of back and forth, we'd be sent on our way.

Until the next checkpoint, where we'd go through it all, again. I wondered if these idiots kept any contact with one another, they were so unaware of what had happened from one checkpoint to the next. Then one driver filled me in that this was merely a method of control used by *dilettantes* with no true purpose.

And there was another word I had to ask use of Father Jack's dictionary for. I didn't quite understand how *being superficial* fit here, since they were deadly serious at every step, but I wasn't going to argue the point.

The driver would swing up St. Columb's Park and drop me then curl back down Glenshane to head on for Belfast. By this point, I'd have my best clothes on and look for all the world like I could be Protestant, and never once did I have trouble. Then on about nine, I'd see Joanna coming and I'd catch my breath each time at the mere sight of her. Silky hair blowing in the breeze. Long legs moving quick and easy. Breath whispering in the cold morning air.

Sunshine or rain, we'd meet and spend the day together, and what we did was...well, we did nothing but be with each other. Sometimes we'd talk about life and meaning, or her friends and mine and how much trouble they'd got into or were about to get into, or her plans for her future. She was taking French, now, and she wanted to teach it, so she was aiming for Queen's in Belfast. I told her Eamonn had been there.

"How'd he like it?" she asked, and she was after a serious report. We were on the side of a hill looking out over the Foyle, that day. Soft clouds in the sky. A few trees about. Some other couples. Birds dancing about in the light air. The world open and honest, for a moment.

"He loved his first couple terms," I said. "He'd write me letters on the courses he was in and pushed me to join him."

"But you're not going."

I shrugged. "I like working McCloskey's. He's fair and pays when he says he will."

"Not what you're worth."

That brought a warmth to my heart. "Jo, I found something I'm good at. Fixing cars. Appliances. Little things for people that make them enormously happy. Which makes me happy. But going to university? I dunno. Seems Eamonn was happier when he was thinking about attending Queen's than while actually there."

"Je ne comprends pas." I gave her a full idiot's look, I'm sure, so she giggled and said, "What d'you mean?"

I shrugged and lay back on the cold damp grass, and made a note to myself to figure some way of bringing a blanket to sit upon, next time. "He doesn't talk to me about it, now. About anything. He keeps his thoughts to himself and his mates, and when I ask him how it's going, all he ever says is, *Fine*. But it's not fine; you can hear it in his voice. He has worries."

"Haven't we all, right now?"

"There's truth in that. And Belfast is proving to be worse than Derry, when it comes to such."

"God, I hope all this madness will be done, soon. I'd hate to be at Queen's in the middle of such hate and anger."

"Something to dream about." I rolled onto one side to face her. She was seated, knees drawn up, flowery hip-huggers tight around her legs, jacket zipped but loose, eyes closed and head tilted back, just a little, as if she were sampling the gentle scents of new flowers off the nearby hedges. It broke my heart to look at her, and I wondered if I should even bring it up. But I had questions and I wanted to be full and honest with her, forever, so I said, "Do you have to go to Belfast?" She looked at me, confused. "What about St. Andrew's?"

"What do you know of St. Andrew's?"

"You mentioned it."

"So far from my family?"

"Well, it'd be better than-than anything here."

"Te me voudrais quitter?" she asked.

"Huh?"

"Trying to be rid of me?" She smiled as she said it.

"No, no, no, no, I-I'd join you," I said, not really understanding what it truly meant. "We'd be in an undivided city, Jo. No sneaking around to meet. I could get a job there, maybe as good as McCloskey's. Find myself a bed-sit."

She sat back, propped up on her arms. "That's a big jump. Different country and all."

"It's still the UK."

She sort of nodded, not looking at me but not committing. So another thought hit me.

"Then what-what about Trinity, in Dublin?"

"I've never been there."

I jumped up to my knees. "To Dublin? You? Oh, Jo, it's a grand city with people running everywhere and happy and cars filling the streets and-and it's joyous to behold."

"When did you go?"

Oops. "Well...I haven't, yet. But I've seen photos and movies and-and will you come with me, some day? If I can arrange it?"

She smiled at me and said, "I would."

Did my heart do back-flips then? Need I say?

What I didn't mention was I'd already heard Mrs. Carroway down the road from us was planning a trip there for shopping, soon. Nothing definite had been set because she was nervous about the checkpoints, but I knew she'd not mind passengers with me paying half the petrol. Same for my lorry mates, though they would be a last resort; I couldn't imagine hours in a truck with diesel fumes and God knows what else being a great way to start a day trip.

Or provide a way back, Brendan. Best think this through before opening your mouth. Bus is far too slow.

Turned out Mrs. Carroway decided against it, but she did mention Father Jack's new housekeeper had told her he was called down to Dublin. I was leery of asking him because I knew it'd be in the middle of the week he'd want to go and I wasn't sure Joanna would ditch work at her father's shop and, well, to be honest, I didn't trust him to not use it in some way.

His recent sermons dealt much with the need for *love from both sides of the divide,* and I had a strong suspicion he'd been trying to dig information from Jackie and Aidan about the true intentions of PIRA. I knew this because he'd then tried working his words on Eamonn, who for once said a lot of nothing to him but certainly filled me in on it. That's when Father Jack, oh, *casually* checked about my feelings on them. I couldn't say a thing since I knew nothing and preferred it that way.

But then I thought, if I present it as Joanna secretly going down to consider Trinity College for University, and her having talked me into considering it, the devil take him for anything else he might think. It meant we'd get a nice ride in a decent car. I'd kept his Cortina in top shape, and we might also get an easier passage through the checkpoints and across the border. That in and of itself could save a good hour's travel time.

So I put it to him after mass, that Sunday. And he reacted about as I expected when I mentioned where we'd need to pick Joanna up, from the Waterside.

"Is this girl Catholic or Protestant?" he asked, removing his spectacles. Already his eyes were dancing in thought.

"I never asked her, Father," I said, which is true. "Do you think it's important?"

"Some might."

Are you one, despite your words about working to make it mean nothing, hit my mind but I was able to keep from saying it.

"We neither one raised the issue," I said, then just had to add, "It didn't matter to me."

"Now, Brendan, it mattered enough for you to keep it quiet."

Which was good to hear. It sounded as if, on the occasions where I'd been seen dancing about town with a fresh-faced lass, one I'd told Jackie was from Claudy, the first assumption would be she's of our faith and just in town to shop. I'd had no fear Danny would have told anyone different, and I'd heard nothing more from him since he'd left. And I'd never introduce her to me other mates. Three questions from Colm in front of Paidrig and it'd be all over the Bogside who she really was and where she's from, and I'd no interest in dragging that sort of attention onto her.

"We only saw each other a few times, over here," I said, which was...pretty much truth. "It was easier for me to drop over to see her."

"I thought you were unhappy with Protestants, Brendan. The language you used against them and some of the actions you and your family have taken..."

"You've mixed me up with Eamonn," I said.

"Right, right," he said kindly enough, but his expression grew hard. "You're the one who works both sides."

"What?!"

"For your repairs." Said with his finest smile. "What did you think I meant?"

I knew better than to answer that question.

"She's different, Father Jack. She sees me. Talks to me like I mean something. She speaks French to me! Because of her, I'm thinking—I'm thinking maybe I'll aim for the A-Levels after all and..."

"You've already left school, and your marks were not as good as they could have been."

"Because I didn't care. My only plan was to work, own a shop, have a family. Now? Now I'd keep on and-and study hard and focus on everything I've not paid attention to and I'd show them all I'm as capable as the next lad." And a bigger liar, but no hurt in sweetening the pot by suggesting he might finally get me to better myself. And I could tell from his eyes he was considering this a big opportunity to advance his public face.

"I'm planning on driving down Tuesday next," he said. "I'd be happy for both of you to join me."

I managed to see Joanna at Marianne's for a few minutes that Wednesday evening and she agreed to come, and I cannot begin to explain the joy this brought me. It was beginning to look like she and I could escape this devil's hole once the time came right. In fact, if she did get accepted to Trinity or St. Andrew's, I could go on ahead and have my nest ready for when she arrived.

So the following Sunday I snuck the Cortina into McClosky's and checked her over, bumper to bumper, to make certain she'd be road worthy. No need to tempt providence any more than necessary by having a mechanical incident on the road. It's while I was replenishing the oil that a knock came to the roll-down and it scared the living Jesus out of me. I couldn't see out but since no one was trying to unlock the doors, I figured it wasn't the peelers or McCloskey so I rolled the door up.

There stood Colm, smiling ear to ear.

"Took you long enough, lad," he said.

I pulled him inside and rolled the door down, snarling, "What the fuck's this about?"

"Jesus, Bren, you gotta be such a bastard?"

"Put a lid on it," I snapped. "I'm doing this without McCloskey's okay. You trying to let him know?"

"Well you didn't answer the main door."

"So what d'you want?"

"Father Jack says you're off to Dublin with him."

I knew it, the gossipy bastard. "What if I am?"

"You thinkin' of movin' there?"

"Dunno. Maybe. Thought I'd see what the jobs were like."

"They're as bad as here."

"You know that, do you?" I got back to the Cortina. Time for another can of oil.

"I've been there a few times."

"Have you? What were the checkpoints like? Border crossing?"

"I-I didn't go the usual route."

Oh, Christ, he was leading up to something, but I knew I'd not know what it was till he said it.

He leaned over the front fender to watch. "Y'know, they got another migration goin' of people lookin' for jobs. I got an uncle down there."

"I thought he was in—"

"From Liverpool. With a job don't pay shite. Just been over a few month. He's thinkin' of going to South Africa."

"Port Elizabeth, with your brother?"

"Yeah. Or America. So, would you do somethin' for me while you're there?"

"In America?" I asked, grinning at him.

"Who knows, these days? I mean, you got family, there."

"By marriage only. In Canada."

"Isn't that part of America?"

I had to think, a moment. "No, Colm, we learned that in geography. It's the same continent, yeah, but I don't think the States includes them."

"Why wouldn't they?"

"I dunno. Tur says Gerry's been to Niagara Falls and crossed the border with just an ID, so maybe I'm wrong."

He laughed. "Doubt it. You paid more attention in that class. But would you drop a letter off, in Dublin? I'd ask Father Jack to do it, but Uncle Finn's in Clontarf."

"*Uncle Finn?*"

"Really a cousin to my Ma."

From a brother to an uncle to a cousin? Yeah, this sounded straight. "Where's it at?"

He pulled out some hand-written directions. "Here, these'll get you there from Trinity."

"Father Jack told you another reason I'm going, eh?"

Colm shrugged. "I'll spot you a fiver. For fare."

I rolled my eyes. "And I've nothing else to do, is that it?"

"Well, you can check the jobs from anywhere. And Uncle Finn might be able to steer you towards a few." He offered up a small envelope.

I took it.

If anyone but Colm had asked me, I'd have said no without hesitation, but all I could say was, "Right, Colm, you're me China."

"It's good to hear you say that, Bren," he said, almost beaming. "And you're mine."

So two days later, I met Father Jack outside the parish door and off we went. And sure enough, we passed through the checkpoints with little trouble. As arranged, Joanna had begged off work and was waiting on Spencer. She jumped in the car's rear seat and we headed down the Dungiven Road.

It was more than two years since I'd come this way, but it seemed changed. It really wasn't, of course. The road was still narrow and a bit more in need of repair. It still curved and dipped past farmland dotted with lambs and cattle. And my memory of the walk to Claudy mingled together with thinking Joanna had been with me on that walk, even though I knew she hadn't. But the truth is, she was, even though I hadn't fully met her till some months later.

Now we were speeding past the place where I sang *The Banks of Claudy*. And the crossroad where I'd tried to flag down cars. And the spot where I'd happened upon the hurt people. And the curve up and over and around a hill to where I'd encountered what I now knew had been B-Specials with the RUC. And it all seemed unreal to me, now, and remained so until Joanna nudged me.

"Brendan, you're so quiet."

"Just thinking," I sighed.

I didn't want to say anything further, right then, since my thoughts were also laced with my first uncertainty about Father Jack and how Billy had helped in the attack at Burntollet. That was the last time I'd seen him, from my plan as much as his. Had nothing more to repair for his mother. I didn't even know if he still lived in the Fountain, since I had no cause to go over there, now. He'd become like a ghost, to me.

That brought up thoughts of how Eamonn had begun to change from then and...

And...

No.

No, no, no, no, no, none of it mattered, now. I was enroute to Dublin with Joanna. I let that wash away every concern and doubt I had. For I just knew we'd both wind up there, some day.

Father Jack spoke only in vague generalities about Trinity College and how impressive it would be to have on one's record. He went on and on about the beauty of Dublin in the spring and summer, and Joanna kept him busy with questions about his life.

Turns out while American born, in Pennsylvania, he attended seminary in Dublin because his father had, almost taking the mantle before moving to Pittsburgh for a job in a steel mill. What brogue he had came from him, and from years in seminary and living around the island. He'd been in Galway, Cobh and Wexford as a parish priest before being sent to Dublin, then taking over for Father Demian. Oh, once Joanna got him to talking about himself, he didn't stop till we were in front of St. Audoen's.

It was just after eleven and he told us to meet him back there by six, when we'd have a bite of supper and head home. I had a map, Joanna had a tiny wristwatch and agreed to keep time on it, so off we went. I had bought a few pounds worth of Punt off Father Jack so when I saw a bus coming, I all but yanked her aboard and paid the conductor in my grandest manner. Joanna chuckled and nudged me in a tender way, and I felt like a king.

The bus took us down to O'Connell and the conductor pointed us to Trinity. We crossed the Liffey, stopping on the bridge to look down the river. Low buildings lined the shore, except for a couple tall new buildings. People and cars and busses hurried towards us on the right and away from us on the left and in the distance I saw the one building I recognized.

"The Customs House," I said to her, all-knowing. "Burnt out by the IRA in 1921. Destroyed tax records and disrupted British rule."

She nodded. "Destroyed so much of Irish history. Papers. Artefacts. And then civil war." She sighed.

"They teach you that in your schools?"

She nodded, not looking at me. "So sad."

"Perhaps some of that history's better gone."

"No, never. The past is too important to be ignored or destroyed. It has to be looked at with honesty. Learned from."

"But isn't that how you wind up with hate based on what happened three-hundred years ago?"

She sighed, again. "I suppose."

We continued on along the street up to a thick stone wall that looked private. I was wondering if we'd made a wrong turn but found a narrow entrance. We passed through into what certainly seemed to be a university. A pathway led us around to an open area of grass—and there was Trinity. Not so big, the buildings close and tight, all so very gray and oddly stolid. Students wandered about, even though it was between terms.

"Probably summer courses," Joanna said as we crossed what she said was *the quad*, but her voice wasn't happy or meaning it.

"University is year 'round?" I asked. "Queen's wasn't."

"No, sometimes you just want to get ahead in them."

I just shrugged in agreement, but it seemed odd, to me. Still, despite how unimpressive it was, it felt to me like a serious college should.

I suppose.

But then Joanna said, "It's dingy."

There was truth in that. And its reputation was hardly in obvious form, just then. I had no idea where to go to know more. So we left, quiet and to ourselves, and went back to the Liffey then turned and wandered down to the Ha'penny Bridge. The buildings were plain and in need of being freshened. Traffic was steady and harsh. Americans called to each other from everywhere, as did busloads of students from a dozen different countries. Music flowed but it was obviously off records and not live. Probably too early in the day.

We crossed the bridge and wandered about some more till we

were back on O'Connell. I was not happy, for Dublin seemed not only busy but brusque, and it was an embarrassment after what I'd promised Joanna it'd be. But she seemed not to mind.

Another bus driver told us which bus was for Clontarf, and we found the address with little difficulty. A line of neat semi-detached homes along a curling street, with trees and walls and drives to keep your car. Rose gardens. All very pleasant and plain in scope.

Only it wasn't Colm's *Uncle Finn* who met us but a sharp, angry woman with coal black hair and eyes. She snatched the envelope from me, her eyes filled with such anger and hate I almost backed away. But I couldn't do that; Joanna might think less of me.

It's fortunate that with her was an older lady, all round, curved and kind. It was she who invited us in. The furnishings were pleasant and comfortable, if a bit old and threadbare, and she sat us in a parlor and fed us tea and cucumber sandwiches as she asked after Derry and the events up there. Joanna kept silent as I told of what little I was willing to. The lady seemed let down that I hadn't some horrors to share, and her associate only came into the parlor once to glare at us before going out. I was not sorry to leave that place.

"So this is Dublin," Joanna said as we returned to the bus stop. "They don't seem happy."

I had no answer. My disappointment had begun to overwhelm me.

Enroute back, we hopped off on O'Connell and stopped in some shops and found they had much finer things available than in Derry. Joanna was looking for earrings to convince herself that she should pierce her ears but seemed unable to find anything to her liking. Then we happened upon a shop on a side lane that offered not only the earrings but piercings, as well.

"My mother is against it," she said, absent and deep in thought. "She says, *Once it's done it can't be undone.*"

I looked at her, finally noticed she wore no jewelry, at all, not even the pendant I'd given her, and said without thinking, "I don't believe your ears need anything in the way of adornment."

She cast me half a smile, sideways, and I felt somewhat better.

She was still thinking about it when I noticed in the back they also provided tattoos. I idly looked through a book of them and wondered at the simplicity of the designs—anchors, dates and animals, and the like, all so uninteresting.

Until I came to a section filled with lettering. One was a lovely flowing script, like handwriting would be if made perfect.

And I started to wonder.

"Joanna, what would you think of me with a tattoo?"

"My father has one from his time in the Navy," was her absent reply. "Got it in Hong Kong, of a half-naked lady. On his left forearm. It's begun to fade. Trop mal."

"Does he have any names on him?"

"Names? Tattooed? No. Why?"

I turned to the girl at the counter and asked, "How much is one?"

"Depends on what you get," she all but snarled.

I felt a snarl coming up in answer so made myself just say, "A name. Six letters here." I motioned across my left upper arm.

"Which letterin'?" she kept growling as she came over.

"Brendan, what're you doing?" Joanna asked, coming close.

"Dunno yet," I said, then I pointed to the script.

The girl eyed my upper arm and said, "Three punt."

"How long would it take?" I asked.

"Just over an hour."

I had five punt on me and seven British pounds, which I've found they take anywhere in the city, so I said, "Let's do it."

Joanna's mouth dropped open. "Brendan..."

"What age are you?" the girl asked, her eyes narrow and wary.

"Seventeen," I said, without hesitation.

She eyed me, unsure. "You look younger, by far."

I took my coolest pose and shot back at her, "We're down from Derry lookin' at Trinity College. We're applyin' to attend, next year, and wanted to see more about it. Isn't that so, Joanna?"

She looked at me, wary, then nodded and said, "I'm not decided. I'm also considering St. Andrew's."

The girl shrugged, howled into the back, and a man the size of Mrs. McKittrick's Cresta come out. I actually swallowed in nervousness at seeing him. "He wants a tatt, right here." She patted her left upper arm. "Letterin' E-6."

"Spell it oot," he said, shoving a slip of paper at me.

I did so.

Joanna was speechless for the first few minutes, then as I was handing over the money she turned me to her and said, "Are you mental? You can't take these things off."

"I'll never want it off," I replied, and I knew deep within that was the truest thing I'd ever said about myself.

"Brendan, this is foolish. How'll you explain this to your mother? To anyone?"

"There's nothing to explain. Nothing. I love you, Joanna." And oh, my God, saying it out in the open, like that, for the first time was like opening a window to a fine spring day. "I will love you till the day I die. Nothing else matters."

"You are mad," she muttered.

"No argument from me."

She shook her head, still wary, but smiled.

The man and the girl smirked at each other, but I knew how deep my feelings were and no one could have swayed me from this course.

"Ooff wit' ye shirt," growled the man.

I removed it and sat beside him. "Does it hurt much?"

He smiled and said, "Put ye arm here, hold this grip an' do NOT move." I did as he said. He copied the script onto my skin with a pen, which tickled giggles from me, to my eternal embarrassment, then started the needle up.

And dug in.

And I bloody near screamed at the sudden pain of it.

"Do not MOVE!"

I didn't! For if there was anything I did *not* want, it's the letters to wind up like my curséd cursive handwriting. I sat there and locked my eyes on Joanna's and crushed that grip and she held my other hand and my focus stayed on keeping from crushing hers.

"Brendan, t'es trop folle," she whispered to me, smiling in admiration. "Wicked mad."

"Have been since the first day I saw you."

"When was that?"

"Bus depot. Remember? I was washing me hands."

She giggled. "In the gutter, and you had dirt on you and you were so pleased with yourself about something."

"It was the first time I fixed a car."

"You really like doing that, don't you?" I nodded. "Well, a degree from university might help you get on with British Leyland. Design cars. Build them."

"I-I-I hadn't thought of that," I whispered, and it pleased me no end that she had considered something so fine for my future.

That's when the words began spilling from me, and I told her of seeing her, again, that day we saw Eamonn off, and of following her down Ferryquay to Woolies, and watching her and her friends dance and seeing what record she bought and how I'd bought the same and the phonograph I'd fixed so's I could listen to it and how I'd seared the words and music into my heart and sung it when I wanted to see her, and this being months before the Liberation Fleadh.

She just sat there, listening to me, looking at me, seeing me and seeming fascinated by my sordid little tales. And her eyes never wavered from my face.

Of course, I said nothing of the nights I'd conjured her up.

And the girl behind the counter said nothing. But she did seem kinder and less—well, less growly as the burly man working on me seemed to grow more gentle and the pain seemed to lessen to the point I could hardly feel it, at all.

I recounted how my heart leapt from joy at seeing Joanna every time we met. How I hated parting from her. On and on and on I babbled, as if the needle was digging a truth drug into me instead of ink as he swiped and outlined and filled in. I grew hoarse from talking so much.

The girl brought us cups of tea and never had anything felt so good on my throat or tasted so fine on my tongue, even without the milk and sugar I preferred.

Finally, I could speak no more, but it was all right, for the burly man did one last wipe of his work and leaned back to smile and said, "Well doone, lad. Ye care to gain a look 'fore I cover it? Last chance fer ten day."

"Why?" I asked.

"It scabs as it heals, then peels away and what ye gain is as lovely as what ye see now."

I nodded. He put up a mirror and I laughed. "It's backwards."

He chuckled and angled the mirror then put up another to catch the first one's reflection. And oh, St. Brigit, how lovely it was. Script flowing together in tender darkness, the hint of an outline in red along the top. Dots of blood that he quickly wiped away. I drew in so deep a breath of pride, I could easily have burst, and I turned to show Joanna her new place in my soul.

She touched it, tenderly. "Does it hurt?"

Yes, it bloody well does, but what I said was, "Never. I'm yours now, no matter what. You've branded me."

She looked at me with eyes so filled with confusion and wariness, I grew afraid. Thought for an instant I'd made a fool of myself. Gone that one step too far for her or done it too soon or too sudden and now she'd back away from me for being too much a child in matters of the heart, still, and oh, dear God, I thought I'd die if that happened.

But then she leaned in and kissed it. Barely brushed her lips over the raw etching, and relief overwhelmed me. I lay my head in the crook of her neck and let out my breath, finally knowing all would be well.

She put her hand to my cheek and whispered, "It's near six. We'll be so late..."

The burly man taped me up, gave me more pads of gauze and said, "Wash it twice a day wit' soap an' water, and do NOT pick at it; let it heal its own self." I put on my shirt and coat, carefully since my arm was now as sore as if I'd been punched a dozen times in it, and we headed off to catch the bus.

I took us back by the Ha'penny Bridge and halfway across pulled Joanna close to me and kissed her. Long and deep and happy. She pulled back, but only a little, only enough to let me know she was still the one in control.

I still had to ask, "Was this too much? Have I gone too far?"

"I don't know," she whispered. "I've never had anyone willing to scar himself for me, before."

"Is that how you feel about it?"

"No. No." And she leaned into me to kiss me, and this one was as gentle as moonlight filtered through a midsummer's evening. It was the tenderness of forever. It was never-ending love. It was home.

"I'll wait for you," I whispered.

"I know," was her soft response. Then she shifted and said, "Isn't that our bus number?"

I made myself look around and saw the big, green, lumbering thing approaching a stop, and damn but she was right. For an instant I hated it. Then I laughed, grabbed her hand and we raced to catch it, and did so just as it pulled away.

It was half six by the time we found Father Jack, but he wasn't angry. "To be honest," he said, "I didn't really expect you till seven. I'm told the café just down the road has a fine stew, if you like. Let's pop in there before we're off home."

Over supper, we told him of everything except the letter and the tattoo. And his response to our feeling about Trinity was, "It matters not what the classroom looks like, or the campus, but what is learned in it, and Trinity has a fine reputation for that."

The drive back to Derry was long but so full of magic as the shadows of trees and fields passed to our left. Before we left the South, despite the night being nowhere near complete, I knew the stars were similing at me for this brazen act.

I sat in the back and let Joanna stretch out in the front. Little was said by any of us; I got the impression Father Jack did not like driving so late, because his few words were tighter than I'd ever heard from him.

My arm now ached from my neck to my fingers, but still I felt good and right. And each time I caught Joanna glancing at me, I'd touch where her name was now mine, forever, and I'd smile, and she'd smile back. And we were so deliriously happy, not even the casual indignity of the customs crossing and silly checkpoints could dampen our spirits.

Internment

Marching season came upon us, again, but this year was not like the previous. Oh, there were the usual fights and anger, back and forth. Catholics against Protestants, of course. But what grew harsher were the disagreements between those in the IRA wanting negotiation against those demanding action. What began to build true horror was how men were being murdered on each side not only by loyalist bastards but also their own. And the Army had to jump in, as well, but they were fool enough to offer up nonsensical excuses for the killings they committed. Now what had finally become too obvious to all was we were caught by this slow-motion spiral into chaos, and everyone sensed it would explode when August came calling, again, which many were terrified of and just as many, deep down, hoped for.

Eamonn was rarely home, now, and when he was he'd appear from nowhere. Either Jackie or Aidan would be with him, and Rhuari and I would be sent to the hutch to sleep, so they could have our beds to smoke and drink and talk with each other in hushed tones. Ma swore it was good for them to be there, and she was happy to have Kieran share her bed.

The first night.

She quickly found Rhuari's complaints about him being restless were not in the least exaggerated. I had to chuckle at that, for any who knew my younger brother knew he hadn't the interest to work up an exaggeration with the intention of filling Ma with exasperation. So on the settee is where Kieran went, and it seemed he preferred his back against the rear panel, blanket tight around him, unmoving.

When I noticed this, I mentioned it to Rhuari. We pushed their bed into a corner, then he settled Kieran against it with his own blanket, which seemed to handle a lot of the trouble. What I found interesting was, that was the bed Jackie would take, and the sheets and covers would look like they were crushed against the wall, like with Kieran. So it never got moved, again.

He sported a beard, now, our Eamonn, with his hair to his shoulders and shining in ways I didn't know a lad's hair could. Jackie and Aidan were frizzy and more ragged in theirs, and the three of them had lost weight, but the fire in their eyes gave them an aura of meaning and invincibility. The first time I saw them together, I thought of Jesus, Matthew and Peter.

And yes, I know, it's sacrilege to compare my brother to *the* Jesus, but that was my thought and so be it. It also brought more nervousness to my heart, for them, because without question they would be at the front lines when trouble did arrive.

So they would appear, do their running about, then after a day or two vanish into the night, as if they'd been naught but ghosts brought forth by the moment.

On more than one occasion, Eamonn would take me aside and demand I bring him that pistol. Each time, I refused. No question in my mind, if he were snatched and had that thing on him he'd never see the freedom side of the bars, again. Each time, he'd huff and growl but then get distracted and that would be that.

Until the start of August.

One of those long days. No night, not in total. Always unsettling to me, not having the darkness to be my companion. You would think after fifteen years I'd be used to it, but as I'd shown when being birthed, I was more a creature of the night.

It still was bright out when Eamonn showed up, with Jackie and Aidan, both. They took over my room so I moved a few items in need of repair down to the hutch. I never knew how long they'd be and I'd made promises about finishing them. Of course, Ma saw them and cast me her sharpest eye, but I said nothing. She already knew about two of them, so no need to expand on her knowledge.

I was about to head out of the hutch when Eamonn appeared in the door and shoved me back against the side wall. Then he sat on the bed. His eyes were as sharp as Ma's, and it made me nervous. I had a feeling what he'd ask me for, and sure enough he said, "I want you to get me that pistol. Pieces is fine; I can put it together."

I just shook my head, no.

"Bren, I let you hide that, trustin' you would return it to me.

Now I want to return it to its rightful owner."

"No," was all that came out of me.

"Why not?" And his voice was soft, but deep and cold.

"It'll get you killed," I all but hissed. "I won't be part of that."

"Don't be daft. I've no intention of usin' it."

"It *has* been used and...well...intentions change. And whether you mean to or not, if it's on you and you're caught, you will die."

"You think that's the only gun I've carried?"

Oh, Christ, oh, Christ, oh, Christ, "Don't tell me that!"

"It's the only one I can't account for. I have to know where it is."

"You don't know where it is."

"I know it's here in this house."

"Do you?"

That stopped him, cold. "Brendan? What have you done?" And now his voice carried a brutal warning.

A warning too much like some I'd tried to forget.

"I-I-I've made it safe."

Suddenly, the anger in his face twisted into a mirror of Da's, the last time he hit me. He rose and grabbed my collar, growling, "You'll tell me what you've done. You'll tell me!"

"I don't think so."

He howled and punched me, so sudden and sharp, I didn't feel it. I just went from facing him, one moment, to lying on the foot of the bed, the next, silence all about me. I was beyond shock into disbelief.

Eamonn had smashed his fist into my chin.

Everything was out of line and could make no sense of it.

Then he yanked me up and slammed me back against the wall, choking me with one hand and his fist about to pummel me even more and I was so confused I couldn't even think to try and stop him and I coughed and he was spitting with fury and I knew I was for it and—

"Eamonn!" It was Maeve's voice, sharp and cold.

It jolted him and he half spun around to find her in the doorway, glaring at him.

She continued with, "Is that really what you want to do? Hurt those of us who love you?" Said in her *Don't push me* tone. And considering how many boys I'd seen her beat to the ground when they did not take warning, small wonder it made him pause.

"Where'd you come from?" he had to ask. "Listenin' in."

"We live here, you eejit," Maeve shot back.

That's when I noticed Rhuari was right behind her, sheets and blankets in hand to make the bed, his judgmental expression in full force but his voice as calm and even as ever as he said, "Eamonn, I heard a pistol was found in the brush."

Oh, Jesus, he was letting Eamonn know the two of them had heard every bloody word. They knew about the pistol, now. Knew what I'd done for Eamonn. What I was still doing and oh dear God, that was never what I wanted.

"It was up the Strand Road," Rhuari continued, impassive.

Maeve took on a far too contemplative look and asked, "Could it be the same one I found hidden here and chucked in a bin on the way to school?"

"That would be no surprise. An army patrol claims they found it and are probably lying about where it was."

His gentle comments shook the anger from my brother. Sent him into shock, almost. Never mind what they were saying showed they hadn't a clue as to what the gun was or where, Eamonn had let out information not meant to be known except by him and me. But thinking on it, that is how secrets always escaped him, not from telling but from him not paying attention and blurting the information out. He fought to think of a response.

Rhuari just took in a deep sigh, as if he hated to state the obvious, and continued, "We won't grass on you, Eamonn. We're not that sort. Are we?"

"Oh, Jackie's looking for you," Maeve added, with the sweetest smile she could muster.

Eamonn send them a look sharp and cold enough to slice meat off the bone. Which had no effect on either one. I had underestimated the abilities of my little brother and sister.

With a final glare cast at me, Eamonn's hands dropped away. He brushed them over his jacket, stumbled back out of the hutch and slipped into the house.

I gave Maeve a look first then Rhuari, shaking inside and out. Too worked up to even think of what to say. Except that bloody cough came.

Rhuari merely held up the sheets, saying, "Help me with this? I brought an extra blanket."

I touched where I'd been hit. It was starting to hurt, not only my jaw but up by my ears. Maeve eyed me and shook her head. "You're not bleeding, but you are going to be sore. You should put a cold rag on it."

"But not for a little bit," Rhuari added. "Aidan was at our window, watching. It's good you two were out of sight and on low volume."

I gulped in a breath and cast them both a smile of thanks.

Maeve grinned and said, "I'll help Ma with supper." Then she bounced inside.

So Rhuari and I made the bed, and I refused to do anything about my chin for fear Aidan or Jackie might wonder, and Eamonn said nothing more about the pistol.

Not that he had time to get to me, again. That was the evening rumors began circulating about internment being instated. Mrs. Rafferty, being her usual contrary self, refused to believe the Army would allow it.

"They've done the best job they can," she said, "to keep us safe from those bastards."

"Let Wilson come here and see for himself how things are," snapped Mrs. O'Canainn. She now lived across the street. The Housing Authority had found issues with the foundation of her new place and had to rebuild that line of terrace homes.

Both were visiting with Ma at the kitchen table, pots of tea already downed and biscuits well-eaten. Ma's response to them was simple. "If the bastards try, they'll find God's own anger will be unleashed on them."

There was much agreement around the table, for that.

There were also God only knows how many meetings around how many similar tables in any number of other homes and halls as the issue was talked down to the satisfaction of all except the *Brits Out* crowd and the *Let's Just All Get Along* groups.

My own thought was the British were putting it out to see what the reaction would be and nothing more. Only a fool would think having rumors like this racing about the Bogside would help them snatch anyone in the IRA. As arrogant as their leaders could be, they weren't stupid enough to stick around for that.

Then the second week of August, full dawn just making herself known, Army trucks roared up to certain houses in the Bogside and soldiers boiled out, screaming and pounding on doors and smashing their ways inside. And don't think it wasn't recognized by one and all that this was just before the Apprentice Boys parade. Men and women were grabbed left and right, their names supposedly *on a list*. Rifles became clubs and fists became cudgels as people were dragged from their beds, half-dressed, and shoved into lorries to be hauled away to Strand Road or Castlerock or Long Kesh.

Our own door crashed open, waking me, Rhuari and Kieran as shouting men lumbered up the stairs to slam into our room, screaming, "Eamonn Kinsella! Lookin' for Eamonn Kinsella!"

I slammed back into a corner of the bed but was grabbed by my hair and yanked forward by an overbuilt para with eyes wilder than a mad dog's as a light shone in my face. "Er ye Eamonn Kinsella?"

I coughed and pure terror filled my voice as I sputtered, "No."

He didn't believe me. He yanked me down the stairs by my arm. I tripped, so he just dragged me after him.

Ma was in the parlor and saw us and came screaming up at him, "What're yous doin'? He's but fifteen! Only a child! He's my Brendan! What're yous doin', you animals? You bloody goddamned beasts!"

She was shoved away and I was half-carried outside to be tossed in the back of a lorry. Ma's curses and howls filled the air as I landed on a group of other men, Mr. Rafferty and Aidan among them. Aidan cast me a quick look of warning and a shake of his head, so I knew not to know him. Before I could get to my feet, the lorry started up and drove away, sending me flat to the floor.

It was only then I realized my shirt had been torn away and I was in naught but my pajama bottoms, and those where halfway down my hips. No slippers on my feet. Two soldiers, rifles at the ready, kept watch on us, and I noticed one kept special watch on me, a near smile on his lips.

Jesus, were half the Paras like priests after boys?

We were taken to Strand Road and packed into a small, dark, wet filthy cell, like animals for slaughter. Aidan and Mr. Rafferty were shoved into a separate one and I did not see them, again. Half the men I knew and the rest I knew of, and none were part of the Republican resistance. One finally told me, I think his last name was Lemass, but he told me, "The IRA got wind of it and they scattered. Left us to it. Bastards.”

I didn’t say it, but I thought, *Of course they did. Why would they wait around to get snatched?*

One man gave me his shirt to wear, and since I was so small I was let sit on the one bench so I could pull my feet up under me to warm them. I coughed, now and then, and another man—a Mr. Tremaine?—asked if I was well.

“Nervous habit,” I said, barely keeping my voice from shaking.

He nodded and squatted before me. “I’ve a sister like that. Any time she has to do the ironing, her cough starts up and continues till she’s done. Then it’s done. What’s quare is, she swears she loves ironing.”

I forced a smile for him.

He looked closer. “Your lips’re almost blue. Cold?”

I nodded. Well, more like a shiver of agreement, then cough after cough, dammit.

He settled on the wet floor, next to the bench, and it was not easy for him; he was a large man. “Come here,” he said. “I’ve three sons and five daughters, and when they were cold this helped warm them.”

He drew me onto his lap and wrapped beefy arms around me. “You should have that cough looked at, to be certain.”

Like a father would say, hit my brain. I nodded.

He held me. And it did warm me. And I near started to cry from never having felt this sort of protection, before. But I refused to weep in front of the other men. Just let his warmth transfer to me. Let myself gain control and put enough worry aside to figure this was only a childish move by bullies, meant to install fear not only in those snatched but those who saw it. *You could be next* was the unspoken message, and in some it might work their way. But it was stupid and would only build anger and disgust in the majority of Derry people. Even then I knew how badly the British had blundered.

Then two soldiers came into the cell and I was dragged into a four-square room for interrogation by a fat, snarling man at a tiny desk. No windows. No papers on the wall. A single light bulb hanging from the ceiling. And I was watched over by those two, both with arms at the ready, which almost brought a laugh to me. I didn’t know I was so dangerous.

First question asked? My name.

"Brendan Kinsella," I said, "and I've done nothing wrong."

"We'll be the judge of that," said the fat one as the two slapped me against a wall, told me to turn around and hold my hands against it, then fat lad stormed around behind me asking questions over things I knew nothing about.

Where's your brother?

Where's Eamonn Kinsella?

Why was I over the Waterside so much?

When was the last time I was in Coleraine?

Had I ever smuggled guns up from the Republic?

Was that me throwing stones at the Army?

With that last question, he showed me a photo of wee Eamonn next to Paidrig, neither doing a thing. I'd have laughed, but my head was spinning so and I was close to losing what sense I had. They even slapped my face with that fine notebook Joanna had given me, asking whose it was, and refusing to believe it was mine.

Meaning they'd searched our house.

Meaning they might have found the pieces of that pistol.

Oh, Christ, I should have given it to Eamonn.

This went on and on for what seemed like hours, and I managed to hold onto my panic, just telling them, again and again and again, who I was and that I knew nothing and fought like mad to keep the fear low in my voice. But I could keep no control over that cough. They would scream into my ear and shove me and slap their sticks against the wall, nearly hitting me. Push me. Kick at my bare feet. Some came in and others went out and it was nonstop and I was getting to be so bloody tired and close to crashing into the terrors.

Then one of the men behind me finally gave a long irritated sigh and said, "I told you he's too young." He sounded proper British.

"Ye don' unnerstan' 'bout these wee bas'ards," his mate snarled. "They fookin' animals an' star' 'em in 'a womb."

"Shall we begin snatching five-year-olds, next? Don't be absurd."

That's when I was yanked from the room, made to sign some piece of paper to get my notebook back, and all but thrown into the street by a couple of peelers. Without a word. Just tossed out like refuse.

I staggered to the middle of the road, fully confused as to where I was, and nearly got hit by a passing car. I stumbled to one side and my pajamas slid down my hips. It was low twilight and the breeze was chilly, but what time was it? I didn't even really know what hour I was grabbed, so could not work it out in my head. Was it to winter, now? Had I been kept in there for months? And why was my notebook in my hand? I'd never have brought it out to use; it was too nice.

Then I heard a yell and my name.

At least, I think it was my name, but I couldn't swear to it. I couldn't think of what to do. I just sort of stood there. Moving about in a loose circle. Coughing. Starving. Desperate for a fag. The world so loose and unreal around me. Maybe I was dreaming all this and about to wake up and find myself next to the window and covers off and cold air whispering in to bring on these chills in the middle of winter even though I would swear it was supposed to be summer.

"Brendan! Brendan!"

I turned and saw Mai. She was hurrying up to me, as fast as she could in her condition, building yet another child. Two other women beside her. She had a coat and slung it over my shoulders. It felt so nice, even though I wasn't so much cold as I was shivering from true confusion.

"Are you well?" she said, her voice cracking. "Brendan, Brendan, answer me, are you well?"

I think I nodded. Can't swear to it.

One of the ladies poured tea from a thermos into its cap and I drank it down in one gulp, even though it burned my throat and was far stronger than I like.

"They took Turlach," Mai continued, now guiding me across to the sidewalk. "Searched the flat for hours. Made a mess trying to find something. Tore it apart."

Oh, Christ, it hit me about that gun, again. They'd searched our house. Had they found it? Shite.

No. No, they'd said nothing to me about it. Just my notebook. They'd not have let me go if they'd found it. Would they?

Mai continued with, "Wouldn't tell me what they were looking for and then they left with him. Called him IRA. He's not; he's not."

"They-they-they asked me the same," I said, surprised I was finally able to find my voice. "And about Eamonn and Jackie. They got Aidan. Where was he?"

"Mrs. Payne's. He's been seein' her daughter. I want to stay until Turlach's released, so I'm sendin' you home."

Walk the streets by myself? Through the checkpoints by myself? Wearing next to no clothing? Without shoes? That did not sound the least bit proper.

I finally noticed a crowd of other women whose husbands and sons had been grabbed. Their voices were neither gentle nor kind as they howled at the guards, nor were their words. But could they have shoes for me, maybe? Slippers would be fine. A nice pair of jeans. The coat would suffice atop the shirt. I'd bring everything back to you, well-washed. Promise. You know I can be trusted, right?

Then it hit me. "Ma's not here?"

"She's with the wains."

Of course. She'd have Kieran, Michael Paul and Jordan Allen to worry about. Of course. So I said, "I-I'm not in shoes."

We rounded a corner to find a black cab parked there, idling.

"Here's Colm's Da," Mai said.

I panicked. "Did they snatch Colm?"

"No, no, no. He's here just to help. He'll drop you."

She guided me into the back and he took me home. Even gave me one of his fags. Some bloody French thing, but I wasn't going to quibble. Of course, he also asked me about a whine coming from his left wing when he turned. I couldn't hear it so told him I'd have to look at it the next day. He agreed to come by after his rounds.

For once, when I walked through the front door Ma didn't greet me with anger or a slap. Instead, she quietly led me to the washroom and set a hot bath going. Then she brought me clean pajamas and said, "I'm popping 'round the chippy for your supper. You all right here?"

I just nodded. I had yet to undress.

"Whose shirt is that?" she asked.

I shrugged. "I-I didn't know him. I think he's from Pennyburn."

Ma nodded. "It's a good shirt. I'll wash it and send out word; he's sure to come 'round for it." Then she left.

He never did. I think he was one of the men sent to that prison ship...uh, the Maidstone, and held.

I undressed and sat in the tub, and it was so lovely and hot and gentle with me, I fell asleep. Woke in my bed, in pajamas. No idea how I got there and did not want to leave it.

Except I realized Ma must have done this and she would have seen my tattoo. Oh, Christ, I'd tried so hard to keep it hid. I knew there'd be hell to pay for this. But when I finally came down for supper, never a word was said about it. Nor did I offer explanation. We just let it be.

As for Mr. O'Faelan's cab, it needed nothing but some industrial tape to buffer the wing from rubbing against the chassis and he was happy for that. I considered it a fair exchange for the ride home. As did he, of course.

Our house *was* bad hit by their searching. Walls broken that needed mending. Most of Ma's plates smashed. Glassware, too. Furniture overturned and framed photos torn apart. I helped Ma clear it up and made some repairs, but not so very much was salvageable. They had taken pure pleasure in their destruction, there.

And yet not one of my hiding places were found. I didn't really understand how not, but I took great pride in it.

I then went to Mai's. She had been sent home, due to her condition, with promises the moment they knew anything she'd be told. Their place hadn't been done as badly to. Smashing was done here and there, but more like just for the sake of it, not as if they were actually looking for anything. Which told me they knew full well Tur was not IRA. They had taken him because they could. The bastards.

It was five days before word came he was to be released. I was at Mai's painting the last repaired wall, with Michael Paul and Jordan Allen making Ma happy, at our home. Mr. O'Faelan dropped by to tell her and Mai was out the door and in his cab the second he spoke. I ran up to Mr. Devlin's and we drove to Strand Road in his estate car, arriving just after Tur had come out.

I almost didn't recognize him, he was so bunched in on himself and was holding onto Mai like a man dying. He was barely able to look at us or even stand erect. I bolted from the car and ran up to help her. Others had been released, as well, so Mr. O'Faelan was free to take them.

We led Tur to Mr. Devlin's car as he muttered, "I was. Was stood at a wall. For hours." His voice soft and cracking. "Hands up on wall. Loud noise. In room. Screamed questions at me. For days."

Jesus, like me only worse.

"Who'd I know in. In IRA? PIRA? OIRA? Was I? Was I part of it all? If I tried to sit, they'd hit me. Curse me. No sleep. Wouldn't let me use a toilet. When I-I-I-I had to piss, they-they had me piss on meself..."

Tears trailed from his eyes as we drove him home, and it was scary how confused he was. He'd forget what he told us and would tell us what had happened, again. Over and over. As if his shaking and the stench wasn't reminder enough.

We got him into the flat and he collapsed in a chair and looked around the room, in amazement. Mai tended to him with a basin of hot water and soap as I heated some stew. She managed to get him out of those trousers and wrapped in a robe, then brought him a steaming bowl and a sup of ale. But his hand shook so, he couldn't even hold a spoon. She had to help. The way he looked at her and she him, you'd have thought she was his Ma and he her child.

Oh, dear God, how angry that made me, and how lucky I considered myself to not have been held more than a few hours. And that a man had been there to warm and comfort me before the interrogation. Something neither my mother nor my father would have done, I was certain. In fact, it amazed me that my sister and fallen so easily into the role of caregiver, since she had no one to model after, but there she was; the one more our mother than our mother.

I mentioned it when she came into the kitchen for more of the stew, and she corrected me.

"Before he grew too lost in his anger and hate, there were occasions, for a while—when Da would come home deep in his cups—he would sit at the bottom of the stairs, crying, and Ma would hold him. Care for him."

"I don't remember anything like that," I said.

"It was just before you were born."

"But you'd have been only four years old..."

"I remember it, well enough. After your birth's when Da began to change. The crying stopped. The more of us there were to feed, the angrier he grew. Ma tried to calm him, but after a point? Well, not even Father Demian could get through to him."

"He hated Father Demian," popped out of me before I could think to stop it.

Mai looked at me, shocked. "How can you say such a thing? Da never said word one against him."

I just shrugged, but I remembered the look of hate he'd sent after the man, and his comments. And I was growing more and more certain Da had been done to like Danny, and my hate of him—the one thing I'd been sure about—it was turning to shame.

Perhaps it was better for me not to know anything about him.

Tur's Da left and came back with his mother and more food and even more bottles of ale. Ma brought Michael Paul and Jordan Allen, soon after, along with Rhuari, Maeve and Kieran, and we had a quiet chat in the sitting room for an hour. Tur never left that chair, and he trembled every time he tried to take a sip of his drink. No one would watch him. They seemed set on ignoring how damaged he was.

Ma took over the kitchen, leaving Kieran with me, and she insisted Mai remain next to Tur, at his knee.

"He needs you there," she'd said in a voice that brooked no dissent. "Just let him see you. Let him touch you. Keep a hand on him at all times."

Mai did as Ma said.

Seeing and hearing that, it offered verification of what Mai had said. Ma had done this with Da before I was here, for I could remember little of them being simply pleasant with each other.

God, the expression on Mai's face as she gazed upon him, it would have broken the hardest of men. They were like that all evening. The whole of her seated on the floor, her head on his leg, her hand holding his and him unable to look away from her. He seemed caught between life and death, at the moment.

Until finally she shifted around to look at him, crossed her arms atop his legs and lay her chin on them. Her eyes never left his as she said, "Call your brother in Toronto."

He grew even more still and gazed upon her, unsure. His head cocked from side to side, like a dog, as he fought to understand what she was telling him.

Everyone else cast quick glances at each other, silent and unsure. Ma came from the kitchen, ladle in hand, apron around her shift, her eyes filled with hurt. But her lips were pursed tight.

I could now see not only a hint of hope in Tur's eyes but also how weary Mai was as she said, "I'm about to have another child. You're no good to them or me if you're crippled, unemployed, jailed or dead, and this is only the beginnin' of what those bastards plan for us. Gerry once said he'd make room, any time we want to come. He's set up, now. I think we should accept his offer."

Tur began to shake, again, his eyes locked on her, but he seemed unable to speak. It was Mr. Devlin who asked, "When do you want to go?"

Tur jolted and looked at his Da as Mai smiled at him.

"On the New Year," she said. "Let this one be born here. Settle what's needed. Have a last Christmas. And that should give us time to prepare for it."

Mrs. Devlin looked away, her hands quivering.

Mr. Devlin just nodded.

Ma glared at Mairead but still said nothing. Just returned to the kitchen. Which made me uncomfortable.

Rhuari came over to sit by me, on the floor, and I put my arm around him. Michael Paul was in his seat, in the kitchen, and Jordan Allen in his bassinette while Kieran paid us no mind as he played with his Hot Wheels, so I beckoned Maeve over and we huddled there, now ignored by the adults. Three kids unaffected by what was about to happen, even though it affected us all.

"So it's just us now?" Rhuari asked. He was reading some book called *Turf Fire Stories*, his finger holding his place.

"And Kieran," I said, "once he's able to sneak past Ma."

"Are you leaving, too?"

I looked at him. Saw he was in long jeans and a rugby shirt. Keds on his feet. I was rather miffed because I wasn't allowed to dress like that till I was near twelve...and then I realized, he wasn't even two years younger than me, right then. How could I forget that?

"I'm not yet sixteen, Rhurai. Where could I go?"

He looked at me for a long moment. Made me uneasy. He might have the appearance of a boy, but there was far more understanding in his eyes. He finally nodded and returned to his book.

He knew what I was thinking. In the back of my head, for just a flash, I'd thought of joining Mai and Tur, but that would have meant leaving Joanna and I couldn't. Not yet. I wanted to be where she was, where she'd be at school, and not once had she discussed the idea of Canada. I could raise that as possible, for she did speak French and even mentioned once they do so in Montreal, and there would be just as fine as anywhere, but I was certain she'd not go for it. She hadn't even liked Dublin, a city with those more our kind, and truth was, I did prefer the idea of Edinburgh. It's where Robert Louis Stevenson was from, and I'd enjoyed *The Strange Case of Dr. Jekyll and Mr. Hyde.* So while I wished nothing but success for Tur and Mai in Canada, I knew it was not for me.

But I was thinking more and more that soon as I was able, Joanna and I should also leave.

Dancers Dancing

Now that internment was the law, there were more arrests to be followed by more claims of torture during interrogations. What's crazy is, thanks to rumors exploding throughout the Bogside, the Army netted no more than five true IRA members—and Aidan, though I don't think they realized their prize in him, for he got released after a week.

And vanished.

I hold no blame to him.

They also proved their blatant bias by arresting one whole Loyalist for every ten Catholics, despite them having been the first to fight back against them. London still insisted it was all *so-very-even-handed*, but even the blind could see how it was contrived to hurt our side. And in their usual brilliance, all the British achieved was to increase recruitment and support for PIRA and the IRA, to the extent both groups were unable to handle them all and actually had to turn some away. But wasn't that how the English work? Do all you can to muck everything up then swear it was the best option possible?

And if that wasn't enough to make things clearer for us as to who was for whom, the loyalists made things a hundred times worse by bombing McGurk's Bar in Belfast. Killed fifteen Catholics, including two children, and injured nearly two-dozen more. Then issued a press release claiming it was an *own-goal* by an IRA man carrying a bomb meant for elsewhere. In the face of all evidence to the contrary. People in the area were so incensed, they attacked the soldiers sent to help in the disaster and killed one.

Which angered the Army even more. *How dare people hold us responsible for the situation and complete destruction of trust that we brought about?* So of course they increased their brutality towards Catholics.

Which gave Protestants cause to rejoice. The fools honestly thought that this horrific act of violence would show us who was lord and master, now, when all it did was spin things faster and closer to chaos. They were no better than beasts.

There followed more demonstrations and marches and riots and accusations of foul treatment from both sides, with the army claiming to be caught in the middle but still more interested in helping the Loyalist cause than ours. Anything that happened, be it bomb, murder or riot, it was first on the IRA and never on those kicking us until proven beyond doubt. Which London went right along with, as did the British press.

As for the world? Words of encouragement were offered so that *both sides might find common ground on which to meet and settle our differences.*

Or, to be simple about it, we got fuck all.

So, what did we Catholics decide to do? Well, NICRA and the SDLP began talking of having yet another march the last Sunday of January, to protest internment. As if any of the previous ones had made a damn bit of difference. They were insisting this one would be different, despite another one in November that was broken apart by water cannons and charging soldiers. But their reasoning was, either we push back in a way that at least tries to be peaceful or, as no one wanted to overtly state, finally acknowledge we had slid into a sort of civil war. I blamed no one for not wanting to admit that this was already our reality, because it would put agreement to that bastard *acceptable level of violence* London so loved.

Christmas was close to a somber affair, but Mai gave birth to Aisling Marie not three weeks prior, so she became the focus of everyone's attention. Once again, all Mai had to do for the first three weeks was nurse her, and I'd swear Ma allowed that only with regret. She was like another person the whole time. Cooing at the wain and smiling! Her voice light and almost feathery, and this wasn't even her first grandchild! It was all very unnerving.

But she was the first granddaughter, so of course every neighbor lady in the twenty blocks around had to come and see the newest addition, and ooh and ahh over her and remark on how perfect she was, with Ma more the center of attention than Mai. There was even a short period of time where I though Ma wouldn't let Aisling be taken to Canada.

As for Tur, once the idea of the move was set, he began to return to life. He knew full well this was the best choice for them, and having his wife behind him complete gave him strength to jump feet first into the abyss. With his brother's help, he pulled together the proper documentation to emigrate with a wife and three children. A garage was made over behind the Toronto house for them to stay in till they were settled. Furniture would be provided from Gerry's furniture shop. To be paid for, of course, but only at wholesale cost; I made sure that was understood.

You don't profit over family.

And don't tell me that's what I've been doing with my hidey-holes. I charged nothing for anything I fixed around the house or for Ma. Of course, even if I'd tried I'd never have seen a penny.

The only truly negative reaction came just before the birth of Aisling, when Mai was upstairs with the midwife, Mrs. Brogan, for a final checkup. Tur was handling the two boys and I'd dropped in after finishing McClosky's hoping Mai'd also feed me, since her cooking was a far sight better than Ma's. Even Tur's was better, for he knew how to use butter and cheese in a spud to make it taste fine.

So I was peeling spuds when Eamonn slammed through the rear door, out of nowhere, snarling like a rabid dog. My heart dropped to my feet, till I knew it was him.

"What're yous doing?" I snapped.

He shoved past me to find Tur, breathing heavy and fast in near terror, holding Michael and Jordan, both, and crushed into a corner of the parlor, deep in shadows, as if to hide. Both boys were wailing.

Eamonn all but spit, "I hear you're desertin' us!"

I tried to pull him back, yelling, "Eamonn, stop it!"

He shoved me away, snarling, "Keep out of this, Bren!"

I near fell over, but still shot back, "It's not your business, either!"

"I-I-I have a family," Turlach replied, his shakes back. He let both boys down, trying hard not to let his terrors take him over. "I've got—I've got responsibilities, and—"

Eamonn grabbed him in such a way he nearly fell to the floor, pushing the boys aside. "So do others, but they're not runnin' like scared rabbits!"

"Eamon, be careful!" I howled as I pulled the boys away.

He ignored me. "We have to fight back, en masse, Tur! We have to show them we can't be intimidated. If you run off, they'll think they're winnin'!"

"You don't know what they did me in that place!"

"I've heard it enough from others!"

"Heard it! You think hearing about it's the same as living through it? You knew what was coming and you and your mates run off, leaving the likes of me to be taken and-and—"

"We had to go! We can't do any fightin' from jail!"

I shoved him, howling, "So you left us to give you cover! You left me to be taken!"

That tipped him a bit off balance. "I don't understand why *you* were snatched, Bren, unless it was they thought that they might find what you—"

"Put a cap on it!" I howled. Dammit, he'd almost revealed that bloody pistol, again. "They were looking for you and let me out but ten hours later. All the time asking questions about things I knew nothing about and pushing and forcing me to stand there and you think they'd have let me go if they'd any reason not to? And not a word till now from you or Jackie or Colm? They kept Tur for days, and him knowing nothing they could want."

Eamonn began to pace, running a hand through his hair and huffing like he was lost and confused as he said, "Bren, I-I-I can't tell you how sorry I am. For what happened to you, but we have to—we're in a war and lookin' to the future."

"Others have left," I shot back. "Why not Tur? What's so hard about him taking our sister and nephews to another land?"

"He-he's married to *my* sister! *My* family! It looks like we can't protect you."

"You can't! That's been proven."

"Eamonn," Tur muttered as he backed away. "What good is a future if my sons don't live to see it? If I don't live to see it? You want me to stay here and hope I don't get killed or sent to Long Kesh over lies or-or even crippled and become a burden to me own wife while you and your mates wander about taking shots at nothing and-and—"

His voice was cracking and his words stumbling and the boys were still crying and me?

Me?

I was being cut to bits by memories of my few moments in

that room, and coughing and furious at my brother for being this way.

"We're not doin' nothin'!" Eamonn snapped. "Every day we're fightin' for you."

I shoved Eamonn, howling, "Fighting by being sneaks with—?"

He rammed the heel of his hand into my chest, knocking me back against the settee. I grew dizzy from it. Breathless. Couldn't get up.

All he did was growl, "You don't lay hands on me, again! What we do is for the better of us all. What we do is stand strong!"

"Oh, yes, you stood strong when the Army came to arrest my husband!" It was Mairead's voice, sharp and cold. We looked up to find her atop the stairs, her massive belly in full view, Mrs. Brogan behind her. "You can hold your tongue or you'll find the back of my hand to your face, Eamonn. People have been leavin' this God-forsaken spot of land for centuries, looking for something better, but now you're angry we're doin' it, too?"

"You back him in this, Mai?!" he shot back. "I never would have thought my own sister would turn against all we believe in and run from those who murdered our father, and let them think they've won."

Oh, Christ, he'd been wound up by Ma. I could see it, now. Her words ringing in his ears had sent him running to Tur's to try and stop the inevitable. I tried to tell Mai, but I still couldn't speak. Too weak to stand or argue back at him.

I didn't need to. Mai stormed down the steps as if she were light as a feather and without a second's hesitation yanked Eamonn back by the hair and hissed, "You live your own life and leave us to ours, or don't we have a right to decide for ourselves?"

He pulled himself away from her, back to nearly spitting with anger as he snarled, "Cowards! You'd have others carry the fight for you!"

"*You* carry the fight? So which are you, today? Connolly or De Valera? Brendan's right. You sneak bombs around. Lord it over us with your *protection rackets* and attack at will those you dislike. Then slither off like snakes when there's real trouble and blame others for what goes wrong. You act more like the bloody British than those fighting for equality and justice. Criminals and mobsters, the lot of you!"

Eamonn's fist bunched up.

Tur howled and started for him and I staggered up to grab his arm to pull him back, but Mai handled it best.

She slapped him.

As hard as Ma ever had Da.

Harder.

Near spun him in a circle. Then she kicked him in the arse. How she was able to, I have no idea, but he crumbled over as much from the shock as the pain of it. After which, she took hold of his collar and dragged him from the house. And I do mean dragged. On his arse. And threw him out to the wet street.

He rolled over to look at her, in shock, nearly prostrate. Saw others at their doors and windows or in the street, watching it all.

"This is my house and you have no say in it," Mai snarled. "Go play tin soldier with your mates. They like to parade around enough. But you best do it quick. The RUC'll have spies out and about lookin' for you. It was you they were after when they took your brother!"

She slammed the door on him. I had never seen her so angry.

I was frozen stock still, my eyes locked on her in complete confusion. Not shaking, now. Nor coughing. My mind flashing between the fights Ma'd had with Da and the interrogation in Strand Road and Eamonn punching me in the hutch, and I could barely sort through any of them so had no words to say. It was like I was in a fog.

I sort of noticed that Tur was holding Jordan as Michael clung to his leg, just as shaken as I, until Mai turned to him and this veil of peace and gentleness fell over her.

Which stopped my thoughts whirling and scared me more than anything.

Mai looked at me, now calm but concerned. "Are you well, Bren? You're white as a sheet. And your lips."

I managed to nod, and my breath was back well enough for me to stand without support.

So she nodded and turned to Tur, saying, "No one but you and I decide what is right for our family. I think he got the gist of it." Then she put a hand to the back of my neck and asked, "Are you stayin' for supper? We've got a nice haddock."

I just smiled a yes. Mrs. Brogan made her good-byes, grinning ear to ear, meaning we knew what tonight's craic would be all about. Mai went into the kitchen to finish the spuds.

Eamonn must have got the message, for we did not see him, again, not even at Christmas or Boxing Day.

Or even on the first Monday of the New Year when, after long good-byes and many tears and much wailing and carrying on, Tur, Mairead and their three wains were driven down to Shannon in Mr. Devlin's estate car, where they boarded a flight bound for Toronto.

I wondered if I'd ever see her, again.

*****

Two weeks later, Faulkner banned all marches and parades throughout the North through the whole of the year. Which set the Loyalists to howling like they'd been whipped. As if it mattered. They were going to ignore the edict as were we.

In fact, our side chose to march on an internment camp at Magilligan Strand Beach, as well. We were bound and determined to show peaceful resistance in the face of the mad dogs barking and snarling our way, and none could convince our glorious leaders of the futility in it.

It was a Saturday, and miles up the coast and wet and cold. I had a record player that needed work so I was going to ignore it, for I knew this would just be another push and shove and shouting match between those not listening to each other, even though John Hume was behind it. But then Colm sent me word he would be there, meaning he wanted me to join him. Well, he was me China so I caught the bus up, and how we managed to find each other in that crowd milling about in the wide-open nothingness was a miracle. What was more of one?

Danny was with him!

I howled and jumped and we pounded on each other from joy at having been so long apart, and damn how we splashed the wet sand. He'd filled in, some, and his hair was long enough for a ponytail, and he had a blond beard! I was sorely jealous, for my face refused to even consider letting me grow one.

"I came by the night bus," he told us. "Be a part of history."

"How long you here for?" I asked.

"Just the day. I'm hopping the late bus to home."

"Still in Armagh?"

"No. I'm in a boarding school, in Belfast. About to take my A Levels. I'm off to the LSE, in London."

"Bloody hell, Danny, you are moving up."

Turned out he'd been set up in a Catholic boarding school because of the fights he'd got into at the local high school, thanks to Armagh being filled with Protestants who thought ganging up on Catholics was the way to prove their superiority. His father had worked up a scholarship for it, through the church, and for once I was smart enough to keep from asking about it, in any depth. But I had a feeling it was more than good scores or mere luck got that for him.

Colm let us talk, keeping an eye about for the crowd. We paid little attention to any of the speakers; they'd be saying the same things as always. And Hume was arguing with an officer at the razor fence about wanting to march down to a certain area and complaining about rubber bullet being shot at women. Again, the usual nonsense.

Until Colm noticed movement.

And it was not from us.

"They're blockin' us off," he said. "Like the RUC did, that October. Can't see better."

"Here, Bren," said Danny, "give us your hands."

I did and we gave Colm a lift up so he could get a better view.

He laughed. "They're stringin' more barbed wire across to hold us back! Soldiers and RUC combinin' in packs."

I noticed Tommy with some other feisty lads throwing what stones they could find in the muck. Others tried to go around the barbed wire. Colm jumped down then he, Danny and I were about to join them when a few people cried out and some Paras appeared to our side and fired rubber bullets at us!

Close range.

One struck Colm in the right arm. He cried out and near crashed to the sand, but Danny and I grabbed him. Which hurt him more. I feared it might be broken for he could not move it. We were checking it when Danny's ear was clipped by another.

That made us fall back in shock, making things even more chaotic.

The Constables made baton charges and the Paras started an even stronger push to drive us back, firing more rubber bullets and laughing, like dogs after a fox. A number of protesters were badly beaten. Some of the Paras went wild in their attacking and shooting and howling, to the point they were ignoring the orders of their own officers and had to be physically restrained! It was madness!

Danny and I guided Colm back to a bus and hopped on. As it filled with wet and angry people, I used an American bandana he had to work up a sling of a sort so it didn't just hang at his side. Done in blue and white, it was, and looked fine against his Anorak.

"You should get this to a doctor," I said. "X-rays and a splint."

Colm shook his head. "That could be used in evidence against me, if they want to make a case for rioting."

Danny chuckled. "Like they need evidence for that."

Colm had to nod in agreement. "I know someone I can get to check it. No worries."

The bus headed back for Derry, and Danny stayed with us so I asked him, "Where you lodging?"

"I'm not. I told you."

Colm shook his head. "After this, you'll be lucky to get away without being snatched. Better you come with me."

"Let's to my place," I said. "You can stay there. Clean up. Leave off in the morning, once all is clear."

"But your ma?" Danny asked.

I huffed. "She likes you, and Eamonn's not around so you can sleep in the hutch. The both of you."

Danny gave me a crooked grin. "And miss another day in lovely Belfast? Oh, Brendan, how could I ever?"

Even Colm chuckled at that.

*****

The bus let us off at Guildhall and we headed for William.

"Do you have some smokes, Colm?" I asked.

He shook his head.

"Two packs on me," Danny said, wary. "Marlboros."

I nodded. "One should be enough."

And normally would have been, but the checkpoint was manned by a pack of very angry soldiers, none of whom I'd seen before...

Save one.

Maybe.

They slammed us against a wall, telling us to put our hands up on it and to spread our legs so they could maul us with full abandon. Which made me a bit shaky, thanks to memories of Strand Road.

Of course, Colm couldn't raise his hurt arm. A Sergeant grabbed it to look closer at it, making him cry out from the pain.

"What's this?" he snarled at Colm. "Bloody rioter?"

He started to rip Colm's Anorak off, causing him even more pain.

Since we were outside, I was still in control enough of myself so gave a small laugh and shot in with, "Me mate? Rioting? Couldn't throw straight to save himself. He was just playing the cod, is all."

"Shut the fook up, ye fookin' taig. That's sand on ye shoes."

I shrugged. "Call me what you want, but I was workin' on a car, at McClosky's, and the sand's to catch up oil from the floor. Me mate went actin' stupid and got under it to play and kicked it off its block. This is from the rear wing hittin' him as it fell. Me boss tied his arm and it took the three of us to set the car right."

"On a S't'ruday?"

"Who said it couldn't be?"

"Ye fookin' liar! Ye fix cars? A nobody like yerself?"

I snorted, this time. "I can fix any car there is!"

He smiled at me, cold and hard. "Yeah? I got a Defender leaks oil. Nobody can tell me why. All the seals are good and no cracks in the block. What the fookin' shite is wrong wit' it?"

"What's the year?"

"Sixty-one."

"Series?"

"...Two-A..."

"Is the head tight?"

"'Course it fookin' is."

"Sure of that? If you put a normal jointing on, it needs to twice be turned, to be sure. I used double joints and compounds when I fixed Dr. Wiler's; went hard on the fastening. Colm helped me with the last turn of the spanner, didn't ya?"

That's when I noticed that one ugly mug who looked familiar was running his hands up and down Colm, slow and grabby. But Colm stayed cold as ice and said, without hesitation. "It was bloody hard. Bloody thing won't come off without major surgery, for certain."

"Hasn't had a leak since," I said, making myself smile.

Christ, that bastard groping Colm was looking more and more familiar.

Then I saw Danny was watching him, his eyes wide and wary. My heart near stopped. Did he not know this was standard at every checkpoint, now? Had he not been through one of the army's maulings, before?

Another soldier came up. "What 'bout a Volvo 122? Shifter comes out the gear box."

"Aw, that's the bloody car's design," I said, keeping my voice light. "Put it back in and screw it closed, is all you need do."

Now Danny was starting to shake.

Oh-no-no-no, this was not good.

"Not what me mechanic said. Needs doin' just right, fasten down just right. Glove repositioned."

I barely kept my voice normal as I said, "Yeah, yeah, yeah, and how much'd he hit you for?"

"Five quid."

"Each time?"

"I-I didn't say it was more'n once."

And now that same bastard was shifting to Danny, and me China was starting to breathe heavy and I was growing scared, myself. I had to make myself chuckle. "Next time it comes out, put it in yourself and see what happens."

"So you know cars." It was a Sergeant speaking, behind me.

I shrugged. "I fix things."

The soldier began mauling up one of Danny's legs, grinning and growling like a hyena, shoving his hand closer and closer to Danny's arse and...

I caught it.

He was the same bastard who'd fingered me, once.

Danny was shaking, his fingers digging into the wall.

Oh, shite, oh, shite, oh, shite, this could go so bad, so easy. If he did the same to Danny and me China freaked out, and the soldiers piled on and we all got snatched or shot and-and-and—

And I noticed some older women in the queue, a couple of whom I knew, glaring at the fat bastard and, without a thought, I suddenly barked, "What the fuck's this? You stickin' your thumb up me arse ain't enough, you wanna do it to me mate, too? Lookin' for dreams to wank off to, when you're alone?"

And I was quite loud with it.

The bastard rose to snarl at me, "What the fook you sayin'?"

I noticed more ladies cast glances our way so grew louder. "What the fuck, yourself, arsehole. It's not enough you grab my bollocks and stick your nose up me arse, you're gonna do it to all of us? Fuckin' poofter! Gettin' your jollies off goin' up boys' jacksies?!"

The bastard howled and punched me in the kidney.

Fuck, did it hurt.

I cried out and buckled as he grabbed the collar of my coat suddenly I'm back in Strand Road and I just know I'm going into that fucking room, again, and that added to my gasps of pain and I'm about to spin into the very howling beast I was afraid Danny would've become and—

A screech roared from that queue of women.

They began howling and threatening and spewing furious curses on the man. Words I'd never heard come out of a woman before, not even Mrs. Keogh when she was in a lather. Spitting at all of the soldiers.

What're you doin' to them boys, you cunts?
You bastards gonna try anything with them?
Big fucks with toy guns beatin' up on little lads?
Motherfuckin' bastards!
Keep your fookin' paws to yerselves, ya sick fucks.
Do this to girls AND boys?
Can't ya make up yer sick fookin' minds?.
And they were beginning to close in on them.

Colm burst out with, "That fookin' bastard groped me! An' he was grabbing me mate's arse. Me mate's an altar boy! Never a stitch of trouble to him and this ape's gonna drag him off for his sick fun!"

Oh, did the ol' cows howl even more. *Poofters* and *Homos* and *Nancy Boys*, and I'd swear I heard a few more *cunts* and *cocksuckers* in there. It was glorious. Others began to come over, from Waterloo, both men and women, to see what the noise was about.

The paras started to get nervous and now held their weapons at the ready, in case this hoard of middle-aged ladies took it upon themselves to attack. If I hadn't been so winded by the bastard's punch, I'd have laughed at the cowardice in them, but then I looked at Danny.

He was still in position, staring at the wall as if frozen, his fingers still digging into the brick, shaking.

Shaking.

Like I had been. For hours.

I started begging in my mind, *Please, Danny, please don't let go, not yet, not now. Please. I held on. I held on. You can, too.*

That's when an officer of some kind put himself between the howling women and his men and snapped at the bastard who'd been mauling Danny, "What the devil's going on, Collins?"

"No idea, sor," he said, his voice suddenly weak and cowardly. "Just sorchin' the little fooks."

I noticed that comment had cut into Danny tension. He was finally looking at me. Confused but calmer. His breathing a bit easier. Colm was still against the wall, as well, and his eyes were on Danny.

The big bastard was fool enough to say, "Sir, I'd swear these little bas'ards was slingin' stones at Magilligan."

That made the officer sigh and shake his head. "Collins, how the devil would you know that? You weren't even there. Christ."

Another soldier backed over, eyes on the snarling crowd, his fingers itching to pull the trigger of his rifle. "Sir, we sendin' 'em off or snatchin' 'em?"

The officer just turned and walked away.

The soldier who'd asked me about the Two-A said, "Off wit' ye." And he called, "Thanks."

As if that made everything fine.

Colm pulled me up by my collar and kicked Danny. He jolted fully into this moment and off we went.

Fast.

So fast, we were halfway down Chamberlain before I stumbled to a stop, I'd started coughing so mad.

Colm pulled me around to Joseph's Place and held me against the base of the flats, Danny right by us. As I fought to gain control, I noticed them both looking at me, their eyes lost in confusion. Then Colm murmured, "You didn't cough once in front of that fat bastard."

I couldn't speak. Just coughed, rough but steady.

Danny's voice was soft. "The way the fook was-was grabbin' at me an'-an' we almost-almost got—almost got snatched and-and—Jesus, Bren—"

Cough.

"But we didn't get snatched, did we?" Danny continued. His voice had strength growing in it, again. He rubbed my back; it helped some. "That was some punch you took."

I could only shrug, my throat was so raw.

"And that story you pulled."

I shook my head and tried to crouch down, to end the aching and the coughing and to hide the slashing memories of that interrogation that cut into me and not let myself get lost in understanding just how close I'd come to it happening, again, but Danny stopped me.

"Lean back against the wall," he said. "Flat. It helps more."

I didn't want to, but his eyes were gentle and far too sure as he pushed me by my shoulders. It was cold, even through my coat, but he was right. I could feel the ache becoming manageable and my coughing slow.

And the memories slow.

And fade.

Fade.

Fade...

My Chinas just stood by me. Kept watch for me until finally I managed to choke out, "That. Fat bastard. Pulled the same. With me. Even more. Just used it. Back. On him." Then another fucking cough.

"Even more?" said Danny. "You-you better, now?"

I nodded. Cough—DAMMIT!

"Colm," I garbled, "the story about you. It-it near happened to-to (cough) to Diarmaid. Being a bloody eejit. (Cough.) I just-just changed it a little."

Colm ran his good hand through his hair, eyeing me like I was a stranger. "I'd never have come up with somethin' so simple and believable. By now I'd be down Strand Road."

I could think of nothing more to say. I was still too aware of nearly going through that interrogation, again, and I couldn't stop thinking of how much harder they'd been on Tur and what it did to him, a full-grown man and to think of Colm and Danny. Danny! Going through that, as well? It had my brain caught in a spin, and

I started to shake, again.

Colm finally noticed and his face grew gentle, then he calmly said, "C'mon, me China, let's to home."

His bad arm was at his side so Danny helped him put it back in the sling. I managed to start walking, that bloody cough still popping up, but only now and again. Colm and Danny paced me. My shaking eased.

Till we turned onto Clíodhna.

I saw Ma looking out the door.

She noticed me and her face screwed into something that told me I was for it, again. She'd gone back to her old self, now that Mai and the wains were gone, picking and angry and demanding. So up she burst to slap me.

"Where've you been?!" she screamed. "I've been callin' you for hours and—"

Colm got between us and said, "It was the checkpoints, Mrs. Kinsella."

"What're you doin' beyond the Bogside! Why would you need to be through them an' what's this with your arm?!"

"You're lucky we're home, at all, and not off to Long Kesh. Bren kept us from arrest."

"You and your lyin' ways, coverin' for each other! What could any of you know that they might want?" She slapped the back of my head and grabbed my collar to yank me inside.

"Mrs. Kinsella!" His voice was sharp and cold. A man speaking, not a boy. We all jolted and looked at him, startled. "I'll ask you not to hit Brendan, again."

Other women had come out to see the commotion and if it could make for some good craic, and all were focused on us. Christ, this curiosity of women could go both good and bad for any.

Ma growled, "You mind your own business, me boy, or—"

He took a step closer and his eyes were dark and dangerous.

Ma froze. For the first time since Da died, I saw fear in her face.

That stopped my shaking, and I said, "Colm! Won't-won't they check my story? Do you know if-if McClosky'll back us up? He knows me but not you."

Colm's voice was like ice. "He will. Once Diarmaid knows."

"Best get to him," Danny said, back to being quick and cool.

He was firing up a Marlboro. I'd forgotten he had those. "Set it straight," he continued, smoke whispering from him. "They always move fast when we don't think they will."

Colm nodded, his eyes locked on Ma.

Danny noticed me eyeing the smoke so pulled out a fresh one, fired it off his and handed it to me. I inhaled, and it was regular tobacco. I could have wept from gratitude. If we'd been snatched and the illegal found on us, we'd have been at Long Kesh till I was seventy.

I saluted him, saying, "I owe you a pack," as I let the smoke out.

He shook his head, smiling. "Bren. You're me China."

Colm gave me a pat on my shoulder. "You're a cool one, Bren. I'm glad you're with us, not them. Danny?"

He looked between Ma and me then nodded his head. "Thanks for the offer, Bren, but I've much to discuss with Colm. May not even sleep before tomorrow's bus. Another time?" Then he winked at me. He was our Danny, again.

I nodded back, sort of smiled at them, and they quietly vanished into the darkness.

Which shocked me. I hadn't realized night had fallen. On top of it, the women had already returned inside their homes, which I'd not even thought about. I needed to pay better attention to my surroundings. I was getting too focused on nothing, of late.

That's when I turned to Ma. And fucking coughed. And said in as casual a voice as I could, "I-I'd not say Colm's a liar, again. I don't think he'd like it."

Then I went up to my room and sat in my bed and gazed out the window at that ugly bloody yard, behind us. It was clouded up and dreary, so no stars available, and I did not move.

I tried not to let myself think.

But the whole situation came crashing in on me. All I could see was how easily that one little encounter could have gone to hell had Danny freaked out and fought the fat bastard. Those soldiers so angry with their batons and guns, he could easily have been just another dead Irish punk, to them. All three of us could have been and-and—I had to fight to make those thoughts leave my head.

And fight.

And fight.

I had no wish for supper, that night. Just sat on my bed till I lost all thought and woke, the next morning, still in my clothes and facing the window. My brain finally, blessedly blank. Except for needing to finish that record player I'd been fixing. I set to it before even getting breakfast.

To no surprise, McClosky actually was contacted by the RUC and he backed us up. As a way of thanks, he was allowed to skip one week's payment for protection.

How kind of our betters.

Mr. Devlin wasn't so well-treated. I learned later that some men from Belfast had forced him to give over a fine, of sorts, *for Tur leaving. It gave out the wrong idea that they couldn't protect their own.*

Eamonn's fucking words, and even more worthless. And stupid.

Those who knew of it figured they just needed some extra coin and that was their excuse. But all that did was convince himself he should close the shop and join his sons. He was in the process of preparing to do so when, three days before my sixteenth birthday, the hell I'd feared came knocking at the door.

Again, courtesy of the stupid fucking British.

30 January, 1972

The authorities-that-be decided—*in the interests of peace,* of course—to allow our anti-internment march to proceed in the Catholic areas of Derry, so long as it did not end at the Guildhall. However, that was exactly what was planned by NICRA, and they were not quiet about it. Just about everyone knew this would *lead to rioting,* as those who had the ear of the media put it, for few in Westminster were willing to allow that it was naught but protest against the ongoing injustices being perpetrated by the Brits. I don't bother with Stormont, because with that crowd anything a Catholic wanted was unacceptable and to be vilified in the strongest terms possible. But naturally this fearmongering gave the Army excuse enough to send more troops to Derry to *defend against hooligans.* In truth, they were meant only to add strength to the snatch and grabs during what was becoming a daily bit of action at William Street and Rossville.

Agro Corner.

In the afternoons, unemployed lads would grab stones from the wasteland and burned-out shops to toss at the soldiers, who would fire CS gas and rubber bullets and chase and snatch, which would continue till suppertime. Then the remaining lads would scamper into pubs to see if yesterday's scruffle had made the evening's news. And sometimes there was a snippet with filmed footage. And if one of them was seen on it, there was loud celebration.

What that footage rarely showed was the soldiers roughing up a lad they'd snatched, or a girl who'd had a bit too much mouth on her, or an older man who'd given one of them a wrong-eyed look. A blind man could have seen the selectiveness of it all.

And the quiet brutality.

Even bloody Paidrig, who's never done a thing in his life that required work, got snatched and taken down Strand Road, once, just for walking near some lads at Agro Corner. He was released a few hours later, much quicker than I had been, but now he was refusing to leave his flat.

I didn't blame him, but it meant he'd miss the march.

"Come along," I'd said to him, after I was off work Friday. I was in much higher spirits, by then, so I'd stopped up the Flats to see if he'd join Colm and me. But he had no interest.

"I'll watch from up here, hi," he said. "No chance they'll snatch me, again."

"Was it rough they treated you?"

He gave a look of pure confusion. "You been through it, Bren, hi. You know."

I had to nod. "It was as bad as that?"

"I dunno. You never speak of it, hi." Then he just looked out his window and said, "I'll watch from up here."

"Like wee Eammon, right? Bag of crisps and Fanta?" I was joking but he kept looking out the window.

"I'll watch from up here."

So I let it be.

I hadn't seen any of Danny that week; not even a letter or birthday wishes. I was fair certain his Da had been difficult about him sneaking off to Derry. I'd finally had to acknowledge he was the sort who believed you should do nothing unless it benefited you in some way. I didn't like thinking it because it reminded me of what I suspected he'd allowed happen to Danny. More than once, I'd had to kick the thought from my head to keep from descending into a full-on hatred of the man, and it was a fight to keep it in the area of supposition, nothing more. However, were Danny ever to truly acknowledge my suspicions, in full, and not in the roundabout way he had, well, it would serve to confirm my distrust of the man.

And dislike.

Which was close to extending to just about everybody. Far too many in this catastrophe had words that did not match their true actions. Calling for peace while doing things that would guarantee violence. I mean, I understood the reasons why they were pushing so hard. If you want change, you can't just sit about and ask for it, not when those who have the control are so unwilling to even talk to you. But be up front with it. *Pay attention and offer some compromise, or we'll bring this house down.* That might actually get them to pay attention.

I had to give a nod to PIRA and OIRA, on this. For all their in-fighting they were of the same mind. *We'll have to make them listen to us. They won't do it from politeness.* But the IRA was still more about talk.

At least seeing all of the double-speak, as Orwell had put it, had lessened my disdain of Father Jack's two-facedness. He was now only one of many, including other priests. Still that made no difference in my wariness of him. And now that my own mother was repeating his sayings as if they were Gospel, I'd begun to feel somewhat isolated in my cynicism. A word the great man, himself had used against me.

I had to borrow his dictionary to look it up.

Anyway, that Sunday, after mass, we gathered in Bishop's Field, up Creggan. Thousands and thousands of men, women and even kids milling about like it was another fleadh. Laughing. Joking. Singing. Calling curses on those who oppressed us. It was grand.

I know *meaningful speeches* were made and instructions were given to not engage with the Army, because there had been warnings about troops moving in and snipers up in the last of Nailors' hovels standing and fresh barricades and some of the paratroopers that were at Magilligan Strand being brought in. Word from the pulpits spread through the crowd along with relays of information from those listening in on army dispatches. It was sounding more and more like an invasion.

In truth, I wasn't paying much attention. My thoughts were more with my birthday. Turning sixteen meant greater opportunities. If I wanted to leave Derry, I could. I'd spoken with Jackie, a few days prior, and he'd mentioned cruise ships that docked in Cobh.

"A lad like you," he'd said, "with your abilities, you could get on with one. Sail the world."

We'd been in the hutch, Jackie seated on the bed, and Eamonn had laughed, "Have another run off?" Then he'd turned to me. "You'd be more help here, Bren."

"In what way?" I'd asked.

"You could join with Fianna Éireann."

Jackie had cut him off with a sharp, "We have more than enough lads to throw stones." Then he'd turned to me and added,

"And Colm says you're with us, already, eh, Bren?"

That was the first time I'd actually been asked. "How could I not be? What they're doing to us all. And I'm good with tools and can fix—"

Jackie had huffed me into silence. "It's better to get some experience in the world. You're quiet, Bren, but my bet is that when you do talk, people will listen. We could use that to get our story out."

Eamonn laughed, again. "Our Brendan? He can't tie two words together without a cough."

I cannot say how deep that had cut into me. My own brother thought so little of me? Had no confidence in me? Joined Ma in seeing me incapable? No, no, *simple*. That was her word. And he joined in it? Christ.

I hadn't said anything, but I think it played on my face, for Jackie had shaken his head and growled at him, "Colm would have a word to say about that. Brendan thinks on his feet and he keeps things to himself. Unlike some."

Eamon had jolted and glared at Jackie, then had stormed into the house rather than reply.

I'd been shocked at how easily my brother was dismissed. And at how it was now obvious others also knew his one true weakness.

I'd gulped in a breath and said, "Jackie, Eamonn's not—"

He'd put a finger to my lips and said, "Your brother is a fine man, but there's times his thoughts don't extend beyond his nose. Like that nonsense with your brother-in-law. Had I known what he was off to do, I'd have stopped him."

I'd just nodded, for it was good to hear that they were unhappy over how Tur had been treated.

"Now then, NORAID is coming together and doing well, but we could always use more money, and a lad such as yourself, looking so fine and Irish and angelic, you would be a good tool in raising some. We could give you suggestions on what to say. Ideas to work out in your own words, if you would."

Angelic? Me? "You-you really think I'd be good for that?"

He'd laughed. "And there's another good thing about you, Bren. You don't take the word of anybody, not on its face. Just consider what I said." Then he'd followed Eamonn and I heard their voices murmuring for an hour, after.

I'd actually gone to a travel agent on Strand Road. Which only took an hour through the checkpoints, each way. They'd found it quite funny I was considering *a career in maritime travel*, as the agent put it. Said I was too young, but he still gave me contact information for a few ocean cruise lines and told me their requirements were mainly that I needed my own passport, a certificate of clearance from the RUC and my mother's permission, till I was eighteen.

Bugger. I had none of that.

Still, I wrote to the ones they mentioned and posted the letters without a word to Ma. Never hurts to ask.

This is why it felt like such a grand birthday, coming up. If I could work this out, proper, with Joanna not even applying to university till the fall, I could build up a nest egg and send her post cards and letters from around the world and when it was all decided, settle myself wherever she was, with an abundance more of experience. Whether it was on a cruise ship or a freighter, I saw Jackie's suggestion as a blessing.

I'd still halfway wondered about the idea of university for myself, but while talking with a bookshop owner on Magazine Street I'd learned it was much harder to do now I'd left school. I'd have a massive amount of work to make up, have to take a hundred tests to show that sort of education wouldn't be a waste on me, and only a few places offered courses in the engineering of automobiles. St. Andrews was not one of them, nor was Queens.

Which put the end to that thought.

But still, it's good to have hopes and dreams.

So it was chilly and clear, that Sunday, not typical of January in Derry. Ivan Cooper was heading it, and Bernadette Devlin and Eamonn McCann were in attendance to speak. People were arriving from all over the North and even London. Of course, Peggy Deery was there. She'd been part of every march since the October '68 one. It wouldn't be a proper march without her.

NICRA was also bouncing around, and word was we'd not be entering the city center but would have the main gathering at the Free Derry Corner, near the Rossville Flats. Crossing the barricade in William was considered too much of a provocation to the army, and after the madness in Magilligan no one wanted a repeat. So a number of stewards had come along to keep the crowds in the right direction. We wanted to make certain this march was as peaceful as possible.

Colm caught up to me at one side of the crowd, where I was crouching on the boot of a Toyota Corona to get a better view of the festivities. Tommy and Brian Boru-to-yous were with him, and it seemed like the near set-to at the fort was now forgotten.

Mr. McGlinchey's coal lorry was being used as a moving platform for the leaders, and was not so far to the right of us. Then just before we started off, Connor rushed up to tell us some lads were already pelting the troops there with rocks and stones. For all the good that would do, beyond making noise.

"They snatched one lad for kickin' a soldier," he'd said, breathless from running.

"Did you shie any stones, yourself?" Colm asked, grinning. His arm was still sore and bruised, but it was only noticeable if you knew about it and knew how much he loved to flex his arms. It hurt him to, now.

"Only a few," said Connor. "Had to be here for the start, with me mates, especially wee Brian."

"Oh, you think I need a nanny," the lad snapped back.

"I think you need treatments to grow."

Brian Boru-to-yous shoved him and snarled, "I throw better'n you. And farther." He puffed up his chest and snarled at us all. "I did so well, I got chased by a couple of Paras, last Monday. It got recorded by BBC and I watched it on a telly in McReady's."

"Yeah, and they said you was but ten years old."

Colm laughed. "Maybe we'll see you in action today."

"We don't want that, Colm," I said. "We're off against internment, not another dance with the Paras."

"What you mean, dance?" Brian snapped, frowning at me. "I don't dance with men, and sure as bloody hell not the Brits."

Before I could respond, Tommy smacked him behind the head and said, "It's a metaphor, eejit."

"What the fuck's that?"

"Symbolism," I said. "It's like—you throw rocks; they chase you; you throw rocks; they chase you; you throw rocks; they chase you; back and forth," illustrating it with my hands going from left to right, then I added, "like you're doing the Twist, together." Then I laughed and did the Twist, still atop the Toyota's boot.

"That's fuckin' stupid," he huffed, but said no more. I think he was still trying to figure out the meaning of it.

The crowd began to move and us with it, down to William Street like a slow-flowing river, banners and placards everywhere. Someone said there must be at least ten thousand of us, laughing and chanting and calling curses on internment and those who enforced it. To my view, that overestimated the number, but many did join along its route. More lads I knew ran around in ways that were almost joyful. Reporters and photographers were everywhere, making Colm happier than I'd seen him.

"Ya think we'll be page one of *The Journal*, me China?" he asked, his sore arm slung over my shoulders.

I shook my head and tried to sound very adult and aware as I replied, "No, page one is for Ivan and Bernadette, as they're in Parliament. We'll probably be the middle of the paper, in a photo section."

"That's fine. I'm keepin' a scrapbook. Cut out everything that mentions anything close to me and pastin' it in." He took on the tone of Winston Churchill to add, "*For Posterity.*"

"Posterity?" Tommy asked, casting him a goofy glance.

He laughed and said, "History, lad. We're at a turning point, and the more that's known of the time, the more history will see us all as right in our cause."

I snorted at that. "Brother James once said, *history is written by the winners*. Let's make sure that's us, first."

Tommy heard me and said, "It will be. You'll see."

We filled William Street, moving on and on, and at the bottom was the Army's barricade. That's when the stewards started directing us to Rossville and they emphasized, once again, it was to be peaceful. Most of us did exactly that, but some still broke through. Lads and men howling curses and throwing stones at soldiers manning the barriers. The stewards tried to push them back and called out over and over for peace, but it did little good.

The organizers used their megaphones to call them out for it, but not before the soldiers responded, firing rubber bullets and CS gas at us. It was silly and childish but not unexpected, and was hardly the worst I'd seen. Tommy and Brian Boru-to-yous joined in the fun, and they were still at it when Colm and I turned on Rossville.

"It's a waste of effort," I said. "That's likely to be what's on page one, now."

"Gas is drifting close," Colm said, sounding troubled.

I made light of it by saying, "Do you have your bandana?"

He nodded. "Soaked in vinegar, but it's dry."

"Better than nothing." Then I pulled my undershirt up over my nose and winked at him.

His focus was on the fighting at the barrier. Gas and smoke bombs and the sound of rubber bullets being fired. "Those're Paratroopers. And they're in cammo?"

I finally caught wind of the worry in his voice. "Oh, I'm sure they think they're hunting. Like at Magilligan Strand. Mad dogs after foxes, they were. One of them's probably the bastard who fired the shot that hit you."

I tugged at his jacket and we followed along with the crowd, shifting more and more to the right.

"Oh, me Da gave me a proper talkin' to, over that. Said I should have ducked better. I told him the bastard was to my left so how was I to know, and he responded, *Stupidity is no excuse*."

That made me laugh. To suggest Colm as stupid had to be the height of idiocy, though I'd never say that to Colm. After all, it was his Da.

The sounds of the rocks hitting and rubber bullets popping and howling were echoing about us, now, almost lost in the murmur of the crowd. Down Rossville between Glenfada Park and the block of flats was a barricade of our own, built from refuse and wire, already manned by a few lads. The crowd flowed around it to reach the Corner. We were keeping up the attitude that this still was Free Derry. As free as the inside of a prison can be.

The crowd was backed up and working around them when I suggested, "We could hop through the Flats courtyard. Maybe give wee Eammon or Paidrig a wave as we pass?"

He frowned at the mass of people to our left and shook his head. "His ma won't let him out and it'll be hard to get across." We wound up pressed against the Glenfada Park flats. "Let's keep to here."

I heard a pop.

Then another from behind us.

I laughed. "Leftover crackers."

Colm frowned. "Don't sound like crackers."

"What else could it be? My birthday's starting early?"

"Yeah. That's come Wednesday, in'nt it?"

"I'll be sixteen, like you."

"Makes a difference in your—"

More pops.

And screams.

Terrified screams.

And the roar of lorries approaching.

We both looked around to see PIGs whisking down Rossville, towards us. More were up Little James, also heading down. People scattered to let them pass but one hit a few marchers then swung into the Flats' courtyard. There were more screams, now of pain and anger, then Paras came pouring out the back of it, rifles at the ready. One took aim and fired at the people running into the courtyard...

And someone yelled, "Those are real bullets!"

Real bullets?

Why would the army be shooting real bullets at us?

Colm and I were close to the barricade and I saw Hugh Gilmour running for it when another Para fired upon him.

And hit him!

And he stumbled but still ran forward to collapse over by the Flats and he was bleeding.

Colm screamed in fury, "They fuckin' killed him!"

It didn't make sense to me. Why would Hugh have been killed? He wasn't even throwing anything but was running away...and to be shot in the back?

Colm grabbed a stone to fling at the bloody bastard and so did I, but more from habit than anything else and I didn't throw it because this was a peaceful march and the angry lads were down on William at the barricade and that was not here so why would they be shooting people?

And running about?

And firing at more of us?

A Para slammed against a wall across Rossville and saw us and focused on us and lifted his rifle and was bloody aiming to shoot us and Colm grabbed the collar of my jacket and yanked me to one side and CRACK!

A bullet clipped the stone by my head and a sharp pain hit above my left eye.

There was more crack-crack-crack coming from them, and another lad running away tumbled to the pavement.

There were screams of, "The bastards are killin' us all!"

But I still couldn't make sense of it. Why were people screaming and howling and words flying and why was it chaos when it was so nice and cheerful and calm just moments before and I could not move? It was madness.

And suddenly I was around the corner of Glenfada Park and on the ground.

How the bloody hell did I wind up there?

And why was I bleeding?

Colm lay next to me, whispering, "Play dead. Play dead."

But I rolled over to lean back and saw others cowering against walls and a medic trying to tend to Hugh as the crowd surged and waved in confusion and people began backing up the street as others hurried into the Glenfadas' courtyards while more Paras raced after them and the crack-crack-crack continued and the screams of pain and fear and pleading, "Don't shoot! Don't shoot!" followed by more of the crack-crack-crack and howls of "You bastards!" and "Murderers!" and "He's going to fire!"

The Army was shooting to kill. No question, now.

Shooting without concern as to who they hit.

Men dropped like sacks of potatoes, and others scrambled to get into flats while others hid behind cars and corners of the building.

Paras began seizing people, beating them and clubbing them with rifle butts, firing rubber bullets at them from close range, screaming threats to kill, and hurling abuse as they dragged some back to the PIGs. They were completely mad, racing through the car park and out the other side, where they shot more men at every corner they could. They even shot at those trying to give first aid to those who'd been hit by their bullets. And they were still beating others and howling curses like it was a hunt for foxes, not fellow human beings, and I was sure I was hallucinating. The same words ricocheted through my mind.

This was a peaceful march. The stone throwing was no more than had ever been before. Why would they fire on us? Did it really happen?

But I saw bodies of men and lads I knew, completely still in death, as blood flowed down the pavement and...and...and it couldn't be.

It couldn't be.

I didn't move for what seemed like forever.

Until the silence.

The silence.

Cold and crisp. A blanket of ice drifting over the blood and smoke. Murmured prayers slowly filled it, more terrifying than anything before.

Then followed sharp orders from the Paras' commanders.

And the cries of those who'd been shot.

Cries for medical help from nearby homes, calling to come tend to the wounded.

Cries from those who now saw others were dead.

Some were driven to hospital in private cars or ambulances.

Wait...were there ambulances?

Yes. Yes. I saw one come rolling in.

One.

Finally, I rose. Slow and careful. The blood on my face had dried. It was from a gash on my temple, nothing more. It felt raw and ragged. I stumbled about in the ungodly quiet. Stillness. Everywhere, I saw only dust and blood and rubble. I had no idea where Colm had gone. Saw no sign of Tommy or Connor or Brian Boru-to-yous.

I saw the bodies of three lads, all dead, at the rubble barricade. Soldiers grabbed them by their hands and feet and dumped into the back of a Saracen, like they were pieces of meat, then drove them away. Others were by them, wounded. I heard one call for them to go to Altnagelvin.

Was it more injured needing help?

Were no more ambulances coming?

I was still too completely lost to know.

The paras shot twenty-eight people. Or was it twenty-nine? Numbers changed. Except for those dead. That was thirteen. No...finally fourteen.

Jackie Duddy was hit while running away from the Paras, in the car park of Rossville Flats. Everyone who saw it said that soldier took careful aim to shoot him. He was seventeen, and unarmed. He was shot in the back.

Hugh Gilmour—I saw him shot as he ran from the soldiers. Shot in the back by the cowards. He was seventeen, and unarmed. The medic who tried to save him was arrested and beaten by the Paras. A fucking Knight of Malta, with a red cross on him!

Michael Kelly was shot in the stomach at the rubble barricade. Shot for throwing stones at his killers. He was seventeen, and unarmed.

William Nash was shot in the chest, beside him. Again, for throwing stones. He was nineteen, and unarmed. What was worse? Three more people were shot while trying to help him, including his father, Mr. Nash.

John Young was shot in the face and killed while also trying to help. He was seventeen, and he was unarmed.

Michael McDaid was shot in the face, next to him, for acting like human being and going to help William. He was twenty and had no weapon on him. Nothing to justify it.

Kevin McElhinney was shot in the back as he was trying to crawl to safety. In the bloody back! He was seventeen. Not one weapon was found near him.

A man I only knew by name, Jim Wray, was not only shot in the back while running away from the bastards, in Glenfada Park courtyard, he was shot, again, as he lay dying on the ground! Crying that he could not move his legs. He was but a year older than Eamonn. Twenty-two. Again, unarmed!

Those were the ones I saw. The bodies. The stillness of them as their blood flowed, soft and red.

Somehow I wound up on Fahan Street at Abbey Park. Mrs. Keogh was wandering about, in shock, her clothes bloody. I went to her, hoping she could explain it all. When she realized who I was she pushed me down to Clíódhna, saying, "Don't go in there, Brendan, don't go in there. I watched those animals shoot Gerry Donaghy. In the stomach. At Abbey Park. Poor wee boy was trying to run for safety. He's—he's gone to Altnagelvin, now. Gerry McKinney was behind him. Shot him in the chest. He was holding up his arms. Shouting, *Don't shoot! Don't shoot!* They shot him, anyway. The bullet went through him...and it and-and don't go in there, Brendan. Don't go near the park. Don't go there. There's naught but blood everywhere, so much blood."

Gerry McKinney? He had a family. He was thirty-five and would never carry a weapon.

And Gerry Donaghy? He was but seventeen.

Both dead? Both?

I blinked and looked around, and realized I had let her push me all the way home. I had no memory of it. Yet I remember her mumbling the whole way about what she'd seen.

I later learned William McKinney was also shot dead in Glenfada because he dared to try and help Gerry McKinney. Killed him for wanting to help a wounded man. He was twenty-six, and again, he was fucking unarmed.

Gerry Donaghy never made it to Altnagelvin. The car he was in was stopped at the Army checkpoint and the man driving it was ordered to leave the car, at gunpoint. A soldier then drove it to what they called a Regimental Aid Post, where an Army medical officer pronounced him dead. Then, as if to prove their fucking stupidity, the Army claimed Gerry had four nail bombs in his pockets.

Fucking nail bombs?

Gerry?

Four of them?

The soldier who drove him to the Army post and the Army medical officer both said that they did not see any bombs, as did the people who first tried to help him and who drove him and-and were the bastards mad? Those things would go off with the wrong touch, and-and it was so stupid and clumsy, not even the commanding officers could accept it.

Mrs. Keogh and I finally reached my home and I gave her over to the care of some women who were there, standing around trying to find out more. I know they questioned me, but I don't remember what I told them, if anything. I know one tried to wipe my face of the blood, but I wouldn't let her. I just went to sit on our stoop, still trying to accept what happened.

That is when Ma wandered up, looking like a ghost. I didn't know if she'd been with the march or not; I hadn't seen her, that morning. She drifted down to sit beside me.

"They killed Paddy Doherty," she murmured. "Shot him in the back as he tried to crawl to safety. Murdered him. A family man."

I only nodded.`

She drew me close, into a gentle embrace, one arm around me. "Were you there. With the March?"

I nodded.

"Even though I told you to stay out of it?"

I didn't recall her saying a word, one way or the other.

"No," she continued. "No, I meant to, after Mass. After

Father Jack's warnin' about the soldiers. But you were gone, already."

I nodded. "With some mates."

"Did you see any of it?"

I nodded.

"Where were you?"

I had to think about it, then said, "By Glenfada North."

"Is that blood thanks to a British bastard?"

"I don't know. I don't remember it. I think so..."

"I doubt you saw Paddy die," she murmured, half to herself. "He was in the forecourt of Rossville Flats. But thirty-one years of age. Barney McGuigan was shot when he walked out to help him. Even as he waved a white handkerchief, showing his peaceful intentions. And I'm hearing John Johnston, was shot on William Street, before it all began. Like he was nothing but vermin to be cut off from life."

I had nothing to say. I still could not understand it all.

"Was Eamonn there?" she asked.

"I didn't see him. Where's Rhuari, Maeve and Kieran?"

"Mrs. O'Canainn's. Twisted her ankle. Couldn't do the march."

"Were *you* there, Ma?"

"To the back." A cruel smile crossed her lips. "Those fools. It was just fun to them. Something to joke about. They have no idea what hell they've unleashed."

I looked at her. "Joke?"

"Made fun of all that death," Ma said. "I heard someone singing *It's a Wonderful Day* and Patty McGuinnan said it was the peelers."

Constables joking about the deaths of so many? Were they that depraved?

"He said there were some up on Nailors shooting down at us. Like-like we were ducks in a shooting gallery."

That made no sense to me. "Could it have been from the observation post?"

"I don't know. Maybe." She was quiet, for a moment, then added, "None of them understand what they've done."

"Don't they?" whispered from me without me without a thought.

Ma cast me a look. "What do you mean?"

"Croke Park," I said.

She hesitated then nodded. "Twelve dead, then. But within two years, Ireland was free."

"*We* weren't."

"We will be."

"That'd be nice."

"You don't agree?"

"I don't know."

Her expression became intent. She almost let a smile come to her face. "So now you see. Now you know. Are you now following Eamonn into the fight?"

I should have said nothing, but the words flowed from me. "No, I'm leaving. No idea where, yet. Just someplace other than here."

Ma took her arm off me and grew stiff. "You'll run?"

"Would you be happier if I was one of those killed, just now?"

"Of course," said with a sneer. "Well, Eamonn will take up arms, if I know my one true son."

"He wasn't there, Ma." My voice was sharp. "Neither were Jackie or Aidan or anyone else I know of that group. Even John Hume and Father Jack stayed away."

"That doesn't mean anything but—"

"But what?" I rose to my feet and fired up a Blue. My voice stayed quiet and calm. "They knew the Army was sending in more men. They knew what trouble there could be. So far as I can tell, they let it happen because now there's not a Catholic in Ireland who will not rise up in anger, filled with fight and curses to tear down the British Lion. But do you truly believe anything will change? The British are stupid in their arrogance and will not be swayed. The Unionists mock us for our dead. They will not back down so nothing will change. And there will be more death. Just like all through history. More and more."

"Of course, you'll whimper and whine about that," she snarled, rising to face me. "But life is a struggle and—"

"Is that struggle made of live men running and then lying dead on the ground? No more future; only a past to be remembered? Shot down like animals by beasts."

"Sometimes you have no choice but to fight."

"Like you did with Da?" I still did not raise my voice. It was nothing but words coming out. "Fight for him or with him or something like that? No matter how many times he blacked your eye or bruised your ribs or cut your lip, or your children's? Fight to let him drink us into hunger and rags and—?"

She slapped me. Everyone around us heard it, and I know they looked over at us, in shock. The cut over my eye began to bleed, again, but I did not react. That seemed to confuse her.

"You always have been a disappointment to me," she snarled.

"Why?"

"What?"

I hadn't meant to ask the question, but now that it was out I wanted an answer.

"You say over and over that I'm a disappointment, but I don't understand why. You pick at me far more than the others and I don't understand why. I cannot think of a time, not one where you've had a kind word for me."

She was startled into sputtering. "You-you never do what I tell you to. Never."

"I fix whatever needs fixing."

"And you keep your money to yourself."

"That's not true."

"And always go against me. Do as you please, even as a wain. Always acting simple but I-I-I could tell you thought you were above us all."

That made me frown. "As a child?"

"Oh, you were wrong from the start."

"Because my birth wasn't easy?"

That made her glare become almost vicious, and her voice grow low and mean. "Not one of the others took more than three hours. But you? Refusin' to leave me. Tearin' at me to keep from coming into this world till you had no choice. It was you and your fight within me that set me off on miscarryin' from then..."

I sighed. "Ma, you had two miscarriages before me."

"Are you correctin' me?!"

"I'm reminding you of the truth."

"Well then, in truth you should have been the third one gone, for all the pain you caused me. Not listenin' to me. Goin' your own way. Thinkin' yourself apart from us. It was clear to any who knew you. Even lookin' down on your own father, with the horrors he'd been through."

"What horrors?"

She jolted and gave me a look like I'd seen on that cat. "Oh, you'd like to know everything, wouldn't you? That's why you went sneakin' around, askin' questions about him behind my back. Seekin' out gossip to tell the world he was unworthy as your own flesh and blood."

"Ma," I sighed, "it's Eamonn who carries tales, not me."

That made her take a step back, her eyes filled with anger and confusion and disdain. And maybe even hate.

"At least he's as much a man as your father."

"Oh? He gets drunk, weeps on the divan and beats women?"

BAM! Another slap. Now there was hate in her eyes. "How can you be of our blood? Any of it?"

I was still too numb to it all, so my voice did not rise or even quiver, and not once did I cough as I said, "So you hate me."

She sank down to sit on the stoop. No longer looking at me. At anything, really. "I-I-I wouldn't say that I hated you."

"It wasn't love. When did it start? Before I was born?"

She seemed confused. Almost lost. "I love all my children."

"Some more than others."

She sent a sharp glance at me. "Who-who wouldn't love Eamonn? Workin' to make himself better? Helpin' the family in every way he could? Takin' up arms for the country? Fightin' for us all?"

God, we were already back to that.

I huffed and said, "Carbine rifles against M-16s. Nail bombs against tanks. Maybe we can find ourselves a grenade or two. That'll show the bloody bastards."

"There are other means beside guns and grenades and..."

Her voice trailed off, but I knew what she meant. Bombs. Real bombs. Like what the Protestants had done at McGurk's. I'd heard of the possibility, already. That would be our weapon of choice, the only one that would truly work against their military superiority.

I nodded. "Make our own slaughters. Prove men are nothing but beasts fighting over a sad patch of land."

That brought her back to her feet, her anger returning. "It's our home we fight for!"

"I didn't want to think that could happen here, but now? Now?"

Ma sighed. She seemed to be—I don't know how to put it—smaller. Less certain. Back to being as confused by my words as I was. I don't know where these thoughts were coming from. When I'd thought of them. If I'd just read about them, once. But there was ice in my heart, right then, and these words rose from it, like tiny daggers.

"What do you care?" she finally snarled. "You continue to work with those who would crush us."

"No," I said. "No more. I will never do another bit of work for a Protestant."

"Oh, the coward has scruples? Isn't that nice?"

Again, I said nothing. Because I was having to remind myself that Joanna was Protestant, and in no way would I cut myself off from her.

Ma let out a long sigh then said, "I'll get the wains."

"You didn't answer my question," whispered from me.

She stopped and glared at me. "What question?"

"When did you start hating me?"

"I did answer it."

"No, you told me why I was a disappointment. But you hated me when I was a wee boy. Why? What did I do to make you hate me? It's not because I'm not taking up arms. This is before that. Since the moment I had memory. Calling me simple. Snapping at me. Ordering me about like I'm a scullery maid. Punishing me."

"I-I-I have no idea what you mean."

"If you cannot say when, then tell me why."

She took a long moment for her to finally murmur, "I-you-you were nothing like your brother and sister. Always so quiet. Always keepin' yourself apart from us. I can count on one hand the number of times you cried. I often felt you were—it's like you were judgin' us, even when still in nappies. I called you simple because you were not. In the least. You were almost too aware. Too different. And it frightened me, at times, the looks you could give. I did all I could to make you like the others, but you never will be. They are all their father's children. But you? You? You're naught but an alien creature."

"So it's all because I wasn't like Da? Is that all it was? I find that hard to believe."

"Believe what you like. And leave when you wish."

"I'll need to get my papers in order. I've no idea how long

that will take."

"What you do is no longer of concern to me."

"It is when I hand over my earnings."

"That which you're willin' to share. You've a dozen holes worked into these walls to hide your money. And other things."

That cut into my mood. Did she know of Eamonn's gun? Had she found it and left it and stopped seeking my hiding places, from that point? But no, no, it had to be something else she meant, because if she thought I was hiding weapons she'd not think so little of me. Would she? And she'd have known Eamonn was desperate to get that pistol back, so she'd have told him, wouldn't she? God, I had no idea. Nothing seemed to want to rest anyplace in my brain. I wanted answers but none were coming. Just weak excuses that meant nothing.

"Now clean yourself," Ma said. "We'll be having our supper cold, tonight. This is not a day to cook anything."

She headed on to Mrs. O'Canainn's. And, most likely, to explain our disagreement and disparage me, greatly.

I lit another Blue and stayed where I was. I was still trying to make sense of what Ma had just told me. Her explanation sounded more as if I'd been some foundling, brought to her by one of the little people and she'd cared for me because she had to. Or like she didn't see me as one of my father's, but that somehow a sprite had come to her in the darkness to sire me. It was not fitting together. But I would get nothing further from her, I knew that.

Of course, she was right, in a way. I'd never been as loose and easy with my emotions as Eamonn. Or as cool and no-nonsense as Mairead. Rhuari was far smarter than I could ever be, and Maeve was like a clever ram butting heads with any who dared challenge her. Kieran? Who knew how he would wind up? But you could see the same blood in him as all of them. Open and aware of themselves in so many ways. Part of Derry and her people while I, in truth, kept far more to myself. Kept apart from them, as much as I could. Even hiding in a bathroom, at Altnagelvin, so no one would see me cry.

Why?

Why?

The only thought that came was, it's just how I am. And with it was my unwillingness to bend when I feel I'm being treated unjustly. Christ, I could be more stubborn than even I thought myself capable of. Not from deliberate thought. But if I was going to do something, I did it, and that was all there was to it.

Now that I was looking back on it as the curséd child of the family, I could see how Mai was as loose and easy as Eamonn, and anything but stupid. Eamonn was willing to dive in-between Ma and Da during one of their set-to's, which I had never done until he had, first. Rhuari was as calm as Mai and kept to himself as much as me, but not in a way that was—I dunno—stand-offish? While Maeve as willing to coldly shut you down with words as well as actions. They were brothers and sisters, members of this family. White wool compared to my black. All showing bits of Da in them.

But not me.

What was in me but a focus that put blinders on, at times. No head-to-head; just, *I will not budge if I don't feel like it, nor will I pay attention if I choose not to, and I will make my own mind up about it all.* None of which was from some conscious decision.

Like no longer doing work for Protestants. That was not carefully thought out for it would hurt my pocketbook. But it came straight from my gut, and I knew I would never go against it.

Not here.

Except, would I for Joanna? Would I? I couldn't see it. Couldn't accept the idea. She was so much more to me than just a member of that religion of persecution. I could never cut her off.

Never.

Never.

Never.

God, even thinking about it tore into me.

Of course, Ma thought me coward for not taking on the Protestant hoards, like Cú Chulainn. But I'd read enough history to see how this would play out. Even at that tender age, I knew. The IRA would come roaring back with the claim *Only we can protect you.* And the British would send more troops. Protestants would support them with death and destruction of their own; my own father was proof enough of that. And like in the past, in conflicts between populace and occupier throughout history, they would fight each other until they were exhausted and bored with the repetition of it and only then would they sit down to find a semblance of peace.

God, how many thousands and thousands of innocent people

would die, thanks to it? How many futures ruined? How much of Derry destroyed? Of course, it was too late to turn. Our side would now set the pace and the British would deliver the dead, be they deserving or not.

Like with Mr. Johnston. He wasn't even part of the march but on his way to visit a friend in Glenfada Park when he was shot. He died not six months later, due to the wounds he received, that day. Martyr number fourteen for that day. A reminder to us all, in the Bogside, of the casual cruelty we were faced with.

The Army was already swearing they'd only shot at gunmen or bomb-throwers, and those were the only ones they hit. Only a fool would not see their claims were lies meant solely for the benefit of the press, Stormont and London. Never mind that not one solder was wounded. Never mind the wealth of film and photos taken during the attack that contradicted them. Never mind the myriad witnesses. Never mind the autopsies showing how many had been shot in positions that were not threatening. That would be the official word, and the only contradiction to it that would be paid any mind was when, a few days later, Bernadette Devlin slapped the Home Secretary in Parliament.

And the main complaint there? *She did not behave in a ladylike manner.*

Her response was perfect. "I'm only sorry I didn't hit him harder."

My thought at the time? *He's lucky she didn't have a knife.* Because by that point, we had all heard more stories of the constables laughing and singing and smirking at the deaths that had come about. As if it were a joyous thing to kill unarmed Catholics.

Stupid men.

Stupid, stupid men.

Anyone who had paid any attention to what had happened on Bloody Sunday could see the writing on the wall. See that it had started. We were, effectively, in a civil war. In our own death spiral.

And I vowed I would not be participant in that horror.

Sharing...and not...

That Wednesday I became sixteen. Without celebration, of course. The day was given over to funerals for eleven of those killed. Every priest you could imagine was at the head of the procession, as were an insane number of politicians. Nice of them to make an appearance once it was safe to do so, and would make them look good and Godly.

They fooled no one.

Tens of thousands filled Creggan to the point it was difficult to move or even breathe. I didn't find Colm or Eamonn, but I was in the middle of it with wee Eammon and once even thought to ask him if I could use his inhaler; he was fighting to keep at my side and I could tell he was having trouble at it. I was glad he hadn't been on the march, but I had yet to ask him if he'd seen any of the murders from his flat. I doubted it; his mother would have been cowering on the floor, holding him close to her.

Paidrig stayed in.

There weren't just protests in the North, in reaction—there were full-on riots, with homes and businesses and vehicles destroyed, much to the shock of the army and constables. They thought they'd showed the stupid Paddies who was boss.

Idiots.

Protests even spread throughout the whole of Ireland in support, and the British Embassy in Dublin was burned to the ground. Only a fool would have thought this wouldn't happen, not with people still alive from events of but fifty years earlier. Of course, the British huffed and puffed and mumbled and fumbled, making matters worse at every turn.

What a shock.

On the occasion of the funeral, the Army was smart enough to keep its distance and harass us only with helicopters hovering above. Granted, they had attacked a march of ten thousand, but only by being cowards and hitting us from the back. There were now far too many reporters and cameras about to risk another bad *public relations incident.*

Of course, then came the finger-pointing, now that Westminster saw the world's reaction to it. The Army continued to scream they'd been fired upon by the IRA as Faulkner repeated the lies from Maulding, and Heath made a big show of appointing Lord Widgery to do an inquiry no one believed for a second would be fair or balanced. The IRA used the murders as proof the British should not be trusted, and I had to agree with them on that, for London was going out of her way to prove they couldn't.

In Derry, what followed, first, was a numbness. A grief throughout the city. Shock. Disbelief, still. Ma's anger at Turlach for taking Mairead and the wains to Toronto gave way to him being brilliant to have seen this coming and doing so. Then came the fury followed by lines of men and women joining the IRA and PIRA and OIRA and every other letter of the alphabet, in response. If the Loyalists wanted a fight, they now had one.

What struck me most was the lunacy of those in control, on either side, who thought they could end this cycle of death by threatening even greater death, but that's what they did.

Stupid, stupid men.

Eamonn finally snuck back into town to see us, the Friday after. I thought he's heard of my injury and it was to commiserate, but when he appeared from nowhere in the back yard he did little more than kiss Ma on the cheek then take me by the arm and lead me to the hutch. I though he was come about that pistol and honestly did not know what I would say, in response. I'd thought more than once about putting it together for myself to use, so might give it over, this time.

Instead, there was Jackie seated on his bed, waiting for me. On the one chair in the place was Aidan, with a pad and pencil. How they got there, I had no idea.

Eamonn was nervous, even seemed a bit out of breath as he said, "You were there on Sunday, Bren. Jackie and Aidan want you to tell 'em what happened. What you saw."

I still showed the wound to my head, but not one word from them about it. My wariness exploded in full force, and I was about to say no, but I heard someone kicking up the back wall and looked around to find Colm, and then Danny, dropping into the yard, from the Payne's side!

Danny took note of my injury, cast me sympathy in his expression, then hopped up to put an arm over my shoulders and say, "Good to see you, me China."

I smiled my response.

Colm nodded, no smile on his face as he said, "We're here to back you, Bren."

"Back me?" I snapped. *Like you did by Glenfada Park?*

"It's not like that," Jackie snarled. Then he looked at me, far wearier than I'd ever seen him. "We're just gathering eye-witness accounts to fight the filth handed out by the Brits and press. We're printing it up to—well—"

He glanced at Eamonn, and that is when my brother said, "I'm gonna visit with Ma."

And left me there.

He left me alone with them. My brother fucking left me alone with them. My wariness grew. But Danny and Colm were there, as if they knew these two might calm me. So what the bloody hell was this all about?

Jackie noticed me growing tense, sighed and said, "This is coming across all wrong. You're in no trouble, Bren. I promise you. We just want you to tell us what happened on Bloody Sunday. Who you saw shot. The aftermath."

"The Army's handin' out all sorts of lies," Aidan said, "and there's already word Widgery's been told by Heath to make it a whitewash. So we need solid eyewitness testimony."

"But on the quiet, so the fuckin' Army doesn't come nosin' about to shut you up," Jackie added.

"They're already seeking out witnesses to intimidate."

So that's why Eamonn was sent off. They knew he was prone to inadvertently letting out information and wanted him to have none to reveal. I still hesitated.

Colm nudged me. "It's not like you're tellin' tales here, me China. They've already spoken to many others, myself included. Got more than just the gossip and fearful stories. They're mainly after knowin' who witnessed the murders and how they happened, and I know you saw as much as me. Maybe more. And your way of-of seein' events is clearer than most."

Danny offered me one of his special Marlboros. As I took it, he asked, "Did you actually see someone? One of the lads...?" He couldn't finish the sentence.

I looked in his eyes to see how troubled he was, but not afraid. Not scared for me.

I lit the Marlboro, inhaled. Held it.

Why were they asking me this? I hadn't seen Colm since he left me at Glenfada. No, abandoned me, and I still felt more than a little betrayed at it. Add in them not even asking me if I'd speak with them, but to just expect it? That, alone, would have shut me down, complete.

Now, I understood the sneaking around to avoid being snatched. What it told me was this group was higher in PIRA than I'd thought. And while I did trust Jackie; Aidan, I was not so sure about. Colm? I could deal with him, later. It was Danny who settled it for me. He had risked being manhandled by those Paras to come back me. He understood me, as I understood him.

I looked at him. He just smiled. I could tell that he'd said nothing about Joanna, and they'd heard nothing from anyone else, that I could tell or they'd be on me about that, as well. At that moment, I felt he was more my brother than Eamonn was. More my China than Colm was. He'd never have left me at Glenfada, bleeding and unaware.

So I took another drag on the Marlboro, nodded and said, "Hugh Gilmour," smoke drifting from me. "And they attacked the medic who tried to help him."

"A Knights of Malta?" Jackie asked, not quite believing.

I nodded, then told them everything. In fits and starts. My voice near death. Hating the images it brought to my mind. The pure surprise of the Paras coming. The armored car striking people. Hugh stumbling after he was shot. The blood.

The blood.

Jesus, God, the blood.

Words flowed from me, and I used the joint to keep them going. I don't recall feeling any of its effects, but I did not stop until I got to when I was home. What happened between Ma and me was between us, alone.

And through it all I did not cough, not once.

Of course, I also said nothing about Mrs. Keogh, nor even about Ma's claim she was on the march. They could look into that, themselves.

They seemed most angered about how the bodies at the

barricade were handled. Aidan even muttered, "Fuckin' animals," as I described it.

I agreed with him.

When I was done, I was shaking. I took a sniff of the Marlboro to see if it truly had been pot, and it smelled right. I just still could not feel any of it.

"Are you still thinking of leaving, for a while?" Jackie asked.

So maybe they *had* already spoken with Ma.

But then I remembered Jackie's encouragement. And I noticed Colm wasn't surprised, while Danny was. Meaning Colm was also higher than I thought, with them. Maybe that's why he left me; he was probably on the Para's list and couldn't risk being grabbed.

I just took in a breath and nodded.

"I lay no blame on you for that," Jackie said. "But would you keep us apprised of your whereabouts? Remember I asked..."

I nodded. "Raise funds for the fight?" I didn't hesitate to continue with, "Yes. I'll tell people what I saw." Which would make me party to the coming slaughter. But I could not find anything in me to honestly justify saying no. And, in truth, did not want to refuse.

Jackie smiled. "That's good. We're done, here."

It was dark, out, so we went into the house. Ma was not to be seen or heard, nor were Rhuari, Maeve or Kieran. Had Eamonn taken them off someplace? For he was not about, either.

I started water to boil then looked in the fridge to find a wrapper of minced meat and a bag of spuds. Somehow, don't ask me how, I knew this was for us, so I said, "I'll work up our supper." I set Danny to cutting up the spuds and Colm chopping an onion, which he was not happy about but served him right. Then I cooked everything together in a large skillet. Aidan was eyeing it, with full-on wariness, but Jackie was fascinated.

"Where'd you learn to cook?"

"Years on," I said. "I haven't any brown sauce to go with it."

"I'll have it as done. Smells lovely."

I nodded my thanks. "It's the onions."

"Which I cut," Colm snarled, still washing his hands in the basin.

I actually chuckled.

I portioned it out as Aidan cut slices of bread and Danny

poured cups of tea, and we ate in silence. Once done, Jackie and Aidan slipped back over the rear wall. Danny put a hand on my shoulder but said nothing. He didn't need to. Then Colm helped him up before turning to me and saying, "We'll see to it your family's cared for."

I just nodded.

"You'll be a great help to us, Bren. Out in the world. Who could refuse money to a lad with eyes like yours?" Then he soft-punched my shoulder.

"Colm," I said. I'd sworn to myself I wouldn't ask, but it still whispered from me. "Where'd you go, that day?"

He looked away. "One of those mad dogs saw me. You were on the ground. Looked half dead. He was comin' over, so I run. Led him away. Bastard fired at me, twice. Lousy fuckin' shot, he was."

"Was?"

He almost smiled. "Soon will be."

I nodded. They were already planning retaliation, which affected me in no way. "What happened with Tommy, Connor and Brian?"

"*Boru-to-yous*? Snatched. Still in jail. Paidrig won't leave his flat, now. And wee Eammon's mother..."

I chuckled. "Enough said about her."

He cast me a sad smile. "It's war now, son."

"*Battle of Algiers*." His expression went questioning so I added. "When the French were driven from Algeria."

That, he knew and shook his head. "It won't be so bad as that. Give us a leg up?"

I did, and he was over the wall and gone.

His claim was wrong. It would be bad as all that.

But I had grown to where I did not care.

Last Walk

Joanna had promised to meet with me the Saturday after my birthday, to have a late celebration. But there was no way she'd be able to. The Army was our occupier, complete, and our status as Derry's Catholic ghetto was undeniable, now. Food still made its way in and those with jobs were able to continue on, though with much difficulty. Couples were married and babies born. Schools remained in session. Somehow redevelopment continued. Folks still snuck across the border to buy what could not be found in Derry shops. Mail came and went, but now no lorry driver would carry my letters to Joanna to be posted from other towns. If they were caught with anything like that, after being searched, it could be the end of their license. So I felt completely isolated.

Ma and I approached each other with a quiet truce. I tried to file my application for a passport, but I needed a copy of my birth certificate and Ma swore she didn't have one. That was bloody hard to get. I had to contact four government offices to locate a new copy, and was told would take at least six weeks to be fulfilled, with the clerk sneering at me, "For someone like you to leave? I'd be happy to get it sooner."

I managed to keep from responding, but the casual cruelty was driving me mad.

Rhuari, Maeve and Kieran changed schools so they wouldn't have to go through the checkpoints, twice a day. So long as Rhuari still had his books, he was fine, while Maeve arrived with her attitude well-known and respected, according to her. Kieran was building a *Don't fuck with me* look in his eyes that would scare the life out of anyone who dared go against him, even as a lad near six. He already had plenty of mates with the same feel about them, and all would be at his school, so I let well-enough alone.

McClosky's was down to two days a week, there being less and less business as well as the usual protests and rock-throwing.

Besides, there was also less money about for people to pay for repairs. Even for me at my lower rate. And with the Devlins gone, I had next to nothing in the way of little jobs. At least the dole was uninterrupted, though I did notice Ma's envelopes at mass now contained only coins, not pound notes.

That was a silver lining; less to the greedy church.

Being down to just two days at McClosky's left me little to do, so I was close to running mad from boredom. Fortunately, himself had trusted me with a key in order to open the shop on mornings when he was *delayed or unable*. Usually thanks to drink, but he was a quiet drunk so I said nothing, nor did I judge. If I'd had the scratch, I'd have been indulging in weed, myself. Instead, when I needed something to do, I would go there, if only to clean and sort the tools, redo repairs as needed. Anything.

Then came a Saturday a couple months after Bloody Sunday. It was the week a full gun battle had gone on between the Brits and IRA, up in the Creggan Estate. The women had quite the craic about it and how it lasted hours, with the Brits even firing from their choppers. The IRA said two soldiers were killed while the Brits said none were even hurt, but there were plenty of bullet shells for the kids to search out all over the fields, for their collections.

Something I did not understand.

But I didn't understand any of it! The back and the forth of it. *I'll show you by punching your face and how dare you punch me back*, from both sides. Republicans and Unionists both laying claim to history to back up their anger and brutality. And I cannot say I did not fall in with it, because I knew our side was just. Had started in being just. Had only wanted the same rights and opportunities as their side, and they had stupidly thought a slap would shut us up. But now it was careening into a hatred too deep to let go of, and on more than one occasion I'd joined with other lads to sling rocks and howl my frustration. And felt I was drowning it all.

That day, we had a jeep whose motor would die and I knew it was a vacuum leak, but neither himself nor I could find it. Come Monday, he said we'd probably have to crack the head to see if there was something in the block causing it. That felt wrong, to me, and I was in the need of something to do so had gone in just to poke at it, a bit more. I'd gone through half a box of Blues before I finally was able to focus enough and let myself locate a crack in one of the hoses, at the very base of the connector, hidden by the glove. Which was easy to replace. I was testing the engine when a soft knock at the door jolted me.

Thinking it was Colm, again, looking for more information, I snarled, "If the door's locked, we're closed! Go away!" I was not in a sharing mood, right then.

"Brendan?" It was Joanna's voice.

I bolted from the jeep and yanked the door open, and there she was in jeans and black parka and white gloves, her cheeks bright and eyes smiling.

"Happy birthday," she said. "Late, but better than never."

She had come to see me! Come through the checkpoints and got past our own lads to see me! How was it possible for her to be here? But here she was and I was so overwhelmed, I began to almost whimper and drew her into an embrace and just held her, close to losing control of myself.

And breathed deep.

Long and deep.

The scent of Spearmint whispered from her; Wrigley's and nothing less, I was sure. With it was a hint of roses. She wrapped her arms around me and caressed my back like she would a child, soothing me more than I could even begin to imagine. I said nothing for I am sure was a full five minutes, just stood there with her until I was able to step back and bring her into the shop and sit with her and still say nothing.

"I thought this was where you lived," she said, with a hint of a laugh. "McClosky's Auto Repair. I should have known. But it made sense, once I saw it. And I figured you'd be working. That's how you seem to handle things, but I never timed it right. This is my third trip over."

Three trips? She'd come over twice before to see me and I'd missed her, and still she'd come, again, and I couldn't believe it, so I just nodded.

"The checkpoints are difficult," she continued. "But I take a bus across and tell them I'm shopping in the city center, or of my aunt in Pennyburn, and that it's my cousin's birthday, and they're not so bad about it. Still, I could have been here an hour ago."

"Will you come with me?" burst from me, without a thought.

"To where, this time?" Her eyes laughed as she said it.

"Into the Republic. It's somethin' I want to show you and we can talk there. I can talk there. Will you come with me?"

"Can we get over?"

"If-if-if we're careful."

"What do you mean?"

"We avoid the Army and peelers. Keep it low and easy."

"Brendan, I have to be home by curfew."

"I'll drive us, partway."

"Have you a license? And what about the checkpoints?"

Well. No, and true, but, "I-I-I know ways around those. Theirs and ours. Will-will you come?"

There was a desperation in my voice, I know, but I was in prison here and couldn't talk or anything and had so much to say.

She hesitated then shrugged a *yes*.

I dropped the bonnet on the jeep and drove us away in it. And it was not easy to do the avoidance I'd so confidently told her of. A couple of times I had to travel down alleys not meant for a car, but the jeep was narrow enough for it. The whole time I keep a scan going about the city and over the countryside, for any notice of the Army or RUC coming to question us. But our prison guards seemed not to notice us, for there was no helicopter racing up or Paras or even a constable's armored PIG sniffing about. They were still focused on the Bogside and furies exploding in Belfast and other towns, doing all they could to blame the evil they'd perpetrated against the Catholics on the Catholics, despite how we'd been done to and now had the audacity to want justice and were daring to fight back.

We finally reached a point where I could just see white, concrete dragon's teeth blocking the road, up ahead. There was a small lane to the right, so I pulled off and parked next to some shrubs and trees.

"We'll need to walk, from here," I said.

"Where are we going?" Wariness now in her voice.

"It's a circle fort atop a hill."

She shifted into bright and happy. "Is it Grianán Aileach? We were going to make a trip, next month."

I shrugged a *yes*.

She laughed. "Why didn't you say? I heard of it in history class and would love to see it."

"Now's your chance."

We walked up the road and around the dragon's teeth to find a hole in the pavement that now marked the border. The British had been kind enough to provide it all. We crossed and were in the Republic, now, and I felt as if a weight had been lifted from my shoulders.

We hiked past wide open fields, close to the hedgerows off the gravel, keeping off the pavement so our profile would remain low. It was good we'd both worn boots, for yesterday's rain had made the earth sticky and mean. We turned and looked up to see the fort was just the slightest of bumps nestled atop a smooth green hill.

"Is that it?" she asked.

I nodded.

There was a frown in her voice when she said, "Doesn't look like so much."

"Wait till you're up there."

So along the rough narrow road we continued, passing field after field of newborn lambs, who came running up to look at us, in shock. She chatted as we went, avoiding mention of anything deeper than how her family followed the Clyde, of Glasgow, in football. And how she'd visited with her aunt's family in Edinburgh on Boxing Day. She, her parents and her brother piled in their estate car, caught the ferry in Belfast and had a grand time of it for several days. Her brothers in London came up by train. And wasn't it awful she and I couldn't get together for the holiday? But she didn't dare bring a present for me, not through the checkpoints.

Words spilled from me about my aunt in Houston with three wains—a boy and two girls. I told her of how she'd married a man half-again her age who owned a *real Irish pub* near some university, and how they'd send gifts at Christmas and Easter, which is why I had my new NASA cap. I got a card on my birthday that hadn't been opened so still had two fivers, but didn't mention Ma snatched them the second she saw them. I'd never been off the island, and I was a bit jealous of her trips away; it sounded wonderful, going someplace else.

Anyplace else.

"I-I've thought maybe of hopping down to Cobh," I said, finally letting out what I wanted her to know. "Maybe over to Liverpool and sign on with a freighter or passenger ship."

"Oh, so you'd be leaving Londonderry?" she asked, sounding not at all wary.

"I-I don't know that I can stay here. I-I was on the march."

I hadn't meant to tell her that, but it came up despite me.

"I know," she said. "I saw an image of you on the telly. Standing alone by a wall. Blood on your face. Were you badly hurt?"

I shook my head. "I didn't know about that."

"It was a French news program. I was practicing it and what they showed looked horrible. Bodies on the ground, and blood."

Hugh Gilmour collapsing.

"It was," half growled from me.

"I wanted to come over, then, but Charlie was being a real brat. Questioned me whenever I went out, like he had some right to know who I was meeting and where I was going. Snooping about. I couldn't even send you a letter. He finally wound my mother up against you, as well. I'm sure she's gone through my room, looking for your letters."

"Kept them hidden, huh?"

"Not until Mum started asking me questions. She stopped believing you were a pen-pal. My friends are being difficult about it, too. It's not fun, being under suspicion all the time. So they're well-hidden."

"How'd you manage to get off, this time?"

"When Charlie and mum were in the kitchen, I simply walked out the front door. And closed it. Very quietly, behind me. Left a note to say I'd be home by five. If I'm not, I'm sure they'll call the police on me."

Shite. "What time is it now?"

She looked at her watch. "Just past one."

"Oh. If you're going to make it home, we should turn around."

"I don't want to. I mean, if you're going be deserting me, soon."

"No, Jo, not deserting. I'm going off to get myself better situated, so I can go wherever you go. For university. I swear."

She smiled. "Do you have documentation? Passport?"

I hadn't even heard back about my certificate of birth, yet, but all I said was, "It's in the works."

She sighed. "And then you'll go see the world and have no

more thought of Edinburgh?"

"No, I mean it," I said. "I worked it out. Sitting on the walls. Looking out over the Bogside. Planning out the possibilities. Travel 'round the world and-and back again. See something other than just this one place. And always where I settled, it depended on where you went." My words were stumbling.

"Even Queens?" she asked, seeming to be genuinely interested.

I shrugged. "If I must." I cast her a quick side glance as I added, "But please don't."

"I won't. I don't like what they have to offer."

"Good. And-and y'know, I-I'd want to get married. Some day. Have a family."

That brought a long silence to her. I feared I'd gone too far, again.

Finally, she whispered, "You don't dream for much."

I'd thought it a perfectly fine thing to wish for, so I snapped, "You said that before."

"I know, but what about designing cars, like we discussed?"

"Jo, I've no head for university. And my abilities are fixing the damn things. And toasters and tellys."

"You never struck me that way."

I snorted a laugh. "Never?"

She was to my left and reached over and caressed where her name was etched onto my arm and said, "Never. I just don't think you've had the support you need to see how bright you are. How capable."

And I felt a moment of life in me, again, and the first honest smile in days came to my face.

We cut left down a road that curved around and I thought was the same road Danny had led us down, the first time we came. But it curved the wrong way, and I realized we should have cut as soon as we'd crossed into the Republic.

"Does this lead up there?" asked Jo.

"It will," I said, for I could see this one led back to the road that did curl up the hill. It made our walk maybe half a mile longer, but I didn't care. I loved just walking there with her, nothing to worry about or fear as I led her higher and higher. What was the height of this bloody hill, anyway? Two-hundred, three-hundred meters to the top? I'd no idea nor cared, before. But now it put the work to Jo.

She held it well, taking only the occasional pause to *take in the view*, as she put it. And I had to admit, the world around us was grand. To one side were rolling hills with dark patches of green that looked like forever shadows on the earth. The rest of the ground between them was partitioned into fields much like the one we'd just gone through, the majority of them square, some angled, all brown and still touched with snow and ready for sowing once Spring made herself known, in full. Tiny white houses dotted roads long built and traveled only by the occasional vehicle. A soft haze covered everything to give it a fairy tale feel, and my breath escaped me at the beauty of it.

And the beauty of Joanna's face as she gazed out upon it. Her cheeks bright pink from the biting breeze. Her breath adding to the haze. Her eyes gleaming from discovery. She was not of this earth. She couldn't be.

When at last we reached the fort, itself, it seemed...I don't know...different. Grander. Not a mere pile of stones rounding a courtyard whose sole purpose was to hide stupid boys from prying eyes as they smoked pot or drank the whiskey they'd pilfered. It carried a sense of meaning. History. Destiny. It almost seemed to say, *So you've finally come.* It was all I could do to keep from replying, aloud, *I've been here before.* But still it heard me and laughed, *Only as a child.*

Jo touched the stones, marveled, "No mortar holds most of them."

She was right, and why hadn't I paid attention to that before? There were spots here and there that had been patched and sealed with awkward cement of some kind, and there seemed to be a line around it as if to say, *This was before and this was after*, as the main part of the stones just lay one atop the other.

Then a bird darted past on the wind. Green wings stretched out, a tan breast under it. Held itself in place for an instant then dashed down into the rough foliage.

I near wept.

I've no idea why, but the sight of so elegant a creature in the midst of all this drab brown and green cover, so free and easy, unaware of the horrors inflicted by men on each other and not caring a damn, it seemed to draw a sense of wonder from me. For all my bravado and the joy it added to my already growing happiness, tears seemed the only appropriate sacrifice.

"Ya comin'?"

I jumped around to find Jo by the low entrance to the fort, a good twenty meters on. She was looking at me odd. Queer. Like she'd not seen me before. I shrugged, jammed my hands in my pockets and joined her, and inside we crawled.

The courtyard still seemed like nothing much, just muddy grass covering the ground. Broken bottles and empty cans about. Trash from crisp packets. We climbed the three tiers of steps and walkways that circled the courtyard, and I saw many of the steps had been reset with a form of mortar and the walkways were uneven, still. Muddy. Littered with stones.

We reached the top walkway and the wind cut harsh against us, now we had not even the least bit of protection. Oh, but what you could see from the summit. To the west...I think it was the west...was a silver dagger of water framed by two high peninsulas. To what I think was the north stood an ice blue inlet, wider than long and snaking its way between the rising hills to join her even wider sister, the sea. I knew without hesitation that this. Here. This is where the world came together. This is where Kings were made. Beauty and grandeur and tenderness and magnificence, all around us, uncaring about the thoughts or concerns of a pair of wild kids. Hell, for anything of man's making.

We looked to the south and far below us, miles in the distance, was a silvery slip of the Foyle nestled between hilltop after hilltop after hilltop, winding its way to the lough and just as unconcerned with any and all other existence. Beyond it, we now saw the shadows of mountains in the distant mist, some still capped with snow. The fields appeared to be less carefully quartered and the houses fewer, with a single tiny town of the Republic nestled there and barely a road to be seen.

We turned to face the east. And there lay Derry, small and clinging to a single hilltop. You could see St. Columb's steeple and across the Foyle to the Waterside, but only barely. Homes circled round the hill. Smoke drifted into the sky. No sign of anything but peace about her, as if that horrible Sunday had never happened. As if chaos had been banished from her.

"She seems so tiny and frail," I whispered.

"She does." It was Jo saying it.

I jolted, for I'd not realized I'd spoken aloud.

"Forget I was here?" she laughed.

"No, Jo, never," I whispered. She looked at me, grinning and not believing a word of it. Her lips the color of rubies. Her bright eyes amazing me. Her pert nose glowing red with cold.

So I drew her close.

And kissed her.

And there was still the taste of Spearmint and my heart leapt and the warmth of her filled me and the wind whispered, *This is good.*

She finally pulled back, much too soon. "You take rather fast liberties, Mr. Kinsella," she giggled.

"I had no choice," I whispered, still holding her.

"So you're not a lad who believes in self-determination?"

I knew she meant it easy, but my voice was harsh when I said, "In this world, you can ask me that?"

"In any world." She was making sport of me, to bring me out of my own mind, and oh how I loved her for it.

"I believe in fate," said I, forcing a grin to my face. "For what else could have brought us together?"

She stepped away, pulling her hood atop her head. "So will you now speak to me as an Irish poet? A spinner of the South using words like a snare for simple young girls?"

"I'm not so well-spoke, as you know," I smiled, pacing her. "Just well-inspired."

My gloves were feeling thin and the scarf round my neck was not doing much to keep me warm. But I cared not.

"Yes, here come the words," she sing-songed. "My brother, Charles, fancies himself a poet, now."

"I'm sure he does."

"He's not," she smiled, her head cocked to one side as if I should know what she meant. "Not in the same way as you. He'll be off to London, in the summer."

"A Proddy's weary of Derry, as well?"

She cast me a look. "Royal Academy of Music."

"Oh. Right. Forgot." And I wished I could take that word— hell, the full sentence back.

"His marks weren't good enough for Oxford."

Okay, fine. That was another world unto itself from me.

"Do you really not intend to go on?" she asked.

"To what purpose?" I shrugged. "As I said, I fix things. I'm good at that. The jeep we drove up..."

"The Land Rover."

"Aye. I rebuilt the timing components for Mr. O'Shea, once."

"He'll not be happy where it is, now. Under a tree."

I shrugged. "It's a pile of junk. Leaks oil. Drinks petrol like it's water. I rebuilt the clutch a year back and the rear brakes, soon after. This time, it was merely a vacuum leak making trouble. He'd be glad if it was gone."

"You brought me here in a car that's stolen?"

"*Borrowed*," I smiled. "I'll return it to the shop."

She laughed, and my heart flipped twice over. "My father will not be pleased, if he finds out."

"He'll not be pleased you're with a Paddy instead of a Proddy."

"True. More than you know. So silly" She leaned against the fort's wall, looking across at the distant, snow-capped mountains. Her hood dropped away from her head and the wind whipped at her golden silk.

"So they've really no idea about us? None at all?" I asked.

She took a moment to answer. "They know I'm up to something, but they don't think it's with a lad *calls himself Billy Corrie*. They're still unhappy at how you fooled them, when you brought me home."

I propped myself against the wall, next to her, and gazed upon the world's most perfect profile, hurt pounding at the back of my chest. "I understand why."

"I wish I did."

"Tell me, Jo, why *did* you come with me?"

She cast me a shy glance. "Your voice. It was so hurt. And that news story..."

Hugh Gilmour shot—blood spit from him. Stumbled and fell.

"No," I said, gasping and shaking the memory off. She cast me a look of concern. "From-from the start. At the Fleadh. When you took my cap and made sport of me. And since. Why are you with me, even after all that's happened? Even though your Charlie knows who I am? And your friends."

She looked my way, her face a mask of wary indecision. Finally, she said, "Your eyes. They're kind and hurt and filled with acceptance. And need. They touched me in ways I never felt before." She almost sighed as she added, "Why'd *you* ask *me* to come? Today? And that Sunday barely two months past."

I shrugged then looked away. Then looked back at her. She was worthy of an answer. "Three days after was my birthday."

"I know." Her voice was kind. Gentle.

"I'm sixteen. Can do what I want. Go where I want. Work as I want. I...I..."

"You weren't just saying that, when you said you'd leave here?"

I shook my head. "My sister, Mairead, and her husband're in Toronto. His brother and uncle already set there so they got on with him, and his Da's taken the rest of his family. I-I'd been thinking I might do the same, but I-I'm wondering—what are you thinking of University? Like where you might go?"

She looked at me for a long moment then said, "I decided that I want to be a doctor, so I'm thinking St. Andrew's, to start, then University of Edinburgh. I could live with my aunt, in Fife."

"Then that's where I'll set up. If I'm there, I can write you without any worries."

"But you already do write me."

"The letters I sent you, I had them taken to be mailed away from Derry. So your parents wouldn't cause a trouble over a Derry postmark."

"They didn't even notice."

"Maybe not, but-but with a return address in Bogside, and them knowing who I am and if-if I was in Edinburgh, we could just set up as-as-as real pen-pals so your parents and Charlie wouldn't know and there'd be no worry. Then once you're there, I could see you without all this trouble. If you want."

"You think too much. Besides, I'm not exactly guaranteed acceptance. What if I'm off to study in London, instead? Or take a gap year?"

"That's why I'm thinking of a freighter or a liner. Give you time, and I could write you from all over the world."

"But why? You still haven't told me why you want to. Why you're with me. Am I a crutch of some kind, to you? Using me as an excuse to get away? Or are you trying to own me?"

The expression in her eyes filled me with worry. Was I being too obsessive? Was she afraid I was trying to control her? Putting her name on my arm, it was a branding for me but was it also for her? I didn't know what to say.

Except...

"I-Joanna, I love you. And-and-and you look at me. You see me. It's like you know me, truly know me. With you, I-I-I..." I slammed my hands against the wall, groaning. My mind was a jumble.

She chuckled and said, "The poet's words fail him?"

I felt a hint of desperation my voice as I said, "Words can't tell you what I'm trying to say. I feel-I-I'm comfortable with you. Right. Complete. You make me want to grow. To move forward instead of hold back and see the world in a new way and-and..." I groaned and spun about, furious with myself and close to despair. "Arra, I'm not putting it right."

She stopped me and turned me to her and took my face in her hands, her smile warm and gentle, and she said, "You put it fine."

And she kissed me. Long and soft and warm, as home should be. As life should be. Tender. Embracing. Protection at its finest. Washing every care away.

At that moment, I'd have died for her.

She ended it an instant before I lost control and looked about. "Is there a faster way back? Don't want my father too unhappy with me."

I turned from her and pressed against the cold wall, trying to force the erection I was gaining back where it came from so it might be called up later, when I was alone. Oh, was I glad to be wearing briefs.

Then in the distance, I saw a helicopter whisper along the border, followed by another. Two of them? Someone must have seen something or got nervous about the jeep—*Land Rover*. Now the border would be rife with Paras seeking someone to trouble.

"We'll need to cross closer to the Buncrana Road," I said.

She followed my gaze, saw the chopper and spit, "Bloody hell."

I laughed at the suddenness of her words then lead her down the steps to the courtyard. "Let's hoof it to Buncrana and try for a bus. Take us back in."

"You know of a stop?"

"There must be one close there."

"What about immigration?"

"Then let's slip through at Coshquin, instead. You up for it?"

"Have I the choice?"

I smiled and led her out. We slipped down to the lane and followed it back to the road then headed right and strode along, silent the whole way. I could tell Joanna was worried. She'd said she'd be home before five and here the light already beginning to fade. I began to fear she'd think the worse of me for getting her in trouble. Fear she'd not want to come out with me, again. I fought to think of something to say that would put her at ease, but half my mind was on keeping watch for that bloody chopper to make sure it wasn't stalking us. From what I could tell, it seemed focused more on the hollow and to the west, and placed no bounty on two kids walking down a lane in the Republic.

It wasn't till we reached a crossroad and turned left to aim for Buncrana I finally had the thought to say, "Joanna, tell your da the jeep broke down. And you were caught on Maple with some mates. Do you have one you can call who'll back you up? I've coins for the phone—"

She cut me off with, "Why would I need to do that?"

"Well, I-I just want you to have a story ready, so your Da'll be less likely to smack you one."

She stopped walking and looked at me as if I were mad. "My father would never hit me. What kind of animal do you think he is, and you having met him?"

"I-I just thought..." I'd no idea what I thought, right then. My mind was a blank. I'd made things wrong by assuming her Da was like mine. Shite, I'd thought all Das were. Colm's wasn't above handing him the occasional lick and I'd seen Paidrig boxed about the ears more times than once. Same for Billy, long ago. Was she honestly saying rich Protestant fathers never punished their kids?

"Brendan," she said, using my full name. And that scared me deep inside. "My father slapped me one time, when I was eleven and being a brat. My mother let him know if he ever laid another hand on me, she'd kick him to the curb. So he hasn't, nor will he. He'll just be *disappointed in me*, and withhold some pocket money, and make me feel the worse for *not living up to his expectations*. I love him, dearly, and would do anything to keep that from happening, but sometimes he can be a bit silly."

"I'm sorry. I didn't mean to-to..."

She frowned and stepped closer, her eyes filled with question as if she'd just realized. "Did yours hit you?"

Did Da hit me? Said in a way that it was not considered

normal or acceptable. It jolted me. It took me a moment to figure out what to say, and then I forced a smile to accompany it as I told her, "Not so much. Not once, since he died."

"Bren!" And she swatted me. And all the worry shot away from my heart. Then she added, "Is there someplace we can stop? I really need to use the loo."

"There's a farmhouse just down there," I said, pointing to a weathered old building that was hedged in off the road. Walls painted white but splashed with mud on the lower quarter. Tile roof. Lights already on, inside.

We slipped up to the black, very weather-beaten front door and knocked. And knocked. And then the tallest, saddest, most slovenly man I'd ever seen answered, holding a shotgun.

"What?" he barked.

I gulped and managed to say, "My girlfriend would like to use your loo, if that's all right." I could have gone, as well, but no bloody way was I asking for both of us.

He eyed her, for a moment, then shrugged and stepped back. We slipped in and he pointed to a short hallway.

"Left."

She hurried down the hall and into a door.

"Other left!"

She popped out and went to a second door, and stayed in.

He looked at me. "Tea?"

Oh, did that ever sound good. I'd had no lunch and was perished from the hunger. But I called, "Jo, would you like tea?"

She called back, "Do we have the time?"

Yeah, there was that. I grimaced at him and said, "We're aimed for Buncrana Road, catch the last bus. So thanks but..."

"Tea," he all but grunted and headed to the back of the house. "An' I'll take ye."

By this time I was looking around the place. It was on three levels, each one only a foot higher or lower than the other. Ceiling beams he automatically ducked under but I had no trouble with. Furnishings that were at least a hundred years of age, and looking every year of it. Whitewashed walls covered with photos of an older woman. No children. A fireplace roaring, which did look very inviting. And a huge Mastiff of a dog lying next to it, just watching me. Neither friendly nor dangerous.

When Joanna came out, I told her, "He's making us tea and

he'll take us down the bus."

She looked around, wary. "Brendan, I don't know."

But he was already bringing a tray out with some amazingly fine China on it, including a fat little teapot that was in perfect shape, and what looked like some massive slices of cake that turned out to be some excellent cheese sandwiches.

So I hit the loo.

And we stayed.

We ate. We drank his tea, which was remarkably good even on the strong side. We tried to get him to chat, but he said a total of five words.

One was his name. "Malcolm."

One was as he pointed to his dog. "Harold."

One was a question. "Milk?" To which Joanna nodded.

Next was, "Back." Then he headed for the rear door. He cast us a glance as if to invite us along, so we followed him out to a barn behind the house. There, he set up a pail and pulled some fresh milk from a fat heifer. He even shot a stream of it at some cats who showed up, to Joanna's laughing delight, then sent some her way and she lapped at it, giggling. He brought the milk into the house and she used that for her tea.

Last word was, "Time."

He led us to this old Citroën CV2 with a van backing, and how he fit in it I will never understand. It creaked and it rolled as he got in. I sat on the other seat and Joanna sat on me, then he drove us down to Buncrana.

And took us across the border!

Apparently, he knew the guards and him having a couple of kids with him was no great shakes. They took a look in the back and passed him on. Didn't even ask for papers. Of course, the soldiers gave us a look, but made nothing out of it.

I understood no part of it, but I wasn't going to say a thing.

Then he dropped us at the bus depot near the Guildhall. He nodded. We got out. And before I could say anything, he was gone.

Jo and I exchanged a look and soft laughter.

"Did you notice his wedding ring?" she said, so very tender.

"I saw the photos on the wall."

"That house is not well-kept. I think his wife is dead and he's just marking time. He's lonely."

"Well," I said, looking closer at her, "next time we go to the fort, let's stop by and say hello. Maybe ask him for some cheese; it was bloody good."

She cast a smile fit for the ages.

Then I saw Mr. O'Faelan's cab in the rank so led her to it, saying, "You need to get home so here. Mr. O'Faelan's a good man. He'll get you there, fine."

"Brendan, this is silly. There's a bus in a moment."

"And you won't be home till late. No arguments."

She laughed. "You are so absurd when you try to be the one in control. Write me."

"I will."

"Post it from your home."

"I will not." Said with a wink.

She kissed my cheek and bounced into the cab.

I said, "Let me know the cost, Mr. O'Faelan."

He cast me a glance then got her address from her and pulled away. I watched till he was out of sight.

I set out to see if I could reclaim the jeep—no, *Land Rover*. Took me two hours to get there but it still where I left it. No one about to bother me. So, I drove it back to McClosky's. When Mr. O'Shea picked it up, he was thoroughly pleased at how well it ran.

She wrote me later, at the shop, to let me know Colm's Da had questioned her about knowing me. She had told him she was over shopping and I'd been chatting her up at a cafe and it had grown late, so I'd walked her to the cab to ride home. That seemed to settle him, for he never asked me anything and if he'd seen Malcolm drop us off he'd have been as tight with the questions as any of the ladies.

Those few hours Joanna and I had together solidified in my mind the idea that life as it was, now, was not the normal way to live. That better ways of existence were available, in other worlds, where one could dream and wish, hope and pray and make himself finer and more educated and didn't have to merely settle for what he'd been handed by an uncaring society.

I mean, Joanna's stupid brother was off to a music academy. She was thinking about university, and she'd wondered at why I wasn't off with her. She'd even been startled that I would consider her father might physically assault her, when she was sure he never would. Nor her mother, by association. She lived in a different sphere from myself. One that seemed far, far better than I'd ever imagined and it built on the questions in my mind about what I'd been accepting, not just from Ma and Eamonn and Colm and Father Jack and the brothers and nuns at the school and all them, but at the whole line of hatred spewed by both sides in the war between us.

So I had a Pope and you didn't? So what? Why should such a detail matter when we were all from the same God? Wasn't there some way to end this mental paralysis? This collapse into hate and anger? Change its direction? Show that we were human beings capable of thought and reason and understanding? Show that we were better than the animals that fight over an imaginary bit of territory?

We could do that, couldn't we?

Joanna and I posted letters to each other once a week, now. Not too often so as not to call attention to them. I used McClosky's address so Ma could never have a gander at them, and I worked hard at making my writing legible. That was a chore.

We never spoke of our plans, in these missives. Just the week's happenings for her and the cars I'd worked on. I always added little hints as to how my feelings were but never dared write them out loud. I don't know where she kept the ones I wrote to her, to keep from her mother, but mine stayed in my rucksack and that never left my sight. I know Ma suspected something, but I never caught sight of her even trying to pick about my room. It was as if were she to do that, it would put lie to her not caring about what I did, now.

Once I received my birth certificate and got the forms completed, I made a special trip to the post office in Buncrana to finish the application. I didn't want Ma to even chance knowing what I was doing. Only had to pass through four checkpoints and be felt up twice. The postal clerk got a bit huffy, wondering why my mother wasn't with me to do this, but I just pointed at the date showing I was sixteen so could do it on my own. I think he was torn between making an issue about it and figuring if I had one I'd be leaving the North. Which to him would be very good. So it was done and off.

Dear God, but did the Bogside begin to feel more like prison, or a sort of ghetto. The Army still kept us hemmed in, making it harder and harder to go anywhere. They and the RUC still ran their occasional patrols just to prove they could, ignoring the barrage of stones sent at their armored vehicles. But they didn't come out of them unless they absolutely had to.

Which made the IRA our police force, now. They were not only judge and jury, but executioner. I saw more and more lads who'd been hurt by them, and the occasional girl in a wig after she'd been shorn of her hair and humiliated for daring to speak to a British Soldier. It was like fascism had taken us over, in full.

I stopped with the pot and whiskey, in part because it was so difficult to get, now, and part because it was so bloody expensive. McClosky had me down to three half-days a week. The only reason I hung on was because I was closing in on having all my documents in order to leave, so no sense finding another job.

If there was one to be found.

I had the horror of our new life brought home to me when I was returning a bike to the Carlin family. A couple spokes were bent and the chain loose, and I'd repaired them in exchange for some spuds and a loaf of brown bread from the missus. Their car had been taken by PIRA and used in smuggling arms then burned, so the bike was the mister's only transportation. I felt it a fair exchange, and Ma never complained when I handed food over.

But I was passing by a row of burned out shops when I heard Paidrig's voice, crying in fear and near panic, "But I didn't know of it, hi! I swear to you, I didn't know."

"I believe you," was in Colm's voice. "But there's too many questions, so..."

"It was just a carton of fags, hi!"

I stopped and peeked inside to find Colm standing in the back of some fallen crossbeams with three lads, two holding Paidrig as he wept.

"Doesn't matter," Colm said in a soft voice, "It was your responsibility to make sure everything was accounted for. This time's just a warning, son. If it happens, again, they'll want you done a real damage."

I started in to them but suddenly Danny was before me and had a hand against my chest, shaking his head.

For some reason, I whispered, "But it's Paidrig. He's only just started coming out of his flat."

"And he brought this on himself," Danny whispered back.

"Colm let him be part of the action? Knowing full well how he is? His whole family?"

"He came begging for a chance and it was given him, and this is what happened."

I snorted, and I know Colm heard me. "That's like giving a junkie the chance to flush his fix instead of shoot it up."

"Just stay clear, Bren. Please. I want one of me Chinas clear of this and—"

One of the lads swung a cudgel into the back of Paidrig's knee. He screamed in pain and fell.

Danny rolled his eyes and growled, "Christ, no patience, them. Give us a minute then go over." And he backed away.

They vanished, like ghosts, without a sound.

Paidrig was still whimpering in the charred wood and muck when I scurried over to him. He was holding his knee and seemed not to know me as I took him under the arms and pulled him over to a pile of collapsed beams, to sit. That is when he finally saw me and asked, "Brendan?"

I just nodded.

"Were you here? Part of it?"

I shook my head. "I was passing and heard. Is it a horrible pain?"

He nodded, then choked out, "They said I'll limp for a while. Not like I been knee-capped or anything, hi. Know what's stupid? I didn't even take the bloody fags. Fuckin' Clubs is all they were, and the box was already open when I got it, hi."

"Why'd they think you did it?"

"I didn't say anything. Didn't think anything of it. And the lad who give it me swore it was unopened." He gave a soft chuckle laced with pain. "Him, they did kneecap, hi."

"I hadn't heard anything."

"He's up Shantalow, hi. Brian something."

"Boru-to-yous?"

"You know him?"

I nodded, and could not believe they'd have trusted that lad with transporting anything and not expect half of it be gone.

"They didn't know which of us was telling the truth," Paidrig grunted, "so punished us both, hi. Some fuckin' justice, eh?" He finally smiled. "Bren, can you help me to home?"

"Is the lift working?"

"Uh—no—no, it's not." He almost began to weep.

I grabbed his shoulders. "Sure you don't want to go to the clinic?"

"No, there'd be too many questions, hi. Shelagh might be home; she can help carry me up."

"Not unless you lose a stone or two," I said, joking.

He almost chuckled. "Pounds, Bren, we work in ounces and pounds now, hi."

"Come on, then. I'm going that way, anyhow."

I helped him back to the bike and he used it to steady himself.

"Is this the Carlin's?" he asked.

"Yeah," I said.

"The mister got lifted, this morning, hi."

"Christ, is the missus still to home?"

"Dunno."

"Well, we'll see."

It took us near an hour but we made it up to his family's flat, then between his sister-in-law and myself, we got him into his room and ice packed around his knee and tea made, and he was all but purring like a fat happy tabby.

So I scooted down to the Carlin's...to find his missus was beside herself with worry.

"Why'd they take him?" she kept asking, over and over and over. "They said he's IRA. He's on a list. But he's not. He'd never."

"I know, I know. See if you can speak with John Hume. He might be able to do some good."

"Him?!" She huffed and said no more, so I left. I took nothing from her. She'd been in too much a state to be baking and they'd probably need the spuds.

Dear God, what I would not do to be done with this madness.

Then three weeks later, I was nearly to home after a full day at McClosky's, thanks to working on a lorry, when Colm came wandering up to me, looking far too casual in his attitude. It made me wary because I had a letter from Joanna in my pocket and had yet to read it, my hands were so caked in oil and muck. I hadn't cleaned them, yet, because I'd found that when they were black with oil, I was treated better when a peeler or squaddie stopped me. It showed I was working and not a hooligan. I guess. I honestly don't know.

So Colm came up, smiling in a way that was almost fake, saying, "Howya, me China? In a rush to home?"

"Have to," I said, not stopping. "I'm fixing supper, tonight."

"Why you? Oh, wait. Women's Auxiliary. Right."

I wasn't surprised he knew of Ma's plans. She was vocal enough about them while disparaging me to others. The one good thing was that she no longer put envelopes of money in the church till, but I'm fairly certain the cash now went to the IRA. In that, I had no argument.

He paced me, his hands in his pockets, eyes darting about. "I'm fine walkin' with you, then."

His quiet nervousness made me jittery, but he was here for some reason, so I shrugged and said, "Up to you. I'm stopping at McCleary's for a haddock. Should I make it large?"

"No, thanks, me Ma's got a stew near done, and I'm eatin' it, she says."

"She makes a good one. Maybe I'll join with you."

He smiled and lit a Marlboro, a real one, his eyes still darting about. Finally, he took in a deep breath and said, "Bren, you been seen with a girl. Blonde. Pretty."

I almost said, *From Claudy,* but he added, "Protestant."

So here it was. The unspoken was about to be spoken and made something to be worried about.

"I never asked what religion she follows," I said. Which was true. I knew what she was, and she I, but that was the end of it.

"Don't be cute," he said, nearly sighing it with hurt in his tone. "I've seen her with you. More than once. Jackie said you told him she was from Claudy, so I thought nothin' of it. But then me Da mentioned you sent her home in his cab, a month back."

Christ, never did I think Mr. O'Faelan would grass on me about this. And he'd charged me three pounds ten for the trip. With all I'd done for him and that pile of junk he drives.

"What if I did?"

"We know her name. And we understand it's on your arm."

Shite. Ma. Let it out during one of her craic's probably. *She's a Protestant? That stupid simple child scarred himself with a Protestant's name? That simply would not do.*

"And, Bren, we know you've been to her house, and you're sharin' letters..."

I managed to keep my mouth shut, but only barely. It was now obvious he'd also been talking with Father Jack. Probably told him all about our trip to Dublin in his usual *isn't this great* manner. And McClosky telling Diarmaid of the address on her letters. So I'd been investigated. Researched. Checked into. Like I was some stranger from afar and not a lad who'd lived here all his life. Well, Colm was leading up to something and it was best to let it out, though I had a nasty feeling I knew what it was.

"Now I'm told you even took her to our fort."

That jolted me. How'd he know? But then my head kicked in. Guards passing us back into the country. Malcolm's Irish van. Mud on our boots and jeans for Mr. O'Faelan to see. Wouldn't take a genius to work it out.

I made myself chuckle. "*Our* fort? Our own private little hideaway? I was unaware we owned it, and it not even in the North."

"You know what I fuckin' mean," he snapped. "There's some not happy about it and only held their tongue to see if you and she would end it. But you keep gettin' letters. And sendin' replies."

Christ, was the post grassing on me, too?

"There's some growlin' going on."

"So men I don't know're gonna tell me who I can and can't love?"

"Not just men. Some women're even less happy about it."

Sure. Ma's Auxiliary mates.

He's seeing a Protestant bitch?

And her name's on his arm?!

I hear he's sneaking around with her!

He'd have seen the back of MY hand the moment I knew.

Oh, Bernadette, he's always been a chore for you, hasn't he?

Shite. Shite. Shite.

Then he added the worst of it. "Your mother says you won't listen to her, about it."

I coughed. Dammit.

Ma was lying about me.

My own mother.

She'd said nothing to me about it, yet now she was exaggerating my actions to make them worse than they were so she'd look better than she was. With never a thought that it could get me kneecapped.

Or maybe that was the goal. Teach me a lesson.

"Bren, her father's up in the UVF," Colm continued, "and as hard a bastard as they come. Some even wonder if you might be feedin' her information. In those letters."

That stopped me, cold, angry and hurt.

"That's bloody mad!" I snapped. "Any who knows me knows that's not my way! And-and-and what would I even know to tell her, for Christ's sake?"

"You don't need to defend yourself to me! I know how you are, and I've told them. God, have I told them! But Bren, I-I-I can't keep them back, forever."

A chill worse than the damp cold whispered over me. "Are they gonna hurt her?"

He almost spit. "It's yourself you should be worried about!"

I took in a deep breath. I knew what he meant. And not just Paidrig's punishment. I'd seen lads who'd been beaten and bound to posts and tarred for the least of offenses. Broken arms. Broken knees. Broken faces. There was even word Shane, one of Tommy's mates, that he'd got the cost of a new bike for turning over an IRA man. Who was then killed. So he'd vanished, and gossip was, into a grave. Vigilante justice dispensed by sadists and thieves, and never mind what claims they made about how right their cause was. Apparently, I was setting myself up for the same form of treatment by daring to love someone not of my own kind, like I was spitting in their eye.

We reached McCleary's and I stopped, not able to look at him. All I could think to say was, "I love her."

He finished the Marlboro and took in a deep breath. I don't think he was looking at me, either. "Bren, you're me China. You backed me without bein' asked, more than once. That's why I'm here." His voice grew uncertain. Even softer. "But here's a real truth—if you don't end it with her, they will. And they will do it in a way as to hold you up as an example. A warnin'."

"Like Paidrig?"

"Worse."

"Shane?"

"No." Then he quickly added, "No one knows what happened with him and-and even Paidrig's bit—I wouldn't wish that on anyone, especially you. I know their stupid worries are for nothin', but I mean it, Bren; it took all I had to get them to let me give you this warnin'. They'll hold off; for how long, I don't know. What I do know is, when they're done with waitin'...well...just...please, don't put yourself on the wrong side of them."

I let out my breath, a crooked smile on my face. "We've traded one devil for another."

"Don't talk like that."

I leaned back against the wall by McCleary's entrance.

Weak. I coughed. He noticed, of course, and stood there, waiting for an answer. I had to give him something. Words he could trust followed by true actions. But first I had to overcome the sense of loss threatening to drown me.

The last four months—near five—had been so lovely. Joanna had sent off her application to St. Andrew's. She wasn't looking for any other option, right now. If they refused her, she said she would take a gap year and travel the continent.

I'd heard from one cruise line willing to take me on if I had my mother's permission, but only as an apprentice in the repair shop. Which was fine, by me. I'd written back to let them know I'd applied for my passport, and waiting to receive it. Then I'd have everything they asked for, and not a word had been raised about clearance from the RUC. Which I knew I'd never get so would have to forge. But with a job like that, I could put money aside and join Joanna, whatever happened.

Only she didn't expect to hear till after the new year, more than four months away. And they were a difficult school to get in to. Hard and demanding. While I had no doubt she was smart enough, she kept reminding me of others who were smarter who'd been refused.

It often depends on the openings they have, she'd written in her last letter. I was hoping this one would give me better information.

They'll take you, I'd written back, filled with certainty. *You're smart. You speak French.*

I felt it in my heart of hearts. Perhaps it was time to prove I believed it.

"Tell our masters they've nothing to worry about," I finally told Colm. "The love's always been more on my side than hers, so I'm sure she'll find another. And it's my plan to leave, soon."

"How's that goin'?"

"I've lined up a position. Once my passport's in, I'm off."

"I'm sorry about all this, Bren." And he truly was.

I nodded. "Enjoy your stew."

He hesitated. Bumped my shoulder with a light fist. The shoulder with Joanna's name written on it. Then he sighed and walked away.

I didn't move.

So there it was; I had three choices. I could end it with

Joanna. Continue to write her and endanger us both, because not for a second did I think they would keep the information about *her* writing *me* from the UVF. I could just imagine how her father would take that. But those did not count. My decision was to leave and join with her in another part of the world, a part where none of this mattered.

I quickly counted how many days it had been since I sent in for the passport. If it were done on time I should have it in the next fortnight. Then I could hop the train to Belfast, maybe even all the way to Dublin, if it hasn't been blown up. Then on to Cobh. The money I had would more than cover that, and I might make even enough to send money home, like so many other lads did.

I could then write her every day. And I knew she trusted I would wait for her and join her, and I knew she'd wait for me.

So I bought the haddock. Brought it home to find Rhuari with his nose in a book and spuds baking in the hearth. I heard Maeve humming in the kitchen. So I joined her, cleaned the fish and set it to fry in a pan. Joanna's letter could wait till I was in bed.

"When'll the spuds be done?" I asked her.

"Now," she chirped. "Rhuari put them in when he was home."

"Ma take Kieran to the meeting?"

She shrugged and poured hot water into the teapot. So I portioned out the haddock, once it was cooked, and peeled the cooked spuds and we sat down to a glorious dinner, just us three, with Maeve ladling out tea like a grand lady.

"You still like yours with half milk and two lumps?" she asked, with a hint of disapproval.

"Yes, very much."

"Oh, Bren, with haddock?"

"It's an acquired taste."

"It's silly to make yourself like something you don't like."

Like Scotch, I thought, remembering Shane's comment. And the response from Brian Boru-to-yous. Who was now a cripple.

"Rhuari, yours is no milk and one lump?"

He looked up from his book, blank, saw her pouring the tea and said, "No milk, one lump, please."

Which she did and set before him, then she and I ate as he took absent bites from his own.

"Rhuari, what's that you're reading?" I asked.

"Hm?" was all he said as he took another bite of haddock, then he focused on me, confused, and let me see the full front cover—*A History of the Irish Speaking People.*

"You don't get enough of that from the brothers?"

His expression grew quizzical. "I'm studying Gaelic. Irish Gaelic, not Scottish or Welsh. This helps me center it."

"Maybe I'll read it after you," I said, smiling.

He shrugged and turned back to his book, and I thought, *This is how it should always be.*

And yet never could.

Leaving

My passport came in Thursday's post, sent to McClosky's so Ma couldn't get to it, first. Himself brought it in, his eyebrows cocked as he said, "What's this, for you? Government stuff. Trouble with taxes?"

"I'm sixteen, Mr. McClosky," I chuckled. "I don't pay taxes on my earnings, yet."

"Oh, you'll soon learn what nonsense that is." Then he shuffled back to his desk.

I slipped the passport into my rucksack and refocused on Mrs. Doyle's Morris Minor. She'd broken a damper driving too fast over a hole in the road, and it was proving a trouble to replace, thanks to some of the frame being bent out of shape. But some hammering and twisting with grips made it work. I ran a hand over the left wing, shaking my head. Mr. McClosky didn't know it, but this was the last time I'd be working here.

A driver I knew was headed for Belfast, that night and he owed me a favor, so I called his hotel and he said I could ride with him across to the train depot. There was a late train to Belfast, then an early bus to Dublin and on to Cobh.

The one thing I had to do first was risk a last visit with Joanna, to tell her. Then I'd be gone before they knew it and could work their evil. But as the train depot was on her side of the river, it worked out.

It being Thursday, she'd be at her father's shop till six, so I told Mr. McClosky I'd finished Mrs. Doyle's Morris and wanted to leave early. He shrugged and took a sip from a bottle on his desk. He'd done more and more of that. I should have felt bad leaving him on his own, but him letting Diarmaid know of my letters put the end to that. I hurried home, scrubbed off the oil and muck with true vigor and dressed myself in my best. I packed few things in my rucksack. Change of clothes, soap, toothpaste and brush, things like that. That driver was set to collect me off Brooke Park, at five. If all went well, we'd pass through the checkpoints at the bridge and he could drop me just before six to get my ticket. I had time enough only to grab a hundred pounds from an easier hideaway spot and scribble a quick note:

I'm off to find work. I'll write you, once I'm settled.

I left six fivers with it. Ma would care more about that, and that there'd be one less mouth to feed on the dole. The rest I could come back to get, once Joanna's plans were set.

I heard Ma working in the kitchen so snuck out the door and ran over to Brooke Park, getting there just before the driver. I slipped my rucksack between my feet and we headed through the checkpoints with surprisingly little trouble. There was another to deal with on the Waterside, but each time I calmly showed the soldiers my British passport and, with the driver being Protestant, they took it to mean I was all right.

He dropped me, I got my ticket and rushed to Joanna's Da's shop as fast as I could, without calling attention to myself. Then I pretended to look at the clothing in the window. It was five-fifty-three.

She came down the stairs and saw me. She frowned and glanced at her watch, but I quickly motioned to the back of her shop. She cast me a wary little smile, so I hurried around to the alley to find her waiting for me at the door.

"Brendan, what're you doing here?" she whispered. "If my father sees you, he'll—"

"I'm leaving." My voice was also a whisper.

"Leaving?" Then she saw my rucksack. "You're really doing it? With no warning?"

I pulled out my passport. "Look what came, today. The way things have-have been going, I-I think it's best...I-I think it's best I leave, for a while and meet up with you when you're set for university. Or whatever. Have you heard anything from St. Andrew's?"

She looked at it, amazed. "I told you, I won't know till Spring. Where will you be till then?"

"Got a job on a ship. Repair. I'll write you for where to write me."

"Brendan, what's happening here? Why such a rush?"

"I have to, Jo. It's that or I have to cut you off, complete, because too bloody many people think my life is their business and-and—"

"I don't understand."

"Please trust me. Please believe me. It's just for a little while. Till we're both away from this place. Like I told you I was going to do."

She just sighed, shaking her head. "You'll forget me."

"No, no, no, no, no, how could I?" I touched my arm where her name was written, then without intending to I said, "I was warned off you. By people. They made threats."

I could see understanding fill her eyes. Such lovely eyes, always looking at me with acceptance and caring. She sighed and nodded. "*People*. Always nosing about. You know, yesterday my mother asked if I was seeing someone from the Bogside. I told her not to be silly; how would that be possible? But it does mean she's been hearing things."

"Like it's anyone's business but ours!"

"That's how people are. Parents. Is your family happy about you leaving?"

"I-I left them a note."

"You didn't tell your mother? She agreed to get you a passport, so she must have known something."

"I wrote her signature in. Did it for classes, sometimes. And I paid the fee and it took a lot of my money but-but there it is." I slipped the booklet into my back pocket.

Then we heard, "Joanna, where are you? Time to close up."

She grimaced. "Second, Da!" Then she whispered, "Meet me at *Marianne's* and we'll have tea and talk more."

"I've got a train to catch."

"Just for a minute, okay? I don't want to see you off like this. Not in the wet and cold. I'll even see you to the depot."

That was brave of her, so I nodded then she gave me a quick kiss on the nose before she closed the door.

I spun and nearly laughed into the skies, then headed on down the alley. To have tea at a cafe, like our first meeting, it seemed the perfect send-off. It would be our last moments together for who knew how long, and no one could tell me it was wrong of us to just sit and talk.

I hadn't realized it had begun to drizzle, as if Derry was also sad to see me go. I reached the drive and cut across to Stanley, remembering to keep my gaze up and straight, and a smile on my face but no attitude, so as not to look too much like a Paddy in the Proddy zone. My boots and trousers were wet but were obviously new and the latest style, so I blended in well. People even smiled back at me as I passed.

Then as I approached *Marianne's* I noticed a lad down the way who looked so much like Danny, I didn't think but called out in surprise, "Oi, me China?"

He jumped around and looked at me with eyes so big, I thought I'd made a mistake.

But it *was* him.

It was Danny.

Another lad was behind the wheel of a car he was about to get into and was scowling at me, in the mirror. But what would Danny be doing on the Waterside? Was he coming in from Armagh? Was I about to miss a meet-up with him? Was he...?

Was...

Was—

Oh, God.

Ice crushed into me.

Joanna's Da was UVF!

I heard children laugh behind me and turned and saw two wains, neither older than eight or nine chase each other from a sweets shop. They danced around, still laughing, and rushed up the lane and I could see straight to the front of Joanna's father's shop and parked before it was a year-old Rover saloon with its rear quarter window broke open. Jagged bits of glass caught in the molding.

It had been broken into...

And my heart dropped.

I spun to look at Danny and saw his shock turn to fury and I knew.

I knew.

I knew.

I backed away. Spun around to head for the shop but slipped on the wet pavement and stumbled and saw the two wains bounce off each other and one of them fell against the Rover and—

Blinding white filled the world.

I was kicked in the chest and flew back.

Twisted in the air.

Landed hard and rolled across the pavement.

Slammed against a wall and bounced to face down. Stunned. Confused. Couldn't breathe. Couldn't think to breathe.

None of this made sense.

I could feel nothing.

Could hear nothing.

Could see nothing but smoke billowing about me.

Not a whisper of a sound. Bits of wood and brick and metal and glass rained down.

Then a hollow whisper touched my ears.

I looked up and could just make out the remains of what had once been a nice clean street now littered with broken bricks, façades torn down and shattered glass and shredded planks of wood and furniture and burning cars and people running about with their mouths open, as if screaming words.

Words I couldn't hear.

Something hit the pavement, before me. The leg of a doll. Its stocking and shoe still attached and red paint on it. It must have hit a puddle because I felt something wet slap across my face. I stupidly thought, *Some little girl is going to be very upset about her dolly.*

Then hands grabbed at me and screaming daggers of pain ripped into me, from my side, from my chest, but I didn't cry out.

I couldn't breathe.

I couldn't speak.

I was pulled up as billowing light appeared in the thinning smoke. Twisting and turning in a demonic sort of dance and-and-and it was fire. Hideous screaming fire taking hold of whatever it could find to feed upon in the debris of those shops and someone was caught in it and that someone looked like a girl.

With long blond hair.

Those fucking hands were dragging me back, away from it all. The pain slamming into me was beyond imagining and a vicious whine was building in my ears, cutting my focus because it hurt.

It hurt.

It fucking hurt!

But I was trying to fight those fucking hands. Trying to get away because I knew that girl!

I knew that girl and she needed help!

Needed help now, now, NOW!

We had to get to her!

Because the fire was dancing.

Dancing.

Dancing closer and closer to her like some evil beast and she was struggling to get away from it but was caught and I needed to help her because it was Joanna.

It was Joanna!

It was JOANNA!

I finally heard screaming, hideous screaming coming from someplace as I fought those hands, desperate to get back to that shop despite the shrieking pain in my body and head and heart and we fell and I tried to scramble away from the bastards dragging me off and even more pain exploded through me and I slipped and I caught glimmers of Danny's face and Colm...

COLM?!?!?

He was yelling something incoherent at me and I fought them even harder until Danny hugged me from behind and Colm slung his fist into me and—

Ma slapped me.

Hard.

I jolted and looked at her and gasped. Choked in breaths. Coughed out air.

I'd been dreaming.

Oh, thank God, I'd been dreaming and was glad she'd hit me, for it was a hideous dream filled with horror and fear and pain. Throbbing pain in every part of my body and I couldn't move and I didn't understand. I shouldn't be here. I should be on a train.

Only this.

This.

This wasn't my bed. The mattress was as hard as a plank of wood.

This wasn't my room. So dark and dirty.

Where was my window?

Why I was crying?

No, bawling?

I was bloody fucking bawling.

And there was Danny. Standing by. So cut and bruised and bloody and terrified and looking between me and Ma and saying something stupid like, *It wasn't supposed to go, it wasn't!*

And why was Ma holding me by the shoulders and yelling at me in words I couldn't understand?

Jesus, Jesus, Jesus, why was this bitch holding me?

She fucking hated me! She fucking told me so and—

I struck at her. Hit her in the nose. Brought blood as—

Blood slapped against me when a dolly's leg hurtled from the smoke to land before me but it wasn't a dolly's leg because it had been attached to a child, one of those playing only moments before the world ended and a girl's blond hair mingled with fire and—

A pillow crushed against me. Smothered me. I didn't fight it.

"This is what you want! Isn't it? This is what you're after! Isn't it? Isn't it?!"

Was that Ma screaming at me? Must be, because she was pulled away by dark men I didn't know.

Whiteness filled the world, again.

Then *Click.*

A dark room.

Men standing.

Seated.

Snatches of voices.

Already leaving.

No one knows of him.

He was there to warn 'em!

How could he know?

He didn't know.

Put him in the grave!

Done nothing wrong.

You do that to him and I will make your life hell on earth.

Click.

A man rose from me to face Ma.

He's mending. That heart should have been tended to, years ago. Another week he can make the journey.

Click.

Me dressed in clothes stinking of starch. Hard and new. So new the collar cut into my neck.

Click.

A black sky and midnight rain. Me led to a car by men I did not know. And me just going along. Just going along.

Click.

Looking across clouds, as an angel does from on high.

Separated from the elegance. From miles and miles of billowing beauty, some far below me. Stars above me in a black sky gleaming with them, bringing me a peace I'd never known.

Click.

Where was I? Seated in an easy chair. Blank wall before me. The sound of air whispering past. A tiny window to my left showing a midnight sky glorious with little diamonds.

What was this?

Had I died in that vile hideous whiteness? Was I being transported to heaven in some strange compartment?

Dear God, I hoped so.

My stupid, childish, uncontrolled heart was screaming at me. I felt so tired and weak. I never wanted to go back to that hideous world.

But a sweet roll appeared before me. Unheated. And a cup of tea, strong and without the milk and sugar I so enjoyed. I ate the one and sipped the other, unthinking. The tea tasted bitter. Tasted right.

Now I knew it was not to heaven I was going. God would never allow such middling food to be served to his minions.

Next came two pills. Which I must have swallowed because the glorious shining diamonds melted away.

Click.

Drifting down a corridor. Gliding, not walking. No, rolling in a chair. Sounds muffled and incessant. Echoing. Surreal.

Until I passed through a sliding door into—

Heat.

Bright and terrible heat.

Blistering heat.

It slapped against me, a wall of it so hard and cruel, I think I cried out. I couldn't say for certain.

I pulled back, fighting to get away from that blazing air.

That fire.

Fire.

Fire!

Dancing.

Dancing fire.

People surrounded me, speaking in tongues I'd not heard before.

I struggled against them, but they grabbed me and held me

down and a pain shot into my shoulder and the whiteness of this new world enveloped me.

And I slipped into what I just knew was hell.

Continued in

A Place of Safety
New World for Old

About this Author

Kyle Michel Sullivan is a writer and self-involved artist out to change the world until it changes him, as has already happened in far too many ways. He used to write screenplays, but now he writes books that range from sunshine and light (*David Martin*) to cold and dark (*How To Rape A Straight Guy*, which has been banned a couple of times) to flat out crazy (*The Lyons' Den*) to mainstream (*The Alice '65*) to a tale of tragedy and redemption (*Bobby Carapisi*). He has ventured into SF-Horror-Suspense with *The Beast in the Nothing Room*, done gay revenge in *Porno Manifesto* and worked up a vicious female revenge thriller in *Carli's Kills,* then taken Capitalism to its logical extreme in *Hunter*. He has also written murder mysteries (*Rape in Holding Cell 6, The Vanishing of Owen Taylor,* and *Underground Guy*), and is working on an erotic gay vampire series titled *Blood Angel,* that will be in several e-book parts.

Most of his novels are gay-oriented but not all. Many contain intense sexual content that fits the erotica category, but not all. Some are even romantic and tender. He's written what he's written, and each one of those books got him one step closer to this point.

He tries to build characters as vivid and real as possible and has a lot of fun doing it mixed with angst, anger, and amazement ... but that's the lot of a writer.

Other Books by This Author

<u>*General fiction*</u>
A Place of Safety-New World For Old
A Place of Safety-Home Not Home
The Alice '65
The Vanishing of Owen Taylor
Bobby Carapisi
The Lyons' Den
David Martin

<u>*Adult Erotica*</u>
Blood Angel series - Léonidès
                    - The Prussian
Carli's Kills
Hunter
The Beast in the Nothing Room
Underground Guy
Rape in Holding Cell 6
Porno Manifesto
Curt (AKA: How to Rape a Straight Guy)